IDENTITY THEFT

A KENNY ELLIOT MYSTERY

BOB AVEY

Black Rose Writing | Texas

ISBN: 978-1-68433-402-5
PUBLISHED BY BLACK ROSE WRITING
www.blackrosewriting.com

Printed in the United States of America
Suggested Retail Price (SRP) $19.95

Identity Theft: A Kenny Elliot Mystery is printed in Sabon

*As a planet-friendly publisher, Black Rose Writing does its best to eliminate unnecessary waste to reduce paper usage and energy costs, while never compromising the reading experience. As a result, the final word count vs. page count may not meet common expectations.

For my mother in Heaven, Ruby Padgett, who managed even during times of domestic turmoil, which was most of the time, to make life good for me.

I'd also like to thank Anne Victory, Keri Ford, Anita Mumm, and Dan Case for editing, and Reagan Rothe, with Black Rose Writing, for believing in me.

IDENTITY THEFT

A KENNY ELLIOT MYSTERY

At 8:30 a.m. Monday I decided to end my career with the Tulsa Police Department. It was not a spur-of-the-moment thing.

Name's Elliot. Kenny Elliot. I'm a cop. It's all I know all I'd ever thought I'd need to know. That changed when I learned a few months ago that I had a son and that Carmen Garcia, the only woman I'd ever truly loved, was his mother.

But there's more to it than that. I'm not exactly psychic. Then again, I'm the first to admit I don't really understand it all. Let's just say I couldn't go to Vegas and come back rich. But when the chips are down, I have a knack for coming out on top. I can't keep myself out of trouble, but in the heat of things, when the other guy makes his move, I have it figured out a split second before he does, whether it be a street fight or a case no one else has been able to solve. As you might imagine, I tend to be a bit unorthodox, and the structure of the department doesn't fit well with that. I'd worked a few cases, trying to make things routine, ordinary. But there was no getting around it. I was not the same person I used to be.

Visions from the past haunted me, and memories of a tortured soul, a man whose identity was unknown to me. Various attempts to track him down had nearly exhausted me. Recently I'd asked the medical examiner to send me photos of any John Does that'd gone through the system within the past few months that remained unsolved.

The ME had emailed me a list two days ago, and I was finally getting up the nerve to look into it. I leaned back in my chair and stared blankly at some old case files sitting on the floor of my office at the Tulsa Police Department. Hesitantly, I opened the email and then the attached file. The images ran across my computer monitor like a bad dream. On another click of my mouse, the nightmare became reality. There he was, the large man who'd stood beside my truck in the church parking lot and asked me the question that'd run perpetually through my mind ever since: *Do you have any idea what it feels like to die in someone else's body?*

The room became noticeably colder. I picked up the phone and dialed the medical examiner's office. "Yeah, this is Elliot. Is Longstreet around?"

"No, but if you're calling about the file of unsolved cases, I can probably answer your questions. Chris asked me to do the research and put the file together."

I stared at the monitor, studying the hideous image. "All right, Jordan. Photo number eight. Have there been any new developments, any leads at all?"

After a pause, she said, "You would have to choose that one."

I let the words sink in. I'd known this was going to be trouble and that it would be easier to just leave it alone, but I could no more do that than I could look the other way while a crime was being committed. After all, that's exactly what had happened. "Why do you say that?"

"Because sometime between after this photograph was taken and the next morning when the night guard made his rounds, the body disappeared."

"Disappeared?"

"Gone."

I increased the size of the image, paying particular attention to the man's eyes. In the photo, they were closed, but that's not how I remembered them. They'd been flat and lifeless. "Any idea how something like that could have happened?"

"I'm afraid not. If anyone knows anything, they aren't saying."

"Thanks, Jordan. I wish I could say you've been a big help."

"Sorry, but you need to stop looking for people who aren't there."

My defenses flared along with a touch of anger, but I reminded myself that Jordan had not meant it that way, that she didn't know enough about my past to have made that connection. "Was no one assigned to look into it?" I asked. "Just vanished, so no forced entry? What about the surveillance video? Who came into the building during the time the body was there?"

"I don't have any answers for you, Kenny."

"I appreciate your help, Jordan. Give my regards to Chris."

I disconnected, then picked up the sterling silver picture frame that held photos of my son, Wayne, a nine-year-old who looked a lot like me, and his mother, Carmen Garcia. We'd met in high school, and after all these years, seeing her image still gave me butterflies. I placed the photo back on the desk, then opened the top drawer and pulled out the resignation I'd prepared earlier.

I walked down the hallway to Captain Dombrowski's office, paused, knocked lightly, then walked over and sat in one of the chairs in front of his desk.

Dombrowski didn't reprimand me for the uninvited intrusion into his busy schedule. It might have been easier if he had. We knew each other well enough, though Dombrowski had sensed early on that I was not your typical detective. He more than anyone else at the department had tried to understand my unusual methods. I glanced at the photos of Dombrowski's family tacked to the wall—his wife, Susan, and two teenage children, a son, the eldest, and a daughter—then slid the resignation across his desk.

Dombrowski lowered his gaze, dropped a pudgy hand onto the resignation letter, and pulled it closer. For what seemed a long time, he stared at the document with no discernable change of expression, and then blotchy red spots began to form on his neck just above the collar line.

He was taking it hard, which made me feel like a jerk. I took a breath and let it out slowly. "I'm sorry. It's something I have to do."

Dombrowski pushed away from the desk and got to his feet. Moving the chair aside, he strode to the window and stared through it, his eyes studying something outside the building. "Remember the old days, when we used to work together?"

I shifted in my seat. I'd seen Dombrowski angry before, his face turning red, the veins in his forehead bulging, but this was something more. "Sure, I do, Bill. I'll never forget that."

"I was on the board of officers that reviewed your application. Bringing you in wasn't a unanimous decision. I kept my eye on you, asked for you as soon as the chance came up. I haven't regretted it."

"Neither have I," I said. But I hadn't known the captain felt that way about it. I'd always thought that I was just a couple of steps away from being driven out of the department.

"Damn it, Elliot, don't do this to me. We're shorthanded as it is. The department needs you."

He turned away from the window and locked his gaze on me. "I need you."

My stomach tightened as I thought back to the Bradford case, the case that had pushed me into my current state of confusion. "I can assure you this is not a hasty decision."

"You're a good cop, Elliot. You have a knack for it. Not everyone does."

Dombrowski didn't know how many nights I'd stayed awake, thinking about this, with my mind vacillating one way, then the other. "I appreciate that. But you know as well as anyone that I've gotten myself and the department into trouble more times than not. I'm surprised by the way you're taking it. I'd thought you'd be relieved to see me go."

He shook his head. "I know I've got a bad way of showing it, but I appreciate the work you've done here, solving cases that perhaps no one else could have."

I worked alone with an unorthodox style, relying more on instinct and intuition than hard facts. Sure, the Bradford case had turned things up a notch, but being back to my old self didn't mean I was like everyone else. I didn't know how to explain my gift or the way it danced around my consciousness in double-edged fashion, never letting me grasp whether it was a blessing or a curse. I wouldn't call myself lucky in the sense that I was lucky in my personal life. Love life a disaster, that time I was accused of murdering my best friend and run from town, plus the fun adventures of a homeless teenager. Lucky like that, no way was I buying any lotto tickets, but lucky with finding answers to other people's problems? Somehow it often ended up unfolding before me. Oftentimes, the path to answers was directly in the middle of some police department red tape I couldn't explain my way around. Dombrowski had, even without understanding what I could do, greased the wheels for me.

"Thanks," I said. "But I've had to fight you and the department every step of the way."

"Yeah, I know. But a cop like you is going to run into that wherever you go."

Dombrowski had a valid point, but I had a good answer. "Maybe I'll do something else, find an area that embraces my individuality." As the words came out, I shook my head. They sounded ridiculous even to me.

Dombrowski came back to his desk, retrieved his chair, and sat down. He folded his hands together and leaned forward. "I don't like admitting it. You have a legitimate argument. But only with respect to your behavior. If you'd follow proper procedure, it would be unilaterally beneficial. You're your own worst enemy, Elliot. I wish I could make you see that."

He slid the resignation back toward me. "You're going through a tough time. Take a few days off and think this over."

"Maybe you're right. Trouble is, for the past month, I've done nothing but think about it."

He smiled. "Think a little more. You'll come to your senses."

I got to my feet and started toward the door. "I'm not promising anything."

"I understand. And thanks. I appreciate it."

I strode down the hallway, unsure if I was happy, sad, or what. I pulled out my phone and called Nick Brazelton, an old friend from high school, to make sure we were still on for lunch, then dropped by my office and turned everything off, picked up my coat and hat, and headed toward the elevator. It'd been cold and wet for a few days, but today was predicted to be sunny, near sixty degrees. I hoped the good weather would help brighten the mood.

The elevator opened, and I crossed the lobby. Several yards later, I pushed through the glass doors and stepped outside, though I was not greeted by the expected freedom of thought or rush of cool air but with a sensation of unrest.

A similar, altered state of awareness had come over me when I'd encountered Laura Bradford a couple of months ago. Laura was a friend from my past, which would have been fine had she not been dead.

I scanned the area, half expecting to again look into the disconcerting eyes of Laura, but she was not there, only ordinary people coming and going, minding their business. My nervousness had gotten to me, precipitated by indecision and the uncomfortable meeting with Captain Dombrowski. But something had caught my attention, a familiar chill up my spine. Curiosity got the better of me, and I altered my path, turning west instead.

It didn't take long. Half a block later, I saw what had drawn my attention. A person who looked out of place in the neighborhood—and that was saying something in downtown Tulsa—stood across the street, their face completely obscured by a garment that more resembled a medieval monk's habit than anything else. A city bus lumbered past, blocking my line of vision, but that didn't leave me with nothing to worry about. The person in the monk habit was no longer in sight, but about fifty yards away someone else, a man, stood on the southwest corner of the intersection.

I thought it might be Officer David Yates. He wasn't in uniform but wore civilian clothes, sunglasses, and a ball cap. He glanced around, slowly raised his arm, and then began to wave as if trying to signal someone.

On the opposite side of the intersection, an elderly gentleman cautiously waved back.

I wondered if it could be Yates's father, but I didn't think so. He, too, seemed curiously out of place, like a time traveler from the past, his manner and style of dress indicating he'd accumulated dignity and refinement along the way. Exhaust fumes from the traffic wafted through my senses, but it wasn't the dirty air that put a knot in my stomach. Something unusual was going down.

Continually monitoring the traffic and the lights, the elderly gentleman prepared to cross the street as if to meet with David Yates. But he abruptly halted those efforts. Shaking his head, he took a couple of steps back, then reached into his coat and pulled out a cell phone.

Something had frightened the old man, and I suspected it wasn't the traffic.

When I turned back toward David Yates, I saw exactly what had frightened the elderly gentleman.

A ragged man emerged from the crowd and lumbered, stiff-legged, toward Yates. About three feet away, the ragged man stopped, his feet spread slightly apart, his arms dangling limply at his sides.

Judging from his clothes and overall appearance, I guessed he lived among the ranks of the homeless. Awareness stiffened my spine, and my detective senses were on full alert.

Without a doubt, it was Officer David Yates, and his body language reflected my own. That cop sense that said something wasn't right.

Yates sent the ragged man a nod of acknowledgment. The ragged man reached for something behind his back, and when his hand was once again revealed, it held a weapon aimed at Yates.

I yelled a warning, but the sounds of heavy traffic quickly swallowed my voice. My pulse pounded in my ears. There was no way I could get there in time to stop the assailant, but years of training kicked in, and I pulled my badge and stepped into the street.

A few of the cars stopped, and still, others slowed their pace, but most of the drivers attempted to swerve around, angrily blaring their horns at my attempt to impede their progress.

I had a notion of firing my service weapon into the air, but I didn't get the chance.

The ragged man took aim and fired off two quick successive shots.

Chaos erupted. People were ducking, crawling, scrambling for safety while others ran in various directions like frightened mice, all of it blocking my access to Yates. But I could see him, and he was still standing, apparently unharmed.

Something beyond the surface level of the horror unfolding was at work. Even someone with no experience would not have missed at that distance. The aim was intentional. I visually followed the most likely path of trajectory and saw that the streetlight at the corner of Elgin had been hit but nothing else. He'd fired high enough to miss everybody.

On the northeast corner of the intersection, the well-dressed elderly gentleman held his phone at eye level and took photos of the scene.

Then, as if questioning his own actions, the ragged man dropped the weapon onto the sidewalk and darted into the street.

I scrambled after him. Again horns blared, and tires squealed, but then the sickening sound of metal striking flesh and bone told me that the ragged man would not be walking away from such an impact. After knocking the ragged man to the street, the heavy delivery truck traveled another ten feet.

The driver clambered out of the truck. He stumbled around in a daze, then ran to the victim and knelt beside him.

I raised my badge high enough so people could easily see, then made my way to the scene.

The noises of the city must have still been there, but for me, the scene had gone eerily quiet. I glanced around, looking for Yates and the elderly gentleman, but didn't see either of them. I lowered myself to one knee and checked the victim's pulse, praying that a remnant of life remained in the ragged man, though I knew that would require nothing short of a miracle.

The man's neck had been snapped, and his head now positioned at a grotesque angle.

The look on the truck driver's face indicated he was about to go into shock.

I put my hand on his shoulder and maneuvered eye contact. "Are you all right, buddy?"

"I killed him, ran right over him."

I lacked the expertise to properly explain to the driver that I knew what he was going through. And I certainly didn't have the heart to inform him that being the cause of the loss of human life, even if unintentional and indirectly, was something you never got over. "It wasn't your fault," I said. It was all I could manage. "There's no way you could have stopped in time."

I slid one of my business cards into his hand. "If you need help with this, anything at all, give me a call."

I got to my feet and turned my attention to my phone, but the area was already crawling with police officers, police cars, ambulances, and other first responders.

A uniformed officer approached. "Good morning, sir. I understand you were a witness?"

I showed my badge, then gave the officer a detailed account of what I'd seen.

"You said the intended victim of the shooter was a police officer, Officer David Yates, who was present during all this?"

I scanned the area. Yates was not there, at least that I could see. The elderly gentleman who'd seemed to know Yates was gone too. "That's right. But he doesn't seem to be around now."

The officer closed his notepad and nodded. "Thank you, sir. You've been a great help."

I hung around for a few minutes, looking around the scene and the immediate area. Later I approached the young officer who'd interviewed me. I motioned to the body still lying in the street. "Have you been able to identify the man?"

"No, sir. He doesn't have anything on him. I mean nothing, no wallet, no keys, not even any money." He paused and shook his head. "I don't know what to make of it."

I thanked the officer, then excused myself and again called the department.

Police Sergeant Carl Long, Yates's supervisor, had showed up and pulled me aside. "I can't tell you much," he said. "There's an ongoing investigation. You know how it is. Anyway, I suspended Yates from duty early Saturday morning. I didn't want to. He's a good man. But sometimes good people go wrong. Are you sure it was Yates you saw?"

I considered my answer. Yates had been wearing sunglasses and a ball cap, and a lot of commotion was going on, but there was no doubt in my mind. "It was Yates all right."

"Well, for Yates's sake, I hope you're wrong. I guess it'd be better that way. I don't really know. The whole thing has me baffled. Yates is one of the best officers I have. He's never caused any trouble. I just don't get it. Anyway, I've said about all I can and probably too much at that."

"Don't worry about it," I said.

"You're a good man, Elliot. I'm sure this is just wishful thinking, but if there's anything you can do to help Yates, I'm sure we'd both appreciate it."

"I'll keep that in mind," I said, then slid the phone into my pocket and walked away from the scene. I had about an hour before I was to meet Nick, and I wanted to clear my head first. I'd lost my appetite, but Nick was a good friend who I didn't see often. Nick was looking forward to it. I didn't want to disappoint him.

2

At Fourth and Boston, I turned the corner, and the lower portion of the Mayo Building came into view. Nick stood near the entrance of Billy's On the Square, checking his watch while glancing around the area. Nick and I had grown up in the same small town. He still lived there, and the city made him nervous. Whatever he'd wanted to see me about must be important to him.

The walk had been good for me, but a menagerie of thoughts still clouded my mind. Like why had the ragged man intentionally missed his shot, and why had he, in effect, committed suicide by running in front of a truck? And then there was Yates. What the hell was going on with Yates? Numbly, my feet reached for the sidewalk as I made my way toward the restaurant, but I might have been nearing a doctor's office or boarding an unwanted flight for the anxiety that gnawed at my insides.

Nick caught sight of me and waved.

I waited for the traffic light, then crossed the street and walked to where Nick was waiting, our handshake quickly turning into a friendly embrace.

"It's good to see you," Nick said. Lowering his voice, he gestured toward the restaurant. "This place looks expensive."

Nick had always been good with his hands, tinkering with things to see how they worked. He'd become a good enough mechanic to earn a decent living in Tulsa. Instead, he opted for the simplicity of life that our old small town of Porter offered.

"It isn't," I said. "And I got this one anyway."

Nick shrugged as we stepped inside. "It sure smells good. I'll give you that much."

"It's the char burgers," I said. "You should try one." We sat at a table near a replica of an antique streetlamp and put our orders in. Through the glass that made up the front of the restaurant, I watched the traffic moving silently down Main Street as people made their way along the sidewalk.

Nick nodded, then leaned back in his chair. "I took Maggie's old truck out for a spin last night. It brought back some memories, got me to thinking about old times."

Maggie Caldwell had been an eccentric but kind old recluse who had played a small but meaningful role in both our lives. She'd passed away a few months ago, leaving the old Chevy to Nick. He'd maintained the vehicle for years, practically free of charge. The old truck had meant a lot to Maggie, and I guessed she figured Nick would give it a good home. However, I wasn't sure why Nick might be bringing that up. The memories Nick referred to were best left in the past where they belonged.

The waitress appeared with our orders, placed the food on the table, and scurried away.

"Man, that's good," Nick said after taking a bite and putting the burger back down. "Like I said, I got to thinking. I know it seemed like bad times to us back when we were growing up, but I miss those days. I can't tell you how many times I've wished I could go back."

"Come on, Nick. Sure, we had some good times, but some of it was bad." I thought back to Johnnie Alexander and Marcia Barnes, friends of ours who'd been murdered outside town years ago. I'd had nothing to do with it, but the incident had resulted in my having to leave town, causing me to lose Carmen and miss the birth of our son. "Some of it I'd just as soon forget."

"Sorry. I didn't mean to drag that up. But you know what I mean."

"Not really. Anyway, you have a pretty good life. You don't need to live in the past."

"Yeah, working at the garage is a thrill a minute."

A grin found its way across my face. "Anything new happening in town?"

"Billy Jones is back. He got married right after college and moved to Colorado. After his folks passed away, he rented the place out. Last I'd heard, he'd given the occupants notice and moved back in, alone. I don't know what happened. That and some young couple bought a few acres east of town and are building a house out there."

Nick's answer seemed relatively genuine, but his behavior indicated that something was bothering him.

"Anything new going on with you?" I asked.

He fidgeted with his plate, moving a few french fries around with his fork. "Linda Cook's still after me. We've dated a few times."

I didn't like the sound of that. I put the burger on the plate. Tom Cook had played defense for the Porter football team during the same time period that Nick and I had played offense. Nick and Tom's relationship had been volatile. Having them together was like dropping a lighted match into a room full of firecrackers. And Tom and Linda had been an item since high school. Nick had always had a strange sense of humor.

"Always the comedian," I said.

He didn't look up but continued to stir his french fries.

"You are kidding, aren't you?"

He didn't answer.

"This isn't funny, Nick."

He put the fork down. "Linda's a nice-looking woman. A guy gets lonely, you know."

I wiped my hands, then put the napkin on the table. I knew all too well about what being lonely could do to a person. "What does Tom think about this?"

Nick shook his head. "I don't think he knows. They split up a few months ago."

"Divorced?"

"I don't think so. But they are separated."

"I know it's none of my business, Nick, but this sounds like trouble. And it doesn't seem like something you would do."

"Yeah, maybe you don't know me like you think you do." Nick looked away for a moment, his expression indicating he was sorry he'd said that. "Heck, maybe *I* don't know me as well as I should. Does anybody really know who they are."

I momentarily returned my attention to the people outside the restaurant rushing up and down the sidewalk. Nick wasn't ordinarily the philosophical type, and his saying such a thing put me on edge. "That's an easy one. I've known you since grade school. You're Nick Brazelton."

He grinned. "Well, that settles it, doesn't it? Now, something's bothering you too. What is it?"

"What do you mean?" I asked.

"I've seen that faraway look in your eyes before, and it usually means trouble. What's up?"

I pushed the plate with the unfinished burger to the side. Nick and I had both suffered through lousy childhoods. I'd grown up in foster homes, some better than others but none good. Nick's father had provided food, clothing, and shelter, but it'd come with a price. He'd been overbearing, even abusive. We had always considered me the lucky one. With our circumstances bringing us together, we'd become more like brothers than friends. With the exception of Carmen, Nick knew me as well as anyone. I studied the reproduced streetlamp beside the table, then turned back and said, "Everything's fine. I'm just a little distracted, that's all."

"So, you're going to give me that tough, silent cop routine?"

He wasn't going to let it go, so I decided to just come out with it. "That'd be ex-cop now."

Nick had started to bring a french fry to his mouth, but he stopped midway, his expression turning sour. "What are you talking about?"

"I turned in my resignation today. Dombrowski didn't take it very well."

Nick tossed the french fry onto his plate. "For crying out loud, Kenny, why didn't you call me? We could have talked about it."

I looked away. The idea of my being unemployed bothered Nick more than I'd thought it would. It wasn't as bad as Nick was making it. I never intended to be without purpose in a purpose-driven world.

"I've known you to do some dumb things, but…" Nick let his words trail off. "Kenny, if anybody was ever meant to be a cop, it's you. It's who you are." He paused, then continued, "Okay, here's what I want you to do. Go back and explain to your boss that you've made a mistake. Tell him you've been under a lot of stress and weren't thinking right. From the way you talk about him, he seems like a reasonable man. He'll understand."

I studied Nick's face. I hadn't realized he'd take the news so hard. But I understood. His image of me had been shaken. Even though we were the same age, he'd always looked up to me, early on assigning me the role of big brother, the one he always came to when he needed help. "If it's any consolation, Dombrowski didn't accept it. He told me to think about it."

Nick held both hands out, palms up. "Well, there you go."

"It's more complicated than it sounds," I said. "It's something I've been thinking about for a long time."

"This is all about Carmen and Wayne, isn't it?"

"That's a big part of it."

"Carmen loves you, Kenny. And who you are and what you are is all part of it. I don't think she wants you to change."

As usual, Nick's responses seemed well thought out, though in truth they were rapid replies to questions he'd had no idea were coming. It was one of the reasons I often confided in him. But neither he nor Carmen knew enough of what I'd seen through the years as a cop, what I'd been through. "I just watched a fellow police officer come within inches of losing his life," I said. "A man just stepped out of the crowd and started shooting."

Nick cleared his throat. "When did this happen?"

I gave him a quick rundown of the scene I'd witnessed outside the department.

"For crying out loud, Kenny, why didn't you say that to begin with? Here I am going on about nothing and…" He paused, then said, "Look, you do what you need to do about the job, but don't try to tell me it's out of fear. I know you better than that. Nothing scares you."

Nick was mistaken, of course, but there was an element of truth to his logic. I'd faced death enough times. Perhaps it was the futility of it all, the squandering of efforts in a vain chase for justice. I just wasn't sure anymore. "That's not true."

"All right then. Lay it out for me. What is it, exactly, that scares Bulldog Elliot?"

It was a nickname I'd picked up in high school. I'd never been particularly fond of it. "Dying alone," I said. "Taking a bullet on some dark corner and melting into the concrete. Disappearing from life without anyone caring one way or the other."

Nick looked away, pretending to wipe his face with a napkin, but he was drying his eyes. When he turned back, he said, "It's not like that, and you know it. You're the best friend I've ever had. I care. I care a lot. And you know damn well Carmen does."

I leaned against the table, folding my hands in front of me. "I'm sorry, Nick. It's been a bad day. I guess I'm a little edgy."

Nick shook his head. "You have every right to be on edge. Heck, maybe it is time for a career change. Too bad you're not a better mechanic, but maybe I could put you to work anyway, cleaning up around the garage."

"That place could use a good cleaning, but don't look at me. I'm taking a few days off to hit the road on the Harley and think things over."

"I don't know," Nick said. "This time of year, the weather could take a bad turn in a hurry." He checked his watch. "Speaking of the garage, I need to be getting back there."

Outside the restaurant, as Nick was walking away, he turned back. "Thanks for lunch. And next time, call me before you do anything crazy."

I waved back and started toward the department where my truck was parked. I'd made it about halfway when my phone vibrated in my pocket, accompanied by a sound tone that indicated a message.

It turned out to be Thomas Meadows, the pastor of my church. The message indicated he wanted to see me and mentioned that it was urgent. A knot formed in my stomach. Pastor Meadows and I were on good terms, but I had a bad feeling about this.

Pastor Meadows slid the book he'd been reading back into its place among the others that lined the shelf that ran behind his desk. "Thanks for coming," he said. "I appreciate your giving this priority."

"No problem. What's this all about?"

He gestured for me to sit in one of the chairs in front of his desk.

After a brief silence, the pastor asked, "Why do I always get the impression that you know my thoughts before I speak them?"

I knew Pastor Meadows fairly well. The details of an unusual case had caused our paths to cross several months ago. Since then we'd become friends, often confiding in one another when we wanted advice or needed a valued opinion on this or that. He'd made an honest effort at fulfilling that trust, but I sensed that the problem he'd called me about was weighing heavy on his mind. "You give me too much credit."

"No," he said. "If the truth were known, I'd probably learn that I haven't given you enough."

Upon our first encounter, I had expected Pastor Meadows to speak with an accent, which he did. However, I had anticipated the accent to be

Irish or Scottish, not Texan. Even now, hearing it brought a smile to my lips.

"Our professions intermingle in a few areas," I said. "Carrying around other people's problems can wear you down."

"Indeed, it can. But the Lord has blessed you with qualities that seem to go hand in hand with police work, Kenny. Are you sure you want to give that up?"

I'd mentioned my intentions to Pastor Meadows a few weeks earlier. "I have mixed feelings about it."

"Well, what are you feeling right now?"

"Sorrow for the poor fellow that lost his life this morning and pity for the unfortunate truck driver who ran him down." I explained to the pastor what I'd been through, pretty much repeating the conversation I'd had with Nick earlier.

In the soft light of his office, surrounded by books, Pastor Meadows seemed to exude wisdom and confidence, and yet his demeanor reflected gratitude for my being there. Whatever was troubling him had left him vulnerable, seeking support.

"In our line of work," he said, "getting too close to those who count on us can be an occupational hazard."

"Would you like to talk about it?" I asked.

Pastor Meadows stared off into space for a moment, and when he returned his attention, he said, "A member of our church is experiencing difficulties. He's asked for help."

I considered that for a moment. I figured similar circumstances would probably make up a good part of the pastor's working day. "Is there something extraordinary about this particular case?"

"It's a friend, someone I've known and respected for many years. He wants me to come to his house and speak with him today."

An uneasy feeling worked its way through my gut. "What sort of trouble has this friend gotten into?"

"Marital problems, I suspect. Maybe more."

"Unfortunate," I said, "but not exactly the stuff of police work."

"Some might call it fate or providence," Pastor Meadows said, "but I believe God puts us where he wants us when he wants us. Whether we respond appropriately is another matter."

"What are you getting at?"

"Your change in career path, or possible hiatus, might have come at a good time. The friend I spoke of not only wants my help but yours as well. He asked me to contact you."

"Why would he do that?"

"He's a fellow police officer."

I considered the facts, and it all fell into place. "You're talking about Officer David Yates, aren't you?"

3

Pastor Meadows guided his Ford Escort across the church parking lot, then pulled onto Mingo Road, heading south.

Easing my foot against the accelerator, I coaxed the old Chevy onto the roadway to follow. Until my resignation was official, I'd have to be careful, keeping my involvement as casual as possible. With Yates being under investigation, the chances of my crossing some lines and breaking some rules were pretty high. Dombrowski was convinced I didn't care about such things, but the truth of the matter was I did care. But I couldn't blame the captain. My past behavior gave him just cause.

A cool breeze blew through the window of the truck, carrying scents of the local restaurants mixed with a touch of traffic exhaust, and my apprehension began to increase. The succession of odd events I'd witnessed earlier outside the department played through my mind, and as I mentally ran through the details of the macabre scene, it seemed even more surreal, like a choreographed play put on by street actors for the amusement of the crowd. The question was had a look-alike scored the starring role, or had the bit actually been played by David Yates? The more I thought about it, the more I leaned toward Yates pulling a Steve McQueen, going out of his way to perform his own stunts. McQueen had it right. Sometimes it was the only way. But what had Yates gotten himself into, and why, out of all the people associated with the department, did he want to talk to me?

When Pastor Meadows reached 101st Street, he turned east. A little farther down the road, the signal of the Escort flashed, and the car turned onto a side street, leading into a semi-affluent neighborhood. A few blocks later, the pastor carefully pulled into the driveway of a well-maintained, two-story brick house.

I pulled in and parked beside him. An array of colorful pansies kept guard over the partially dormant flower beds, accenting nicely against the white picket fence that separated the front lawn from the backyard. Rising out of the lawn near the street, a real estate sign announced an upheaval of some kind was underway. Yates had put his family home up for sale. I climbed out of the truck and joined Pastor Meadows, who was standing near the front door, and it was then that I noticed an old Mercedes—a 1950s era, I guessed—parked alongside the curb just up the street. The vintage automobile looked as out of place as I felt.

A noise came from behind, and Pastor Meadows and I turned to see David Yates standing in the doorway of the home.

Yates was not a small man, but at that moment he looked as beat down and defeated as I'd ever seen him. Following the pastor's lead, I stepped forward and shook Yates's hand.

Moments later, Pastor Meadows and I stood in the foyer on the other side of the closed door. The house was not what it appeared to be, but was a remnant, reflecting a false example of what suburban life should be, its secret deftly hidden, giving evidence to the contrary. It wasn't so much the untidiness. In fact, everything looked pretty ordinary. But my senses were picking up on a sadness so heavy that I doubted it would take someone with heightened abilities to notice. I wondered what had happened, and though I had no intention of verbalizing my thoughts, I threw a questioning glance at Pastor Meadows.

The color drained from his face.

"Never underestimate the power of evil," he said.

The knowledge that I was not alone in sensing the heavy, troubled atmosphere that had settled about the home of David Yates offered no comfort.

Suddenly Yates, who'd gone for coffee, came back into the room. When it occurred to him that he'd left the pastor and me standing in the foyer, he grabbed a coaster from a set on the table, then placed one of the mugs he'd carried onto it and rushed over to where we were standing. "I'm sorry," he said, "but I'm afraid I haven't been myself lately."

He gestured for us to follow him into the living room where he directed Pastor Meadows onto a sofa near the coffee table.

I sat the other end. I'd turned down the offer of coffee. Having had trouble sleeping lately, I'd thought it might be the caffeine and had decided to cut back.

Choosing an art deco–style chair made of leather, Yates sat across from us. Using both hands, he held his coffee mug near his face and blew air across the hot liquid, then took a sip. Afterward, he glanced away and gazed silently toward the front of the room where light filtered in through windows partially covered by wooden blinds.

Pastor Meadows shifted in his seat but said nothing.

I wasn't ordinarily the impatient sort, but the situation didn't seem to be going anywhere. I took the initiative. "Officer Yates, I understand you have something on your mind that you wish to discuss with Pastor Meadows and me."

"I'm sorry. I've gone over the details more times than I care to count, thought I had it sorted out or at least knew what direction I would take, but now that I'm confronted with it, I'm not sure where to start."

I hadn't been around Yates enough to know his casual demeanor, but he exhibited signs of being overly stressed about something. Whatever haunted Yates's mind, I needed to know more. I drew on my skills in trying to get people to talk by shifting forward, casually resting my elbows on my thighs and, for all appearances, gave the look of someone who could be trusted. Honestly speaking, I was. "I understand your apprehension, but you thought this important enough to get us here. Just relax and tell us what this is all about."

"Thanks, Detective. I'd hoped you would understand."

"I'm here to help," I said, "but I am curious about something. It appears you might be dealing with sensitive issues of a domestic nature, the kind that Pastor Meadows might handle more effectively. Where do I fit in?"

Pastor Meadows sat forward and placed his coffee mug on the table. "Gentlemen, before we go any further, I suggest we pray."

The pastor led us into a lengthy prayer, covering everything from friendship to honesty. Afterward, not being able to let go of the question about my involvement, I asked it again. That's when Yates dropped a bombshell.

"I thought you might be willing to help me out," Yates said. "Find out exactly what happened to me last Friday night and Saturday morning between the hours of 9:00 p.m. and 3:30 a.m."

The pastor quickly responded. "Let me make sure I'm understanding you correctly. Are you saying that your memory of certain events is obscured or just unclear?"

"Just"—Yates said with a bit of hesitation—"a bit fuzzy."

I'd suspected something out of the ordinary was behind my being called in, but I hadn't expected anything like that. And from the look on Pastor Meadows's face, he hadn't either. "Have you ever experienced anything like that before?" I asked.

Yates shook his head. "Not that I'm aware of. I realize how this must sound. I'm not crazy. At least I don't think that I am."

"And neither do I," the pastor said, "though you have piqued my curiosity. Why don't you start from the beginning and explain how you came to that conclusion?"

Officer Yates lowered his gaze to the coffee table, and when he looked up, he said, "I'd known something wasn't right. Saturday was my day off, and I was sleeping in. I tossed and turned, in and out of strange dreams. Around 9:00 a.m., I got a call from Sergeant Long. He wanted to talk to me, said it was urgent. He sounded upset, so I didn't waste any time. I got dressed and drove right over. I got there around ten."

I wondered about the content of Yates's dreams, but I decided to put that on hold. "What happened during the meeting with Sergeant Long?"

Yates glanced around the room. He kept wiping his palms against his pant legs. "He started asking questions about my shift Friday night, wanted to know where I'd gone, what I'd done, stuff like that."

"Is that unusual?" the pastor asked.

Yates shot a quick glance in my direction. "You could say that. I don't know what Dispatch showed. He wouldn't tell me. He asked for my badge and service weapon, said I was under suspension until further notice." He paused. "I gave him my badge, but I didn't have my service weapon. I don't know what happened to it."

Pastor Meadows shook his head. "I'm sorry to hear that. I know how much your work means to you. Have you spoken with a doctor about this, about your memory, I mean?"

"Not yet. I need to sort it all out first. It's why I called you, Tom. I need you to pray for me, help me get through this."

Pastor Meadows stood and walked to where Yates was sitting. He put his hand on Yates's shoulder. "Of course I will. I'll do whatever I can for you."

Yates nodded, his eyes filling with moisture. "I need your help too, Detective Elliot. Will you find out what happened, why I was suspended?"

"I'll do what I can. But I need to ask you something. I saw someone outside the department earlier today who looked a lot like you. Were you downtown this morning, wearing dark glasses and a ball cap?"

Yates shook his head, avoiding eye contact. "I've been here all day. Sergeant Long called though and asked me about it."

Yates was lying. What's more, he knew that I knew he was lying. There was a lot more to the story than he was giving up. He wanted to tell me that too, but he was holding back. I suspected I'd be talking with him again soon. For now, I'd let it ride, see where it went.

"David?" Pastor Meadows asked, a curious expression coming over his face as he visually explored the room. "Where's Linda? How is she taking all this?"

Yates massaged his temples. "She's gone, walked out Saturday afternoon after I got back from the meeting with Sergeant Long. I haven't seen her since. I don't even know where she is."

Pastor Meadows shook his head. "That doesn't sound like something Linda would do."

Again, Yates fidgeted, avoided eye contact. "She needed some time to think, said she'd get back to me later. I worry that might never happen, that I might never see her again."

I decided it was time to ask about the nightmares. "You mentioned having strange dreams earlier. Could you tell us a little more about that?"

Yates shrugged. "You know the kind, something's chasing you, but you can't run, like your feet are mired in clay. I've had similar dreams before, but never like that."

Pastor Meadows checked his watch. "We'll get through this," he said. "And I do apologize, but I have some appointments I must keep. Why don't you come over tonight, have dinner with Becky and me?"

Yates stood and hugged the pastor. "I'd like that," he said. After that, he walked us to the door.

Moments later, standing in the drive outside, Pastor Meadows paused beside his car. "I need to be going," he said, "but I need to ask you something. Was David being straight with us?"

I looked across the front lawn. The real estate sign indicated that Yates's marital problems were probably not as spontaneous as he'd made it sound. "More or less."

"That's not a clear answer."

I glanced past the real estate sign. The old Mercedes was still parked across the street. While I didn't believe Yates was lying about the core issues, I had the impression that he had withheld information. However, the pastor was taking this pretty hard, and I needed to be careful. "Let me put it another way. He seemed to believe what he was saying."

"Are you being purposefully evasive?"

I shrugged. "I was getting mixed signals. He admitted to having experienced memory loss. If he's unsure about the details, it would explain why I was having trouble reading him."

"Can you obtain the information he asked for?"

"Most of what he's after should be in Dispatch's records. That being said, there's little doubt that an ongoing internal investigation has been launched. The department might have asked him to take a few days off and see a doctor, but I don't think he would have been suspended on the basis of memory loss alone."

"I was wondering about that," the pastor said. "Along similar lines, I suspect there is more to his wife leaving him too. I've known David and Linda since they were children, attended both their confirmations, even presided over their marriage. Linda would never have walked out on him simply because he couldn't remember a few things, even if it had resulted in his losing his job."

While climbing into his car, the pastor added, "Can you find out what's going on without getting yourself into trouble?"

The car I'd been watching pulled away from the curb and started out of the subdivision. "I'll do what I can."

I got into the truck, then backed out of the driveway. Keeping a safe distance, I followed the old Mercedes out of the neighborhood.

In what appeared to be a haphazard series of turns, the Mercedes maneuvered a purposeful route, heading in a northwest direction which ultimately led to an older section of Tulsa.

The uneasy, mausoleum-like feel of the Yates house kept running through my thoughts. I knew that in order to be effective, I needed to maintain a certain level of detachment, or maybe objectivity was a better word, though I certainly wasn't neutral on the subject of David Yates. Then again, had I ever been neutral on anything? I guessed that was part of the problem. I always managed to make things a little too personal. So why should Yates be any different? I didn't know. And I still wasn't convinced the man didn't need a psychiatrist instead of a detective.

Again I caught sight of the old Mercedes, traveling north on Peoria Avenue and then west onto Eighth Street.

I followed the old car into the Village at Central Park, a collection of two-story brick structures, relatively new condominiums, and townhomes that looked as if they belonged in Boston or even London. Like a planned backdrop, the buildings of downtown Tulsa rose into the western skyline.

I knew the area well. Seven months ago, in the heat of May, I'd worked a case in which the body of a victim had been dumped in the trash facilities of the same complex.

The garages for the condos were located directly behind the units they went to, and after watching the Mercedes pull into one, I knew which condo I would need to visit. I drove out of the complex, then parked along the street and waited a few minutes before attempting to confront the driver of the vehicle. Knocking on the door of a stranger who might be expecting the intrusion was never without risk, but I had found that giving the suspect time to settle in helped in some cases to lower the tension a degree or two. It didn't always work out that way. When it came to detective work, there were few absolutes. The law of probabilities was on the side of the man having a perfectly good reason for being in Yates's neighborhood that had nothing to do with Yates. I didn't believe that though. I couldn't shake the notion that the condo resident's reason for being there had been very much in line with my own, trying to gather information on Yates. The question was, *why?*

The blinds covering one of the upstairs patio doors moved.

The door led to a small balcony belonging to the unit on the northwest corner of the complex, which confirmed my suspicion of which condo the Mercedes driver had gone into. On the downside, it also indicated that the driver knew he'd been followed.

I reached for the door handle of the truck, but my phone going off stopped me.

The ID showed unknown.

I brought the phone to my ear but said nothing.

"That you, Elliot?"

I knew who it was, but, the knowledge of this didn't alleviate my concern. I played along. "Who wants to know?"

"It's me, David Yates."

I'd suspected Yates would be contacting me, but his timing couldn't be worse. I couldn't decide if I should put Yates on hold and knock on the door of the condo before the driver had a chance to leave again or stay in the truck and hear the man out. I chose the latter. "I'm in the middle of surveillance right now, so this had better be good."

"I have a feeling you already know this, but we didn't finish our conversation earlier. There's more to it."

"All right, I'm listening, but I'm not in the mood to be toyed with. Lay it out straight this time."

"That's what I want to do, get it off my chest, but not over the phone. I was hoping you might agree to come back to the house."

I looked beyond the condos and studied the Tulsa skyline where the clouds had thickened into a gray overcast blanket. This problem I was dragged into wasn't going to go away. But I'd known that from the start. It wouldn't take long to question the driver of the old Mercedes, but I needed to get to Yates before he changed his mind. "I'll be there in a few minutes."

I threw the phone onto the seat, then started the truck and drove away from the condos. Questioning the mysterious resident would have to wait.

Half an hour later, I was back with Yates. He'd brought in a chair from the kitchen and placed it beside his office chair, and now we both sat there, staring at the blank computer monitor on the center of his desk. Yates seemed to be losing his nerve again, having second thoughts. "Seems to me you were in the right place with Pastor Meadows," I said. "Maybe throw in a little psychiatric help on the side. Why me, Yates? You probably have friends at the department who could get you the information you asked about."

"I'm getting to that. Let me start by assuring you that, while maybe incomplete, everything I've told you has been the absolute truth as I understand it."

"Why do I feel like I'm being set up?"

He shook his head. "I don't mean for it to be like that, Kenny. May I call you, Kenny?"

I thought about that for a moment. Not many people used my first name. "Sure, why not?"

"I've been praying nonstop, asking God to help me, to lead me in the right direction. Your name keeps coming up. It's God's way of telling me that you're the only one I can trust with this."

"All right," I said. This case had trouble written all over it, but I couldn't deny my compulsion to follow it through. "But why didn't you tell us everything the first time?"

Yates switched on the computer. "There's only one way to do this, and that's to just show you."

He placed his hand on the mouse and made a few clicks, and when the intended content was revealed, it showed a young woman, her fingers clumsily working the buttons of her blouse.

My pulse quickened as I anticipated what the woman shown in the video might do next.

The blouse slid from her body and dropped to the floor. She ran her hands up her torso and then lightly touched the area around her nipples. As if this excited her, she began to squeeze and fondle the soft flesh of her breasts.

I quickly turned away. Had Yates actually sunken to these depths so quickly, or had he always harbored dark desires, somehow managing to hide the secret from his peers? If so, had it been such behavior that had finally driven his wife to call it quits? Then again, if this was Yates's private downfall, why would he dare to share it with me?

Anger threatened to overtake me, and I took a deep breath to calm down. I was tempted to bust Yates's chops and walk away, but I couldn't do that. I needed to know more. "What kind of sick game are you playing, Yates?"

Yates hit the pause button on the computer. He was trembling, and the color of his face had changed. "You don't know what I've been through. In fact, I don't know how much more I can take."

"That makes two of us."

Yates massaged his temples. "You've got it all wrong. And there's more. The video, I mean."

"I've seen enough. Maybe I should just leave."

"Don't give up on me, Kenny. God is faithful, and he wouldn't lead me astray. You're my best hope for getting out of this or at least figuring out what's going on."

I stood and walked to a double window that looked over the front lawn. Yates appeared to be opening up, trying to be honest about whatever it was he'd gotten himself into. I turned back toward him. "All right then. Let's back up a little. What were you doing downtown this morning? Who were those people? And why did you lie about it?"

"I was scared, Kenny. I still am. I don't know what's happening to me."

"All right. But if you want my help, you're going to have to be completely honest from this point forward."

Yates took a deep breath, and after letting it out, he said, "I do want to get this off my chest. I'm not the type of person who wants to be dishonest about anything. But I have to warn you. Some of what you're going to hear is going to sound... incredible."

"I'd be surprised if it didn't," I said.

Yates's expression reflected his uncertainty. "Around 8:40 p.m. Friday, I answered a disturbance call. Some guy had had too much and was busting up the place out at Arnie's over on Second Street. I guess by the time I got there, he'd gotten it out of his system. He didn't put up a fight. When he saw I was a cop, he pretty much gave up and let me cuff him. My guess is he was no newcomer to being arrested. I loaded the poor old sot into the patrol car, but as soon as I slid behind the wheel, I heard about a possible breaking and entering at an empty building over on Elgin. I was only a few blocks away, so I answered that one too. I got over there pretty quick, and I was getting ready to call for backup, but the suspects bolted from the building and ran right past the patrol car. It was cold and rainy, but I left Crawford—that's the guy's name I picked up at the bar, Dewey Crawford—and went after them. It didn't take long to catch them. Turned out to be an old homeless couple. Dispatch said the owner of the building was pitching a fit. I guess he'd been hit too many times and he was tired of it. But it was pretty obvious that the old couple was just trying to get in out of the weather. It was about 9:00 p.m. by then, and I was just going to give them a good talking to and let them go." Yates paused and shook his head.

Yates's words had described the details of the events, but they had also conveyed commitment to his job and compassion for the people he dealt with. I walked back and sat in the chair next to him. "What happened after that?"

"I'm not sure. The next thing I know, Linda's shaking my shoulder, telling me to wake up and get in the house. I was in the patrol car, which was parked in the driveway of my house. I told Linda I must've fallen asleep. The truth is I have no idea how I got there or what exactly happened between."

I leaned back in the chair. A question hung in the air that had to be asked. "So how does the pornography fit in?"

"A chunk of missing time would be difficult enough to deal with," Yates said.

He reached for the computer mouse, and when the video of the sensuous woman was once again revealed to its unwilling audience, it showed a scene of lust, its content explicit, from which came incriminating evidence. The woman was no longer alone but was engaged in sexual intercourse with a man. The camera had been used in a way that left no doubt as to the identity of the man. It was David Yates.

"Turn it off," I said.

Yates quickly shut down the video, then turned to face me. He wiped his eyes with his hand, then said, "This showed up in my wife's email. I love Linda with all my heart, and I would never do anything like that."

"So how do you explain it?"

"That's why I asked for you, why I need your help. The word around the department is that you have experience with this kind of thing, a history of dealing with unusual things like possession."

"Is that what you think, that you were possessed?"

"What other explanation is there?"

I considered the question. I'd hoped my involvement with certain cases had gone unnoticed, but I knew better from the questioning glances, coworkers lowering their voices when I walked past. I wanted to tell Yates that amnesia was a more likely answer, but the truth was that complete and total memory loss is highly unusual. And in this case, compounded by Yates's assertion of it only covering a specific time period. "I don't know," I said, "but jumping from memory loss to possession is a pretty big leap. Let's try piecing some of this together. Maybe it'll start to make sense."

Moisture clogged Yates's reddened eyes. "I debated all night about whether or not I should tell you this. Tell anybody, for that matter."

Uncertainty about the direction of the case coursed through me. Based on what I'd heard so far, I didn't know if I was ready to gain knowledge which Yates had been holding back because he thought it too risky. "If it's pertinent to the case, let's have it."

"I kept telling myself it was a dream." He shook his head. "It wasn't."

The room became quiet, and I thought Yates might lose his nerve. "Go on."

"I thought I was paralyzed," he said. "I was in bed, and I couldn't move. It was a struggle just to breathe. It occurred to me that things were wrong, bad wrong. I kept thinking about Linda. Suddenly I broke through and came out of it, and her name fell across my lips. It was then that I noticed a person sitting up in bed beside me. She was upset."

"Your wife, Linda?"

He shook his head. "She said it was the third time this week and she was tired of it. Her language was a little more colorful, but that was the gist of it."

I mentally raced through the scattered details. Had Yates contradicted himself, saying he couldn't remember cheating on his wife only to confess it through the guise of a dream? I gestured toward the computer. "Was it the woman in the video?"

An expression somewhere between fear and confusion crossed his face. "No," he said. "I might be able to deal with a spat of amnesia and affiliated infidelity."

I tried to remind myself we were talking about a dream but had it been? Yates had indicated he wasn't sure. If the events, even some of them, had been real, I needed to know. "If it wasn't your wife and it wasn't the woman in the video, who was it?"

"At first I thought maybe it was Linda. I mean it had to be, didn't it? She was getting madder by the minute, whoever she was. I told her I'd felt like I was drowning, and that's why I'd called out her name when I woke up. That didn't help matters any. In fact, it seemed to make it worse, so I slid around and dropped my feet over the side of the bed, but when I touched the floor it was bare and cold, not the carpeted floor of my bedroom. She wanted to know where the hell I thought I was going, and I told her I needed a glass of water. She informed me I wasn't going to get it there unless I was planning on climbing out the window. That's when she flipped on a lamp, and when my nightmare solidified. It wasn't my bedroom, and it definitely wasn't Linda in the bed. Even more puzzling, if anything appeared out of the ordinary to the lady, she certainly didn't show it."

He shrugged. "I asked her where I was. It was just a natural reaction. She rattled off a string of foul words that would embarrass a seasoned pastor. I told her I was sorry and that I didn't know how or why any of this was happening. She picked up an ashtray or something and hurled it at me. Figuring she would continue the assault, I ducked into the bathroom. I could hear her screaming behind the closed door, but that wasn't the worst of it."

"What do you mean?" I asked.

"I saw my reflection in the mirror," he said, "and it wasn't me. His hand moved when I told it to, and it stroked his face just like I commanded, and the pressure registered against my skin or his skin, but it wasn't me."

I paused, wondering if Yates was suffering from a mental lapse brought on by the pressure of what he'd been through, or if he'd completely snapped and was lost in his own warped reality. A question formed in my mind, surprising me when I actually verbalized it. "Who did you see in the mirror?"

A bead of sweat trickled down Yates's face. "Dewey Crawford. The man I arrested at Arnie's, the bar on Second Street."

Most cops—most anyone, for that matter—would have probably walked away at that point, told Yates to get professional help, and left it alone. But unusual people and strange situations had a way of finding me. Nothing surprised me anymore. But I had to admit that this came close. "What did you do?"

"That's when I came out of it with Linda shaking my shoulder and telling me to wake up and get in the house."

"And that was around 3:30 a.m. Saturday?"

A smile tried to turn the corners of Yates's mouth, but the impulse was outnumbered. "Your knack for detail gives me confidence," he said, "a trait that's been worn to the breaking point in my case. I was there, Kenny, in Crawford's house. With every ounce of my being, I want to believe it was a dream, but it wasn't. It happened. It was real. I keep going over it, can't get it out of my head."

I put my hand on Yates's shoulder. "Take it easy. I said I'd help. We'll get this sorted out somehow."

Yates got up and paced frantically about the room. "What if he did drugs or something? What if he killed someone? My God, what if he had killed himself with me in his body, Elliot?"

Yates's expression said he was about to mentally check out. "What in the world would it feel like to die in someone else's body? Would I actually be dead? Would I have gone back to my old body?"

Do you have any idea what it feels like to die in someone else's body?

Yates's words slammed into me like a right cross, transporting me back to that day in the church parking lot when a man, the John Doe that was now missing from the medical examiner's lab, had asked me that question. I jumped up and grabbed Yates, hauling him to his feet. "What's going on, Yates? What kind of game are you playing here?"

"I'm being straight with you, honest. I don't know what's going on."

I let go, and Yates plopped back into the chair. "Don't walk away, Kenny. I can't do this alone."

I strode back to the window and stared at the lawn, already beginning to fade into darkness. I had to calm down, focus on the details of the case that were of substance and not from ethereal ramblings. A few seconds later, I turned and walked back. "You never told me why you were downtown this morning. Let's get back to that."

Yates sat silent for a moment, his eyes glazed over and distant, as if complying with my request to climb back down to the physical world was difficult. "Yesterday," he said, "I was sitting alone in the living room, trying to sort this out, when my cell phone rang. I thought it was Linda. Instead, some gravel-voiced guy told me he knew what I'd been through, had some information that would help."

I stepped forward. Yates had been a cop long enough to recognize a break when he saw one, and yet he'd thrown the last bit in as if it were a trivial detail. "Were you able to gain information from the caller, who he was, where he was calling from?"

"I did what anybody in my position would do. I jumped at the chance and agreed to a meeting."

I paused, thinking it over. Things were starting to fall into place.

"Was that what I walked into this morning outside the station?"

Yates nodded.

"And the guy who took a couple of shots at you, was he the one who called and set up the meeting?"

"It had to be. He told me how he would be dressed, said I'd know him when I saw him."

"Why was he trying to kill you?"

"I'm not so sure that he was. The look on his face, all my years on the force, I've never seen anything like it. It was closer to anguish than anger. He saw that truck coming. He had to have. He jumped in front of it on purpose."

"They haven't been able to ID the man yet. Do you have any idea who he was?"

Yates shook his head. "It's just like with the girl on the video. I don't know. I've never seen either of them before."

I put the questioning on hold and mentally ran through what Yates had just told me. Nothing about his demeanor indicated deception. "What about the elderly gentleman standing on the northeast corner near the crosswalk? He seemed to know something. He was waving at you."

Yates wiped his forehead with the back of his hand. "I know this sounds incredible, but right after I got through talking with the gravel-voiced guy, I get another caller telling me pretty much the same thing, that he had some information. So I told him to meet me at the same time and place, figured I'd get everybody there at once, you know."

"It looked like the old man intended to cross the street," I said, "to get to where you were standing, but he stopped just before the commotion began. Something must have alerted him. Maybe seeing the old guy caused the younger one to miss his shot."

"Yeah, I wondered about that too, especially after getting back-to-back calls."

"Like you said, pretty incredible. Has anyone else contacted you in relation to this?"

"Yeah, Detective Monica Campbell called right after you, and Pastor Meadows left, grilled me again about where I was Friday night and Saturday morning." He paused, then added, "She also asked about my service weapon."

"Sergeant Long probably informed her you didn't have it."

"Yeah," he said. "I guess that's it."

"Where was the last place you saw it?"

"I've looked everywhere. I don't know where it is."

I had a good idea of where the weapon was located, and if I was right, it wasn't good. "How about the weapon the John Doe dropped on the sidewalk this morning?"

"That thought crossed my mind as well, but I didn't bring it up during either of the interviews. God forgive me, but I haven't told anybody but you about that part of it."

I considered Yates's words. I hoped his confidence in me wasn't misplaced. "I honestly don't know how much I can do for you," I said, "with the department already looking into it. I'll have to be careful."

"Every time a car drives by," he said, "I run to the window thinking it's a squad car coming to take me to jail."

"I wouldn't worry too much about that just yet. The missing gun is troublesome though. Have you erased the call log on your phone?"

"Not lately."

"Scan through it and give me the numbers of the two callers and any associated names or information. Maybe I'll have some luck, and they'll have used phones I can trace."

"I appreciate your help, Kenny. I thank God for his wisdom in bringing us together."

"Is there anything else you should tell me, information you might have left out?"

Yates stared at me for a moment, then said, "Not that I know of, but you saw the video. What else might I have done that I don't know about?"

4

Outside the home of David Yates, I sat in the cab of the pickup. The phone numbers Yates had given me from his call log turned out to be dead ends. No surprise there.

I started the truck, then backed out of the drive and headed out of the neighborhood. Under ordinary circumstances, I'd have ample reason to think that Yates was attempting to spin an elaborate lie, that he'd done something crazy and was trying to use me as a distraction, a cover of sorts. I didn't believe that though. On the contrary, I suspected Yates was in more trouble than he realized. The fact that Sergeant Long had questioned him about his whereabouts and then suspended him reinforced the notion. And why was Detective Monica Campbell involved? She usually worked theft and robbery.

I didn't like the idea of going rogue, climbing around beneath the radar, but my instincts were telling me that, for David Yates's sake, someone needed to, not because the department was corrupt but because certain unrecognized details might go unchecked, even unnoticed, otherwise. Sooner or later I'd have to talk with someone inside the department, but not just yet. Earlier, I'd intended to question the Mercedes driver who I'd followed. I pulled out of Yates's neighborhood, and several minutes later, I arrived once again at the Village at Central Park, the condos where the Mercedes driver had gone.

I climbed the stairs to the condo, then rang the bell.

Seconds later, the door opened. An elderly gentleman stepped into view, then clicked his heels together and bowed slightly. "Ezra Barrington," he said. "How can I be of service?"

I took a step back, mentally reprimanding myself for being careless, as my hand instinctively patted the area just beneath my left arm, verifying the availability of my service weapon. Standing in the doorway of the condo was the same elderly gentleman I'd seen waving at David Yates just before the John Doe had opened fire. "Name's Elliot," I said. "You were downtown near the police station this morning. I believe we have a lot to talk about. May I come inside?"

A wry smile turned the corners of the old man's mouth, hinting at ages of mystery that hid behind the expression. "Of course," he said, "but shouldn't you first show me your credentials?"

I hesitated then. "I could do that, but my business here is unofficial, a private matter I'm handling on my own."

"Forgive my presumptuous manner," he said. "Ordinarily under such circumstances, I would ask you to leave, but guessing the true nature of people is a hobby of mine. Sometimes I get it wrong, but not often. Yes, please come in."

The man, who had called himself Barrington, led me into the living area of the condo. "Feel free to sit wherever you want. Can I offer you coffee or tea?"

I chose an art deco–style chair covered with brown leather. "That's kind of you, but I'm fine, thanks."

The condo was crowded but not untidy, rather like an old well-stocked museum where abundant artifacts seemed a part of the background, coming to life individually when noticed, brass nautical items, intricate clocks, and timepieces. "Expanding on your previous game of perception," I said, "what were you doing downtown earlier today?"

"I observed you as well, as soon as you descended the steps leading from the police department. You took notice of my presence as a bystander, which I was merely an accidental witness to a string of unfortunate events and nothing more to it than that."

"I'd like to believe that," I said, "but my instincts are telling me otherwise."

Once again, Barrington displayed the wry smile. "As I implied, I happened to be at the wrong place at the right time."

More like this was mystery caller number two who wanted to speak with David. "Does the name David Yates mean anything to you?"

"Can't say that it does."

Once again, I let my gaze leisurely fall across the multitude of varied objects that stuffed the room. An oil painting, which hung over the fireplace, caught my attention. I was no art critique, but the painting appeared to be the real thing and quite old. "Yates tells a different story. He says you called him, claiming to possess helpful information relevant to some recent problem areas in his life. You agreed to meet him at the time and location where I saw you."

"Your client must have me confused with someone else."

"Come on, Barrington. I was there, remember? I saw you wave at him."

He shrugged. "Just a friendly gesture."

"What about the man who took a shot at Yates? Do you know who that was?"

Barrington shook his head. "I wish I could be of more help to you. You strike me as someone who has an eye for detail. Tell me, what do you think of the artwork?"

Barrington was referring to the painting over the fireplace.

"Meaningful art has always fascinated me," I said, "though my knowledge of the subject might be contained in a nutshell. However, I've seen this before. Van Gogh, I believe, and yet it appears to be authentic. How can that be?"

Barrington smiled. "The longer one lives, the more they realize how little they know about life, except that it's mostly illusion. I saw you coming out of the police station and surmised you a cop, but the truth of the matter is that you could be anybody—a lawyer, a convict, an elected official, a zombie who works nine to five and comes alive at night as a bass player for some mediocre band."

I couldn't stifle the laugh that found its way to the surface. I wanted to remain serious, but I liked the old guy, and I couldn't help it. As packed with memorabilia as his place was, I suspected each item carried significance, had a story behind it. "What about the painting, Mr. Barrington?"

"A few years ago—back in the 1960s, I believe—I went through a phase where I'd thought I'd found my calling in applying oil to canvas."

"You did this?"

"In a manner of speaking, and yet I cannot claim it as my own."

"What exactly does that mean?"

"Well, as you pointed out, the artist's name was Vincent Van Gogh. It's called *The Painter on His Way to Work*, but it's also referred to as *The Painter on the Road to Tarascon*."

"It's amazing," I said. "You could have told me it's real, and I would have believed you. It's that good. Why did you give it up?"

"Thank you, Mr. Elliot, but that would be impossible. The original work was destroyed by fire during the war—World War II, that is. I moved on from the phase by choice. It seemed I was pretty good at copying but not so good at being myself."

I picked up an old clock from the table beside me. Like many of the other pieces, it was made of brass, its internal workings, gears, and other moving parts exposed. Barrington's condo resembled a backstreet haberdashery in a steampunk novel. "That's interesting," I said. "It's exactly the impression I've been getting of you."

Barrington's eyes twinkled, but he offered no rebuttal.

"I would have liked to have met you under more favorable circumstances, Mr. Barrington. From all indications, you've lived a long life, and judging from the variety and complexity of your collection, you've enjoyed experiences beyond the reach of most people. An impression of malice doesn't present itself convincingly, but one of secrecy does."

Barrington shook his head. "I had a feeling you were going to be troublesome. You have the kind of eyes that see too much. I once knew someone very much like you, a champion of the downtrodden with an instinct for the truth."

"What happened to this fascinating acquaintance?"

"He caught the disease that awaits the lucky. He got old."

Barrington's character continued to unfold, and it occurred to me that he might be lowering his defenses, hinting at secrets ordinarily reserved for a dwindling number of those close to him. I returned the clock to the table. "All right, Mr. Barrington. As you have admitted, you were there this morning during what I suspect was an attempted engagement with David Yates. Later I found you parked outside his home. The fact of your involvement in whatever is happening here is of little doubt in my mind. I don't know how or why, but I intend to find out."

"Yes," he said. "I expect you do. However, things aren't always what they seem to be. Samuel Rosenberg, an old and dear friend of mine, was to be in court this morning, counsel for the defense of a man accused of armed robbery. When you saw me, I was on my way to meet with Rosenberg. We were to have coffee while we talked of old times."

I'd thought that Barrington was going to open up, but now it seemed he'd thought better of it. "It looked to me like you were preparing to cross the street. You had recognized David Yates, and you were on your way to meet with him."

"Appearances can be deceiving."

"What about later?" I asked. "Why were you parked outside Yates's home?"

He shrugged. "As you might imagine, I was shaken up by the commotion of gunfire and seeing that poor man run down by the delivery truck. I gave up on coffee and went home. Sam called later for a reschedule, and we talked in the privacy of his home. As fate would have it, Mr. Rosenberg apparently resides in the same neighborhood as your friend, Mr. Yates. Sam has a large family, and his drive was full. To avoid complication, I parked along the street."

The only time I like coincidences was when they occurred to me. Which was often, and it was acceptable. But coincidences in others always smelled of lies. "We've both been evasive and guarded with one another," I said, "perhaps understandably so. I'll take the first step. David Yates could be in a lot of trouble. He's a good man, Mr. Barrington." This case had intrigued me, and since I was taking time, I figured I should use it well and do something I couldn't do on the clock. "I've taken a leave of absence from the department to gain latitude and freedom to fully investigate his case."

I grabbed the notepad I kept in the breast pocket of my jacket and scrawled my number across it, then tore off the page and gave it to Barrington. "Any relevant information you could give me would be greatly appreciated. No need to get up. I'll let myself out."

I left Barrington's apartment with an increased suspicion that the trail I was following would become increasingly complex. The enigmatic old gentleman was somehow tangled up in the nightmare David Yates had stumbled into. I'd caught a glimpse of acquiescence in Barrington's eyes, but as quickly as it had come, the inclination to cooperate had faded. I had yet to gain his trust. I grabbed my phone, and a few minutes later I had the information I was after, the phone number for Samuel Rosenberg, the attorney Barrington had referred to.

A cool wind blew across the darkened area of what used to be Central Park. The old city park had been modified, improved, some might say, and incorporated into the grounds of the complex of condominiums where Barrington lived. His alibi had checked out. Samuel Rosenberg, a longtime Tulsa attorney, had confirmed his story, including the botched coffee break and the meeting later at Rosenberg's house that just happened to be down the street from David Yates. It was all too convenient, but there wasn't much I could do about it at this point except to give Barrington time and hope that he came around.

Going on the assumption that Yates had told me everything he knew, Barrington was the only good lead I had. The way I saw it, the next best course of action was to retrace Yates's steps and talk to the people who'd been around him just before he checked out. Finding the homeless couple he'd roused from the abandoned building would be next to impossible, but locating the man he'd arrested at the bar shouldn't be too difficult.

5

Dewey Crawford, the man David Yates had arrested Friday night at Arnie's Bar, lived in a white clapboard house located in one of the more mature neighborhoods of Broken Arrow, not far from the downtown post office. Yates had given me the address. He'd tracked it down and come here just to see if it really existed the way he remembered it. Yates claimed he'd been too nervous to do much more than drive by, but when he saw the woman he'd encountered during his waking nightmare standing in the yard, he'd nearly run into one of the cars parked along the street. At least that's what he'd told me.

A lady with dirty-blond hair and a face etched with trouble answered the door. She maintained a stoic expression, but her eyes moved quickly, like a frightened animal.

A tinge of pity worked its way into my consciousness, and I fought off an urge to turn and walk away. It appeared that the lady of the house had lived a hard life, and I didn't want to add to it. "Good evening," I said. "The name's Elliot. I'm looking for Dewey Crawford."

The lady didn't respond right away, but her quick eyes searched my face for answers. "I'm just guessing," she said, "but if Dewey knew someone like you was looking for him, I don't think he'd want to be found."

"It's nothing like that," I said. "I just need to talk to him."

Several bad tattoos decorated the lady's arms. A cigarette smoldered between the fingers of her left hand. "You a cop? You sure act like one."

I'd certainly been guilty of being evasive in the past, even bending the truth on occasion, but I'd gone through a lot of changes lately. I guessed finding out you're a father would do that to you. "You nailed it, but I'm off duty, working a personal case on my own. Does that bother you?"

She shrugged. "It doesn't make much sense to me, but it doesn't matter anyway. Dewey's not here. Hell, I haven't seen him since Saturday. He came home all drunk, nothing unusual about that, but he was acting strange even for the sorry excuse that he is. He pulls crap like this all the time. I shouldn't put up with it. Hell, I don't even know why I should worry."

"I wouldn't know," I said. "Is there a particular place he goes when things get bad, like a fishing cabin or something?"

"You're kidding, right? He can't even afford this dump let alone a vacation spot. Hell, he wouldn't know a fish from a can of beer anyway."

I tried not to smile. "Is there a particular bar he frequents?"

She took a drag on her cigarette, mulling over the question. "If he finds out I put you on to him, he won't be happy. But yeah, the beer joints, any of them, would be a good place to start."

"You mentioned he was acting strangely," I said. "Could you tell me a little more about that?"

She shrugged. "It's kind of hard to explain. He was just different, using fancy words that aren't usually part of his vocabulary, and looking at me funny too, like he was all confused or something. It was downright scary. I got to thinking that maybe he'd finally had one too many, pickled his brain or something." She paused, then said, "Ordinarily I wouldn't be telling you all this, but I'm worried about him. He ain't much, but he's all I got."

A question formed in my mind. Dewey Crawford couldn't be spending all his time in bars. He had to be sleeping somewhere. However, the pain-filled expression on his wife's, or girlfriend's, face caused me to reconsider going down that path. "I mean him no harm," I said, "and I appreciate your cooperation. Could you put together a list of places he might hang out?"

The lady's face alternated between giving up and hopeful. "Yeah, I can do that for you."

She hesitated, then turned and walked into the house.

I stood on the small porch and waited, listening as muffled voices coming from somewhere up the street echoed through the area followed by the slamming of a door. Dewey and his wife, if that's what she was, fit right into the neighborhood.

A few minutes later, the lady reappeared and frowned as she tore a page from a yellow legal pad and handed it to me. "If you happen to run across the sorry excuse, tell him his woman wants him home, that there won't be no hard feelings."

I scanned the page, which showed only three locations. Finding Crawford might be easier than I'd thought. Then again, Dewey could have numerous places his lady didn't know about. "I'll do that," I said. "I just have a couple more questions, and I'll be out of here. Does Dewey own a gun?"

A look of fear crossed her face. "Not that I know of. He is in some kind of trouble, isn't he? You just don't want to tell me."

"All right," I said. "I'll level with you. There are a lot of details about this case that I haven't figured out. With the gun, I'm hoping it's just a matter of confusion. Did he have a weapon on him when he came home Friday night?"

The lady shook her head, her hand darting up to cover her expression.

"I'm sorry to upset you," I said. "Everything will probably work out fine. Does the name David Yates mean anything to you?"

Again she shook her head but said nothing.

At the mention of a gun, she'd clammed up. I wasn't going to get anything more out of her. "Thanks for your help, ma'am."

The lady shrank deeper into the house, then closed and locked the door.

As I stepped from the porch, I caught sight of someone walking across Crawford's yard, going toward the rear of the house.

Using the other side of the house, I made my way around too.

When I reached the area, a change in the shadows caught my attention, and I visually followed the commotion to a broken-down shed.

I pulled the flashlight I kept in my jacket pocket and shined it toward the area.

Two people stepped forward, a couple of teenage boys, big for their age. The one with the darker hair pointed to the flashlight as if he thought it some kind of weapon. "What you going to do with that?"

"That depends," I said. "What are you doing here?"

"We ain't doing nothing. Maybe we live here."

"I don't think so."

"You think what you want. I ain't seen you before. What's you doing here?"

I reached inside my coat and pulled my badge. "I happen to know the Crawford family. Personal friends, you might say."

The boys took a step back, their expressions softening. "I meant it when I said we wasn't doing anything. We saw you and got scared, that's all. Dude as big as you ought to be used to that."

"All right," I said. "No harm done. But I want you to leave, and I don't want to see you around here again."

"Yes, sir."

"The family has my number. If I have to come back, it won't be pleasant."

A few hours after talking with Dewey Crawford's wife, I pulled into the gravel parking lot of a yet another bar. I hadn't had much luck. The guy at Arnie's hadn't worked Friday night when Crawford was there. He'd heard about it and knew the bartender who'd worked that shift but claimed he didn't know how to get in touch with him. It'd be four hours until he was back at work again before I'd be able to speak with him.

The lady who worked at the second bar on the list admitted to knowing Crawford but said she hadn't seen him in a while. She couldn't remember exactly how long it had been.

Now at the last location, a bar just off Main Street in Broken Arrow, my spirits lifted a bit. The place was within relative walking distance of Crawford's house. It made sense that it would be one of his favorites. I'd started with Arnie's because that was where Crawford had caused trouble and Yates arrested him.

The reason behind Crawford's disappearance still puzzled me. He'd managed to slip away from David Yates, so the possibility that the police might still be looking for him had no doubt occurred to him, but being drunk and disorderly wasn't exactly a capital offense as a reason to run. Based on what I'd puzzled so far, Crawford ought to be used to the routine of sleeping off a night of drinking in a cell. He was running from something. And I suspected for a guy like Crawford, the problem would have to be something more serious than being arrested for disturbing the peace.

I climbed out of the truck, then strolled across the lot to the door of the bar on Main Street and stepped inside.

A thick layer of cigarette smoke filled the dimly lit room where the sound of voices buzzed in the background. A short, rotund man leaned over a pool table, ready to take a shot, while several other people stood against the wall.

I was encouraged to find the place busy. It meant I might have a bit of luck. I let my eyes adjust to the darkness, then made my way to the bar where a thin man with a pitted face glanced in my direction but stayed where he was, talking with a couple who sat at the bar. I remained patient, but after a few minutes, I gestured for the bartender to stop ignoring me.

He frowned, then pulled away from his friends and strolled over. "What can I get for you?"

"Sorry to bother you, but I'm looking for someone, a man named Dewey Crawford. I heard he hangs out here."

The bartender didn't say anything. He stepped away and grudgingly waited on another customer who had stepped up. After that, he busied himself washing glasses. Taking his time, he wiped his hands on a towel and returned. "You a cop?"

"Not exactly."

"One of those kind, huh? Well, maybe I'm not exactly a bartender. One thing's for sure. I'm not your local lost and found."

I took a deep breath, letting it out slowly, an exercise that often had a calming effect. It was during grade school that I'd first acquired the tough-guy image—out of necessity, I liked to think. It's hard enough being a kid, but when you only had yourself to fall back on, you did the best you could. I'd never had to look for trouble, that's for sure. I had to admit that I'd found the childhood persona useful during my tenure as a cop. Not only had I resurrected the charade, but I had honed it far beyond its original form, making it quite real. By the time I'd come to learn that the behavior might be harmful, it had become a part of me. I'd been working to change that. According to Carmen, I'd made progress.

But setbacks were to be expected with behavioral problems, and it was a reflex action, like blinking when the optometrist blows air into your eyes. You're told not to, but you do it anyway, kind of like when this bartender got lippy with me. I grabbed him by his collar and yanked him forward.

An eerie silence crept across the room. The customers had taken notice.

I released my grip. "Sorry, but I'm not in the mood for games. Now, do you know where I can find Crawford?"

He glanced at a booth near the front door. "Take a number," he said. "Guy's invisible for years. Now everybody's looking for him."

In the booth, wo men sat across from each other. I didn't recognize either of them, but they seemed restless, on alert that I'd taken notice. They had that armed, dangerous, and pain-in-the-backside look about them. The bartender had the look about him that said he wanted the pair of troublemakers gone. "Do you know them?"

"No, I don't, and who the heck are you?"

"Name's Elliot. Dewey's wife is worried about him. I told her I'd look into it."

"Peggy asked you to do that?"

"That's right."

"How is it you know Peggy, but you don't know Dewey?"

"Life's complicated like that. The truth is, I'm trying to get to know him, but he's not making it easy."

The bartender's gaze slid toward the pair in the booth at the front. I was unsure if it was intentional, but either way, his gaze returned to mine as he threw a towel over his shoulder. "Yeah, well maybe he's got a reason."

I gestured toward the men in the booth. "I'll make you a deal. I'll get rid of the goons if you will cooperate and give me any information you might have that could lead to Crawford."

"How do I know you're not worse than they are?"

I didn't want to tell the bartender that I'd already reached that conclusion, otherwise, I wouldn't have made the offer. It wasn't conceit. I'd just spent enough time with my back against the wall that I knew my limitations, and I'd gotten pretty good at guessing those of others. "You don't," I said. "But here's the deal; I only need to talk to Crawford because I believe he has information that could help my client. I intend him no harm. I'm not so sure you can say that about the thugs in the booth."

The bartender walked away, and when he returned, his expression had not improved, but he said, "All right. You do, and we'll talk. Don't expect miracles, though. I don't know that much."

I turned away and walked to the booth where the goons were seated. I positioned myself near the end of the table, approximately equal distance between the pair. "The bartender tells me you're looking for Dewey Crawford."

Neither of the men made a move that looked threatening, though the big fellow on the left took the initiative of speaking. "What's it to you?"

I considered the question carefully. I doubted either of them knew enough about Crawford's whereabouts to be of any help. Otherwise, they wouldn't be hanging around his favorite bar, hoping to get lucky. "It seems we have a common interest," I said.

The big fellow spoke again. "If you're looking to team up with us, you can forget about it. And we were here first, so why don't you shove off."

I shook my head. The amateur retort coupled with the fact that neither of the goons had made an aggressive move, indicated that bluffing them wouldn't be difficult. I slid into the booth next to the big guy. "That's not going to happen," I said. "I don't know how your day's been going so far, but my guess is it just took a turn for the worse."

Doing the best he could, the big fellow turned to face me. "Just who the hell do you think you are? You got about five seconds to get your ass out of this booth."

"I don't know," I said. "I kind of like it here. No one can come in or go out without my seeing it. It's probably why you chose it."

The big guy's partner leaned forward, toward the table.

Acting on instinct, I slid my right hand beneath my coat.

The partner shook his head, his arms on the table with palms open so I could see them. "We don't want no trouble, mister. My guess is you don't either. We can't make you leave, so all we can do is ask. Go on and sit somewhere else."

"What business do you have with Dewey Crawford?" I asked.

"He owes me," the little guy said. He gestured toward the big fellow. "We're not professionals. Something tells me you already knew that. We aren't looking to hurt Crawford. I just want my money back, that's all."

I looked at the big fellow. "Is he telling the truth?"

"Yeah," he said. "That's all there is to it. Now, will you please leave us alone?"

"How much are we talking about?"

The big guy started to speak, but the little one cut him off. "Two big ones," he said.

"Looks like you haven't done your homework," I said. "Do you honestly think you'll get two thousand out of a man like Crawford?"

"Two hundred," the man corrected. "But I know what you mean. I'd be lucky to get two cents out of that deadbeat."

I wondered what kind of lowlifes would waste time and effort on such a trivial amount. Could be more to it, but I didn't think it related to my interest with Crawford. "If you got the money, would that settle it?"

The pair of wannabe goons glanced at each other. "Yeah, sure. Like I said, that's all we're after."

I slid out of the booth and reached beneath my coat.

Both the men flinched.

I found my wallet and counted out the money.

The smaller goon opened his hand, reaching for the cash.

I held the payment out but then withdrew it. I wasn't in the habit of doing things like that, paying people, taking the easy way out, but this was just a trivial part of a much bigger problem, and I didn't need these two misfits stirring the waters. "The payment comes with a contingency," I said. "I don't want to see either of you around here again or anywhere near Dewey Crawford, for that matter."

The men glanced at each other, nodded, then got to their feet. "Sure," the smaller one said. "We can do that."

"And don't worry about the bar tab," I said. "I'll take care of it."

I waited for the wannabe goons to clear out, and when I was satisfied that they wouldn't be back anytime soon, I turned and went back to the bar. "All right," I said. "I improved the quality of your clientele. Now, tell me where I can find Crawford."

The bartender shook his head. "I never said I knew where he was. Fact is, I'm starting to get worried about him. But, hey, I was watching you with those guys, saw the whole thing, how you got Dewey off the hook and all. Not many people would do that, especially for a guy like Crawford. I don't know who you are or what you're after, but it looks like you're a straight-up guy. I don't know how much help I can be to you, but I'll try. Dewey showed up here Saturday around noon. He was in bad shape too."

"So you're saying he'd already started to drink?"

"No, man, it wasn't that. In fact, if I had to guess, I'd say he hadn't had any at that point." He paused. "Give me just a minute, okay?"

The bartender waited on some customers, and after taking care of them, he returned and continued. "Okay, it's like this. Dewey and I go way back, went to school together right here in Broken Arrow. He's had a tough life, probably brought most of it on himself, but hey, don't we all? I know he ain't much on character, but he's not a bad guy really. I mean he's not going to throw himself on a hand grenade for you, but he wouldn't go out of his way to hurt nobody either. What kind of trouble has he gotten himself into? Come on, I need to know."

"Like I said earlier, a client of mine is in a jam. I don't think Dewey had anything to do with it, but I think he was there and saw what happened. That's why I need to talk to him. You said he was in bad shape. What did you mean by that?"

The bartender glanced around, then lowered his voice. "He was scared, stone-cold terrified, if I had to guess. At first, I thought he was out of his head or something, talking all crazy and such, but when somebody's that shaken up, there has to be some substance to it."

I leaned closer. The bartender's sudden change in demeanor had my attention. "Did he give you any indication as to what might have caused him to behave like that?"

He shook his head. "Dewey doesn't usually strike people as being the religious type, but he and his family used to go to church. I don't think he's been in a while though."

"What does religion have to do with it?"

"He was going on about spooks, spiritual possession, and stuff like that. He asked if I knew of any priests and if I thought they'd be able to help. I had to ask, you know, what do you need with a priest?"

Crawford's worrying about possession seemed to somewhat fit in with David Yates's claims of their identities being all tangled up. "What did he say?"

"Something plumb crazy. He said he'd looked into the eyes of a demon. Honest to God, that's what he told me. This friend of yours, the one you said was in trouble, does he have something to do with this?"

I thought about the question. I didn't yet know enough about the details to honestly answer it. The bartender cared about Dewey though, and he wanted to help, but anything I might say could be misleading. "I can't be sure at this point," I said, "but it's beginning to look like Dewey, and my client witnessed the same thing. Whatever it was, it apparently had a traumatic effect on both of them."

The bartender glanced around the room, and when he turned back, his face held an expression of fear. "Do you believe in ghosts, Mr. Elliot?"

I thought back to the prior case I'd worked where forces beyond my control had been at work. "Let's not jump to conclusions," I said. "In all likelihood, there's a logical explanation behind it."

The bartender nodded. "Yeah," he said, "that's what I'm thinking."

I looked around the smoky room where people, couples mostly, occupied the booths, and I thought of Carmen. "Let me clear something up," I said. "I don't want to leave you with the wrong impression. I don't know Peggy any more than I know Dewey. I was looking for him earlier today and found her at home. I asked her some questions. She hasn't seen Dewey since Saturday either. It looks like he came here right after he left home. Are you sure you don't know where he is, where he might have gone?"

The bartender shook his head. "I wish I did, but I don't, and that's the truth. And with a guy like Dewey, it's hard to guess what he might do."

"You said he asked about a priest. Is he Catholic?"

"Yeah, I think so. But like I said, he ain't religious or anything. It surprised me when he brought it up."

I made a mental note to check with the Catholic churches nearby. "What did he say before he left? There must be something."

"I wish there was. He told me he'd see me later, then walked out. I haven't seen him since. I sure hope you can find him, mister. I've got a real bad feeling about all this."

I did as well, but I didn't want to elaborate on the subject. "I'll do what I can," I said. "Thanks for your help."

After that, I turned and walked out of the bar. It was late, and I'd exhausted my leads for the night, so I climbed into the truck and pulled out of the parking lot onto Main Street and drove west.

Minutes later, I pulled into the garage of my home in Broken Arrow. Once inside, I brewed a cup of coffee, decaf, which I kept on hand for such occasions. I wanted to think about the case, but I didn't want to stay up all night in the process. When the machine hissed to a stop, I grabbed the cup, then added cream and sugar.

I went to the living room, then plopped into the recliner and settled in for a good bit of thinking. David Yates had claimed he didn't know the lady in the incriminating video, and from what I'd gathered, he hadn't appeared to have been lying about it, which brought up another interesting point. I'd half expected the lady in the video and Crawford's girlfriend to be one and the same, but it didn't turn out that way. They were about as different as two people could get. And Dewey Crawford, the only other person that Yates knew to be involved, didn't want to be found.

I sipped the coffee and tried to slow things down, smooth out the collage of details tumbling in and out of sequence through my head. I wondered if Yates or any of the other people I'd interacted with during the day had said anything important that I had not caught or had not attached significance to, but nothing came to mind. At times like this, I would typically look for the unusual, odd details that didn't add up or seemed out of place. With this case, everything fell into that category. It occurred to me that perhaps I should do the opposite and concentrate on anything that seemed ordinary. Nothing came to mind.

I kept going back to Ezra Barrington, the refined old gentleman who'd claimed to be nothing more than a victim of circumstance. I didn't believe that. On the contrary, I suspected that Barrington, like Dewey Crawford, knew much more than he wanted to know, and he'd tried to distance himself for that reason.

At some point in my line of reasoning, it occurred to me that Samuel Rosenberg, a longtime Tulsa attorney, and Barrington's alibi, might be a source of useful information. I resolved to contact him in the morning.

I finished the coffee, then took a hot shower. In bed, just before I drifted into sleep, I replayed through my mind the scene where the John Doe came from the crowd to confront David Yates. As the scene unfolded, my attention was drawn not to center stage but to the dark corners where a man who wore a dark hooded garment which obscured his face stood away from the crowd.

6

Early the next morning, I sat in the office of Samuel Rosenberg, the attorney Ezra Barrington had claimed to be meeting.

"Thanks for seeing me on short notice," I said.

Rosenberg, a deliberate man with dark piercing eyes, sat behind an antique mahogany desk. "Not a problem. Always a pleasure to lend a hand to Tulsa's finest. Now, what's this all about?"

"Before we go any further," I said, "an important detail needs to be clarified. I'm not representing the department on this case. I'm working privately."

Rosenberg raised an eyebrow.

The old attorney was a long shot, but I was running out of leads. I'd arranged to contact the Catholic churches near Dewey Crawford's house and the surrounding area, but the effort hadn't paid off. If Crawford had contacted any of the churches, he hadn't made much of an impression. Given the nature of his problem, it's doubtful his inquiries would have gone unnoticed. The churches would, of course, have nondisclosure policies, but I hadn't made the calls personally. I'd convinced Pastor Meadows to do it for me. More than likely, Crawford had ditched the idea of finding a priest.

"Is that a problem?" I asked.

"I guess that depends on why you're here and what you hope to gain from it."

I suspected Rosenberg knew perfectly well why I was there. "Let me get to the point," I said. "I'm representing a client who has found himself in a somewhat precarious situation. I have reason to believe that Ezra Barrington is withholding information that could be helpful in my efforts to restore my client's reputation."

Rosenberg folded his hands together and leaned against the top of his desk. "What exactly has led you to believe that Mr. Barrington might possess this information?"

I wasn't going to tell Rosenberg that I was basing my investigation on a gut feeling. "Let's just say Barrington seems to have a habit of showing up every time something relevant happens."

Rosenberg shrugged. "I was under the impression that Mr. Barrington had already explained that to you."

"Indeed, he has. However, I find his alibi a bit unconvincing."

Rosenberg smiled. "I hope that wasn't intended as a direct insult."

"You can take it like you want. I've been an investigator for long enough to know a good lead, and my instincts are telling me that Barrington's all tangled up in it."

Rosenberg rubbed his chin. "In that case, I hope I can eventually clarify things for you. I took the liberty of inquiring about your background. You have a reputation for getting the job done, not someone to be taken lightly."

The fact that Rosenberg had taken the time to check up on me meant that he and Barrington were taking me seriously, which in turn meant that they had reason to worry. Rosenberg had probably been talking to Captain Dombrowski.

"You're a no-nonsense kind of guy, Elliot. I like that. If it's not confidential, could I ask the name of your client?"

Rosenberg's question caught me off guard. With my background of working for the department, I didn't ordinarily deal with client confidentiality. I considered stepping from the room and calling Yates to get his opinion, but I stopped short of doing that. I couldn't imagine his being concerned about it. "His name is Yates," I said. "David Yates."

Rosenberg, a rotund man with thick, bushy eyebrows, didn't say anything, but his eyes gave him away.

I didn't want to let the conversation end there, so I continued. "Do you know him?"

"Yes, more or less. He lives in my neighborhood, down the street from me, as a matter of fact. However, I have known Ezra Barrington for a long time, and I believe him to be a good man, one of the best."

I couldn't deny Rosenberg's assessment. Barrington had given me the same impression. But that didn't negate my suspicion of his involvement, however benign it might have been. "I saw Barrington at the scene of an attempted crime involving my client," I said, "and again later, parked near the home of the same client. If you were in my position, what would you think?"

Rosenberg smiled. "Perhaps you are short on leads, so to speak. You're searching for information anywhere you can find it."

"You could be right. But it's been my experience in the public sector that when a suspect becomes evasive, it's an indication of guilt. I think I made a good tactical move in coming to see you, Mr. Rosenberg. You're protecting Barrington. The question is, why?"

"Mr. Barrington doesn't need my protection. Of that, you can be sure."

I was anything but sure. I was inclined to believe that Rosenberg would have been right about that at one time, but not so much now. "It seems we've played to a draw," I said, "for now."

Rosenberg relaxed into his chair, but his dark eyes never wavered. "Don't be so sure, Mr. Elliot. It might play out that we have some common interests. And as fate would have it, I am currently in need of someone with your talents. The investigator I've been using has decided to retire. Would you be interested?"

It seemed strange that someone I might end up in conflict with would offer me a job. It made little sense, but I decided to play along, see where it led. "I'm not a private investigator by trade. I'm doing this as a favor for a friend."

"Oh, come now, Mr. Elliot. I believe you have found your future, and a good one I would wager. I'm prepared to make you an offer."

"I'm not looking for work. I'm looking for answers."

Rosenberg smiled. "If things turn out the way I think they will, you could well find both."

I paused. Rosenberg had been dropping phrases designed to pique my interest. He hadn't come out and said that our current cases were related, but he was hinting at it. "What do you have in mind?"

"A client of mine is alleged to have taken something that wasn't his from a local establishment. He has brought to my attention that a certain lady friend of his could verify his whereabouts just minutes before the robbery occurred. This evidence could bring doubt upon his participation in the event. The trouble is, we can't locate the witness. That's where you come in."

"What do I get out of it?"

Rosenberg shrugged. "What are your terms?"

I considered my answer. I hoped I wasn't falling for a trap. "After I find the witness, you come clean on Barrington and make available any related information you might have. Something tells me we're working the same case, just from different sides."

Rosenberg stood and extended his hand. "Mr. Elliot, I believe we have a deal."

"I'll need the lady's name and any other information your investigator might have dug up."

"Not a problem."

"Just one more thing. I gave you the name of my client. It seems only fair that you return the favor."

Rosenberg was silent for a moment, as if unsure if he should comply. When he spoke, it was with a lowered voice. "James Goldstein," he said. "Please keep that confidential."

Three hours after leaving Rosenberg's office, I sat in the truck, parked alongside the street in an older neighborhood of Sand Springs, a small town just west of Tulsa. Through the windshield, I watched someone who I thought might be Roxie Taylor, the person Rosenberg had asked me to find. She wore a jogging suit with the hood of the sweatshirt pulled over her head, but even with the disguise, if that's what it was, she looked vaguely familiar. The file Rosenberg had given me contained several photographs. They weren't very good. Whoever had taken them had done so from a distance and with shaky hands. But the photos had been enough to put an uneasy feeling of familiarity in my gut and to now recognize that I had the right person. And that's when it hit me. I'd suspected before, but now, seeing her in person, all doubt was erased. Roxie Taylor, the lady Rosenberg had hired me to find with hopes of her panning out as a witness for his client, was none other than the stunningly attractive blonde I'd seen in the video, engaged in an act of passionate sex with David Yates.

Roxie glanced around, then got into one of the cars, a brown Nissan parked near the house and backed out of the drive.

I had no idea where she might be going. Without the head start offered by Rosenberg's information, it would not have been easy to locate her. She had, it seemed, gone into hiding. Rosenberg hadn't told me who his investigator was or why he'd decided to resign from the case, but his groundwork had been nearly complete. I'd easily picked up where he'd left off and followed it through. Roxie Taylor was staying at her sister's house in Sand Springs, not a good plan of action for someone serious about hiding, but it had been enough to throw everyone off for a few days.

Keeping a safe distance, I pulled onto the roadway and followed the brown Nissan east along Eighth Street for a mile or so then south to Sixth Street where the car resumed going east. A few minutes later, the Nissan pulled off the road, stopping near a small city park just down from the high school.

Upon realizing the driver's intention, with her wearing running clothes, my spirits lifted. Due to the season and time of day, with parents at work and kids at school, the park would be somewhat deserted. Talking to the person I'd been following would be easier in such a setting, provided she didn't panic and run.

She got out of the car and climbed over a grassy incline, a berm created to shelter the park from the street.

I waited a few minutes, then followed the same route over the berm, and when I crested the small hill, I saw the lady standing in a grassy area with her back to me. She took something from her pocket and tossed it to the ground near a group of mature oak trees where several squirrels scampered about.

I paused. It wasn't unusual for me to experience apprehension upon approaching someone related to a case, but this was a little different, and there was no denying the hesitation in my step.

As if she, too, sensed the uneasy energy in the air, the lady stiffened, then turned toward me.

Offering as nonthreatening an image as I could muster under the circumstances, I stopped at a distance, and even though I was working a private case, I pulled my badge. I thought it might lessen the tension.

"Who are you?" she asked. "And why are you following me?"

I suspected the lady had no way of knowing that my own surprise exceeded hers by a long shot.

"Name's Elliot," I said, extending my badge out a little farther to help ease her mind. "You're not in any trouble. I just need to ask you a few questions."

The lady relaxed a little, the expression on her face closer to resignation than fear. "About what?"

A menagerie of questions fought for attention, but the one that topped the list dominated my response. "A friend of mine is in trouble," I said. "Please don't be offended, but I need to talk to you about David Yates."

She studied my face for a moment, her eyes making slight but rapid movements. "Who?"

"He's a police officer," I said. "Nice guy, five feet ten, 185 pounds."

I pulled the only photo I had of Yates. It was recent enough for her to recognize him.

She studied the photo, then shook her head. "I've never seen this person, and I don't know anyone by that name." She handed the photo back to me. "What's this all about anyway?"

I collected my thoughts and refocused. Seeing a photo of someone she'd had that kind of encounter with would have drawn a reaction, even from a seasoned liar, which I didn't think she was. My guess was, like David Yates, Roxie had no memory of the event. "As it turns out, Mr. Yates is not the only party involved. How about James Goldstein, that name mean anything to you?"

Roxie Taylor's expression went from a look of slight nervousness to one that bordered on being scared. "What's going on, and why you're asking these questions?"

My bringing up Goldstein's name had definitely gotten her attention. "I'm working for Samuel Rosenberg, an attorney from Tulsa. It appears Mr. Goldstein has gotten himself into some trouble. Rosenberg seems to think you have information that could help clear it up."

"I don't understand any of this," she said. "And I don't know anything about an attorney."

"But you do know James Goldstein," I said.

"We run into each other now and then, that's all. He seems like a nice man, but it's not like we're friends or anything. I barely know him. I don't see how I could be of any help to you."

I paused to regroup. Roxie Taylor's nervous demeanor told me there was more to her relationship with Goldstein than she was letting on, but I needed to approach it carefully and not scare her off. "I apologize," I said, "if I've come across too strong. I'm a police detective, but I've taken some time off to sort things out. I'm considering a career move. I've taken this case on a private basis to test the waters and help out a friend at the same time."

"And this friend of yours is James Goldstein?"

"Actually, David Yates, the other man I mentioned, is my client, but the more I work this case, the more it expands. It looks like Goldstein is part of it. You mentioned that you run into him now and then. What exactly did you mean by that?"

She stiffened and stepped into a more defensive stance. "There's nothing to it really. We both do volunteer work. Sometimes we end up in the same place, that's all."

I was running out of options. Roxie Taylor was one of the few tangible leads I had, and I didn't want the opportunity to gain useful information to slip through my fingers. She knew Goldstein, but from all readable indications, the name David Yates meant nothing to her. Setting aside the mystery of why a classy lady like Roxie Taylor would be in a small-town park, feeding squirrels, how could it be that neither she nor Yates remembered the encounter showed in the video? It just didn't add up.

"What kind of volunteer work?" I asked.

She studied my face for a moment, then reached into her coat pocket and pulled out a handful of peanuts, still in the shell, and tossed them to the squirrels. "Different things. Helping people in need for the most part. What sort of trouble is Mr. Goldstein in?"

"Rosenberg was rather vague about that," I said, "but from what I could gather, Goldstein was involved in some kind of robbery."

"That doesn't sound right," she said. "Mr. Goldstein is pretty old, somewhere north of eighty, I'd say, and he's kind and gentle."

"Sounds like you know him pretty well after all."

"Not really. A single lady has to look out for herself and learn to read people quickly. But still, I can't imagine Mr. Goldstein being involved with any kind of robbery. I mean, why would he? I last saw him Friday night at the homeless shelter over on North Denver, doing volunteer work. I don't know if that's what you're looking for, but it's all I have."

"It might be. What time period are we talking about?"

A look of anxiety flashed through her eyes. "I left around 9:00 p.m., a little after, perhaps. I'd been there for about three hours. Mr. Goldstein was there the whole time. What might have happened after that is as much a mystery to me as it is to you."

Once again, I reached for a business card. I'd already told her I was a cop. I wasn't sure if she'd intended her statement to be cryptic, but it certainly sounded that way. "Thank you, Ms. Taylor. Would you be willing to testify on Mr. Goldstein's behalf if it came to that?"

A caged and fearful expression came across her face. "Testify, like in a court of law?"

"Yes, ma'am. It might not turn out that way, but if it does, I'm sure Mr. Goldstein would appreciate your help."

She shook her head. "I don't know if I can do that."

It seemed Roxie Taylor led a private life and feared being seen in public. I wasn't sure why that might be, but for reasons I didn't fully understand, I wanted to help her, even protect her. I was inexplicably drawn to this strange lady. I suspected that keeping a low profile was a constant part of her life, her need for privacy running deeper than superficial desire. I handed her the business card. "I'll make you a deal," I said. Already my mind screamed I shouldn't be too sure about this. If I made this deal, then finding out more on my case from Rosenberg wasn't going to happen. But my gut screamed for this, so I followed it. "I won't tell anyone that I found you if you will agree to keep in touch and not go into hiding."

She examined the card but offered no comment.

"If your description of Mr. Goldstein is accurate," I said, "he wouldn't last long in prison. Sending him there would be a death sentence."

She nodded, her face reflecting weariness and a need for someone to talk to, someone she could trust. "You have a hard face, Mr. Elliot, etched with life, but your kind eyes defy you. I'll take you at your word if you will take me at mine. I'll stay where you can find me for a few days, but if anything transpires that's not to my liking, the deal's off."

"All right," I said. "I understand."

An idea occurred to me, and I pulled my wallet and found one of the cards the church had provided—for circumstances less mysterious, no doubt—and handed it to her. "We all need a little help now and then," I said. "It's a nice church with lots of nice people, but big enough to get lost in if that's what you choose."

She smiled. "Thank you, Mr. Elliot. I'll take that under consideration."

With that, she turned and walked away.

I waited a few minutes, then went back to the truck and got inside. I didn't know if I would ever see Roxie Taylor again. Her end of the bargain, like everything else about her, had been cryptic at best.

From my position inside the truck, I could see the bare branches of the oak trees swaying to the breeze, a gentle reminder that colder, harsher weather was on the way. Fall in Oklahoma was a season mostly experienced as a state of mind, like admiring vibrant, colorful leaves and steaming bowls of beef stew on the pages of magazines. Of course, there was occasion to break out the sweaters, though even those cool mornings were often laced with the threat of afternoon heat with temperatures starting out in the low sixties only to end up in the high eighties. Most typically this part of the country dropped from the heat of summer and plunged into the cold of winter within a few days, or so it seemed.

With the haunting loneliness I'd seen etched into the face of Roxie Taylor still fresh on my mind, I thought of Carmen. I fished the phone from my pocket and called.

She picked up, and after a brief period of silence, she said, "It's fascinating how you do that, Kenny. I don't know how many times I've thought of you only to have you call. I cannot decide if it's comforting or unnerving."

"Radar love," I said. "We have a wave in the air."

I made the statement jokingly, though I knew all too well that Carmen was not the only person to have noticed such peculiarities about me.

"Maybe you're right," she said. "Anyway, I need to buy a gift for a friend, and I'm on my way to Broken Arrow to that sporting goods place, the one up on the hill by the highway."

"That would be the Pro Shop."

"I was wondering if you would like to have lunch while I'm in town?"

I gripped the phone. We'd been out together several times since I'd learned of our son, Wayne, but Carmen had never been the one to initiate such things. She sounded cheerful, but I hoped it would be a good thing and not a pleasant way for her to indicate a desire for us to go our separate ways. "That would be great," I said.

"Is it okay? I don't wish to get in the way."

I thought back to our high school days and the tragic way we'd been torn apart, an incident that had thrown the town of Porter into chaos. Chief Charlie Johnston had known all along that I was innocent, but many of the townspeople had not shared his knowledge or his belief. "You could never be in the way of anything I do, Carmen. Besides, I've taken a few days off, working a private case. It won't be a problem."

"That doesn't sound like you, taking days off. And what do you mean, private case? Is everything thing all right?"

I detected uncertainty in Carmen's voice. She had never been comfortable with my being a police officer, but she liked even less the thought of influencing me to do otherwise. Once again, I looked at the lonely branches of the tall oaks contrasted against the dreary sky. How could I reply honestly to a question I hadn't the answer to? "I'm doing well," I said, "especially now that I'm talking to you."

"You're impossible," she said. "And you know where I like to go, so I'll see you there, okay?"

A little later, I secured a table at Carmen's favorite restaurant, and not long after that, she walked in.

She caught sight of me, then waved and made her way up the isle toward the table.

I slid out of the booth and gave her a quick, but not inconsequential, hug.

Her eyes indicated that she felt some the same emotions that overtook me whenever we were together, joy and anticipation, fear and uncertainty: A guarded love that had once been free but now—due to our lives having taken different paths, if not by our own choosing—remained restrained.

"It's good to see you," I said.

She held the embrace for a moment, then stepped away and maneuvered onto the bench seat.

I sat on the opposing bench, fascinated, the daylight from the front of the restaurant diffusing around her, captivating me to the point of staring.

She became aware of it and shifted farther into the booth.

"How's Wayne?" I asked.

"He's doing well. He asked about you, told me to say hello for him."

I'd known Wayne for only a few months, but I'd already developed a deep love for him. The feeling had, in fact, been nearly instantaneous upon our first meeting. "He said that?"

"Yes. He's been worried lately. His friends and some of the coaches have been insisting he play soccer. He made the mistake—his words, not mine—of giving in a few days ago and practicing with the team. They want him to join, but he has no interest in the sport." She paused and shook her head. "He's hard to understand. He loves only football and nothing else. He wants to be like you. He's never said as much, but I know that's what it is."

"He's a good boy, Carmen. You've done a wonderful job with him."

She sighed. "He is his own person, and I am proud of him for that."

She reached across the table and took my hand. "Now, let's talk about your taking this time off. Nick told me about what happened yesterday with that poor man getting run over. Is that what this is about?"

Carmen wasn't completely wrong. My deciding to help David Yates was indeed an integral part of what was going on except it more closely aligned with the result and not the cause. "It's a bit more complicated than that."

"I thought it might be," she said.

I shook my head. Our conversations lately always seemed to come to this. And I knew that Carmen probably suspected that what I'd witnessed the day before wasn't at the heart of it. She was hesitant to face the problem head-on. "I've been a cop for a long time," I said. "I've experienced much worse than what I saw yesterday. I don't want to accept that all that is now part of who I am, that I've become jaded, and if that alone was the entire left side of the equation, we probably wouldn't even be having this conversation."

Carmen's attention drifted across the table. When her gaze caught mine, she gave a nervous smile. "Something else is bothering you," she said.

The case I'd been involved with a few months ago had nearly devastated me, but it had been a catalyst for change as well. The resignation plans had been there, but that wasn't all. I'd always had a certain sense about me, the heart of my edge on the street, but it had evolved and intensified in an unnerving way.

"I'd dropped by the church not long after my recovery from the prior case. Pastor Meadows and I had a long talk. Afterward, as I was leaving, I kept noticing how empty the parking lot was, how different it seemed from busy Sundays, with my old truck sitting alone on the lot like some relic from the past."

Carmen's expression of concern deepened.

"Have you ever had a deer run through the glow of your car's headlights at night?" I asked.

She nodded.

"That's how it was," I said. "One second everything was fine, and the next it wasn't."

"I'm not sure I'm following this."

"There was only my truck," I said. "I parked alone on the lot, and then the man showed up, standing beside the truck, waiting for me."

As if a chill had run over her, Carmen hugged herself, rubbed her hands across her arms. "One of your visions?"

I nodded. "The look on that man's face is something I will never forget. It was like I was his last hope, and he was pleading for my help."

"What did he want?"

I shook my head. "He said only one thing: *Do you have any idea what it feels like to die in someone else's body?*"

"Kenny, that's creepy."

"Tell me about it. It's also connected to the case."

"What case?"

"Whatever's going on with David Yates," I said, "the man who was being shot at by the John Doe that Nick told you about who later ran into the traffic."

"If you go through with this and decide to resign from the police department, what would you do? Where would you go?"

Carmen still held my left hand, and I placed my right one atop it. "Being a part of your life and a part of Wayne's is more important to me than any of this. I'm not planning on going anywhere. And completely giving up on my occupation isn't what I have in mind."

"Then what do you have in mind?"

"Other than you?"

A hint of a smile crossed her lips. "Kenny, this is serious."

I decided to just come out with it. "I've been thinking about going private."

"You want to be a private investigator?" She shook her head. "I cannot see you taking stealthy photos of unfaithful spouses to supply ammunition for divorce settlements."

I smiled. Carmen was always so straightforward and honest in her conversation that, while I never forgot how intelligent she was, I was often lulled into being surprised by the depth of it. "Good point," I said. "But that's not what I had in mind."

"What will you do then?"

"I plan to handle the department's unusual, unsolved cases, the stuff no one wants to deal with, only on a contract basis. It's pretty much what I've been doing anyway."

"Well, when you put it that way, it makes even less sense to quit your job, if you're already doing what you want to do."

I shrugged. "I guess the idea of flexibility, of not being tied down by rules and regulations, appeals to me."

"And you would be happy with that, and it would keep you busy?"

"I don't think that would be a problem, but even if it came to that, I've got it covered. A local attorney has expressed interest in my services. Something tells me he knows other people in the industry that would be interested as well."

"I don't know, Kenny. I hope you are not jumping from bad to worse." She paused. "Johnnie once told me something about you."

She was speaking of Johnnie Alexander, one of our high school classmates. Johnnie had been what every boy dreamed of being: He came from a wealthy family, he was tall and handsome, captain of the football team. But he'd had one seemingly inexplicable flaw: he had developed an unwavering, unending friendship with one of the local bad boys, that being me.

It wouldn't have been anything the town couldn't handle if Johnnie hadn't been murdered during our senior year of high school. Over half the town had suspected me. I hadn't killed Johnnie Alexander. I'd loved him like a brother. Johnnie's death was the reason Chief Charlie Johnston had secreted me out of town.

"Okay," I said. "You've piqued my interest. What did Johnnie have to say?"

"Actually, it wasn't so much Johnnie's words but something you had told him, what you believed about yourself, that you were the type of person people wanted around as long as they needed you but not so much when they didn't. Kenny, you should not think of yourself in this way."

To some, Carmen's words might seem to be irrelevant or out of left field, but that part of our past was so intertwined with who we were at the time and our relationship in those days that the subject often surfaced in one form or another.

"But it's true, isn't it? The gunslinger is only welcome in town as long as the bad guys are around."

"There might be some truth in that, but you made yourself into that tough guy. It was your decision."

"But only because people seem to accept me that way."

"No. Like you said, it is when they need you. There is a difference."

I paused, again overwhelmed by Carmen's understanding of things. "How about you? Do you need me?"

A bit of color flashed across her cheeks. "Why do you put me on the spot? It is not your usual way."

Carmen was right. It was wrong of me to direct her into a trap, to corner her emotions. "I'm sorry. It just sort of slipped out."

"You don't have to apologize for letting your feelings be honest around me."

"I've been working hard on improving myself, Carmen. I want to be a good father for Wayne. And I..."

She squeezed my hand. "It is good that you are concerned."

Carmen's reply had been intentionally interjected before I could finish saying what I had intended, that I loved her and that I wanted us to be together as a family.

"Has it never occurred to you that the controversy within me is more complicated," she said, "that your rogue spirit is part of what attracts me?" She let go of my hand and pretended to busy herself by rummaging through her purse. "I cannot believe I just said that."

I paused to process Carmen's words. It was true that I'd never considered that she, or anyone else for that matter, might actually like me for who I am. I'd spent the bulk of my adult life trying to tone it down and conform so that others might find me more palatable. Was it possible that she had not refused me as a husband and a father because I hadn't changed, but because she was afraid I would?

The waiter appeared with our food, and as he spread it out before us, we switched our conversation to small talk while we ate.

Afterward, as Carmen was preparing to leave, I said, "It was good seeing you, and our talk was interesting. Thank you."

"For what, for confusing you?"

"For warming my heart."

Outside the restaurant, Carmen leaned close, and we kissed, not an empty and meaningless touch, but an indication that I should not give up on pursuing our relationship.

I watched Carmen drive away, and my mind drifted back to the case. Growing ever stronger was my suspicion of the people I'd interviewed being somehow connected. Barrington, Rosenberg, and Goldstein had one thing in common. They all had names typically associated with the Jewish community. I didn't believe that was overly significant, but Barrington and Rosenberg were friends, so it stood to reason that both of them knew Goldstein as well. My client, David Yates, seemed to be the odd man out. And then there was Roxie Taylor, a sufficient mystery within herself, and valued by Rosenberg as a witness for his client. Roxie was also the star of David Yates's sex video. To further complicate matters, neither Yates nor Roxie Taylor seemed to remember the affair. Somewhere in the middle of that there was Crawford too.

I wasn't sure why Rosenberg might try to include me as an associate. The thought that I was being used had definitely crossed my mind, but I wasn't overly keen at the moment to upset the plans. Our collaboration could be useful. For that reason, I would be running a risk by talking to James Goldstein, but not enough to deter my curiosity. Goldstein might know something the others didn't, and he might let something slip.

8

Just off Wheeling Avenue near Utica Square on the lawn in front of a redbrick house, I saw who I thought to be Rosenberg's client, engaged in gardening, working fertilizer or something into the soil of a flower bed that ran along the front of the house.

I climbed out of my vehicle, then walked up the drive. Pausing at a comfortable distance, I said, "Hello, I'm looking for James Goldstein. Would that be you?"

The man, who was kneeling on a cloth spread across the ground in front of the flower bed, did not respond to the question, vocally or otherwise, but continued to toil away in the soil.

I took a few more steps, stopping at a sidewalk that led from the drive to the front door, a serpentine pathway made of the same brick as the house. "The name's Elliot. Please excuse the intrusion, but I'd like to speak with you for a moment."

Once again, the man gave no discernable response.

Stepping off the drive, I walked across an expanse of dormant Bermuda grass until I reached the area where the man worked. "I'm truly sorry to bother you," I said, "but Mr. Rosenberg hired me to find Roxie Taylor. After speaking with Rosenberg, I got the impression that she was a friend of yours. I'd hoped you might be able to help me locate her, or at least point me in the right direction."

I didn't mention that I'd already found Roxie. I wanted to get Goldstein's response.

It didn't matter anyway. The man still wasn't responding.

And with him kneeling over the flower bed, it was difficult to be sure, but I guessed him to be of average height and weight. He was bald on top, but close-cropped salt-and-pepper hair grew on the sides. I looked around the yard, then extended my visual search to the neighboring houses.

I saw nothing except unoccupied yards and empty streets. I imagined being alone, caught up in some Rod Serling tale with an unknown force having removed the people from the city while leaving behind the houses and buildings. I'd certainly been in more threatening situations, but the sensation of being at risk had seldom run so heavily along the base of my spine. Returning my attention to the kneeling man, who still worked busily though silently, I said, "I apologize if my presence troubles you, but the matter is of extreme importance. Could I please have your attention for a moment?"

As if he were some sort of robot programmed only for gardening, the man continued.

If he had heard me or even noticed my being there, he gave no indication of it.

I had begun to believe that the man was either ignoring me, or was incapable of comprehending, but suddenly Goldstein responded and turned to face me.

The unnatural visual image that followed caught me unprepared. Goldstein's face held no expression, and his eyes offered no indication of belonging to a cognizant individual. I wondered, though he stared right at me, if his flat, lifeless eyes were even equipped to deliver messages to his brain.

I had yet to fully process what I was witnessing when my phone went off.

A strong compulsion that I should answer it overrode my inclination to let it go, and I brought the phone to my ear. "If you find what you've come upon as unsettling as I do, Mr. Elliot, then perhaps we have enough in common to further our relationship in this matter."

The caller was a relatively new acquaintance, but when the voice registered, I said, "It's good to hear from you, Mr. Barrington, though I'm not surprised. With every turn of this case, I seem to find you."

The man I thought to be James Goldstein returned to mechanically work away at the flower beds. "What's going on here, Barrington? Come on, you always seem to have an answer."

"Check the inside of his left forearm," Barrington said, "and tell me what you see."

I didn't see anyone around the area, but I suspected Barrington was close enough to observe my actions. Taking care to remain aware of my surroundings, I knelt beside Goldstein, then took his left arm and slowly extended it. Goldstein made no movement or noise to indicate awareness that I had physically adjusted him. A faded tattoo ran along the inside of his forearm: a prisoner of war, the Holocaust. I let go of Goldstein's arm, then rose to my feet. "What does any of this have to do with the case?"

"There is no direct connection that I've been able to determine, and this I would know. I bring it to your attention to establish the man's character and to demonstrate my dedication to him. We were at Auschwitz together, just children and yet we survived. He would give his life for me, if it was required, and for him, I would do the same, if I still can. I'm trying to figure out what happened. He wasn't always this... *frail*."

I glanced at the house. I figured Barrington was helping Goldstein get by from day to day in such a condition. I wondered if Barrington was inside. "I'm truly sorry you had to go through that," I said. "You're a man of courage and honor, but none of this is making sense to me. What does David Yates have to do with Goldstein or any of this for that matter?"

"Mr. Goldstein has been accused of armed robbery, and my involvement has come about due to my efforts to clear his name."

"I gathered as much from talking with Rosenberg, but I still don't get your interest in Yates."

"Let me see if I can clarify it. When the police arrived at the liquor store on First Street, they found Mr. Goldstein standing outside on the sidewalk. He had in his possession a brown paper sack full of money, which he'd presumably taken from the store, and a 9mm Glock. The pistol was later identified as being the service weapon of Officer David Yates."

The palms of my hands had begun to sweat, and I gripped the phone as the words of David Yates ran through my head: *What else might I have done while I was out?*

"How is it, Mr. Barrington, that you know all this?"

"It's a complicated matter, but what is important here is that I know Mr. Goldstein as well as anyone can know another. He is a man of extreme character. He would never, under his own volition, do anything like commit robbery. And I think you will agree that in his current condition he would not be capable of orchestrating such an endeavor."

Barrington had known I would end up at Goldstein's place, and if Barrington had known, then so had Rosenberg. Rosenberg had asked me to find Roxie Taylor because he believed she could help establish the whereabouts of Goldstein just prior to the robbery. Roxie had indicated she'd seen Goldstein Friday night. David Yates had said he'd arrested Dewey Crawford around the same time period. I gripped the phone. "How long has Goldstein been like this?"

"I'm not exactly sure," Barrington said, "but it seems to have gotten worse. I took him home right after Sam got him out of jail Saturday morning. I could tell that something was wrong with him, but he could still converse at that time."

"I take it you believe David Yates is responsible. Is that why you set him up Monday morning for a meeting that nearly got him killed?"

"At the time, Mr. Yates was the only lead I had, and I am sincerely sorry for putting his life in danger. However, I was as surprised as anyone by what developed."

"That's an interesting way of putting it, Barrington. What exactly did develop?"

"I've yet to sort it out enough to identify the shooter, which is I'm sure what you're after."

Barrington had a way about him that kept me from getting angry with him, but his cryptic nature was beginning to frustrate me. "Well, perhaps you could tell me what you do know about it?"

"Actually, Mr. Elliot, contrary to what you might believe, I'm only a few steps ahead of you in this game."

"It's no game, Barrington, and those few steps could prove to be helpful. Whatever information you have, I need to know about it."

"Are you not being presumptuous, taking for granted that we desire the same results?"

I glanced at Goldstein. Barrington had a point, though I wasn't sure why he might tip his hand if he was on the wrong side of things. No doubt he was tangled up in this, but I did not suspect him as the perpetrator. "You're all about illusion," I said, "using anonymity and evasiveness to your advantage. It's why you tiptoe around the shadows that puzzles me."

"Your intuition is impressive, Mr. Elliot."

I took a moment to consider Barrington's answer. Was he purposefully trying to confuse me? "So, which side of things are you on?"

"Only time will tell. Were you able to locate the witness for Mr. Rosenberg?"

"Now it's time for me to be evasive. Maybe I have, and maybe I haven't."

"I would expect nothing less of you. With that behind us, what I tell you next is extremely important, so listen carefully. Please walk around the house to the backyard."

The backyard? Was Barrington setting up a trap, or was he finally trying to help?

"Why?"

"No time for questions, but I do urge you to comply."

I scanned the area, turning clockwise in a complete circle. Since I was working independently, I'd left my service weapon behind. But I wasn't unarmed. I'd brought along a .38 Smith & Wesson from my personal collection. I glanced at Goldstein, then pulled the .38 and walked slowly across the yard until I reached a black wrought iron fence. I hesitated, then opened the gate and followed a cobblestone pathway that meandered through several garden areas until I reached an irregular-shaped patio made of brown-painted concrete. "All right. I'm in the backyard. Now what?"

"At the edge of the patio," Barrington continued, "you will find a garden shed."

I made my way to the shed, which resembled a micro version of the main house, complete with window boxes, one of which was empty. "Yes, I see it."

"Open the door to the shed and look to your right where you will see a workbench."

I put the phone on speaker and placed it in the empty window box, then holding the weapon in front of me, unlatched the shed door and pushed it open.

In the dim light coming from a small window, I saw an envelope sitting atop the workbench.

Using the barrel of the .38, I nudged the envelope slightly, then picked up one corner and looked beneath it.

The letter-sized package, puffed at the middle from its contents, seemed harmless enough.

I leaned through the doorway of the shed and spoke to the phone in the window box. "Okay, I've found your little present. What am I supposed to do with it?"

I got no response, but the cranking of a car around front was loud enough to reach me. It dawned on me what had happened. Barrington had coaxed me to the back of the house for a reason, which was to hide Goldstein.

I retrieved the phone and slid it into my pocket, then grabbed the envelope and ran back to the front of the house.

I arrived just in time to see Barrington's old Mercedes leaving the area. Goldstein was gone.

There would be no use in trying to follow the Mercedes. By the time I reached the truck and got it started, Barrington would have gained enough distance to be out of sight, and that would be enough to keep me from finding him. I tried recalling. It didn't surprise me that I got no answer.

I held the envelope up to the light but couldn't see through the packaging, so I lowered it and tore off one end.

A small bundle wrapped in brown paper fell into my hand.

I thought of Barrington sitting comfortably in his condo, sipping tea while he gazed at the brass and copper gadgets that filled the apartment. I carefully unfolded the paper, my actions revealing a large brass key, which I turned over and over in my hand. The key had no markings, but written across the paper it'd been wrapped in was the following message:

Greetings, Mr. Elliot, though I'm not sure whether to congratulate or to console you for getting to this point. Tell no one about the key. Keep it safe and do not lose it. If it becomes necessary, further instructions will follow.

I felt like an actor, directed against my will in a dark play where I continued to obediently follow the lead given me. I stepped onto the brick sidewalk that led to the front door of Goldstein's house, and once there, I attempted to insert the brass key into the lock. It didn't fit. I hadn't expected that it would. I had the same luck with the back door.

I considered breaking in, but the action seemed pointless. I would find neither Goldstein nor Barrington inside and probably nothing else that would be of use in solving the case.

In a near-mesmerized state, I left Goldstein's yard and went to the street where I'd parked the truck. After climbing in, I sat back and considered my options, ultimately choosing to go along with the insolent director of the dark play.

I left the Utica Square area and drove to the Village at Central Park where Barrington lived. Upon arrival, I bailed out of the truck, then dashed up the stairs and tried the key on the lock to Barrington's condo. Even though the logical side of me cautioned against it, I half expected the uniquely configured slab of brass to slide into the mechanism and disengage the lock. That did not happen. The barrier between the outside world and Barrington's domain remained sealed.

I slipped the key back into my pocket and descended to the parking lot. A light rain had begun to fall, and the temperature had dropped. When I reached the truck, I climbed in quickly to get out of the weather and reduce the chill that had come over me. I'd parked on the street about a block away from the condos. It seemed prudent to keep a low profile and not be perceived by anyone who might take notice as spending an inordinate amount of time in the proximity of Barrington's residence. I hadn't seen anyone other than Barrington monitoring my movements, but trusting my instincts had become a practice I gave little resistance to.

Inside the cab of the truck, out of the wind and rain, I relaxed into the seat cushion and wondered about James Goldstein and the phone conversation I'd had with Barrington, who appeared to be looking after his old friend. The line of thought splintered, and I reconsidered what David Yates had told me and the guarded demeanor of Roxie Taylor. Something had taken place Friday night, an unusual string of events that had driven Dewey Crawford into hiding, removed certain memories from David Yates and Roxie Taylor and left James Goldstein in a catatonic state. Barrington had been right about Goldstein not being able to rob a liquor store on his own. The question was, who would have done such a thing? And what had been the point of it all? The meager amount of money that could be taken from a liquor store would hardly seem to warrant such an elaborate scheme. And the act of allowing for increased exposure inherent in involving so many people, making complex what should have been simple, made little sense.

The robbing of the liquor store couldn't have been the point, which meant that there had to be another reason, an unknown motive for an unestablished crime. Some private investigator I'd turned out to be. I couldn't even figure out what crime I was solving. The only course of action I could conjure was to do what I'd always done in uncertain situations, and that was to keep pressing forward. The way I saw it, the liquor store in question should be in the general area of where it all, whatever it was, had transpired.

Just before Yates had lost his memory, he'd run an old couple out of an abandoned building at First and Elgin. Barrington had mentioned that Goldstein had been arrested outside a store on First Street. I grabbed my phone and checked for stores matching the criteria. Within a matter of minutes, I'd determined what I thought to be the location.

The drive from Barrington's condo was short and uneventful, and as I got out of the truck, I noticed the sign above the door of the liquor store, an open-face clock with the name of the establishment surrounding it, made in the old style like it had come out of the 1930s.

I had learned not to ignore symbolism that came to my attention, and I made a mental note that time, or perhaps the timing of events might become important in determining the how and why of Yates's service weapon ending up in the hands of a would-be robber. From what I'd been able to determine, David Yates had not been lying about his memory loss. It was also necessary to keep in mind that Yates could have withheld much of the information, the sex video in particular, but he had not. He'd told me that no one else knew about the tape except for his wife and me. Of course, she could have told others, but I didn't believe that she had. It had been a painfully private matter between two people that, prior to that, had been inseparably close in their relationship.

Once inside the place, while the clerk behind the counter waited on customers, I glanced around the small, well-stocked store. Colorful bottles lined areas along the walls while shelves full of merchandise created hallways through the interior.

"Could I help you with something, sir?"

The clerk had finally gotten free. Even then, his greeting seemed less than cheerful, and I wondered if it was me if I didn't look the customer type, and perhaps the staff was still on edge.

"Name's Elliot," I said. "I was hoping to speak to someone who was here during the recent robbery or perhaps had knowledge of the event."

The clerk studied me for a moment. "That would be Dan, or Mr. McKenzie, I mean. He owns the place."

"Is Mr. McKenzie available?"

"Well, sort of. He's in his office. He doesn't like to be bothered when he's back there, says he can't get his work done."

The clerk wasn't trying to be obstinate. He was doing his job and relating the nature of the situation as he understood it.

"This is pretty important. Perhaps you could tell him I'm here? I was hired as a private investigator by someone else, for other purposes, and figuring out this robbery has become part of my case."

The clerk nodded. "Yeah, I can do that."

Grabbing a phone from the counter, he turned away, and when he spoke his words were soft and muffled to the point of being unintelligible.

When he turned back, he said, "Yeah, you can go on back. Just knock when you get there and wait for him to let you in."

I thanked the clerk, then followed a pathway lined with spirits until I reached the office. Using the back of my hand, I tapped lightly against the door.

The door swung open to reveal a man of medium build who looked to be in his early thirties. "What can I do for you, mister?"

His speech was direct and to the point, a hard and tough business owner. One would almost have to be to run a liquor store located in the heart of the downtown district.

"Name's Elliot. I'd like to talk to you about what happened here Friday night."

"Lots of things happened Friday night. What's it to you, anyway? You a cop?"

He asked the question as if he already knew the answer. He'd no doubt been around a while, had been in some tough situations. He probably suspected something wasn't right. I hadn't identified myself as such, hadn't shown any ID.

"Not exactly."

"What does that mean? Either you are, or you're not. You sure look like one, then again maybe not so much. For all I know, you're just another thug, casing the joint. It's been hit before. You'll do it again. Well, I got news for you. It won't be that easy next time."

I stifled a smile. What kind of crook would talk to the staff and interview the manager before he decided if the caper was worth his time or not?

"That's not why I'm here, Mr. McKenzie. Like I told your man upfront, I'm a private investigator. The robbery of your store is tangled up in my case."

He cut me off. "Yeah, yeah, whatever. Now get to the point."

McKenzie's office wasn't much more than a closet in the back of the store, but it was organized and functional. In spite of the guy's attitude, I was starting to like him.

"I'm here to help a friend, Mr. McKenzie, a police officer. He's a good man, goes to church, always willing to do whatever he can for anyone who asks it of him. Now he's in trouble, about to lose his job, his wife, everything."

"Is he the one who came in the store and tried to take the money?"

"No, but it was his service weapon that was used during the holdup."

"And he's about to lose his job over that?"

"It's more complicated than it sounds. He doesn't know how or when he lost the weapon or how it ended up in the hands of the perpetrator."

McKenzie leaned back in his chair and rubbed his chin. Later he raised both his arms up slightly and held his hands out, palms up. "So, how do you plan to help this friend of yours, this cop?"

McKenzie's voice had softened, and his facial expression reinforced his change in mood. Something I'd said had hit a nerve, and he now seemed more willing to cooperate.

"I'm trying to find out all I can about what happened that night, get the details, then work backward and piece it all together."

"And how's that going to help?"

"Hopefully by showing the truth, that my client is guilty of nothing more than inadvertently stepping into... whatever it was he stepped into."

"If you don't know what you're looking for," McKenzie said, "how you going to know when you find it?"

Among the neat stacks of paper, a bottle of water sat on McKenzie's desk. The organized space reflected his hard work, his proactive nature. He was a no-nonsense type of guy, and as clichéd as his question was, it was also, in the ordinary sense, quite valid. He just didn't understand that dealing with the unknown was something I'd become accustomed to or that I would make it my mission to uncover and expose whatever it was that rode beneath the currents of this case. I would, in short, know it when I found it.

"I'll just have to do the best I can."

McKenzie leaned back in his chair and smiled. "So, you used to be a cop, huh?"

I thought about the question for a moment. It seemed strangely prophetic, talking about a career change as if it'd already happened.

"That's right, a homicide detective for the city of Tulsa."

"If I had to guess, I'd say you were pretty good at police work."

McKenzie seemed interested, intrigued even, by my association with the police department, as well as that of my client's. "Some people think so."

McKenzie shrugged. "So, what do you want from me?"

"I would ask that you bring in whoever was working Friday night and let me conduct individual, private interviews."

"That'll be easy. You're looking at him."

Maybe things were starting to turn around and work in my favor for a while. "You worked that night, saw what happened?"

"Yeah," he said, "no one but me. And I'm thankful for that, that no one else had to go through it, I mean. I've seen a lot of crazy stuff, but nothing like that."

I'd been mentored by Captain Dombrowski, who was old-school, and I'd picked up some of his habits. I pulled the notepad I kept in my pocket and flipped it open.

"I appreciate your cooperation, Mr. McKenzie. I'll try to be as brief as possible. To the best of your knowledge, what time did the robbery occur?"

McKenzie smiled. "I don't ordinarily pay much attention to that kind of thing, but it was a little after nine. I know cause that's when we close and I'd just finished up with a late customer. But did I listen to the little voice in my head and lock the door behind the customer? No, I didn't. So, I'm heading back to the register when I hear the door open again. I didn't think much about it. Figured it was another late arrival or a wino looking for sympathy."

He paused and shook his head. "I sure wasn't prepared for what happened next."

McKenzie had fallen silent, and I looked up from my note-taking to see him staring into space, a worried look on his face. Reliving the event wasn't easy for him. For a tough guy like McKenzie to be rattled, something pretty bad must have happened.

"And you were working alone that night?"

"Yeah, that's right. I don't usually do that, but sometimes circumstances call for it."

I waited briefly to see if he would continue, but when silence again threatened to take over, I asked, "So what exactly did happen, Mr. McKenzie?"

McKenzie tried to speak, but nothing came out. He took a drink of water from the bottle on his desk, then set it back down. "You probably already know the rest of the story, else you wouldn't be here."

McKenzie's demeanor had changed from a hard-nosed business owner to that of a person who was confused and afraid. He just wasn't sure if I was the right person to spill it to.

"Getting robbed at gunpoint is a terrifying experience," I said. "There's no shame in being upset by that."

McKenzie studied his desktop, straightened some stacks of paper, then looked up. "You look like a tough guy, Elliot. If you'd been me, what would you have done?"

McKenzie was going under the assumption that I knew the details of the case. He'd stated as much, and now he was acting on that premise.

"I guess that would depend on the circumstances."

"Yeah, that's exactly what I'm talking about. I can't tell you how many times I've gone over it in my mind, asking myself why I just stood there and let it happen. The old guy had to be in his eighties. Sure, he had a gun, but his determination was in the toilet, and he had no focus at all, no drive. I could have taken him, but I didn't. I just let it happen."

"It's all right," I said. "You did the right thing. Money is never worth dying for."

"I get what you're saying, but it shouldn't have happened like that, a sheepish old bald-headed man who looked like somebody's friendly old grandfather. As soon as he walked in, everything got all Twilight Zone."

McKenzie's description of the suspect fit exactly with the catatonic gardener I'd been with earlier. It had to have been Goldstein. "Was the man alone, or did he have accomplices?"

"No, it was just me and the old guy. Funny thing about it, I wasn't really scared. If I felt anything, it was a sort of pity. I don't know why I went along with it. I just don't know."

I thought about my experience with Goldstein earlier, his flat, lifeless eyes. "How did you know the old man intended to rob you?"

McKenzie shrugged. "He didn't say anything, just pointed the gun and held out a sack. It didn't take long to figure out what he wanted."

Again I thought back. Goldstein hadn't answered my questions, but when I'd asked him to look at me, he'd complied, as if following a command. The thought of what that might imply sent a tremor of fear coursing through my senses. "You mentioned Twilight Zone. What did you mean by that?"

He shrugged. "It's kind of hard to explain. Things just didn't feel right, that's all. Then again, things weren't right, were they? I mean it's not every day that you get held up, thank the Lord. But still, I can't shake the feeling that there was more to it than that. I don't want to come off sounding like a nutjob, but I've been in business for a long time, experienced some crazy stuff, though nothing like that."

McKenzie paused and shrugged again.

I used the time to think things over. Based on what I'd seen so far, I doubted Goldstein could have pulled off the robbery on his own. He would have needed help. "Did you happen to notice how the old man got here? Was he driving a car, or did he come on foot?"

"Yeah," McKenzie said, "I wondered about that too. I sure didn't see any cars pull up, and in this business, you get tuned in to noticing that sort of thing, especially when you're working alone. Maybe he parked a block or two away. It would make sense, I guess, if the guy wanted to seem anonymous."

"Did you notice anything else out of the ordinary, people coming into the store just to browse, cars parked nearby that'd been there awhile?"

McKenzie leaned forward and spoke in a hushed tone, as if he were telling me a secret. "Yeah, when I let the last customer out, just before the old guy showed up, I thought I saw a patrol car parked up the street. Not all that unusual, I guess. And the officer wouldn't have known what was going on inside the store. I mean, if it hadn't been called in or anything."

Once again, the words of David Yates came to me: *What else might I have done?*

"I wonder if it was it the same patrol car that arrived to arrest the suspect?"

"That thought crossed my mind a few times, I can tell you. It could have been. They sure got here awful fast. Could be somebody was walking by, saw what was happening, and alerted the officer. Yeah, that would make sense."

"Yes, it would, but you don't sound convinced."

"I don't know. It's like I said. Everything about it was weird, like some kind of dream or something. The guy was old, slow, and obviously out of it. I could have taken him, but I didn't. Something inside me kept telling me to keep calm and don't cause trouble, that doing anything else would be a mistake."

The more McKenzie spoke of the ordeal, the more nervous he became.

"You said the perpetrator was out of it. What did you mean by that?"

"I don't know. It was like the old guy was operating on autopilot or something. I guess that sounds crazy, but I don't know any other way to explain it."

9

I exited the liquor store and quickened my pace along the sidewalk toward the truck. I was certain that Goldstein had not acted alone during the robbery. In addition, I couldn't shake the notion that whoever had helped him had acted as more than an accomplice. Goldstein couldn't do much on his own, which left open the possibility of his following commands.

I thought of Ezra Barrington, but no sooner had the idea of his involvement come to mind than I dismissed it. There was just something about Barrington that commanded respect. I couldn't bring myself to think of him as anything but honorable.

With Barrington on the back burner, the remaining players were David Yates, Roxie Taylor, Dewey Crawford, and Samuel Rosenberg. The trouble was, none of them seemed a proper candidate to have thought up and executed the crime I had begun to visualize. Of course, considering what I'd found so far, the possibility existed that any or all of them could have been involved without their knowledge. Even for someone like me, who had experienced more than his share of unusual cases, that seemed a far-fetched idea.

A gust of wind whipped the cold rain-filled air against my face.

I pulled my overcoat around me to block the onslaught. The weather had been just as bad, if not worse, Friday night when Yates had found the homeless couple, taking refuge in the abandoned building. I paused and glanced around the area, examining both sides of the street, finally extending the visual search in an easterly direction. Like I'd said earlier, it had all taken place in this area. The abandoned building in question, an aging, three-story structure of faded red brick, occupied the northwest corner of First and Elgin about a block up the street. I turned and began to walk toward it.

Once there, I walked slowly around the structure, examining the exterior, searching for a point of entrance. On the west side of the building, I found what I was looking for. Plywood covered the narrow arched windows, and the third sheet from the front moved when I applied pressure to it. I pushed the wood covering out of the way and gazed into the gaping hole.

I checked to see if anyone was watching, then threw my left leg over the sill. Hesitation could get you into trouble, but for a moment I straddled the window sill, one foot in and one out, wondering if I should proceed. Knowing that I didn't actually have the authority to enter the building gave me reason to pause. Being a police officer does at times lend an eerie sense of confidence. I shrugged off the apprehension and maneuvered my way inside, sliding off the window and onto the floor of the interior.

My cautious nature showed no signs of weakening as I imagined adversaries hiding in every dark corner. Then again, the possibility existed that my fear might not be totally imagined. The thought of that sent a chill running through me.

I grabbed my flashlight and shined it into the interior of the building. "Anyone there?"

No answer. I stepped forward, sweeping the light from side to side.

Broken bricks, stacks of lumber, busted furniture, and various other forms of debris-covered the floor. It appeared as if the place had been empty for some time.

I stepped over a pile of debris and walked deeper into the interior, small pieces of brick crunching loudly against the floor and the bottom of my shoes.

If anyone was hiding inside the building, my intrusion into their world had been blatantly announced. I shined the light downward.

Tile covered the floor. That explained the amplified noise of my footsteps. Considering how long it had probably been there, the tile was in remarkably good condition. Where the debris had been cleared, makeshift trails snaked deeper into the cavern-like interior of the old building. One of the trails went off at an angle toward the east side, eventually disappearing into the dark hollow.

Choosing my footsteps carefully, I followed the pathway for what seemed about thirty yards until I reached a structured area beneath one of the sealed windows. A small amount of light filtered in from a hole in the plywood covering the window, and it illuminated with just enough of a glow to make it ghostly, a collection of wooden crates positioned around a pile of ashes. A section of tin bent in a semicircle was attached to a PVC pipe that had at one time run through the hole in the plywood, a makeshift hood designed to vent off some of the smoke and gasses from the campfire.

I shined the flashlight around the area.

Footprints disturbed the dust atop the tile around the clearing while several empty cans testified to a meal of sorts. Someone had recently sat around the campfire, probably the old couple that David Yates had found.

A sensation of pain and sorrow laced with fear raked across my senses, and I began to believe that I should get out of there.

I turned to do just that, but before I could, the beam of the flashlight ran across something curious near the crates that drew my attention.

I leaned over and pulled a rectangular piece of cardboard from beneath one of the crates, then shined the light onto it.

A drawing of a child, a boy about six years in age, had been sketched onto the cardboard with remarkable skill.

The image awakened a memory, and I thought back a few years to a time when I was new on the force. It had been late at night but with enough ambient lighting coming from the hazy glow of the streetlights for me to see a child walking along a back street in Tulsa, accompanied by two ragged adults—his parents, I'd presumed—one on each side, holding the child's hands, leading the kid who wore a hooded sweatshirt off into a future that was dismal at best. At some point, as if he'd sensed my presence, the child turned toward me, and I saw his face. The thought of it still haunted me.

A noise crackled from somewhere in the expanse, the sound of someone else's shoes crunching against the tile floor.

I swung around, panning the light across the dark expanse.

I saw no one.

I reached inside my jacket and touched the .38 in its holster but did not pull the weapon. I had no desire to put a bullet into the chest of some unfortunate indigent. I would use it if I had to if it came to that.

"I know you're out there," I said. "Show yourself. I mean you no harm."

Nothing but silence came back to me.

An image of the person who had worn the hooded garment that I'd seen just before the John Doe had taken a shot at David Yates formed in my mind.

There had been other people in the area, walking to their cars, going to work. Why did I keep coming back to someone who had stood at the other end of the street, away from the action?

I had no answer to my question, but I knew with certainty that I needed to get out of the dark chasm I'd climbed into. Keeping one hand on the handle of the holstered .38 while holding the light and the cardboard artwork in the other, I began to walk along the pathway that meandered around the piles of debris.

The trip back to the window where I'd come in seemed to take much longer than it should have. I had a strong suspicion that whoever I'd heard walking among the crates was watching me.

When I reached the area where I'd entered the building, I kept the light trained in the direction of the dark interior while I shoved the plywood covering aside and climbed through the window, back into the cold but welcomed air of the outside world.

On the sidewalk that ran alongside the abandoned building, I paused briefly, then started up the sidewalk toward the truck, mentally reviewing the details of the shooting incident involving David Yates. It had been my experience that those who lived on the street for any length of time, whether by choice or by fate, had a discernible look about them. With the man who'd taken a shot at Yates before jumping in front of a truck, that hard-luck aura had been present in abundance.

Back inside the truck with the cardboard portrait on the seat beside me, I called the medical examiner's office and punched in Jordan McClain's extension.

"This is Elliot."

"Calling about the John Doe again?"

"As a matter of fact, I am, but another one, more recent. He took a shot at a police officer, then stepped in front of a delivery truck. He would have come in Monday around 11:00 a.m., a man in his late twenties, medium build, brown hair, wearing a gray Oklahoma Thunder sweatshirt. I need to know if there's been an ID on the body yet if an autopsy has been done, anything you got on it."

"Let me get back to you, okay?"

Before I could say another word, Jordan disconnected.

Something was wrong. Jordan had been courteous and businesslike, but a slight hesitation in her voice had betrayed her.

I laid the phone on the seat cushion, then leaned back and stared through the windshield. My theory about the case having a possible connection with the homeless community played around the corners of my mind. With respect to the people of interest in the case, a curious pattern had begun to emerge. Both James Goldstein and Roxie Taylor had volunteered at the Emergency Shelter Friday night, and it was on that same night that David Yates had run a couple of street people from the abandoned building. In furtherance of the line of reasoning, both the John Does had, or so it seemed, fallen from the ranks of the homeless.

Moments later, my phone went off. The caller ID showed unknown.

"That you, Elliot?"

It was Jordan McClain.

"What's up?" I asked.

"I took a short break," she said, "stepped out of the building. I haven't exactly been told not to discuss this, but it's a sensitive issue around the office. Dr. Longstreet said he'd handle all the inquiries and to direct the calls to him. So far, I don't think there's been many."

My earlier suspicions had been confirmed. I'd known Jordan for a long time. She had an eccentric personality and a propensity for walking along the edges of rebellion, but when it came down to the wire, she was a person you could count on to do the right thing.

Then again, my dealings with everyone had been extraordinary the past couple of days, as if I'd inadvertently stepped into another dimension where everyone was the same as before but not quite. Dombrowski hadn't been as upset as I'd thought he'd be over my career indecision; Nick Brazelton, the freest sprit I'd ever known, had lectured me about my attitude with a tone of conservatism; even Carmen, who had always been my rock, had maneuvered out of character, coming close to encouraging my reckless nature.

"Be careful, Jordan. I wouldn't want you to jeopardize your career over this."

"Well, that's mighty chivalrous of you, hon, but the way I see it this ain't no small problem. Someone needs to get to the bottom of it, and I figured if anyone could do that, it'd be you."

"I appreciate the vote of confidence," I said, "but what exactly are we talking about?"

"Well, I'm not sure how to tell you this. You're going to think we're the most incompetent bunch of nuts you've ever met, but I guess I'd better just come on out with it. It's just like before. Nobody around here knows anything, and it's not because they don't want to talk. Hell, we just don't know."

"Slow down. You're not making much sense."

"Oh, for heaven's sake, Kenny, it's the John Doe. He's gone missing."

Jordan McClain's words settled over me like a dark cloud. Within a timeframe of two months, two unidentified bodies had disappeared from the morgue at the medical examiner's office, and no one had a clue.

The question seemed redundant, but I had to ask. "How can that be?"

"I wish I had an answer for you. God knows I do. I'd hoped you might be able to dig something up on it, no pun intended, I assure you. But this kind of thing can't go on around here. The department's breathing down our necks, and we won't be able to avoid the media forever. And I think we both know that even in your world, hon, those cadavers couldn't get up and walk out on their own. The whole thing's got me so shook up; it's all I can do to concentrate on my work. Please tell me you'll look into it."

"I'll do what I can," I said.

After that, I disconnected the phone, then fired up the truck and pulled onto the road. I was headed for the emergency shelter on North Denver Avenue where James Goldstein and Roxie Taylor had volunteered Friday night.

10

The lady behind the reception desk at the shelter busied herself, shuffling through stacks of paper around her workstation. Pieces of her hair stuck out at awkward, but probably unintentional, angles. She glanced in my direction but said nothing and kept working.

"Excuse me," I said. "I'm looking for information, and I wonder if you could help?"

"Information? What kind of information?"

"I need to talk with someone who was on duty Friday night. I suspect I'd need to clear that through the proper channels. If you could assist with that or point me in the right direction, I'd appreciate it."

She smiled. "If you're needing assistance, sir, with finding a place to stay or even getting something to eat, don't be shy about it. We all need a little help now and then, nothing to be ashamed of. Now, what can I help you with?"

The receptionist had found her calling. Her disheveled appearance, calm demeanor, and down-home attitude all worked in unison in achieving the goal of making everyone feel welcome.

"No," I said, "it's not that."

I realized, and not for the first time, how much less weight revealing my new credentials would carry as compared to letting someone know I was a cop. Both endeavors had a stigma attached to them, one quite sobering, the other not so much. "I'm an investigator," I said. "Do you know who I would need to talk to gain permission to interview some of the employees or volunteers who worked Friday?"

"That'd be Major Hornell. I can call him if you like, but I have to wonder why you might want to do all that. We were busy that night, over capacity when the nasty weather hit, stacking the poor souls in the hallways before it was over, but other than that, nothing comes to mind that might pique the interest of an investigator. What kind of investigator are you, anyway? Are you with the police?"

"No, ma'am. I'm independent of the police department."

"Then who do you work for?"

"Myself, ma'am, and my clients, of course."

She smiled. "So, you're a real-life private investigator? I've always wanted to do that, you know, traveling around, solving weird cases and all that. I guess you love what you do, huh, living a dream and all?"

I shrugged. "Like all jobs, it has its ups and downs."

The receptionist started to say something, but before she could, a small, slender man walked across the room and came over to stand near her.

"Is everything all right here, Bessie?"

The receptionist took a moment to answer. Finally, she smiled and gestured toward me. "Everything is fine, Major. This charming gentleman...goodness, I didn't get your name."

"Elliot," I said. "Kenny Elliot."

"Yes, Mr. Elliot would like to..." She paused and winked. "Well, I'll just let him tell you all about it."

I briefly explained my reason for being there.

"I see," the man said. "As it turns out, I have a few spare moments. Would you like to step into my office where we can discuss this further?"

Inside his office, an adequate space though spartan in décor, the gentleman introduced himself as Major Sterling Hornell. After we were seated, he leaned forward, placing his arms on his desk, his hands folded together. His office chair was positioned to make him appear much taller than he was. "Now, Mr. Elliot, I'd like for you to explain the exact nature of your visit today. Keep in mind that I am aware that there must be a reason for your interest because there was another gentleman here just yesterday asking questions. Were you aware of that?"

The atmosphere had gone from casual to serious in a hurry. "No, but it doesn't surprise me. Was the interrogator a police officer?"

"He was not, which makes it all the more curious because, by your own admission, neither are you, Mr. Elliot."

It didn't take long for my confusion to give way to understanding. It seemed my old friend Barrington had beaten me to the punch. "Was he an older gentleman, dressed in proper business attire?"

"I'd say we're talking about the same man. Do you know him?"

"You could say that."

The major leaned back in his chair, his intense stare never wavering. "Well, Mr. Elliot, you've hit upon the exact point of my confusion over the matter. For you see, I was here on the night in question, and I don't know that anything out of the ordinary did happen. However, to keep things in perspective, one must keep in mind that we are talking about a shelter where we, by the nature of the subject, deal with people who are a bit down and out, shall we say. Of course, some things could have been going on that night which might seem odd, even drastic, to the uninitiated, but all in all, it was, to the best of my knowledge, a night much like any other. Then again, you are here, aren't you? I suspect something a bit unusual must have captured your interest, and you are under the impression that it has something to do with my shelter. So, let's have it, Mr. Elliot, what is it exactly that you think you might find here?"

I paused to gather my thoughts. Curious things had happened, to be sure, but the only real crime that had been committed was the robbing of a liquor store. And the perpetrator had volunteered at the shelter that night.

"It's my understanding that a Mr. James Goldstein occasionally volunteers at the shelter and that he had chosen to do so Friday night. After leaving here around nine o'clock, Goldstein stepped into a liquor store over on First Street, pulled a gun, and demanded the money from the cash register."

The color drained from the major's face. "You must be mistaken. I find that extremely difficult to believe."

"So do I. But the evidence says that's how it happened."

"I see. Where is Mr. Goldstein now? Has he been arrested?"

I didn't want to say that I didn't know where the man was, though that was the truth. "He's out on bail. A friend is looking after him."

The major let out a heavy sigh. "Well, that certainly changes things, doesn't it? Of course I'll help in any way that I can. Something puzzles me though. If you're not with the police, what exactly is your interest in the matter?"

"The client I'm working for is somehow caught up in it. I'm trying to help."

Major Hornell shifted in his chair. "I reiterate that nothing about the night in question stands out in my mind, but I will answer your questions to the best of my ability."

Thoughts of the abandoned building I'd visited earlier, the remains of the campfire, and the empty food cans unfolded in my mind. "I understand it was an inclement night, and the shelter was full, overcapacity. Is it possible that anyone was turned away, and if so, could James Goldstein have been involved?"

An expression reflecting concern tinged with a bit of trampled pride crossed the major's face. "Highly unlikely, Mr. Elliot. We have numerous facilities throughout the area and an adequate resource of staff and volunteers. It is not our intention to turn anyone away. Of course, there could be circumstances, someone seemingly apt to cause trouble, for instance, or perhaps exhibiting signs of being under the influence. However, even in those situations, we would seek assistance from the police rather than turning them away."

I thought about Goldstein and my experience with him. He'd certainly appeared to be under the influence of something. "What about Mr. Goldstein? Did you notice anything unusual about him such as odd behavior, acting out of character?"

The major shook his head. "I wasn't actually around him that much, but, no, I did not."

I thought about that. Whatever had happened to Goldstein could have taken place after he'd left the shelter. "There is another person of interest to the case," I said, "who also claims to have been here Friday night. Do you know anyone who goes by the name of Roxie, or Roxanne Taylor?"

Before the major said anything, his expression gave the answer. Even for someone who tried to resist such things, it was hard not to notice someone like Roxie.

"Again, I must answer in the affirmative. Ms. Taylor is another highly valued volunteer. Please tell me that she did not also engage in illegal activities after leaving here."

I thought about the sex video. "I'm not sure at this point just how Roxie Taylor figures in, but to the best of my knowledge, she was not present at the liquor store while the robbery was occurring."

"I'm happy to hear that, though I must admit that your tiptoeing around the subject is of little comfort." The major paused and glanced at his watch. "Considering the weight of this matter, I am reluctant to cut our visit short. Unfortunately, other things demand my attention."

"I understand," I said. I handed Hornell a business card. "If you happen to think of anything else, give me a call."

He took the card and placed it on his desk. "I am sorry. I truly wish I could be of more help."

I walked out of Major Hornell's office somewhat disappointed over the results of the meeting. The major delved enthusiastically into control, trying to overachieve, but beneath it all, was a man who cared about those he looked after, necessary for someone who shared the pain and suffering of others on a daily basis.

Before leaving, I stopped again at the receptionist's desk. "Sorry to bother you again," I said, "but do you keep track of the people who volunteer at the shelter?"

She glanced toward Hornell's office, hesitated, then said, "Yes, Mr. Elliot, I do. Why do you ask?"

"I know James Goldstein, and Roxie Taylor volunteered last Friday night. Could you tell me if they were here at the same time and, if possible, what time they left?"

Again she hesitated. "The major runs a tight ship, if you know what I mean. I don't wish to get on his bad side."

"I understand. This is important. I just need it for my own information. No one will ever know where I got it."

"Yes, to your first question," she said. "As to what time they left, I'm not quite sure. People usually let me know when they come and go, but..." She paused, straightened some papers on her desk. "I think they left around 9:00 p.m. Anyway, I don't recall seeing either of them after that. And I haven't heard from them since. I called a couple of times, left messages, but so far, no callbacks. I'm worried. And now, with you being here and all, I hope they are all right."

I nodded. "I've spoken to both of them since. That's about all I can tell you right now."

I made my way across the lobby, then exited the shelter. Once outside, I strolled across the parking lot, though as I drew near the truck, a sensation that someone had taken an interest in my movements and was watching caused me to pause.

I quickly spotted the reason for my concern, a man who had the look of the street, walking toward the truck. I resumed my approach, but before I could open the door, the man hurried over, stopping just inches away.

"Are you a cop?" he asked.

"Not exactly. Is there something I can do for you?"

He reached inside his shirt and pulled out a crucifix suspended from a string around his neck. "I've got Jesus," he said. "It's the only thing that saves me."

A mixture of pity, respect, and awe waved through me. The man probably had nothing in the way of material possessions, and yet he reached out to a stranger, hoping to share the gift of salvation.

"I'm happy to hear that," I said. "Are you staying at the shelter?"

"Yeah, but it's not forever, only till I get myself back together."

I nodded, though I doubted he could ever get it together. I pulled a few bills from my wallet, and stuffed the money into the man's hand, holding it closed around the gift.

"Promise me," I said, "that you won't use this for drugs or alcohol."

The old man grinned. "Not a problem. I've been sober for twenty-one days now."

I thought of Major Hornell and Bessie and the good work they were doing. "Are you attending church services at the shelter?"

"Yeah," he said, "but there's something else I need to talk to you about."

I let go of the man's hand, then leaned against the truck, my back to the door.

"All right, I'm listening."

The man glanced around, then leaned in close, and spoke with a hushed tone. "I heard you talking to Bessie. It was bad that night for sure, real bad. And they don't know the half of it. I've never known him to come out like that."

I had no idea what the man was talking about or where he might be going with it, but I played along. "What exactly are you trying to tell me?"

"People were coming from every corner," he said, "filling the lobby, and those that couldn't hanging around outside, all of them trying to find someplace to get in, away from that cold rain, even some that don't do that or ain't supposed to anyway. I'm not supposed to know about it, but when you been on the street as much as I have, you gain a certain amount of trust and tolerance."

"Are you saying that there were people who were turned away from the shelter?"

"I wouldn't put it quite like that. Folks that run this place wouldn't let that happen if they could help it. Maybe some got tired of waiting and just walked away, others didn't like all the questions, you understand, value their privacy over anything else. It scared me enough that he would push the envelope so much, but it was who he came after that shook me to my soul."

I pushed away from the truck. The old guy was obviously dealing with mental issues. I wasn't sure if I could trust anything he'd said. "Thanks for your help, partner, but I need to be going. You keep your promise and stay off the booze, okay?"

"Suit yourself," he said. "I thought you might be different, but just like the rest, you don't listen. I'm telling you that his being here was no accident, of that you can be sure. He singled out the old Jewish man and the pretty lady, who doesn't belong here, and he took them right out from under their noses."

I stepped forward. The old man was talking about James Goldstein and Roxie Taylor. He had to be. "What did you mean, his being here was no accident? Who did this, who took the old Jewish man and the lady?"

He shook his head. "I didn't actually see him, but he was there. There're some things a man just knows. And his minions were with him, sure enough, did his bidding and herded his prizes into a police car and drove off with them."

I thought of Yates, but that wasn't all. A vision of the suicidal shooter blossomed in my mind. I ran with it, like an extra sense I'd learned I somehow had. "Was the one who did this wearing a gray Oklahoma Thunder sweatshirt?" I asked.

An expression of fear engulfed the old man's face. "I've said too much already."

Before I could ask another question, the old man turned and bolted away, but I didn't pursue him. A limousine with dark windows pulled into the parking lot and glided toward me. The limo neared my position, then stopped, and for a moment nothing happened, but the strange vehicle sat there idling.

I turned to get into the truck, but the hum of the vehicle's window coming down stopped me, and then a raspy, masculine voice said, "Excuse me, sir. So sorry to bother you, but I wonder if you might assist me with something?"

Apprehension riddled my senses as I stepped toward the rear of the limo where the window had been brought partially down. I reminded myself that it had been an unusual day with strange things going on, and it was for that reason that it seemed I was approaching a ghost car with ghostly inhabitants. I thought the occupant of the vehicle was a man, though in the waning light of an overcast evening in December, I couldn't be sure. As if taunting me with my own cautious behavior, in the darkness of the partially exposed interior of the limousine, the complexion of the unknown person inside appeared to be the color of paste.

"What do you need?" I asked.

"Would you be so kind as to give me directions to the Brady Theater?"

I wondered why the passenger, a young but pasty-looking man, would ask and not the driver, but even with that, the benign request acted to calm my nerves. The timing was right. A concert was happening at the Brady that night, and the vehicle wasn't that far off course. I gave the occupant of the limo the information he'd requested, then climbed into the truck.

Through the rain-spattered windshield, I watched the limo exit the parking lot and silently glide away, heading, if the strange man's story could be trusted, toward the Brady.

As the taillights dimmed and the car pulled away from the lot, a whispering of ideas floated through my head. I suspected that it had been the John Doe, the one who'd shot at Yates, that the homeless man, who'd been frightened away by the arrival of the limo, had seen at the shelter and that it had been he who had coerced, perhaps even forced, Goldstein and Taylor into the police car. The homeless man's reaction to my question about the sweatshirt the John Doe had been wearing was at the heart of it. Had the patrol car in question been the one David Yates had been driving? I suspected that it had.

And where did that leave me? Not only was the John Doe who'd shot at Yates dead, but he was missing as well. All hope of identifying the man was lost.

I started the truck and followed the path the limo had taken. I hung back, not exactly worried about being seen by the inhabitants of the limo, but not specifically wanting to be either.

A few minutes later, I drove through the area of West Brady and North Boulder where I spotted the limousine parked in front of the theater and letting off a few passengers. It seemed the guy's story checked out.

I began to drive away. A theory, whether fantastic in origin or premonitory, had begun to coagulate in my mind. What had happened revolved around the homeless couple Yates had rousted from the abandoned building. The couple had been there because they harbored a desperate need to find a warm place to sleep for the night. What exactly had developed to put them in such a position I had yet to ascertain, but it was the couple's relationship to Yates, Goldstein, and Taylor that was at the heart of this.

Goldstein and Taylor had volunteered in a highly visible position at the shelter, and what if they had been perceived as being instrumental in the couple being turned away? After that, Yates had then run them from the abandoned building, their last hope of a roof over their heads.

And what of Dewey Crawford and the others? Where did they fit in? The way I saw it, Dewey Crawford was nothing more than a victim of bad timing. He'd managed to get himself arrested just before David Yates had come upon the old couple. Ezra Barrington and Samuel Rosenberg, on the other hand, had been dragged into the mix through their association with James Goldstein.

Of course, I could be mistaken. I'd been wrong before. For about the hundredth time, I wondered if David Yates was on the level. It was the motivation behind why a person might try to pull off such an elaborate hoax that kept tripping me up and the fact that I inherently believed Yates was telling the truth.

I now believed that what I had on my hands was a crime of revenge. But who would avenge the wrong by exacting such harsh penalties?

A friend or relative came to mind, but the idea seemed lacking. Such a relation would, by allowing the couple to sink to such a deteriorated state of existence, be as guilty by default as anyone who had later refused the couple help or stood in the way of them getting it.

Would a father or a mother or a son or a daughter allow their relations to exist on the street and then take offense at others who also refused them help?

It didn't add up unless...

I slid my hand across the truck seat and grabbed the crude cardboard artwork I'd found in the old building, and as I drew the portrait near my face to examine it in the darkness, I again thought back to the homeless couple I'd seen years ago leading a child along the alleyway.

Such a person who had grown up in similar conditions might take offense at his parents being abused by the system. A chill ran through me. How would I go about finding such a person if, indeed, he even existed? It occurred to me that he could have been the John Doe who'd shot at Yates and was now dead and missing. And if not, what kind of person was I up against, who could remove memory and cause others to do things against their will, perhaps even unknowingly?

As I considered the possibility of the portrait in charcoal as being that of the suspect, albeit a much younger version, a feeling of loneliness and a sensation of darkness that far surpassed the gloom of a cold and sunless December encompassed my thoughts. This was no ordinary criminal. Of course, I'd already begun to suspect as much, but any doubts I might have had about the dark nature of who I was dealing with quickly faded.

I needed to find the old couple. But accomplishing that task, with the parties of interest desiring the opposite, perhaps even coveting their anonymity within the vast wilderness of the homeless, would be difficult, could be in fact nearly impossible.

11

I left the Brady District and continued to drive the darkening city streets, reviewing the idea that Barrington had remained a step ahead of me during the investigation, including his visiting the shelter where his old buddy Goldstein had been prior to the robbery. I'd drawn conclusions as to the relativity of the homeless community, and Barrington had as well. Getting together with the old investigator and comparing notes could prove to be beneficial, but that wasn't likely to happen.

I checked my watch; nearly 5:00 p.m. Due to the darkening conditions, it seemed much later.

I turned south onto Cincinnati, and when I reached Sixth Street, I followed it to Peoria Avenue where I went south again. When I found Eighth Street, I turned into Barrington's neighborhood.

I parked on the street and kept to the shadows as I walked through the rain until I reached the stairs that led to the condo. I didn't expect Barrington to be there, but a compulsion to check drove me forward.

The porch light near Barrington's door cast a soft glow across the landing.

I didn't know if that was a good sign, but I didn't remember it being on when I'd been there before. As I neared the door, an uncomfortable sensation of loss and failure crept through me, and when I rang the bell, the action brought no response, no lights came on from inside the apartment, and no indication of movement sounded from within.

I stood quietly on the dimly lit landing, letting my thoughts drift, then I closed my eyes and leaned forward, placing my hands against the door.

My unusual ability is not a subject I'm comfortable talking about, or even thinking about, but when I can find no other option, I extend my senses a bit farther than most. The concept frightened me. It always had. But through hours of prayer, I'd reconciled the gift and the use of it sparingly.

The result of my outreach settled over me with unusual clarity. There was no one inside the condo. It was as empty and devoid of life as a mausoleum in some forgotten cemetery.

I descended the stairs and crossed the parking lot to the street. Once inside the truck, I drove away from the condos and took Peoria Avenue to Twenty-First Street. Later, I parked along the curbside just down the street from the house of James Goldstein.

I got out of the vehicle and started toward the house, pulling my overcoat around me. When I reached the front door, I rang the bell several times, then knocked. With no less reluctance, I leaned into the door and repeated the process I'd performed earlier at Barrington's condo.

The result was identical, that of absolute certainty that the residence was empty. I turned away, though I did not leave the protected area of the porch but remained there momentarily, a darkened shadow man, unnoticed in all likelihood by the neighbors. It didn't surprise me that I hadn't found James Goldstein at home. However, the absence of Barrington weighed against my senses like a harbinger of things to come.

I stepped into the weather and made my way to the truck, pressing forward under the assumption that if Goldstein was still in the condition in which I'd last seen him, it stood to reason that when I found the old gentleman, I'd probably find Barrington as well. The trouble was I had no idea where that might be.

My sensitive state of mind was further exposed when the sound of my phone announcing a text message rattled my nerves. Inside the cab, I quickly checked the message. There wasn't much to it, only an address and not a specific location, but a general area, a certain intersection. It had come from someone who went by the tag of *valley girl*.

I ran the address through my mind, trying to visualize where it was and what was there. Most people would ignore such an intrusion and delete it without hesitation, but with the kind of day I'd been having, which had left me with more questions than answers, I dropped the truck into gear and pulled onto the roadway. I didn't know what I was getting myself into, but the enigmatic text was all I had right now.

About twenty minutes later, I pulled up to the intersection and slowed to a stop at the traffic light. I didn't have to wait long for my answer. The passenger door to the truck opened, and Roxie Taylor climbed in.

She managed a weak smile but said nothing. From the look of things, she'd been there awhile. She was soaking wet.

She was also the last person I expected to encounter. This had all the markings of a bad idea, but I couldn't just leave her. "What's going on?" I asked. "What are you doing here?"

"There's a shelter nearby," she said. "You know, for women. I just couldn't make myself do it. There would be questions. I didn't want that."

"What about your sister? Do you want me to give you a ride back to her house?"

"It would be better if you didn't, for her and her family, anyway."

I'd been staring straight ahead through the windshield, intentionally averting my attention away from the lovely woman sitting in the truck next to me, but after her last remark, I allowed myself a glance.

She was shivering.

I turned the heat up in the truck and increased the rate of airflow from the fan. "Why? What's happened that would change things?"

Roxie warmed her hands near the air vents, but to my question, she gave no reply.

"Are you hungry? We could go somewhere, get something to eat."

She ran her fingers through her wet hair, glanced at her clothes, then shook her head.

My guess was she just didn't want to be seen, partially because of the way she looked, with her clothes and hair a mess, but also because she feared public attention.

"We don't have to go inside," I said. "Most places have takeout windows if you don't mind fast food?"

She hesitated for what seemed a long time, then asked, "Where would we eat?"

I shrugged. "In the truck, I guess."

A hint of a smile crossed her lips. "Yeah, I guess that would be all right."

I found a restaurant that offered a selection we could both agree on, then drove around until I found a suitable spot, a grocery store with a large parking lot where we could stay for a while without drawing much attention. We were halfway through the burgers and some small talk when I revisited an earlier question. "So what's up with your sister that caused you to move out?"

Roxie had spread the wrapping the burger had come in across her lap, and she laid the sandwich down and took a sip of cola.

In the silence that followed, I began to regret having intruded on this strange lady's privacy, and a thought that I should apologize came to mind, though the urge was cut short when she began to answer.

"My husband always told me that if I ever left him, he would kill me."

The beginnings of regret I'd experienced earlier now turned into a full-blown emotion. I shouldn't have pried into her personal affairs, putting her through unwanted memories, but now that I'd thrust myself into the middle of it, maybe I could do something about it. "Does your husband live around here?"

She shook her head. "We're from California. As far as I know, he's still there, but..."

"Maybe I can help," I said. "Persuading people to change their minds just happens to be one of my talents. If you know where he is, I'd be willing to have a talk with him."

She shook her head. "A few months ago, he went on a fishing trip with some old buddies of his. He left me there by myself. He'd never done that before. I actually considered waiting for him, thinking that maybe such a display of obedience might afford a degree of tolerance, maybe even lay the groundwork for a real relationship. It took me two days to work up the courage, but I finally decided I wouldn't get another chance, so I grabbed some clothes and ran. Never thought I'd end up soaking wet in the cab of a stranger's truck."

I considered my answer. I didn't want to sound condescending, but the question hung in the air. "It seems logical that your husband would know about your sister and where she lives. Didn't it occur to you that this would probably happen?"

"I stretched the truth earlier. I grew up in foster homes. I don't really have a sister or anyone else for that matter. I met Eileen online. She offered to help. I didn't think he'd find me, or else I wouldn't have put her in danger."

I didn't need to hear that. Knowing that Roxie and I were both orphans only strengthened the kinship I felt for her. "What makes you think there is any danger? Have you seen your husband or heard from him?"

"No, but people have been watching the house."

"And you think your husband is behind it?"

"Who else could it be? It is kind of freaky though. They just sort of stand there and stare at the house. I decided it wasn't right for me to put Eileen and her family at risk, so here I am."

"You did the right thing. And don't worry. I'll help you find a place."

"I know this is a little forward," she said, "but maybe I could stay with you for a while?"

I glanced away. Through the rain-spattered window, I could see a couple loading groceries into the trunk of their car. Roxie's words had caught me off guard, and it took a moment to regain my footing.

"That's probably not the best of ideas."

"I think I get it. You're married, aren't you?"

I turned back. "Not exactly, but I am seeing someone. She means a lot to me."

"Lucky girl."

I thought about my past and my life up to this point. It hadn't exactly been the stuff of dreams. "Thanks, but I have more than my share of problems, trust me."

At that point, the conversation seemed to taper off, and we finished our burgers in uncomfortable silence. Finally, she started up again.

"There's a few things I need to tell you, kind of related to what you're working on, I think."

We'd finished the food, and I collected the wrappers and leftovers and stuffed them back into the sack. "All right," I said. "I'm listening."

"It's about Friday night. I haven't been completely honest with you concerning my involvement, what I remember of it, anyway. At the shelter that night, it was busy. I'd never seen it that bad before. We were over capacity, and people just kept coming. The lobby was crammed full of desperate faces, and plenty more were outside, trying to get in. It was awful. I felt so bad for them."

"Was anyone turned away?"

"There had to have been. But we were doing the best we could, trying to make arrangements for everyone."

"What about an elderly couple? One of them might have been sick."

"I can't be sure. There were so many, but yeah, I think there was someone like that."

"Anything else? Whatever you can remember could be important."

She rubbed her forehead. "It's all kind of cloudy after that, kind of like trying to remember a dream. At some point, a man shoved his way to the front of the line. He said there'd been an accident, an emergency outside, and he needed our help."

I leaned forward. I was pretty sure I already knew the answer to my question, but I had to ask. "Was he wearing an Oklahoma Thunder sweatshirt?"

"Yes, I think he was. Do you know him?"

"I have a pretty good idea," I said, "Did anyone go with him as he requested?"

Roxie paused and stared through the windshield of the truck.

I waited for her to continue, and when I could stand it no longer, I asked, "What happened after that?"

When Roxie turned toward me, her face showed the stress she was under. "I don't know, Mr. Elliot, and that's the truth. I remember going outside, and after that, there's nothing, like a part of my life was just taken away or something. The next thing I remember is waking up in a police car."

"How do you think you got there? Were you arrested or detained?" I paused, then added, "And please, call me Kenny. Mr. Elliot sounds way too formal."

"I don't think it was like that," she said. "I was in the front seat, and there were no cuffs or anything. Besides, we were parked in the driveway of a house in some fancy neighborhood. It was dark, and the police officer was still there, except he was asleep or passed out. I'm not sure. I kind of panicked, you know. I didn't know what was happening, so I got out of the car, and walked away, found my way out of the neighborhood. When I reached the main road, I saw a convenience store. I didn't have anything with me. My purse, my phone, even my jewelry, all of it was gone. I talked the clerk into letting me use his phone, and I called Eileen."

"Can you tell me approximately what time all this happened?"

"When I got to the convenience store, it was a little after 3:00 a.m. I noticed the time at the shelter because I was getting ready to leave for the night anyway. When Mr. Goldstein and I went outside with the man, it was around 9:00 p.m. That's six hours and all of it gone. What's going on, Kenny? What's happening to me?"

"I don't know. But I intend to find out."

"There's more. I'm not sure why I'm even telling you this. Maybe it will help you with your case, or maybe I just need to talk to someone, but something happened while I was out, something that shouldn't have."

"What do you mean?"

Roxie's hands began to tremble, so she clasped them together and put them in her lap. "A woman knows when she's been violated."

I turned away. I'd suspected where this was going, but I wasn't prepared for the pain I felt for this strange lady. I thought of Yates and the sex tape. "Do you think it was the police officer?"

She shook her head. "I can't be sure. Nothing like this has ever happened to me before. Am I losing my mind?"

I took a moment to gather my thoughts. Roxie's story went along with what Yates had said.

"No, I don't think that's it. However, there is something you need to know, and I'm not sure how you're going to take it, but I know the police officer who was in the car with you. In fact, he's my client. He told me pretty much the same thing you did about the missing time and waking up in his patrol car parked in the driveway of his own home."

I decided not to mention the sex tape. I couldn't see that doing anything but harm.

"And like you, he can't remember anything. The time period lines up too."

Concern creased Roxie's face. "How could that be? What's happening to us?"

"I'm not sure. And as hard as it is to wrap my head around who might be behind this and why I've never been so compelled to follow a case to its end."

I paused and examined the parking lot. It was nearly empty, which left us looking a little conspicuous, sitting in the old truck. And while the rain had not become a downpour, it had become steady, the kind that was going to hang around for a while. The only thing to hope for now was for the temperature to remain above freezing. The way things had been going, I wouldn't bet on it.

"It's getting late," I said, "and the weather's only going to get worse. I think letting you spend the night at my place would be the right thing to do."

I thought about saying that tomorrow we could make better arrangements but didn't. Perhaps I should have.

A few minutes later, we turned into my neighborhood, then onto the street where I lived. I was preparing to enter the driveway when Roxie stopped me with her words.

"Don't pull in, just keep driving. I've changed my mind."

Her change of heart didn't surprise me. "All right," I said, "I understand."

"No, it's not that, not what you think. Look, do you see them? I don't know how it could be, but they're here, they've followed me."

For the first time since meeting Roxie, the subject of her sanity began to run through my mind, but the uneasy concept had yet to take hold when I, too, saw them. A shadowy figure stood near the southeast edge of the house, another peeked around the corner beside the garage, while yet a third unknown person leaned against the maple tree in the front yard.

I stopped the truck and reached for the door handle, but Roxie grabbed my left arm and pulled me back. "No, Kenny, please. Just keep driving. I don't like this. I don't like it at all."

I dropped the truck into gear and did as Roxie asked. I didn't like the thought of leaving strangers alone to mill around my house unchallenged, but I had a feeling Roxie might be right. I drove away and out of the neighborhood.

A few seconds later, an idea came to me. I jumped onto the Broken Arrow Expressway, and when I saw the place I was looking for, a hotel that offered inside suites, I exited the freeway.

I had a bit of luck. There wasn't much going on in the Tulsa area, and the hotel had a two-bedroom suite available.

Once I got Roxie settled, I gave her instructions to not let anyone in, and if someone tried, she was to call the front desk. I told her I was going out for supplies and a change of clothes, but I had other plans. I needed to have another discussion with David Yates.

As I was about to leave, Roxie put a hand on my shoulder, causing me to pause.

"Why are you doing this for me?" she asked.

Her eyes reflected fear, hope, and a menagerie of other emotions. I'd seen the look before on others who'd hit bottom and didn't know where to turn.

"Because you look like someone who needs it," I said.

I left Roxie standing in the doorway of the hotel suite, took the elevator to the first floor, then started across the lobby with a head full of confusion. There was no denying the rapport between us, like old friends, immediately comfortable with each other. I could not allow it to go too far. Carmen meant too much to me. As I exited the hotel, I did my best to clear my mind.

Twenty minutes later, I passed by the convenience store where Roxie had called her friend after her ordeal with Yates, whatever that had been.

Yates lived a few blocks up the street, and when I pulled into his driveway, I remained inside the vehicle, the essence of trouble emanating from his house affecting my senses even from that vantage point.

I grabbed my phone and called, and it didn't surprise me that Yates didn't answer, but I didn't expect to receive a text just as I was calling, as if the call had triggered it, which it had.

It was from Yates, and it read:

You need to get out of there. Don't ask, just back out and leave.

I'd already decided that heeding Yates's warning might be a good idea when, as if to punctuate the notion, a man came out of the darkness and stepped in front of the truck. In the glow from the headlights, I saw that his eyes, like those of James Goldstein, were as empty as those of a mannequin.

My career had been anything but ordinary, sprinkled with enough oddities to season me for the unusual, but a town full of zombies wasn't something I was prepared for.

Another one stood beside the driver's side of the truck, his face hovering only inches away, separated from mine by only the window glass. With a speed which defied his appearance, the man grabbed the door handle and began to open it.

I threw the truck into reverse, not caring what I might hit, and as soon as I had a workable angle, I shifted into drive and floored the old buggy.

In the rearview mirror, I saw the men, or whatever they were, staggering around in the street, watching me as I left the area. If these were the same people that'd been watching Roxie's friend's house and mine, we'd just shifted from a bad dream to a nightmare.

I reached the exit from the subdivision and turned onto 101st Street, not completely sure where I was going, and it occurred to me that such a dilemma might be a good thing in a weird sort of way. I didn't want to be followed, and what better way was there to confuse a potential tracker than to not have a specific destination?

I thought of going north on Mingo but did the opposite to create more confusion, I guessed, though I wasn't sure. I wasn't sure of anything, though the simple act of driving randomly had a calming effect on my nerves.

The route I'd taken wasn't busy, only a few vehicles, and while the faces of the other drivers held an assortment of expressions, none of them appeared to have a clue that something bizarre, perhaps even sinister, was happening a few miles away at the house of a onetime model citizen and probably former police officer.

I began to wonder if David Yates would ever be able to pull his life back together, even with my help. It seemed unfair. He was a good person, and he'd asked for none of the trouble he was caught up in.

At some point, I ended up at a store. Once inside, I found a cart and began to shop. I was used to it. I'd been on my own for long enough. But this was different in that I was now shopping for two. I roamed the isles, then made a loop through the clothing section, opting for sweatshirts, sweatpants, and blue denim jeans. How could I go wrong with that? And I did my best with the necessary items.

Sometime later, I pulled into a spot in a dark corner of the hotel parking lot and shut off the engine. I'd tried calling Yates several times in addition to sending multiple texts. He wasn't answering.

Making sure I hadn't been followed, I remained in the truck a few minutes, observing the area. The idea of returning to the hotel had been troubling my mind, and I suspected it might be best if I didn't, but I didn't know what else to do. With the zombies we'd seen hanging around, my house was out of the question.

Exasperated and confused, I gathered the items I'd purchased, then made my way to the hotel.

Inside, everything looked okay, nothing unusual.

I reached my floor and started down the hallway. I was still several feet from the room when Roxie opened the door and pulled me inside, shutting the door behind us.

She pressed me against the door and put her arms around me. "I didn't think you would come back."

She wore a terrycloth robe supplied by the hotel, and the scent of her freshly shampooed hair softly flirted with my senses. I reminded myself that Roxie had been through a lot in her life, and she was now reaching out to anyone who might offer a bit of hope.

I gently pulled away and walked into the room, placing the items from the store on a table which had been set up to serve as a desk.

"Just a few things I picked up," I said. "I had to guess at your size. Hopefully, I wasn't too far off."

She quickly stepped over to the desk where she began to rifle through the sacks. Examining the clothing. She laughed, not out loud, but the quivering of her head and movement of her shoulders gave her away.

"What is it?" I asked. "I did my best on short notice."

She shook her head, and when she turned toward me, an expression somewhere between happy and sad covered her face and her eyes were reddened.

She hadn't been laughing at all but was crying. "I'm sorry," I said. "I didn't mean to upset you."

Without explanation, she grabbed the clothing and disappeared into the bedroom, closing the door behind her.

I stared at the closed door for a moment, then lowered myself into one of the chairs in the living area. I wondered what I'd gotten myself into, and though nothing had really happened, it mattered to me what Roxie might be going through right now; had I offended her or made her angry? I didn't like the idea of adding to her pain, and thoughts of what I might do to make things right filtered through my mind.

Finally, the door opened, and Roxie stepped back into the room. She'd put on the blue jeans and one of the sweatshirts. Like a model on a runway, she strolled through the room, then twirled around and returned. "What do you think?"

Her actions brought me out of the chair and to my feet, which left us once again near enough to touch. "Stunning," I said.

And she was every bit of that.

She caressed my left forearm, then wrapped her fingers around mine. "No one's ever done anything like this for me."

"No one ever bought you clothes?"

"Not like this, and not without having been asked."

I shrugged. "Yours were all wet and everything, so…"

"You got the size right too."

"A lucky guess?"

She smiled. "More like careful observation."

I let the comment ride.

Before I could say anything else, Roxie wrapped her arms around me, and then her lips were pressing against my own.

12

In many ways, Roxie was intoxicating, but my reasoning returned, and I pulled away.

"Roxie, I can't do this. It's just not right."

"Why not? Is it me?"

"No, but I can't."

"Why?"

The hurt that showed in Roxie's eyes prompted me to go further. It was then that I told her the whole story of Carmen and me, beginning with our early days in the small town of Porter, where things had come to an unfortunate conclusion, and ending with where I was now, trying to win the hand of the woman I'd always loved, especially after having recently found out that we have a child together.

Roxie's eyes glistened with moisture. "That's the most romantic thing I've ever heard. You're an unusual man, Kenny." She smiled. "I've never known a real live knight before. If it were possible, I'd change places with your Carmen in a heartbeat."

Roxie's words raked across my senses, and I turned away.

Finally, I turned back and said, "If for some reason, it doesn't work out for me and Carmen, and if by some miracle you're still available, I'd be honored to talk to you about it."

Roxie clamped her eyes shut. "Yeah, if it turns out that way, we'll talk."

After a short period of gazing into each other's eyes, Roxie and I walked to the small sofa and sat down. Neither of us knew what to say. It was then, like some electronic cavalry, that my phone came to a rescue of sorts. Through the otherwise silent room, the message indicator reverberated like an alarm, reminding us that we were not caught up in a fairytale but were still very much involved with the outside world, which was as problematic as ever.

I hesitated, considered ignoring the phone, then hesitantly fished it from my pocket.

It was David Yates, getting back to me.

Roxie shifted her position on the sofa.

Her effort wasn't in trying to gain comfort, though I suspected she was in some way attempting to belay additional discomfort.

"It's the police officer, isn't it?"

Roxie's question was stated in a rhetorical manner, and its answer was not something she should have known. From her vantage point, she could not see the screen of the phone, much less read the message. "Why do you say that?"

"He's your client, isn't he?"

"Yes, but he's not the only one who might text me."

"I need to ask you something, Kenny. And I want you to be honest."

I nodded, but I didn't like where I thought this might be heading. "All right, I'm listening."

"Your client, the police officer who was in the car when I came to, did he rape me?"

My face grew warm. I felt sorrow for Roxie and anger at Yates for what he'd done to her, but neither reaction was truly warranted. After all, how did one define rape, an act of sex forced upon an unwilling partner? Based on the evidence I had, it hadn't happened that way. Yates was as confused and unsure about it as Roxie was.

"No," I said. And I felt that to be the truth.

Roxie's eyes darted back and forth, her gaze searching my face, measuring my sincerity.

"I'm not like that, not that kind of woman."

"I know that. Your innocence in all this has never been a question in my mind."

"I don't throw myself at every man that comes along. In fact, I hadn't flirted in so long I thought I'd forgotten how."

I shook my head. She had not forgotten how to get a man's attention but now didn't seem like the time to remind her of that. "Nothing negative about your character has ever entered my thoughts. I promise."

"Then what did happen?"

An uneasy feeling came over me. I'd built my reputation as a detective around hiding my emotions and protecting them beneath a façade I called a good poker face. Even though I'd never actually played the game, I'd gotten pretty good at that part of it. I knew of only two other people who could read me that well, Nick Brazelton and Carmen Garcia.

"I don't have all the answers, Roxie, but to the best of my knowledge, David's memory is the same as yours with chunks of missing time. There's some video. I didn't see all of it"—that much wasn't a lie as I had turned my head away—"but of what I did see, the two of you were consensual. I suspect it has something to do with those people we saw watching my house. You were right about one thing. There's definitely something odd about them."

Roxie looked as if she wanted to say something more, but instead, she got up and started toward the north bedroom, the one she'd changed clothes in. The other bedroom was west of the living area.

I sat forward. Our conversation felt unfinished. "Roxie?"

She paused, her face remaining expressionless, then turned and continued toward her bedroom.

I kicked off my shoes, then leaned back into the sofa.

The phone chimed again, reminding me of the message from Yates. Time had passed, but only a small amount, I thought. Had I become confused to the point of forgetting about a friend who was counting on me?

The text read: *Are you okay?*

Yates's concern acted to multiply my guilt for being distracted from the case. I tapped in my reply: *Where are you, at home?*

You're kidding, right? You were there. You saw them.

About that, how did you know I was at your house?

Security camera. I can check it on my phone.

I breathed deeply, then let it out slowly, had to pull myself together. Yates was a police officer, familiar with crime. It wasn't surprising that he would have a sophisticated security system.

Who were those people?

I don't know, zombies, I guess.

So, the same term had occurred to Yates. *Zombies?*

Forgive the facetiousness, but it's happening, Elliot, the end of days. I always thought I'd be caught up in the rapture when it came time, but I guess my sins, even those I don't remember, have kept me here.

The phone grew heavy in my hand as I actually considered Yates's reasoning. After all, things were happening that I could neither understand nor explain. I cleared my mind and tried to recall some related scripture.

Hold on, Yates. Isn't it written that there will be clouds, angels, trumpets, that sort of thing?

Yes, the twenty-fourth chapter of Matthew, but it also says: Two men will be in the field; one will be taken, and the other left behind. What if the announcement is only for the righteous?

My thoughts raced. Yates knew the Bible as well as anyone. He was stressed, near delirious.

I reminded him: *The Book of Revelation says all eyes will see.*

A short time later, Yates posted: *You're right. The Son of Man will appear in the sky, and all nations will mourn. They will see Him coming on the clouds.*

What's going on, Elliot? What's happening to me?

I responded: *It's not the end of days, though it's understandable that you might think that. Pull yourself together, David. I have some questions I need answered.*

You have questions? That's all any of us have. We need answers.

I squeezed the phone. Yates made a good point. I was the detective, the one everyone was counting on to remove the smoke and mirrors from this strange game of illusion.

Right, I replied. *Now calm down and concentrate. I need you on this. The old couple you rousted from the empty building over on First Street, what do you remember about them? Could you describe them?*

We've been through this. I've told you everything.

Through the curtained glass door of the hotel suite, I saw the shape of someone as they walked past the room.

I went to the door and peeked out. It appeared to be a hotel staff member, nothing to worry about. I went back to the sofa.

Come on, David. You're a police officer, trained to observe. There must be something.

I was kind of preoccupied, he replied, *with Dewey Crawford. He was still in the back seat of the patrol car and none too happy about it. Wait, I do remember that both of them were rather short, small in stature, I mean.*

Are you saying they were little people?

No, but my guess is the lady was somewhere south of five feet. The man wasn't much more than that. Then again, he was wearing cowboy boots, which could have made him look taller than he was.

Now we're getting somewhere. Anything else?

For a few minutes, nothing happened, but then:

Sorry, my friend, but that's about it. I'm surprised I recalled as much as I did. Hope that helps. Talk to you later.

I laid the phone on the sofa cushion beside me. Yates had signed off. I wouldn't hear from him again tonight.

At some point, the bedroom door opened and Roxie came back into the living area, again wearing the terrycloth robe. "I couldn't sleep," she said, "knowing you were out here, worrying about things."

I hadn't thought much time had passed, but I wasn't sure how long I'd been there, thinking, staring at the walls of the hotel suite. "Sorry. Didn't mean to keep you awake."

She came over and sat beside me on the sofa. "I'm the one who should be sorry, not you."

"Why do you say that?

"For dragging you into this and laying all my problems on you."

A vision of the John Doe being struck by the vehicle bloomed in my mind. It seemed like a well-established memory, a tragedy that'd happened weeks ago, and yet the macabre event that'd launched me into the investigation had taken place only yesterday. "You haven't been a problem," I said.

"But you said it had something to do with those people who were watching my friend's house... and yours. I know you don't think my husband is behind all that, but who else could it be?"

I considered the question. I had some ideas, but my theories had yet to develop to the point of being reliable. "That's what I've been worrying about," I said. "But the way I see it, if you hadn't been at the right place at the wrong time, you probably wouldn't even be involved."

"I'm not sure I understand."

The dual implication of what I'd pointed out occurred to me. If Roxie had not inadvertently become tangled up in this mess, in all likelihood, we would have never met. "The shelter," I said. "Whatever happened there, including the part you don't remember, has something to do with your being caught up in all this. I don't think your husband has anything to do with it."

An expression of misunderstanding crossed her face.

I thought about trying to explain further but decided against it. With my thoughts as jumbled as they were, I'd probably add to her confusion.

"It'll all work out," I said. "It's just a matter of time."

I'd no more than gotten the words out when my statement seemed a falsehood even in my own mind. Who was I trying to kid? And what, exactly, was I trying to do?

"Are you okay?" Roxie asked.

"Not really."

The ease at which I was able to open up to Roxie continued to surprise me. "The truth is I've been sitting here staring at the walls because I can't come up with anything else. I've hit a dead end, and I don't know what to do next."

"Is it unusual for you to draw a blank like that? I mean, if I was a detective, it'd happen to me all the time."

Roxie presented the question with such innocence that it tugged at my emotions. "It's not unusual," I said, "but, thankfully, it's not all that common either."

"What would happen if you simply walked away from it?" she asked. "I know that sounds crazy, but it seems to be working out pretty well for me so far."

Again with the innocence, and yet one might make the case for a teasing offer, not exactly thrown in for good measure but laced lightly around the edges and perhaps born from the same honest nature.

"I like the idea," I said. "I could hop a flight to Mexico and leave it all behind."

"I know you don't mean that. There's too much of you wrapped up in things here."

Roxie was vulnerable and having just come out of a bad relationship, she was more so now than ever. I didn't understand how someone could mistreat such an open and straightforward person.

"You're right," I said. "Since becoming a detective, I've never walked away from a case. And I have Carmen and Wayne to think about."

I tried to subdue my feelings, which were too close to the surface.

"I don't know what you've been through, Roxie. I can only guess. But I can tell you that you should never think that you have to live in a bad relationship."

After what seemed a long time, she said, "I walked away from that relationship over a year ago. It's only recently though that I filed for divorce. I guess that's why I thought it was him, reacting to what I'd done. I'm not on the rebound, reaching out to just anyone. You're special, Kenny. I'm not just saying that."

A notion to respond to Roxie's admission welled up inside me, though it lacked the strength to overcome my current inability to express my thoughts. In the silence that ensued, a chill much like that which I might later experience in the cold dampness of the world outside the hotel suite trickled like an electrical current through my senses. I wondered if I had changed so much in one day that my identity might be questioned, even compromised.

"You have a hard face," Roxie said, "but kind eyes. And like those of a child, they show your feelings. I hope you're not so troubled because of me."

I thought to say *of course not* but realized this thing with my eyes would probably tell her otherwise.

"To drop something once I've picked it up goes against my nature, but I have questioned the validity of this case, even the necessity of my involvement, from the start."

"Then why is it so hard for you to let it go?"

I considered the question. The answer was so tangled up in who I was that explaining it would be difficult, though the need to try was there as well. "Because I can't shake the feeling that fate pulled me into it and that it's about to escalate into…" I paused, searching for the right description. "A nightmare," I said, "or something pretty close. Bad things are going to happen. But it will be even worse if I don't try to help."

Roxie's eyes grew intense, and when she spoke, it came out strained like an urgent whisper. "If you believe that, then you have no choice but to see it through."

A small sense of accomplishment settled upon me, though adding to Roxie's troubles had never been my intention, so I didn't tell her that I feared she had every right to be frightened. "Yeah," I said, "that's the way I see it too."

The sound of another text coming in reverberated through the room. The source showed as unidentified, but that didn't stop me. It read:

The time has come. You will find me where you saw me last.

The identity of the sender was not a mystery. It could have been the construction of the text, or the content, even a combination of the two, but I immediately sensed who was on the other end.

Roxie pulled her robe tighter and snuggled into the sofa. "Is it the police officer again?"

"Not this time."

I had answered Roxie's question, but not completely. She deserved better than that. "It's a man named Barrington. I might have mentioned him earlier when I found you at the park in Sand Springs."

"Does he have something to do with all this?"

The events of the day, which had been many, filtered through my mind. "You could say that. Maybe you've seen him, elderly gentleman, who dresses like a wealthy businessman?"

The solemn expression that crept across Roxie's face answered the question before she could. "He's one of them," she said, "one of the people I saw outside my friend's house."

I struggled to gather my thoughts. The concept of Barrington falling into such a category was outside any line of reasoning I'd tried to establish. Or was it? Goldstein couldn't have pulled it off alone. Who better than his old friend to stand in the background and pull the strings? It just didn't add up. Neither of them needed the money. "Are you sure about that?" I asked.

She shrugged. "Someone like that was there, older than the others and wearing fancy clothes. He seemed odd or out of place, even more so than the others."

I jumped up and walked across the room to the desk chair where I'd hung my overcoat. I straightened the coat and slid my arms into it.

Roxie sat forward. "What are you doing?"

"Barrington sent me an invitation. After what you just told me, I believe I need to accept it."

Fear and uncertainty clouded Roxie's face. "Right now?"

I went back to the sofa, taking care not to stand too close because of the dampness of the overcoat. "It'll be all right."

"But it's late, and it's raining."

"Which is why you will stay here where it's warm and dry."

"Please don't go, Kenny. I'm scared, and I don't want to be alone."

"It's something I have to do. I thought you understood that."

"Why can't it wait until morning?"

I let the question run through my mind. Perhaps Roxie's idea carried some merit. I was tired, my senses dulled. A good night's rest would do me good. I shook my head. This whole ordeal carried a sense of urgency I couldn't ignore. "I need to take care of this, Roxie. I can't explain it any better than that."

"Then take me with you."

I actually considered her request, but only briefly. "That's not a good idea."

"Why not?"

Her helpless, almost childlike, demeanor tore at my heart. It demanded no less than brutal honesty. "Because I don't know what I'm walking into, and it would be irresponsible of me to ignore that."

"Which is exactly why I don't want you to do it."

I looked away, gazing through the curtained window of the entrance. "It'll be all right," I said. "I'll come back for you. I promise."

13

The house on Wheeling Avenue where I'd previously found James Goldstein working in the yard now gave no indication of anyone being there, and while I hadn't seen Barrington during the ordeal, I had communicated with him, which led me to believe that this was the place where he wanted to meet.

The serpentine walkway was nearly indiscernible in the darkness, and I chose my steps carefully as I made my way toward the entrance. Once there, the doorbell glowed dimly as the door began to creep open, its hinges emitting a sound that might have gone unnoticed among the noises of the day but was now quite disconcerting.

I reached inside my overcoat and pulled out the Smith & Wesson, then stepped inside the house where I paused, intentionally leaving the door open behind me.

A rustling sound came from somewhere within the darkness of the house, and I tightened my grip on the .38, wishing I'd grabbed the flashlight as well, but I dared not relax and retrieve it now.

A small flame flared into existence, appearing to combust from the air in which it floated. A match or a lighter had been lit, and when it was brought to a candle, the flame fueled by the paraffin grew, and a dim but sufficient light flowed across the room, revealing someone sitting on an overstuffed couch in what appeared to be the living area of the house.

It was Ezra Barrington.

A smile crossed his lips. "I was beginning to wonder if I'd misapplied my faith in you."

I lowered the weapon but did not holster it. "Well, that makes me feel a lot better, Barrington. You see, all this time, I thought you had the advantage of me, but it turns out neither of us has a clue as to who we're actually dealing with. You're up to your neck in this mess, and I'm getting tired of your evasive nature. I want some answers."

"And you shall have them," he said. "It's time we pooled our resources. Have a seat."

Barrington had a point. I wasn't exactly making headway with the case. I needed his help, and I wanted to trust him, but an uneasy feeling had come over me when I'd entered the room, and I couldn't get past it. The house was much too silent and empty for comfort. "What have you done with Goldstein?"

"I did what I could. Unfortunately, it wasn't enough. Goldstein is dead."

The words Roxie had spoken earlier returned to me: *He's one of them.* "Dead?" I asked. "How did that happen?"

"The doctors said it was cardiac arrest, but I'm telling you that the cause was anything but natural."

That should have surprised me, but it didn't. Nothing about this was ordinary. "What are you trying to say?"

Barrington leaned back into the couch, trying to exude confidence, but this thing had him rattled as well. "That he was murdered, and no one will ever prove it."

"You're not making sense."

"Oh, come now, Mr. Elliot. Don't play dumb. Mr. Goldstein's mind was not his own. You should know. You saw him."

"He couldn't have robbed the store on his own," I said. "That's for sure. I suspect he had an accomplice. Maybe it was you."

"You wound me, Mr. Elliot. It's true Mr. Goldstein and I share an illustrious history, but our escapades never included criminal activity."

"Then what did it include?"

Barrington's face harbored multiple emotions. "I'm not a vengeful person, and it's quite ironic that near the end of my life I should feel obligated to entertain such thoughts."

"If you want my help, Barrington, you're going to have to stop speaking in riddles."

"Forgive me, but it's become such an inherent part of me that not doing so is unnatural."

"What seems inherent to me is your propensity to tiptoe around the truth."

"Please don't mock me, Mr. Elliot."

"Sorry, but frustration tends to make me somewhat abrasive."

A slight breeze found its way inside the house, causing the candle to flicker, which cast shadows around the room. Barrington seemed to be trying to open up to me. I needed to lighten up.

"How careless of me," Barrington said. "In all the excitement, I neglected to remind you that you left the door open."

A sharing of Barrington's concern came over me. I glanced back, then walked slowly toward the entrance. "I've learned to be cautious, that's all."

"A wise philosophy," he said, "but it makes your decision to choose such an option puzzling. Considering all the poking around you've no doubt engaged in, I suspect you have encountered them."

I figured Barrington was talking about the people Roxie and I had seen watching the houses. I leaned through the doorway and scanned the area, then closed and locked the door and returned to the seating area where Barrington waited. "Yeah, I've seen them. Who are they?"

"The question might be more properly posed as what are they."

"An interesting way of putting it since a friend of mine saw you with them. She thinks you're one of them. Are you?"

"Hardly, Mr. Elliot. Are you familiar with the concept of Messianic Judaism?"

I holstered the .38. Through my reading, I had been introduced to the idea of Jewish people who might not go so far as to call themselves Christian though they embrace the belief that Christ Jesus is indeed the Son of God, the Messiah. "I am, yet I fail to see your point."

"Please understand that I am not attempting to compare myself with the Messiah," he said. "I reference the subject because it so clearly makes the point, as you put it. In the book of Matthew, Jesus warns his disciples of those who would come, imposing in his name, and that they would recognize them by the fruits of their labor."

"That's just it," I said. "I don't know anything about you or your labor."

Barrington crossed his legs. "Are you so blind as not to realize that I have enough of my wits about me to not be mistaken for one of those… drones, for lack of a better word?"

An image of the empty-eyed stare of James Goldstein formed in my mind. "Very well put, but like your text message said, the time has come, the time for you to tell me exactly who you are and how you came to be tangled up in this mess."

Something close to a smile crossed his lips. "Someone who has been around as long as I have has had the opportunity to experience many lives. However, more to your point, I spent several years with the Federal Bureau of Investigation."

"That's interesting," I said, "though it barely scratches the surface of whom, much less why."

He shrugged. "In relation to the problem at hand, my story isn't all that important. The greater need at present is for you to grasp the nature of what we're dealing with."

"I have some ideas. More often than not, people underestimate my abilities. You could even say I've come to count on it."

"Intriguing words," he said, "but humor an old man and explain what your intuition has told you about the case so far."

I hesitated, though, for reasons I didn't completely understand, I was compelled to comply. "Two elderly people, a man, and a woman, possible long-term members of the homeless community, attempted to gain refuge at the shelter on North Denver Friday night. Things didn't go well. The couple ended up breaking into an empty building over on First Street. It went downhill from there. Later someone connected to the indigent couple, possibly a relative, perceived that the pair had been mistreated. Whoever that person is, he's singling out those he thinks responsible and meting out his own brand of punishment."

Barrington raised his eyebrows. "Very good. Very good, indeed."

A fabric-covered wingback chair occupied a space near the couch. I stepped over, then lowered myself into it, facing Barrington. "Thanks, but my theories have done little more than leave me at the starting gate with not much in the way of ideas on what to do next."

"Actually," he said, "you've narrowed the field considerably. Unfortunately, the homeless community is far more encompassing than most people realize."

"Don't I know it," I said, my words being closer to thinking out loud than an actual expression.

"Am I to understand that you've had experience with the matter?"

I leaned back in the chair. "A few cases have led me in that direction, nothing extensive."

"It seems we have more in common than I had thought. I, too, have had occasion to mingle with those less fortunate."

That was an understatement. Being a prisoner of war during the Holocaust, Barrington had no doubt seen and lived through horrors I could only imagine. "The FBI thing, right?"

"It was a long time ago, but certain aspects of my research continued to intrigue me well into my retirement years. Perhaps *haunt* would be a more descriptive word."

I shifted in my chair, wondering where Barrington might go with this. "And then this thing with your buddy Goldstein came along and stirred it all up again."

"Precisely. And how could I not get involved? Considering my experience and my relationship to the man, it was nothing less than my duty." He paused, then added, "One in which I failed miserably."

I felt bad for the old guy. I knew exactly what he was going through. How many times had I let people down or at least thought I had? "I don't see it that way. Seems to me you did what you could."

Barrington shook his head. "I tried to get through to him, took him to Woodward Park, talked about old times. He always liked that. Nothing seemed to work. He just kept getting worse."

The candle flame faltered, looked as if it might go out, then regained its position. "I don't like to put you through this," I said, "but do you have any idea how Goldstein ended up like that?"

Barrington nodded. "It was like you said, an act of revenge."

"Do you know who is responsible?"

"Once again, you've already answered your own question. I, too, suspect it was someone connected to the homeless couple."

"Do you know where we could find this person?"

"That's the question, isn't it? You could say it's why I summoned you. I've neared the end of the trail, Mr. Elliot, and I need your help."

"What about the man who took a shot at David Yates, then stepped in front of the truck? Do you know anything about him?"

Barrington shook his head. "I'm afraid not, other than my suspicions of his being under the influence."

"Do you mean like James Goldstein?"

"That's precisely what I mean."

I sat forward. Barrington had said earlier that Goldstein wasn't in control of his own mind. I thought about David Yates, Roxie Taylor, and Dewey Crawford. "I think I know a few people who might have come under the influence as well. Why is it that some seem only mildly affected while others end up like, well, like Mr. Goldstein?"

"I suppose it has something to do with the makeup of the individual and how direct and sustained the contact was."

"So what are we talking about here, some sort of highly proficient hypnotist?"

Barrington remained silent for a moment, then said, "Several times I woke up to find Mr. Goldstein standing over me, watching me. On one occasion, I was sure I'd even heard him call my name."

"I'm not sure I'm following you."

"When I awoke to the face of my old friend, for a brief moment, his eyes were no longer empty, but someone was there, and it wasn't James Goldstein. This is no parlor trick, Mr. Elliot. It's real, and it's dangerous."

An image of Roxie Taylor formed in my mind and how her eyes looked on the video. I began to wonder how much of the lady I'd been with in the hotel room was actually Roxie Taylor. "All right," I said. "We've made some progress identifying the suspect. Now, what do we do about it? What's our next move?"

A sound like that of a distant and muffled thumping came from somewhere outside the house. "We pray," Barrington said, "that they haven't found us."

He held out his hand, which shook visibly. "As you can see, this has all become too much for me. I called you here in hope that I might persuade you to take over, assume full responsibility for the case."

I stood and walked across the room, stopping at a window which I thought might offer the best available vantage point to check out the sound we'd heard. The shade had been drawn, and the curtains pulled tight. It was the reason for the candlelight too. Barrington didn't want any light escaping. He wanted to give the illusion that the house was empty, unoccupied. Being careful to disturb as little of the cover as possible, I peeked outside.

My efforts were wasted. I could see nothing in the darkness.

I strolled back to the seating area, and my intuition, for lack of a better word, flared. "If it comes to that, I'll do what I have to do, but I sense that you're holding back. Your work with the FBI led you into some questionable areas where you witnessed things you thought you were never meant to see. And now this case is getting eerily close to resurrecting feelings and emotions you'd rather not have to deal with again."

I took a moment to gather myself. I'd begun to raise my voice, show my frustration.

"Look, Barrington, I don't mean to come down on you so hard, but this thing's put a knot in my stomach, and I believe it's going to get worse, that what we've seen so far is a severely watered-down version of what's to come."

In that room of the otherwise empty house of James Goldstein, where the animated candlelight pushed back the darkness, Barrington reminded me of some gracefully aging mafia boss who was forced to render disciplinary action upon a favored protégé. He motioned for me to again sit in the chair near the couch. "Your reaction," he said, "is perfectly warranted, and your uncanny ability to perceive that which is below the surface is impressive, to say the least. You are absolutely correct. What I discovered, during the course of my investigations, scared the hell out of me. The only reason I got involved with this nightmare was to help my old friend. Now he's dead. Your underlying insinuation is also dead-on. I have an obligation to society that transcends personal connections. In consideration of the subject we've been skirting, have you ever given thought to what or who might exist beyond hard luck, drug addiction, mental illness, lack of ambition? The list goes on, but the point remains valid if you're following it."

I thought about the charcoal drawing I'd found in the abandoned building. "I've wondered about the children of those people caught in such situations, what kind of life they might lead, and why they might choose to continue such a lifestyle."

An appreciation of my understanding showed on Barrington's face. "The group I'm talking about, that particular segment of the population from which I believe the drones come, go back generations, Mr. Elliot, a ghost society, existing beneath the population of those we call homeless. They take care of their own, coming and going, for the most part, completely unnoticed. There are no birth records, no medical or dental trails, no Social Security numbers, and as you're about to discover, no record of death. For all practical purposes, these people do not exist."

The weight of what Barrington was telling me settled in, and I was glad I was sitting down. The idea that two unidentified bodies might vanish from the morgue now seemed more plausible. "And you believe our suspect hails from this shadowy segment of the population?"

"I do. And like any society, they have their bad apples. Occasionally one of them will break ranks and come to walk among the regular population. The result can be anything from harmless pranks to... well, to murder." Barrington paused, then added, "I believe you can understand my reason for concern. One more thing. He suffers from a condition which renders him... shall we say allergic to sunlight."

I leaned back in the chair. "The suspect?"

"Precisely."

For Barrington to know so much about the subject suggested that one of his prior cases had led him down that trail. "And it was something similar to this that you were working on, the case that drove you into retirement."

"It would be more correct to say that an inordinate amount of concern over the potentially disastrous nature of my findings followed me out the door. However, as with my superiors at the bureau, and even with your unusual depth, you are skeptical."

Barrington grabbed the arm of the couch, and for the first time since I'd come into the house, he rose to his feet. "Come," he said. "Let me show you."

14

The terrain began to change, sloping downward in a steep grade, and Barrington tugged at my shirt, indicating that we should stop. At a distance of about fifty yards from the road, through heavy trees and undergrowth, we crouched into a thicket and peeked over the tips of the leaves, and though a thick layer of clouds blocked the moon and the stars from sight, my eyes had begun to adjust to what had been total darkness only minutes earlier. At a distance, not much more than that of a basketball court, a barely discernable cluster of darkened shapes moved across the floor of the deep-wooded hollow.

I'd never frightened easily, but my pulse rate felt like it was about to go off the charts. Barrington had already warned me through a series of silent gestures that if the people in the woods, the segment of the homeless population he'd referred to earlier, became aware of our presence, it would not fare well for us.

After we'd left Goldstein's house, Barrington had directed me to a remote area on the west side of the Arkansas River. We'd parked the truck in a deserted industrial area, stacking stuff around the vehicle to make it blend in, then walked through the woods to our present location. It'd been quite a distance. Barrington's agility and stamina continued to amaze me.

A flame appeared in the hollow.

I ducked farther into the thicket. A torch had been lit and then another and still another, the process continuing until there were five of them in all.

The torchlight further revealed the unusual gathering, a group consisting of fifty to sixty people, though there could have been more outside the reach of the light.

Those who held the torches stood apart from the others, wearing black hooded robes, which added to their distinction, and they seemed to be in charge or at least to carry a certain amount of authority.

The leaders formed a circle around a large stack of tree branches where they began to march in a slow procession. On the third revolution, they began to chant, uttering a few words at a time which were then repeated by the entire congregation. Reinforcing the dark nature of the ordeal, what appeared to be a body wrapped in blankets lay atop the stack of wood.

I glanced at Barrington.

He shook his head.

We were at too great a distance to hear what the shadowy people in the valley were saying, but squatting there in the woods, it was easy to fantasize that we'd been transported back a few thousand years where we now watched a group of druidic priests as they led their followers in some type of bizarre ritual.

The priests, or whatever they were, stopped marching, and with it, the chanting ceased as well. The congregation grew silent. Moments later, the priests turned inward within their circle, then simultaneously lowered their torches to the stack of wood, which instantly rendered the consistency of its makeup to fuel a raging fire.

I crouched deeper to shield myself from the increased light. Some type of accelerant had been used to cause the wood to burn quickly. With that much heat, there would be nothing left of the body except for some ashes that would most likely go unnoticed. Barrington had said there would be no record of death of these... Well, I wasn't sure what to call them anymore. The full realization of what was happening hit me. We were witnessing a funeral.

Some of the smoke, which carried a sickening odor, reached our location.

I looked at Barrington, who nodded in affirmation of what I had already determined. Redirecting my attention to the unclean ritual was not something I wanted to do, but I reminded myself that I had to, that it was my duty to gather as much information about the strange proceedings as I could because it was related to what had set this whole thing with David Yates in motion.

I turned away from the apologetic face of Ezra Barrington and once again stared down into the valley.

The fire blazed, the light it cast showing that there was indeed a larger gathering of people than originally estimated. It also revealed something far more disturbing. Standing near the outer edges of the congregation was another person who wore a hooded garment. He did not look at the fire as the others did but hid his face, using the hooded garment to shield himself, not from the heat, for it would have dissipated into the night air before it reached him, but from the light, it gave and possibly what it showed. The hooded man was not of the priestly sort but dressed in such a manner for reasons of his own. Barrington had said the suspect suffered from a sensitivity to light. Another peculiar man stood beside him, and his identity, with defining characteristics of shortened stature and style of dress, acted as a catalyst that brought the pieces together.

David Yates had said that the couple he'd run from the abandoned building were petite in height and that the man had worn Western-style clothing. My senses kicked into full stride, and it all began to unfold in my mind. The dwarflike man, who was part of the congregation, was the same man David Yates had encountered. His wife had grown ill, and in her weakened condition, her exposure to the elements had proven fatal. It was she, or at least her remains, that was now all but consumed by the fire, and the hooded figure, who shielded his face from the light, was the inspiration for and the subject of the charcoal drawing I'd found in the abandoned building. He was her son. He was also the man I'd seen standing in the shadows while David Yates was being attacked.

Down in the bottom of the wooded hollow, the strange hooded man straightened his posture and cocked his head in my direction.

It was then that I realized that something beyond my intuition was at work within the stream of information that had begun to flow through my senses. A bond, a connection of sorts, had been forged between the strange man and me. And the man, who seemed to instinctively hide his face from others, had become aware of the connection as well. He now knew that there were people in the woods who did not belong there.

I swung around to alert Barrington of the danger, but he was already gone.

Had I felt a tug at my shoulder seconds earlier? Yes, I thought I had. Barrington must have sensed the problem as well and had tried to warn me.

A clamoring of voices arose from the valley, and seconds later the cacophony was joined by the sound of footsteps climbing the sloping terrain, coming toward my location.

My first instinct was to run, but I fought the urge. The mob was practically on top of me now, and the noise would give away my position.

I moved deeper into the thicket and prayed that I would not be discovered. I hoped Barrington had made it. He would instinctively go to the area where we'd left the truck, hoping I was not far behind and would arrive shortly to drive us out of there. That wasn't going to happen. I regretted being so mesmerized that I hadn't followed his lead.

Footsteps and murmured voices came from all directions.

The congregation had spread throughout the area. They wouldn't give up until they found something. I had to get out of there. Keeping low to the ground, I scrambled away from the sound of stomping feet. I had no idea where I was going, but putting distance between the crowd and me was the only plan I could conjure at the moment.

It didn't take long. About twenty yards later, I thudded into something, and I found myself staring down at a pair of boots.

Thankfully, it wasn't the man wearing the hood nor, judging from the guy's actions, one of his minions. He was simply a member of the shadowy society Barrington had described. A mixture of fear and disappointment coursed through me as I rose to my feet, deciding to play it cool, just part of the gang. "Having any luck?" I asked.

The man shined a light in my face. "Yeah," he said, "I believe I am."

He wasn't buying the act. I hadn't really thought that he would. Without saying another word, I stepped to my left and drove a hard, right uppercut into his chin.

The man hadn't expected such a thing, and the punch caught him off guard. He stumbled back, then fell to the ground.

I glanced around, didn't see anyone else, but from the sound of things, they had to be close. I thought about finding the flashlight the man had used but decided I didn't have time. I turned and stumbled down the sloping terrain toward the smoldering funeral pyre. It wouldn't take long for someone to discover the man I'd decked and figure out what had happened. I had to keep moving.

I reached the bottom of the hollow, then turned left. If I kept my directions straight, my path would take me toward the general direction of the area where I'd parked the truck.

I hadn't made it far when someone stepped in front of me, and the shadowy form of a man wearing a hooded robe came into view.

My pulse quickened, but my instincts told me it wasn't the hooded figure who avoided the light but one of the priests, or whatever they were, that had performed the ceremony. I dug my feet into the terrain and charged, driving my right shoulder into the man.

The momentum took us both to the ground. I tucked into the roll, found my balance, and maneuvered on top of my adversary, then planted my knee onto the center of his chest.

The action knocked the breath out of the man, allowing a fraction of a second within which he was powerless to react. His eyes held a mixture of fear and surprise, but mostly they reflected contempt.

The fraction of time had yet to expire when I drove the heel of my hand into the priest's throat. It was a precautionary move and not a lethal one. The man would live. He was preparing to scream an alert to the others, and I couldn't let that happen.

Thankfully, it had been one of the priests and not the deranged son of the deceased. I regained my footing and started again in what I thought to be a southerly direction, but the sounds of the other priests and funeral attendees doing their best to find the cause of the trouble reminded me that I had to move fast. If their efforts proved successful, the smoldering funeral pyre would not be wasted but would offer itself up for another cremation.

I tore blindly through the woods, barely dodging the trees. I knew that if I misjudged and hit one at the speed I had attained, it would all be over, but I did not let up. At some point, a bit of clear reasoning cut through the clutter, and I realized that I should not go straight for the truck but should try to throw my pursuers off the trail. Even though I seemed to be gaining ground, my chances of finding the vehicle and getting it started before the crowd caught up to me were not good.

I turned west. The darkness was nearly impenetrable, and I had no idea how I was managing to maintain the speed I'd reached. A few minutes later, I turned north, more or less circling back, or so I thought. The truth of it was I didn't know for sure.

The floor beneath me disappeared followed by a momentary sensation of flotation, which ended abruptly as I slammed belly first onto the ground.

I rolled over onto my back, then explored the area with my hands.

Rocky walls were within touching distance on both sides. I'd fallen into a small gulley or ravine that wasn't but seven or so feet deep.

I maneuvered myself into a sitting position and leaned against the rocky wall behind me. A chill went through me, and I pulled the overcoat tighter, thankful that I'd worn it. Caught up in the chase, I'd become oblivious to the weather. The rain had stopped, but the ground was damp, and the temperature was near freezing. I struggled to clear my head as I ran through my options. I could survive the night here if I had to, but the idea did not appeal to me. Then again, neither did being burned alive by a bunch of would-be druids.

I pulled myself up and peeked over the edge of the natural foxhole.

I seemed to be alone. I didn't hear any voices or anything else for that matter. If any of my pursuers were in the area, they were doing a good job of hiding.

I climbed out of the gulley and started off again, choosing a direction I hoped would lead me to the road where Barrington and I had entered the woods.

At some point in time, I stopped and leaned against a tree to rest. I had no idea how long I'd been running or where I was. With no discernible landmarks, everything looked the same. I could have been going in circles, stumbling over the same ground, for all I knew.

I pulled my phone from my pocket, worrying whether or not its light might give away my position. I hadn't seen anyone for quite a while. If they had been tracking me, I figured they would have shown themselves by now. I positioned the phone in my hand and hit the power button.

Nothing happened.

I suspected that it must have busted when I fell into the ravine. I kept the phone in a protective case, but only a film of plastic covered the screen, which I could now see had been penetrated.

I pushed away from the tree and resumed my escape.

Sometime later, I saw a clearing, a parting of the trees about fifty yards ahead.

I trudged ahead, picking up the pace as I went toward the area, ignoring for the moment any noise I was making. As I drew near and confirmed that it was what I'd hoped for, I nearly fell to my knees but stumbled to keep my balance. I stepped out of the trees and crossed a grassy area, then stepped onto the pavement. I'd found the road.

I considered crossing to the east side of the pavement to put distance and a barrier of sorts between the clan and me but decided against it. The area was barren of vegetation and offered no cover.

I went back to the tree line, then headed in what I thought to be a southerly direction. It seemed like the thing to do, though with all the running, hiding, and circling back I'd done, I wasn't sure. I was all too aware that if I'd already passed the area where the truck was, I might be walking for hours to find nothing.

I maneuvered through the edge of the woods, struggling to keep the disturbance of my progress to a minimum, but within a few minutes, I again began to detect the sound of voices. The funeral party had not given up the search. The discovery dampened my spirits, but it held a redeeming truth. It was an indication that I was heading in the right direction. I kept my mind on my destination and pushed forward.

The trampling of feet along the forest floor increased in intensity, and suddenly the form of someone diffused from the darkness.

About ten feet ahead of my position, two people walked past, heading back toward the area where the funeral had been. They were talking, but I couldn't make out what they were saying.

The idea occurred to me that the participants had perhaps shifted their immediate agenda from finding me to cleaning up the area, removing any evidence that such a thing had happened. Barrington had said they were practically, if not completely, anonymous. If I made it out of the area to report what I'd seen, who would believe it? And even if I managed to convince someone to inspect the area, what would they find? If such a gullible party was to be found, and I doubted the chances of that, they would quickly conclude that I'd lost my mind.

I waited until the sounds made by the two people became nearly indistinguishable, then I resumed my efforts to escape.

Not long after that, I emerged from the woods near the industrial area where Barrington and I had hidden the truck. We'd done a good job. From my vantage point in the darkened wood, I could make out the hulking forms of the vehicles we'd parked between, but I could not determine if my truck was still there.

An urge to run across the yard toward the area raced through me, but I held back. If anyone from the funeral had discovered the vehicle, they might have guessed it was mine and could be standing guard, waiting for my return.

Keeping inside the tree line, I worked my way to the western perimeter of the industrial yard, then jogged across the graveled lot, stopping near a battered chain-link fence that surrounded the business, an old defunct repair shop, I guessed.

Forklifts, trucks, cars, and other miscellaneous machinery sat like abandoned hulks along the fence line. I sprinted across an exposed area, and when I reached one of the forklifts, I stopped and hid behind the machinery, using the time to observe and listen. I repeated the process until I reached the area where Barrington and I had hidden the truck.

Finally, I reached the rusted-out vehicles I'd parked between, and as I drew near, the familiar shape of the '65 Chevy came into view.

The truck was still there.

I squeezed through the gap between the first rusted-out vehicle and the '65 until I came out the other end, near the back of the vehicle. To hide the truck, Barrington and I had placed scrap plywood across the bed, then threw various junk items we'd found around the yard on top of it. The trick had worked well. In the darkened yard, the camouflaged truck did not stick out among the derelict vehicles but looked as if it belonged there. But the cab of the truck was empty. Barrington was not there as I hoped he might be.

I scooted to the side of the vehicle, and while keeping an eye on the woods, I quickly began to remove the items of junk. A few minutes later, I took off the plywood and stacked it behind one of the abandoned vehicles.

Again I scanned the area around the yard, then extended the search to the tree line, where I'd exited the woods a few minutes earlier.

No movement caught my eye, no sounds reached my ear.

I fished the keys from my pocket, then unlocked the door and climbed into the cab.

The interior light popped on, and I closed the door quickly, hoping no one had noticed. If the unusual gathering was still in the area where the funeral had been, it was doubtful that any of them would have seen the light from that distance.

Sitting in the cab of the truck, with the adrenaline easing back, I became aware of how cold I was. My hands were stiff, my fingers swollen. It took effort to fumble the key into the ignition, but it paid off, and the engine rumbled to life.

I uttered a prayer of thanks, then slid the truck into reverse and backed from between the old vehicles and into the yard.

A flash of red came from behind me, and I caught my breath.

I'd refrained from turning on the headlights, but the flash had come from the brake lights when I stopped the truck to change directions.

I gathered my nerve, then dropped the gear selector into drive and eased down on the accelerator.

As I picked up speed, the tires crunched against the graveled lot, sounding with the intensity of gunshots in the quiet of the night.

I glanced through the side window to check the wooded area one more time, and that's when I saw them.

The unusual people, the entire funeral party, it seemed, streamed from the woods and were now coming toward the vehicle.

They intended to stop me, block my escape. A few of them had already taken position across the narrow exit.

I didn't want to run anyone down, and I couldn't tell how deep the bar ditch was, but I decided to try to jump it. I twisted the wheel hard to the right and stomped on the accelerator.

The rear wheels spun against the loose gravel, but the action wasn't enough to keep me ahead of the horde.

Some of them had caught up with me, and they pounded their fists against the sides.

I glanced in the rearview mirror.

Three or four of them had grabbed onto the tailgate and were trying to climb in.

I whipped the wheel to the left, then back to the right, causing the old truck to swerve wildly.

The ploy worked but not completely. One of the pursuers had managed to hang on and was now straddling the tailgate, one of his legs already inside the truck bed.

The others were still chasing me, but they were losing ground. I was winning that battle for now, but if the bar ditch turned out to be too deep to jump, it would all be for nothing.

Again I slung the truck from right to left.

The man on the tailgate was still there. His grip on the truck was too strong. I gave up the evasive maneuvers and pushed the accelerator to the floor. It was now or never. I swung the truck toward the ditch and sped toward it full blast.

As the headlights panned eastward, a better plan showed itself. Near the south end of the lot was another exit.

I twisted the wheel and banked hard to the right. The momentum of the truck carried it partway into the ditch, and I slid against the driver's side door but kept the pedal to the floor. The old truck threated to bog down in the muddy ditch, but I kept going, and when I finally wrestled the vehicle back onto the lot, it lurched toward an exit blocked by a gate made of steel tubing.

This had come down to my only chance of getting out of there, and I wasn't giving up without a fight. I braced for the impact and kept the truck moving. The truck busted easily through the rusted steel, and when it hit the pavement, I turned south and gave the old buggy all she had.

The guy, who'd hitched a ride, had climbed into the bed of the truck and was now hunkered down near the cab, searching the bed, presumably looking for something he could use to bust through the window. Luckily, I kept nothing back there. But if he had something heavy in his pockets, in his adrenaline-pumped state, he might attempt it, and I would be at his mercy to be put in a chokehold, or even worse, have my head bashed in by the maniac. It all added up to one thing. I had to get rid of the guy. There was no way around it.

I'd put distance between the rest of the funeral crowd and me, and it would take them a while to catch up. I'd seen no other vehicles in the area, which made sense. They would have no driver's license, and it was doubtful they would risk all the questions which would ensue if caught driving without one.

I made the decision quickly and brought the truck to a sudden stop beside the road, then jumped out. I suspected the man was hiding against the cab, and as I hurried toward the rear of the vehicle, I slid my hand inside my coat for the .38 but found an empty holster. I'd lost the weapon as well.

The man rose to his feet, a black silhouette, challenging me to make the first move.

Working slowly, I removed the latches from both sides, then lowered the tailgate. "This is where you get off," I said.

He neither moved nor said anything but remained as he was.

Keeping my attention trained on my adversary, I climbed onto the tailgate. "I don't know who you are," I said, "and I don't want to hurt you. But I will if I have to. I'll extend the offer again. Get out of the truck while you still can."

The strange man lunged forward.

I prepared myself, though I did not deck the man but used both hands to shove him back.

He stumbled, falling against the cab of the truck. For a moment, it appeared it might be over, but no such luck. He sprang to his feet and charged again.

I'd had enough of this little game. I sidestepped, then landed a right hook flush against the man's face. Almost in the same move, I dug my left fist into his rib cage.

He tried to come forward, but when the pain caught up to him, he dropped to one knee.

The man was big and strong, but like the others of his kind I'd encountered, he seemed to lack fighting skills. I pulled him from the truck bed, then rolled him into the bar ditch. I'd hurt him pretty bad, but he would recover. I jumped back into the truck, but as I pulled onto the road and sped away, a disturbing thought ran a sobering realization through my senses. The man's eyes had not been empty but had been full of life. He had not been like James Goldstein.

15

I had the truck heater on high, but I couldn't seem to break the chill that had sunk deep into my bones. The clock said it was around 12:30 a.m. It was original equipment, but I'd found it to be fairly reliable, though more importantly, it indicated that about two hours had passed since Barrington and I had first come upon the funeral.

I'd worked my way into a commercial area where a fast-food restaurant had caught my attention. I used the drive-through to order coffee, then pulled back onto the road. I wondered about Barrington. The thought of the old guy being out there somewhere, alone in the cold, kept me in the vicinity. I hoped the coffee would clear my head. Until then, I would keep driving around the only commercial area that was anywhere near where the funeral had been. Barrington was smart enough to come here if he got free.

I was halfway through another pass around the block when the ringing sound of an old-style phone filtered through the cab.

I knew it couldn't be mine, but I checked it anyway. Sure enough, it was still dead.

And the sound was muffled as if it was coming from beneath the seat or some other hidden location.

Keeping my attention on the road, I reached across the cab and opened the glove compartment.

The ringing immediately became more intense.

I fumbled around inside the compartment until my hand closed around something that did not belong there, and from the small storage area, I pulled an old flip phone that was still ringing.

It was not one of mine. I hadn't used one like it in years, and I never kept them but turned them in. It could only mean one thing. Barrington had left it there. I pulled into the nearest parking lot, flipped open the phone, and brought it to my ear. "This is Elliot."

"It's good to hear your voice, young man. I thought you would never pick up."

It was Barrington. My respect for the old gentleman continued to grow. "Where the hell are you?"

"In a relatively safe place, for now."

Barrington's voice sounded like he was out of breath as if he'd been running or exerting himself. "If you're still in the woods, just give me an approximate location. I'll find you somehow and get you out of there."

"You're an honorable man, Mr. Elliot. However, while you were busy carousing through the woods, I was tailing the suspect."

"How did you know who to follow? There must have been a couple hundred people at the funeral."

"There you go again," he said, "playing the bumbling detective. You saw him, standing along the perimeter, shielding his face from the firelight."

I thought about the man hidden behind the hooded garment and how he'd also sensed that I was there. It stood to reason that if the man had become aware of my presence, he'd probably known about Barrington as well. I'd also sensed that the strange man was not like the other funeral attendees, even the priests, a part of the group, yes, but still different in some significant way.

"He's dangerous," I said, "probably more so than anyone you've ever encountered. If you're anywhere near him, you need to get out of there. You need to do it now."

"On that, I tend to agree with you. I was hoping you might offer to assist me with that endeavor."

"You got it, old buddy. Just tell me where you are."

"Are you familiar with the Vandever Building?"

I wondered how Barrington had gotten to a location that was such a distance away, but I did not ask. It didn't really matter at that point. Barrington was talking about an old building in downtown Tulsa. "Can you make it to the corner of Fifth and Boston," I asked, "without drawing attention to yourself?"

"Yes," he said. "I believe I can."

"Good. I'll be there in ten to fifteen minutes."

"I knew I could count on you."

"Yeah, well, don't do anything crazy, but just wait until I get there, all right?"

"Of course. However, just as a precaution, I need to give you some information. I informed you earlier concerning a certain item and that further instruction would follow if it became necessary."

A knot formed in my gut. Barrington was talking about the key I'd found in Goldstein's backyard. I grabbed a pen and notepad from the glove compartment. "I'm listening, but make it fast."

"Impatience is never a virtue, my good man." He gave me a four-digit number, then continued with, "Though useless when separated, the town of a broken treaty harbors a tiny door of brass."

"That's it?"

I got no reply. The old guy had disconnected. I tossed the phone onto the seat, then threw the truck into gear and followed the route I thought would get me downtown in the least amount of time.

Several minutes later, I reached the intersection where I'd asked Barrington to meet me. The traffic light showed green, so I slowed the truck to a crawl but drove on through.

The area was nearly deserted, with only one man stumbling along the sidewalk skirting the avenue. It wasn't Barrington.

I figured it was probably some drunk looking for a place to sleep. I looped through the area, a deliberate maneuver which landed me on Fifth Street about a block east of Boston Avenue where I pulled alongside the curb and parked. I didn't want to keep circling the block. Quite a few members of the strange subculture had seen the truck. I wasn't sure how they communicated or how fast news might travel within their ranks, but the chance of being recognized, which could spell trouble for Barrington, was a risk I wasn't willing to take.

My keeping vigil from inside the truck near the pickup point didn't last long. Barrington had not showed, but others had; several more men stumbled along the sidewalks near the area, much like the one I'd seen earlier. I didn't like it. The unusual manner in which the men moved reminded me too much of the way the John Doe had behaved. Virtuous or not, my patience had expired.

A block and a half ahead of my position, the Vandever Building rose like a graceful part of Tulsa's past from the south side of Fifth Street. Etched into the façade of the building in cursive writing large enough to be seen from the street was the name of W.A. Vandever, a businessman who'd been lured to Tulsa by the opportunity for wealth offered by an oil boomtown. He would go on to form the Vandever Dry Goods Company, a variety store that would thrive in the building on Fifth Street from 1924 to the 1990s. What the building had been used for since then, I wasn't sure, but now it was under construction, completely gutted from what I could tell. The intention was to turn the space into upscale apartments.

I lifted the Styrofoam cup of coffee I'd purchased earlier and drained it. Fatigue had set in hours ago, and I guessed that was why all the extraneous information kept flowing through my head. One thing was becoming apparent. Barrington wasn't going to show up.

I didn't relish the thought of mingling with the strange people I'd seen on the street, but I couldn't just sit here and do nothing. I grabbed the flip phone, then climbed out of the truck. Keeping to the north side of the street, I quickly walked toward the area.

When I reached a point directly across from the Vandever Building, I paused and surveyed the area. In the dim light that filtered through the darkness, I could see that the first-floor window glass had been removed, and an opening about the size of a garage bay now served as the construction entrance. A six-foot chain-link fence enclosed the site, but if the temporary barrier was intended to keep people out, it had been a halfhearted attempt at best.

Beyond the construction entrance was only darkness. During the day nearby the construction site, an occasional street person or two might be seen or even encountered, but things changed in the city when the sun went down. The cover of darkness gave courage to those who lived in the shadows.

I wondered about Barrington during the time he'd been with the FBI. What could he have possibly gotten himself involved in to have discovered the existence of these people? A disturbing question ripped through me. With Barrington's knowledge about the people we'd observed at the funeral, why had he followed some of them to this location? And what did the strange man, who had a propensity for hiding his face, have to do with it?

A sickening realization formed in my mind. The man had known Barrington was tailing him, and he'd purposely led him to this place. It had been a trap.

I gathered what hope I could find. Barrington had proven himself to be surprisingly resourceful, and it was possible that he had once again used his wits to avoid whatever he might have needed to. It was also highly probable that he'd gone inside the old building.

I considered using the flip phone, then decided against it. If Barrington was hiding in some darkened corner, the call could give him away.

I hesitated, then stepped off the curb and walked across the roadway, stopping when I reached the chain-link fence that surrounded the construction site. A chain and padlock secured the gate, but enough slack had been left that anyone who had a mind to could easily step through. I was off duty, and I would be entering the construction site illegally, but the thought that Barrington might be inside and could be in trouble overrode any other judgment.

I grasped the sections of fence and pulled them apart to slide between them, but the sound of someone coming up the sidewalk caused me to pause.

One the odd fellows I'd seen earlier stumbled directly toward me.

I reached for the .38, then remembered I'd lost it in the woods and took a defensive stance, left shoulder toward my opponent. "I was supposed to meet someone here," I said. "You haven't seen anyone, have you? Elderly gentleman dressed like he doesn't belong here?"

The man slowed his pace but kept coming, ambling forward as if lost but driven by some unknown purpose. As he closed in on my location, I sized him up.

He was of average build, five foot nine, 175 pounds, dressed in ragged clothes, but his face held no expression, and his eyes, like those of Goldstein, were as empty as a cadaver's.

I didn't ask any more questions. I stuck a left jab between the man's eyes, then blindsided him with a right hook.

The man stumbled along the sidewalk, paused as if regarding me with his blank face, then turned and walked away.

I thought about going after the zombie, or whatever he was, but decided against it. The punch I'd given him, hard and completely unblocked, would have sent an ordinary man to the concrete, possibly to the hospital. Barrington wouldn't stand a chance against someone like that. I slid through the gap in the gate and stepped into the darkness of the Vandever Building.

A chasm of darkness unfolded across the underbelly of the old building as I edged deeper into the cave-like atmosphere. My foot caught on something, and as I struggled to regain my balance, it occurred to me that I might step into a hole, an open shaft, or an unguarded stairwell.

I glanced back to where I'd come in, assuring myself in the dismal gloom diffusing around the construction site that the entrance was still behind me. The knowledge of that did little to raise my spirits. Barrington could be sprawled across the floor only a few feet away, and I wouldn't know it. I had to choose between being stealthy and being effective.

I fumbled the cell phone from my pocket and flipped it open. "Barrington?"

The bluish light given off by the phone illuminated various pieces of construction equipment, bricks, and pieces of wood. Crude lighting fixtures hung from the ceiling, suspended by wires, but I didn't know how to turn them on, and I suspected the power had been cut, and I wouldn't be able to if I tried. Footprints dotted the dirty floor, but it was impossible to tell if they were from Barrington or from the construction workers or even the zombies. The light fell across something which looked out of place among the debris, and I bent down and scooped up a high-quality fountain pen.

Barrington's. It had to be. Who else would carry such a thing these days? He wasn't a careless person. I wondered if he'd dropped the pen, hoping I would find it.

I gathered my bearings and continued, taking small steps to avoid tripping over something. Any thoughts I'd had about turning back were gone now.

The light from the phone fell across what appeared to be a piece of plywood leaning against something I couldn't make out.

It turned out to be metal scaffolding that extended deep into the building, set on either side with an aisle between that lined up with the construction entrance.

The glow from the phone barely penetrated the darkness, offering little more than a few feet of visibility. I went a few feet down the aisle between the scaffolding, checked the area with the light, then moved on. If the battery held out, I would be able to search most of the bottom floor construction site that way. There were, of course, other floors, five, in fact, above me. I would worry about that when the time came. Every minute I wasted diminished my chances of finding Barrington.

I started down the next aisle between the scaffolding, and an uneasy sensation blossomed in my mind, a dark undercurrent that ran a chill up my spine. I wasn't alone, not by a longshot, but more unsettling was the awareness that someone was attempting to access my consciousness.

I was not without experience with malevolent entities trying to alter my thinking, influence my actions, but this was different. I couldn't wrap my mind around how or why, just that it was. But the same dangers existed. If allowed to hang around, the entity might gather potentially dangerous information, could plunder my thoughts of Carmen and Wayne and obtain knowledge of their whereabouts. And there was Roxie, alone in the hotel room.

To block the intrusion, I thought of the Bible, specifically Philippians, chapter four, and recalling the words as best as I could, I began to recite verse eight. Soon the dark sensation began to disperse, but the remnants of my earlier cognition of not being alone would not allow relaxation. Logic suggested that I leave the area, turn around and tiptoe toward the exit, but I could not do that.

The phone had cycled off, and when I again turned it on, the light filtered across a small crowd of people standing in the gloom, the bluish glow casting an eerie tint across their blank, empty-eyed faces.

I struggled to catch my breath, my heart pounding in my temples. I was no stranger to nightmares, but the twisted depths of my consciousness had never conjured anything like this. I could only guess at how many of them there were and what they might do.

I lowered the phone, veered left, and started toward the exit. A few steps into my retreat, I leaned over and scooped up a three-foot section of a discarded two-by-four.

Several drones, zombies, or whatever they were scooted to the middle of the aisle and blocked my escape route.

I turned around and walked the other way, going deeper into the interior of the construction site. I made no sudden moves but maintained a slow, steady pace.

The zombies again closed ranks, blocking that path as well.

Suddenly the construction lights came on and illuminated the area.

Someone had turned on the power. I pocketed the phone and gripped the two-by-four like a baseball bat. My hands were shaking. So much for showing no fear. "Take another step, and the first one to reach me gets this board wrapped around his head."

The zombies did not remain motionless at my threat but started walking slowly toward me.

Though it was cold, even more so in the basement-like construction area, sweat oozed from my pores, dampening my clothes. I gripped the makeshift bat with both hands, and when the first stoic man came into range, I pulled the board back and swung.

The zombie crumpled to the ground, but another one immediately stepped forward to take his fallen comrade's place.

I took a step back. I wasn't going to club my way out of this. There were just too many of them.

Acting in unison, like an army operating in slow motion, the group of blank-faced men continued to stumble toward me.

I backed away, edging toward the scaffolding.

The expressionless army raised their right arms, each of which held a four-foot section of pipe, and as they formed a semicircle around me, they slapped the pipes against their open palms, like a group of deranged cops threatening with their batons.

Not an unfamiliar calm came over me. The fear was still there, but it was my mind, slowing things down so that I could assess each action more effectively. I readied the two-by-four. I was trapped and severely outnumbered, but I wasn't going to make it easy for them. I would take a few of them down before they got to me. I moved backward, feet shuffling against the concrete floor, but when I glanced over my shoulder to gauge the distance to the scaffolding, I saw more than metal pipes strung together.

Like some modern-day crucifixion, Ezra Barrington, dressed in his nice clothing, hung from the scaffolding, a section of pipe—like those the drones were wielding protruding from his chest.

A rush of heated emotions coursed through me. "You heartless bastards."

If my words had been understood by the mindless robots, it did not register on their faces. They continued to press toward me, pounding the pipes against their palms in a relentless drumbeat.

I grasped one of the pipes of the scaffolding, which rose ten feet from the ground. I was exhausted, but if could reach the top, I could maneuver along the metal structure above the heads of the drones and perhaps gain enough of a lead to beat them to the exit.

I twirled around, found a foothold, and scampered up the metal structure.

Hands grabbed at my feet while still others clutched the fabric of my trousers, but I shoved the thought of resignation aside and reached for the next bar.

Like bees swarming a hive, a sea of climbing hands carried blank faces up the scaffolding toward me.

I kept climbing, and when I reached the last connector, I pulled myself onto a patchwork of plywood panels that ran across the metalwork. I stepped onto the platform and began to make my way toward the front of the building.

The structure began to shake, and I glanced behind me.

Several of the drones had reached the top, and more were on their way. The shaking increased, followed by a subtle tilt toward the center aisle.

My newfound sanctuary would not remain safe for long. The combined weight of the drones was too much. The scaffolding was going to fall. The reality of what was happening settled across my thoughts. I considered trying to make it to the end of the metal platform before it toppled, but it soon became clear that wasn't going to happen. It was coming down.

Several zombies who hadn't made it to the scaffolding stood at the bottom, still pounding the pipes into their palms. All of them seemed to be focused in some odd way on me and my assured descent into the midst of their ranks.

A current of fear slipped down my spine. They had already killed Barrington, and I was next. I grabbed the section of plywood in front of me and heaved it downward onto the crowd of mindless faces, then balanced on the connecting rod next to the edge and stepped into the void between them, letting myself free-fall. Halfway into my descent, I grabbed the outermost bar and swung like a crazed gymnast.

The added weight sealed the fate of the scaffolding. It started to fall.

I had to make this count. There would be no more chances. I stiffened my legs and planted each foot onto the foreheads of two different drones. The crashing metal and falling bodies did the rest. I tumbled to the ground.

With the lights on, I could now see clearly. I scrambled to my feet and stumbled toward the exit, extracting from my weakened legs all they would offer.

The construction area went dark again.

I focused on the exit and slowed my pace, but just enough to keep from tripping over something.

Footsteps slammed against the floor behind me.

I was tempted to increase my speed, but if I lost my balance and fell, it would all be over.

Something raked across my back.

They were closing in, possibly only a few feet behind, driven by a force only they understood. I cleared the exit and bolted across the open yard.

Only the chain-link fence separated me from freedom, but I had to choose between squeezing through the gate and climbing over. Neither option seemed adequate. My chances of making it to the other side before the zombies dragged me down were not good. Without breaking stride, I jumped, and when I hit the fence, I grabbed handfuls of metal and scampered upward. I reached the top, cleared it, and dropped to the other side.

I came down hard against the sidewalk, and as I lay on my back, looking up at the buildings that rose up into the night sky, people started to gather around. They stood motionless, staring down at me as if wondering what they should do with the scruffy-looking man they'd found.

Realization came to me in a flash. It wasn't concerned citizens who hovered over me. I rolled over and tried to get to my feet, but when my worn-out muscles refused to cooperate, I reached for the fence, found it, and pulled myself up.

Most of the drones had followed me over the fence, and the rest were struggling to make the transition, but as if awaiting instructions or programming, the minions stood blank-faced and motionless on the sidewalk.

I didn't wait for answers. I turned and scrambled away.

Halfway up the block, a couple more zombies walked along the sidewalk. I quickly stepped around them and continued on. A car drove slowly along the street, but if the operator of the vehicle had noticed anything, it did not show in their driving.

I glanced over my shoulder.

The lobotomized army had not given up but followed my movements, walking calmly if not sedately five or six steps behind.

Driven by an understanding of the dangerous nature of the mindless people who would fade back into the shadows only to reappear later, I found an untapped reserve of energy. I increased my speed and loped toward the area where I'd left the truck.

When the vehicle came into view, I jabbed my hand into my pocket and grabbed the keys. There was little thought behind my actions. I worked on gut instinct. That tactic had pulled me through before.

Three blank-faced men stepped between me and the vehicle.

Without stopping, I lowered my shoulder and slammed into them.

The action temporarily dazed the men, but they would quickly recover. Fueled by adrenaline, I spun around, fumbled the key into the lock, then flung open the door and slid onto the seat.

Before I could close the door, one of the drones got to his feet and stumbled toward me. Blood streamed from his nose as he grabbed my arm with one hand and my lapel with the other.

I coiled my leg toward my chest, then let it loose against the man.

As if the move had been choreographed, it worked perfectly. The drone flew backward and thumped into the one behind him, sending them both to the ground.

More of them were coming.

In what seemed like one fluid action, I slammed the door shut, started the truck, threw the shift lever into reverse, and backed onto the roadway where I shifted into drive and sped forward. Only when I'd rounded the corner onto Boston Avenue did I glance into the rearview mirror to see what was going on behind me.

Several of the mindless men were on their knees, trying to regain their footing, while others stood in the middle of the roadway, causing quite a disturbance with the few cars that happened to be traveling through the intersection.

None of it seemed real.

I turned at the first opportunity—Fourth Street, I thought—and traveled east until I reached Cincinnati. Confusion surged through me, though the sensation of a foreign intelligence hovering outside my own began to diminish. I found the entrance ramp to the Broken Arrow Expressway and headed east. The truck's clock showed that time had slipped into the next day, around 2:00 a.m.

I wondered what kind of mad world it was that I'd stumbled into, where no one seemed to be in possession of their own faculties.

A mixture of fear and exhaustion coursed through my senses as I wondered where I might go to get some rest. I couldn't go home. Roxie and I had both seen the guards there. I couldn't go to Carmen's house or the hotel room where Roxie was. The same went for Pastor Meadows or anyone else, for that matter. I could have been followed. The way things were going, having picked up a tail was not a far-fetched idea, and I couldn't risk bringing that danger to my friends or loved ones.

I toyed with the idea of calling Pastor Meadows, not to gain permission to come to his home—no doubt he would give it—but to ask for his advice. It occurred to me that I could always get another hotel room, but another foggy notion vied for my attention, the key Barrington had left in the garden shed in Goldstein's backyard.

I leaned over and retrieved the key from the glove compartment, glancing at the instructions I'd received from Barrington, though his words were already running through my thoughts. He'd mentioned a town of a broken treaty.

The answer to the riddle crept into my tired mind with clarity. In the past, Native Americans had used the breaking of an arrow to symbolize a broken treaty. Barrington's reference was to the town of Broken Arrow. I pulled the key I'd found in Goldstein's shed from my pocket and reexamined it. It looked like one that might be issued by a post office. The door of brass might be referring to the post office. I drove to the main post office in downtown Broken Arrow. Inside the post office box that corresponded with the number Barrington had given me, I found another key.

Less than an hour later, I parked along Eighth Street, then climbed out of the truck and strolled across the grounds toward the condominium. Once there, I glanced around, then grasped the wrought iron railing and climbed the steps to the landing. Just as I'd suspected, I'd found the key inside the post office box in Broken Arrow. I pulled it from my pocket and slid it in the lock.

It turned with ease.

I stepped inside the condominium where Ezra Barrington had lived and closed the door behind me. I was tired, exhausted, but there was something I had to do. I used the phone Barrington had left in my truck and called the department to report Barrington's murder.

16

The reality of Barrington's death permeated my thoughts as I relished the cleansing steam of the hot water that poured over me. I fervently wished the old guy would come busting into the room and pound on the shower door, demanding to know what I thought I was doing, breaking into his home like some thief.

That wasn't going to happen. I'd walked in, promptly slept for six hours, and Barrington hadn't magically come back to life yet.

I twisted the knobs until the water stopped, then reached for a towel. Stepping over my dirty, tattered clothes that sprawled across the tile floor of the bathroom, I grabbed a terrycloth robe that hung from a hook attached to the door and slid into it.

Barrington had treated his guests well.

I exited the bathroom, then walked through the bedroom toward the closet. I outweighed Barrington by at least fifty pounds, and his clothes would not fit, but I thought it was possible that he had left some hanging around for guests.

No such luck.

The condo turned out to be a townhome, with the bedrooms upstairs. Unlike the living area, which was cluttered with interesting items, the top floor was clean and tidy. I strolled down the hall to the master bedroom and checked the closet there.

Like the other closet, this one held plenty of nice clothes, but none that I could squeeze into.

It occurred to me that when I'd been in the hallway, I'd noticed another door. In a condo this size, there would be a utility room. I retraced my steps and swung the door open.

Sure enough, the small rectangular room housed the washer and dryer I'd hoped for.

I went back to the guest bedroom and gathered my clothes, then took them to the utility area and put them in the washer. In the cabinets that lined the wall above the appliances, I found the soap and softener. With everything in, I played around with the washer until I got it started, then trotted downstairs to find something to eat.

Barrington kept a well-stocked refrigerator, though his preferences were a little different than what I was used to.

Once again, the pangs of regret for what had happened to Barrington rushed through me. It seemed wrong being in his house, making myself at home in a place he'd made so personal. But he'd given me the key. He'd known the odds of something going wrong were high, and he'd left his sanctuary available so I would have a place from which to work if it became necessary. He'd thought that whatever was going on in the city was dangerous enough that he was willing to risk his life to try to stop it, and he'd entrusted me to pick up where he'd left off and follow it through. And through it all, Barrington had remained calm and gentlemanly. I didn't know what to make of it.

I would not let him down.

From the refrigerator, I grabbed a carton of blueberries and some cream cheese, then went to the pantry and foraged a package of bagels. Rummaging through the kitchen drawers, I found a knife and a fork, then carried the food and utensils into the dining area and piled it on the table.

It felt as if days had passed instead of hours since Roxie and I had downed some burgers in the cab of the truck, but the full extent of my hunger didn't hit me until I started eating. I couldn't get the food in fast enough.

Later I pushed away from the table and went back into the kitchen. In my haste, I'd forgotten to make coffee. I wondered if Barrington stocked it or if he abhorred the stuff and refused to keep it around.

My spirits lifted when I spotted a coffeemaker on the countertop near a toaster and some sort of drink mixer. A rack beside the coffeemaker held various flavors in single-serve containers.

I chose a dark french roast, and when the final drops fell into the cup, I doctored the brew with cream and sugar, then strolled into the living area. I detoured to the patio door and pulled back the curtains, but just enough to peek through the glass door. The patio chairs looked inviting with the midmorning sun pouring over them, but I dared not chance going outside where I could be seen. I turned away, then plopped down in the same chair where I'd sat a couple of days ago when Barrington and I had talked.

Barrington's death should have drawn some attention at the department. It wasn't out of the question for that kind of murder to go unsolved for a while, maybe even forever, but when the police had been notified, things went faster. I'd been exhausted, but the memory of calling in and reporting the crime right before I'd fallen asleep was fresh on my mind. I wondered if they could have traced the call. I'd used the phone Barrington had left for me. The department wasn't state of the art, but they had enough sophistication to lock in on a phone if they chose to do so. Yet no officers had shown up. No one had called or knocked at the door.

The question was: Had they taken the call seriously, or had they laughed it off as just another sick prank?

I searched my memory, trying to recall whether or not I'd identified myself when I'd called. Surely, I had. It was in my nature to do so.

Thoughts of the strange funeral I'd witnessed during the night and the bizarre chain of events that unfolded later at the construction site swam through my head. The invasive mental energy I'd encountered in the wooded area had also manifested itself beneath the Vandever Building, and it occurred to me that the drones or zombies had been present at both places as well. I suspected it was the man in the hooded garment I'd seen at the funeral. An army would not be effective and probably wouldn't exist without the cohesive force of leadership. Someone was behind it, and whoever it was had been responsible for the death of Ezra Barrington. An army and its general might typically be separate entities, but in this case, they might as well be the same. Based on my observation of the drones, their leader exercised complete control over them.

They had targeted Barrington because he'd gotten too close to endangering their secrecy.

I glanced around the living area, which was stocked with brass clocks, compasses, and other curiosity pieces. Barrington would have been old-school in his methods, and he would have kept files associated with the case.

The painting over the fireplace, the Van Gogh replica that Barrington had so expertly reproduced, drew my attention.

I stood and walked across the room to the artwork.

It would have taken a lot of time and energy to reproduce the Van Gogh in such masterful detail, and Barrington's true motive for doing such a thing was as mysterious, as the man himself, but when I slid my hand behind the artwork and gently tugged at the frame, the hinged painting swung away from the wall, revealing the gray metallic door of a safe.

I wrapped my fingers around the handle, twisted it downward, and pulled.

It opened with ease.

With reluctance, I removed a brown fiberboard file from the safe. Even though Barrington had wanted me to find it, had left the safe unlocked so that I could, a sense of intrusion still lingered. With the file in hand, I strolled back to the chair and lowered myself into it. I hesitated, sat quietly for a few minutes, then slowly opened the file.

Photographs from the shooting on the street that had unfolded with David Yates clung to the inside cover, three of them, all focusing on the same subject: the man wearing the hooded garment that I'd noticed that day, the one who'd stood in the shadows on the other end of Sixth Street away from the action.

The photographs, which had been printed onto regular letter-sized paper, confirmed the information pertained directly to the case. I'd personally witnessed Barrington taking the shots. His notes on the subject, neatly arranged in outline style, made up the rest of the file. There wasn't much to it, but that was to be expected. Barrington had become involved with the case only a few days ago, because of the inadvertent involvement of James Goldstein. I imagined Barrington's last thoughts dealt with regret for his not being able to save his old friend.

I directed my attention away from the photographs and began to read the notes, which reiterated the inherent difficulty involved with finding the subject. Below the section labeled PERSON OF INTEREST, a caption in bold letters read NO IDENTITY.

Thoughts of the man who'd taken a shot at David Yates and the horde of mindless people I'd encountered snaked through my mind.

A bead of perspiration ran down the small of my back, not because I believed an anarchical mob of zombies was behind the madness, but because I did not. Barrington's file all but confirmed my assumption that an individual, most likely the person depicted in the photographs, was responsible. The trouble was, as Barrington had pointed out, the subject he'd digitally captured did not, for all practical purposes, exist in the real world.

I turned to the next page, which was the last of the file.

Barrington had made notations of probable crimes he'd believed were connected to the suspect.

On February 15, Kimberly Denbury, a twenty-eight-year-old computer programmer, was found dead, floating facedown in her swimming pool. The death was ruled an accident.

Klaas Siegler, a genetic specialist, walked out of his office on the twentieth of May. He was never seen again.

The last entry indicated that a bank teller named Jeremiah Turnbull packed a briefcase with funds from the safe, then strolled out of the bank, no questions asked. Two days later, on October 6, the bank teller's sister discovered Mr. Turnbull slumped over the bathtub in his home with his wrists sliced open. The money was never found.

That was it, a rather shortlist, but Barrington had only worked the case for a few days. Given the time he had available, the information he'd gathered gave testament to his exceptional investigative abilities. And having known him even for a short time, the fact that he went to such lengths to prepare the case file was proof enough of its relevance.

The plight of Jeremiah Turnbull caught my attention. Why would someone go to the trouble of stealing a large sum of cash only to take their own life? It didn't add up.

Then it struck me as to why that particular event stood out from the others. The date of death was listed as October 6. That would have been right around the time that the first John Doe went missing from the morgue.

Neither James Goldstein nor Roxie Taylor could remember the events that occurred after they had left the shelter. Perhaps the same thing had happened to the banker.

An onset of fear and doubt threatened to derail my thought process. How could I fight something like that? Where would I begin to search for such a suspect, who theoretically existed within the confines of an unknown society?

I looked away from the file and allowed my gaze to fall across the rich but odd collection of brass curiosities that characterized Barrington, who had lost his life trying to expose the forces, whatever their nature, behind the ruin of James Goldstein.

I returned my attention to the list, and after a few minutes of study, I began to wonder about the doctor who'd gone missing and what his connection to my suspect could be. The suspect seemed to have a habit of hiding his face and avoiding the light. A person like that could have a need for such a specialized doctor, probably suffered from porphyria or some other genetic disorder that rendered its victims sensitive to light, especially sunlight.

The banker wasn't difficult to figure out. The suspect needed cash. The computer programmer was anybody's guess.

I closed the file and placed it on the table beside the chair, then stood and walked into the kitchen. While rummaging through the cabinets and drawers earlier, I'd noticed some phone charges. I found one that fit, plugged in the flip phone, and then trotted upstairs and transferred my clothes from the washer to the dryer. With that done, I went back down and fixed another cup of coffee.

Sometime later, when the dryer announced the clothes were ready, I got dressed and retrieved the phone. I had some calls to make. It was around 10:00 a.m. and Carmen would be at the bank, but she would be taking her break right about now. Her phone probably wouldn't display the number, and she wouldn't recognize it if it did, but I hoped she would take the call. I was about to give up when she answered.

"Yes?"

"It's me. I was afraid you wouldn't pick up."

"Kenny?"

Emotion riddled the tone of her voice.

"Yeah, sorry I didn't call sooner."

"I was starting to wonder if you'd fallen off the face of the earth, and yet we talked only yesterday."

Images of the blank-faced drones formed in my mind. Carmen was closer to the truth than she realized with respect to her comment about falling off the earth. "I miss you too," I said. "Remember my mentioning that I might take some private cases? Turned out it didn't take long to land one."

"Where are you?"

I hesitated, wondering how to field the question. "Undercover. That probably sounds like a Mickey Spillane fantasy, but it isn't. It's as real as it gets."

"What does that mean?"

"The case is…" I started to say dangerous but decided to play it down. "Sensitive, and a bit more than I'd bargained for. I'll be checking in from time to time, but you probably won't see me for a few days."

"Kenny, what's this all about? What are you up to?"

The sugar coating wasn't going down very well, but if I told Carmen the truth, she'd think I'd finally lost my grip on reality. "I didn't want to worry you, Carmen, that's all. I'll give it to you straight. I'm tracking an extremely dangerous suspect, and I won't take the risk of exposing you or anyone else I love to that threat."

"I thought you were considering a new occupation so you could get away from that kind of thing."

"Yeah, that was the plan. I didn't go looking for this. I just sort of fell into it."

"You have a real knack for that."

A smile came across my face. Typically, Carmen understood, even supported my propensity for getting tangled up with someone else's problems, but on occasion, her frustration showed through. "It seems that way, doesn't it?"

"Could you not turn the case over to someone else?"

Carmen's voice carried a genuine tenderness that tore through my heart, but at the same time, a feeling closer to acceptance than resignation tiptoed near the back of my thoughts. The person who was essentially responsible for the deaths of Ezra Barrington and James Goldstein was out there somewhere. I could not turn this over to anyone. Who would understand it? Who would even believe it? And I certainly couldn't walk away from it. "No," I said, "I can't."

"How did I know you were going to say that?"

The small rounded phone began to feel unnatural in my grip, slick with the sweat of my hand. There was something else I had to do, feelings I needed to express. A swarm of words flew through my thoughts, but what came out was, "I love you Carmen."

"I know."

Her voice was soft, almost a whisper.

"It's always been you," I continued. "No one's ever come close to understanding me or reaching me the way you do."

The phone was silent, and for a moment, I worried that I'd lost the connection, but finally, she said, "I guess I'll see you when I see you then."

"You can count on it, no guessing needed."

"I have to go now," she said. "I need to get back to work."

"All right. Give my love to Wayne."

"I will," she said and then, "Kenny?"

I gripped the phone and tried to prepare for the bad news I thought was coming. She would tell me that I was getting too serious and that we should just be friends.

"I love you too."

The phone went silent. This time the disconnection was for real.

I leaned back, relaxing into the cushion of the leather chair, not wanting to think of anyone else but Carmen, but I needed to check on Roxie Taylor, not for personal reasons but because she might be in trouble and possibly had nowhere else to turn. It occurred to me that I didn't have her number. She'd called me yesterday, but not on this phone. I hadn't thought to memorize the hotel number.

I wondered if Barrington had a computer or a tablet he'd stowed somewhere, but I'd yet to get out of the chair when my gaze fell across the solution. Sitting on the table beside me was an old-fashion phonebook.

I grabbed the book and flipped through it until I found the number, dialed it, put the book back on the table, and then leaned back in the chair.

Moments later, I closed the flip phone and stared at the Van Gogh replica over the fireplace. There had been no answer in the room where I'd left Roxie. I'd convinced the hotel clerk to send someone up to check on her. The room had been empty and void of clothing or any other indication that someone might have been there.

I did not blame Roxie for wanting to get away from all this and as the traveler she'd become, that was most likely what she'd done.

I had another call to make, and I wouldn't need a phonebook or a computer for that one. I flipped open the phone but stopped short of making the call. It occurred to me that my current whereabouts might be a matter of interest not only to the man in Barrington's photos but to certain members of the department as well. I slid the phone into my pocket, pushed myself from the chair, and then strode down the hallway toward the door that led to the garage. It was the only part of Barrington's condo I hadn't searched.

Inside the neatly organized garage, a small workbench ran along the back wall, and metal shelving that held cans of oil, brake fluid, antifreeze, and other automotive-related items lined the one adjacent. But it wasn't the miscellaneous items that held my attention.

I rubbed my hand across my face as if doing so would bring answers to the swarm of questions that spun through my head related to the automobile which undeniably belonged on the slab of concrete, parked over a swatch of fibrous material designed to catch unwanted drips of oil. That knowledge did little to take away from the idea that the car shouldn't be there.

I opened the door to the old Mercedes, then with one hand on the doorframe and the other braced upon the top, I leaned forward and scanned the interior.

The keys dangled from the ignition. A garage door opener clung to the sun visor. It was Barrington's, all right.

I wondered how Barrington had managed to get the car back into the garage, but only for a moment. He'd arrived at Goldstein's house, where we'd had our meeting, the same way he'd gone from the funeral area to the Vandever Building. It didn't take a logistics wizard to figure out that Barrington had been using a cab the whole night, except when he'd ridden with me in the truck.

Even in his absence, the old detective remained one step ahead of me. I pulled the keys from the ignition, then walked to the rear of the vehicle and popped the trunk.

A clean rubber mat lined the storage area. A bundle of tools and a spare tire claimed their rightful spots.

Nothing was there that shouldn't be, and I lingered for a moment in relief. I'd hoped I would not find the body of James Goldstein stuffed into the space. After that, I checked inside the car, including the glove compartment. No registration information or insurance card.

Finding the car in the garage, as if it had been purposefully left there, caused me to gain an idea. I closed the trunk, then put the keys back into the ignition and went back inside the condo. Reimagining the notion of lying low, I left everything as it was and drove my truck to the airport.

Less than an hour later, I guided the old Mercedes onto the familiar street that led into my neighborhood, and from there I zigged and zagged until I was on my street, driving past my house.

Nothing looked out of place, and I didn't see anyone who didn't belong there, but I kept driving. I wouldn't risk going inside. Instead, I circled around and parked about a block away on an intersecting street. I'd left my phone, which I'd busted in the woods, stowed inside the glove compartment of my truck parked at the airport. I had to see this thing through, and I wasn't going to let something like being tracked on a phone or being spotted in my own car stop me.

I flipped open the phone and punched in the number for the department. The receptionist sent the call through, no questions asked. Time would tell whether or not that was a bit of luck.

"I'm glad you called," the lady said. "I was hoping you would get back with us."

It was Monica Campbell. A pause followed the greeting, and I imagined Detective Campbell signaling for someone, probably Dombrowski, and putting the call on speaker.

"What's going on, Elliot? What's this all about?"

Dombrowski. I'd guessed it correctly. "Just following up on the call I made this morning," I said.

Another pause.

I glanced around to see if the area was clear, saw nothing unusual. They hadn't had time to home in on the call, and if anyone had been watching the house, I saw no indications that they had noticed me.

"Yeah, about that call."

It was Detective Campbell again.

"Could we rehash those details?" she asked. "You were slurring your words, not making a lot of sense, you know."

I gripped the phone. It'd been a long day and a worse night before I'd called. It wasn't surprising that I'd come across a little incoherently. At the moment though, I didn't have the patience or the inclination to try to explain. Making sure Barrington received a proper burial was at the forefront of my thoughts. "Were you able to recover the body?" I asked.

"Not exactly. According to the investigating officer, all they found was a construction site, with no indication that anything unusual had happened there. Why don't you come down to the department? We can have coffee and get this all straightened out."

"I don't think that's a good idea," I said. "At least not for now."

"Why not?" Dombrowski asked. "Where the hell are you, anyway?"

"I'm on vacation, remember?"

"That's not what I meant, and you know it."

"Oh, I see. You want my exact location. Give me a few minutes, and I'll email you the coordinates."

"Don't get cute with me, Elliot. I don't have time for it."

"All right guys," Detective Campbell added. "Let's all calm down. We need to work together on this. What do you need, Elliot? How can we help you?"

I scanned the area again. Campbell was doing a good job, trying to keep me on the line. "The name I gave you," I said. "I need to know who Ezra Barrington was and why he'd involved himself in this."

"Sure. We'll talk about all that when you come in, okay?"

I started the Mercedes, slid it into gear, and pulled away from the curb. Something was definitely up. Both Detective Campbell and Dombrowski, in his own way, were trying a little too hard to slip into the role of a patronizing friend. Campbell, I could excuse. She didn't know me that well. But having Dombrowski think I might fall for such a ruse was disheartening at best.

I left the neighborhood and drove in an easterly direction. I had no particular destination, but the important thing was to keep moving. I needed to know what they'd found on Barrington. "What did the name check turn up?"

Once again, a pause of silence put me on edge. Finally, Detective Campbell came back on.

"Well, that's just it, Detective. We didn't find anyone named Ezra Barrington living in Tulsa or anywhere else across the country, for that matter."

"You must have missed something," I said. "The man was murdered last night. I saw it."

"I don't know who or what you saw, Detective, but the only Ezra Cohen Barrington II we could find didn't meet his end at a construction site in Tulsa, Oklahoma. He died in 1944 at Auschwitz, a German concentration camp."

I pulled to the curbside to keep from crashing the car. Barrington had said he'd been in a concentration camp, and a tattoo testifying to the same fate had stained Goldstein's forearm. I thought of the first John Doe that had disappeared from the morgue. The one I'd encountered on a previous case and what he'd said to me: *Do you have any idea what it feels like to die in someone else's body?* Just how many dead people was I seeing these days? I suspected the answer to that question might haunt me for years to come. And how had I come up with the complete name for Barrington that I'd given to Campbell? I barely remembered going through some documentation I'd found at the condo. I'd seen the name there. It was the only explanation. "The man must have been using an alias," I said.

"Maybe so, but we didn't find anyone, Detective. And we certainly didn't find any indication that someone had been murdered there. You said you were tired. Maybe somewhere between sleep and consciousness, you imagined the whole thing."

I fired up the Mercedes and pulled back onto the road. I had the impression that Detective Campbell wasn't trying to be cute, but actually suspected I might be losing my grip on reality. That could only mean trouble. "I didn't imagine anything," I said. "Barrington, or whoever he was, had ties to James Goldstein, the man who robbed the liquor store Friday night."

"Interesting you should bring that up. Do you know where we can find Goldstein?"

I turned onto Ninety-First Street. Barrington had told me Goldstein was dead, but he hadn't elaborated the details. I considered suggesting to Campbell that she check the hospital morgues but decided against it. There would be too many questions. "No," I said. And it was the truth. I didn't know.

"You seem to be familiar with the robbery. Why is that? What are you not telling us, Elliot?"

"Seriously, Detective Campbell? You're bound to have reviewed the security camera files. I didn't have anything to do with it, and you know it."

"Maybe so, but you're all mixed up in it. Why is that?"

"Come on, Campbell, you already know the answer. I was trying to help Yates."

"So, we're back to Yates again?"

"That's where it all leads."

"Are you saying David Yates is responsible for robbing the store?"

My head swam with unanswered questions. I'd really gotten myself into a jam this time. I turned north on Memorial Drive. Detective Campbell, or whoever was investigating the robbery, must have realized Goldstein couldn't have pulled it off alone. "No," I said. "That's not it at all. But when Yates rousted a couple of homeless people Friday night, he might have inadvertently set the whole thing in motion."

"I want to help you, Elliot, but you're not making much sense with all this."

A patrol car drove past, going east. The officer didn't seem to notice me, but it was enough to make me nervous. I started to tell Campbell that I was making perfect sense, though she couldn't see it just yet, but decided against it. "I have to go," I said. "I'll be in touch."

17

The person in the mirror executed each movement, mimicking my actions with flawless perfection, though even to my own eye, the reflection appeared to be someone else. It wasn't, of course. I'd just pulled off a good transformative disguise. Some psychologists might suggest that my role as a police detective had become my identity, that I'd been swallowed by an innate fear of owning a life that did not matter. They would be wrong.

Much like my reflection in the mirror, the man I had known as Barrington had pulled off an elaborate hoax, pretending to be someone other than who he really was. Then again, who was to say that he had given any less credit to the name than would have been achieved by the real one, had he survived the genocide that had claimed him?

Nothing was straight up anymore, nothing point-blank.

I'd shortened my hair and changed the color and style, which accounted for the odd reflection in the mirror. I wasn't surprised that Barrington kept an assortment of hair dye, which I'd found in the cabinet beneath the sink basin in the guest bathroom. I'd lost weight too, the unusual activities of the past few days having taken a few pounds. With that and a stubby growth of beard, the result was remarkable. Dressed in blue denim jeans and a sweatshirt, I might be able to move around the city unnoticed if I played it safe. The spiky blond hair contrasted sharply with the beard. For all practical purposes, Kenny Elliot, the one most people knew anyway, wasn't standing in front of the mirror. But I was.

I flipped off the light, then exited the bedroom and trotted down the stairs to the garage. I couldn't simply walk away from this. I had to see it through, put a stop to it, and my reasoning went beyond truth for David Yates, beyond avenging Barrington's death. The whole ordeal had sprung into existence due to a spirit of evil, an overreaction born of revenge that had triggered an epiphany for its creator, the man who hid his face. There would be no turning back. For even though the revenge had subsided, leaving the perpetrator in strategic retreat, a position of defense, the power once tasted would be impossible to relinquish and hide on a shelf until it again became necessary to resurrect.

With trepidation, I backed the old Mercedes from the garage, then maneuvered out of the complex. My old friend Casey, who ran a nearby bar, had provided a solution for Barrington's cell phone. I'd simply left the phone with him at the bar. It would be there if I needed it. In all likelihood, the department would not go that far to track me down, but I wasn't going to take that chance.

I turned onto Peoria Avenue, then headed west on Sixth Street toward the downtown area. If in fact the perpetrator belonged to an obscure segment of the homeless population, finding someone who knew something about that particular community shouldn't be impossible.

Maneuvering the downtown streets, I drove cautiously, though not so much as to interfere with the flow of traffic. I wanted to keep alert, be aware of my surroundings, but as much as possible with the old Mercedes, I also wanted to blend in and not draw attention.

When I reached the Brady District, an area under renovation for the past few years in an effort to make it more attractive to the general population, I pulled into the parking lot of a restaurant, then guided the Mercedes between several other vehicles. The place was busy with the lunch crowd, and if it stayed that way for a few hours, the old car wouldn't stand out as being there for any unusual reason.

I hadn't brought along Barrington's entire file, just one of the photo printouts which featured the hooded figure as its subject. I hoped the shadowy depiction of the character would be enough for someone to recognize. I retrieved the manila folder from the passenger seat, then climbed out of the car and locked it.

I walked past the restaurant, then strolled north along the east side of the building, and when I turned the corner at Cameron Street, it seemed I'd stepped into another world. The area wasn't deserted but certainly stood in contrast to the bustling restaurant crowd a block away.

A shabbily dressed man leaned against the east side of an old sheet metal building that had been turned into a coffee shop. In contradiction of the clear sky and sunshine, the day was cold, and the man had hunkered against the building to block the wind. He wasn't a regular patron of the coffee house but had the look of the street about him, just the type I was looking for.

I smiled and tried to appear non-threatening as I ambled toward him, but he immediately turned to walk away.

I blocked his exit. People who survive the streets depend on their senses, and the man wanted no part of me. "Sorry to bother you," I said. "I don't mean you any harm. I just want to talk."

He shook his head and again tried to move away.

Experience had taught me that those who appear meek and nonconfrontational could quickly turn on you if they felt threatened. Taking him down would not be a problem, but I didn't want to cause a scene, and I had no desire to hurt the man. "I'm looking for someone," I said. I pulled the photocopy from the folder and held it out.

The man kept his head down and said nothing.

"You have your reasons for not wanting to talk to me. I get that. But this guy's bad news, and he needs to be stopped. He's particular about his victims too, preferring to choose them from the street."

The man glanced up, and though he avoided eye contact, he allowed his gaze to fall across the photo. Suddenly, he dropped to his knees, squirmed away, then scrambled to his feet and took off running.

I paused to gather my thoughts. I had tried to remain nonthreatening. It must have been the photo. I did not go after him. Even if I caught the man, he wouldn't be of much help, scared out of his wits that way. And I wasn't there to frighten people. I was there to find answers. I slid the photo back into the folder and began to walk toward the homeless shelter where the lives of David Yates, Roxie Taylor, and James Goldstein had begun to unravel on an otherwise ordinary Friday night.

The deeper I walked into the northwest section of town, the more pronounced the sensation of avoidance I had begun to experience became. It was as if the man I'd cornered near the coffee shop had somehow sent out an instant alert, warning everyone to avoid the strange man with the photo.

About an hour later, having found only a few people of interest to talk to about the photo, I decided to head back to the restaurant where I'd left the Mercedes. The small number of people I had managed to question had all demonstrated differing responses, either feigning disinterest or pretending outright ignorance of the subject. Their behavior had a common denominator. An underlying, though detectible fear dwelled at the heart of it. The identity of the man in the photo might be illusive as smoke, but knowledge of the negative side of what his nature represented was beginning to emerge from the shadows. With the community from which the hooded figure hailed coveting anonymity, his burgeoning reputation would soon become a problem if it hadn't already. But I could neither count on his own taking him down nor could I afford to wait around for such a thing to happen.

I turned east onto Cameron Street, then headed toward the coffee shop. The walk through the streets had left me chilled, and a hot cup would do me good right about now. Keeping alert, I approached the shop, glancing around the area for any down-and-out people I might have missed earlier. I saw no one in the vicinity, but something else caught my attention.

A patrol car moved steadily along Cameron, and when the officer spotted me, he slowed the vehicle to a crawl.

I angled for the door to the coffee shop. I'd gone to the trouble of changing my looks so I wouldn't be noticed, but I wasn't sure if my disguise had been busted or if the officer was merely being curious. I soon got my answer. Before I reached the door to the shop, the patrol car pulled to the curb, and the officer leaned toward the passenger side as the window came down. "Excuse me," he said, "but I need to ask you a few questions. Would you please get in the car?"

My mind raced for answers. The officer's request was completely unorthodox. We weren't familiar enough to be friends, and I doubted the officer knew me, but I'd made it a point in my career to keep up with the personnel. It was Danny Craigthorpe. From what I knew of him, he was a good cop, though his current disregard of protocol didn't support that assumption. To make matters worse, Craigthorpe's eyes, much like those of James Goldstein, indicated an absence of awareness. "I don't think I want to do that, officer. I'm on my way to get a cup of coffee. Why don't you join me? It would be a more comfortable situation, don't you think?"

The officer continued to stare at me, his eyes unblinking, his focus unchanged. Seconds later, he unbuckled his seat belt and jerked open the door, then stepped out of the patrol car and circled around to the front of the vehicle. As he stepped onto the sidewalk, he pulled his service weapon. He didn't tell me to stop, and he didn't state that I was under arrest. He shoved the weapon into my side and said, "Start walking and don't stop until I tell you."

Everything about the encounter was wrong, but in it, I found a bit of hope. The fact that Craigthorpe wanted me to walk away, probably to a more deserted area, meant that he was hesitant to do anything now where he could be seen.

"What's this all about?" I asked. "Am I under arrest? If so, don't you think you should read me my rights?"

"Shut up and do what I tell you."

"What's your name, Officer?"

Instinctively, the man glanced down at his name tag. Halfway into the action, he caught himself, then snapped his attention back to me, but it was too late.

The small break-in time was all I needed. I stepped away, then swept my left arm down, moving the weapon away from my side.

The officer stumbled but quickly regained his balance. More importantly, he'd maintained his grip on the weapon. Steadying his aim with both hands, he leveled the barrel.

For a brief moment, I didn't know how to proceed. An officer of the law had me in his sights, and he meant to kill me.

Then instinct took over, and I slowed things down, but even in that dreamlike state, where I could react in a manner that seemed to come before the action, it could still go wrong.

Ignoring what the fall might do, I dove for the ground, tucking and rolling as my shoulder struck the sidewalk.

At some point, Craigthorpe fired his weapon, and the sound of the discharge blasted through my ears.

I came out of the roll and found my footing, but when I got to my feet, I stared into the blank eyes of Officer Craigthorpe.

An instant later, I slammed my elbow into his face, then grabbed the wrist of the hand that held the weapon. Continuing with the momentum, I twisted Craigthorpe off his feet, then slammed him to the sidewalk. While he was down, I wrenched the weapon from his hand and then turned and ran full force away from the scene.

A small crowd had gathered along the sidewalks, but no one made a move to stop me. On the contrary, they seemed to be cheering me on.

I ran along the same path from which I'd come beside the restaurant. Just before I cleared the edge of the building, I dropped the weapon into a storm drain near the sidewalk. It was deep. It was unlikely anyone would find it there. I straightened my clothes and hair and stepped onto the parking lot in as composed a manner as I could manage.

I thought about going straight to the Mercedes and driving away from the madness, but instead, I climbed the steps leading to the restaurant and went inside. I suspected that the person or entity who'd taken the mind of Craigthorpe might have needed to be in close proximity during the attack. I didn't want whoever it was to see me getting into the Mercedes, didn't want to give him anything additional to go on.

I ordered a cup of coffee, and when my order arrived, I leaned back in the chair, savoring the aromatic brew, but with the relaxation afforded by the action came also a sensation of someone trying to get inside my head, gain access to my thoughts.

Instinctively, I touched the crucifix beneath my shirt and began to pray for protection.

A well-dressed young man walked up and sat across from me. His eyes were distant, not his own, and I'd seen enough of this by now to not be caught off guard or to think that some stranger had decided to dine with me.

"Nice to sort of meet you," I said. "Who are you?"

The young man pulled a wallet from his pocket, then fumbled through it. "Says here I'm Jeffery Martin." He put the wallet away and smiled as he said, "but you can call me Ishmael."

The man's mannerisms reminded me of a comic book villain. The Joker or the Riddler, I couldn't decide which. "Is that your real name?"

He dropped his head and mimicked a pronounced frown. "Oh, come now. Don't spoil it for me. I've always wanted to say that. I get the chance, and what do you do? It's from Moby Dick. I know you've read it. I mean, who hasn't, right? The character doesn't say my name is Ishmael or I'm Ishmael, glad to meet you. It leaves room for doubt, part of the whole Melville magic sort of thing."

I had a feeling I was talking to the man who liked to hide his face, the hooded figure, though not in person but through someone else. I was surprised at his lighthearted approach. "All right, Ishmael. Let's get down to business then."

"Perhaps, but first things first, and fair is fair. I showed you my ID. You show me yours."

I stood and patted my empty pockets. "You're out of luck," I said. "I don't have anything on me."

"What kind of man walks around with no ID?"

Ishmael's tone of voice indicated that he'd actually taken offense over my lack of credentials, but even better, it seemed he truly was at a loss as to my identity. I recalled the invasive sensation I'd experienced and how I'd felt something similar at the funeral when the hooded figure had become aware of my presence. "Why don't you ask the John Doe who walked in front of the truck?" I asked. I paused, then added, "You can call me Barrington."

"Oh my. You are a clever one, aren't you?"

"Fair is fair," I said. "Now, for the business side of things. I could ask a lot of *whys*, but let's settle on a big one. Why did you kill the elderly gentleman beneath the Vandever Building?"

The young man did not answer but sat blank-faced and motionless. I was about to conclude that the foreign influence had tired of its whereabouts and had moved on, but then Ishmael spoke.

"Technically, I didn't kill anyone."

I set the coffee on the table. Ishmael's delayed response indicated that he'd given careful consideration to the question, which could mean a lot of things, though hopefully, remorse was a part of it. "Yes," I said, "but your minions, acting under your control, did. How many have there been? How many more will there be?"

The young man offered a sly smile, again the comic book villain. "Minions? I like that. Sort of like that cartoon, Despicable something or other."

"I don't know," I said. "The character in the movie wasn't actually despicable. He turned out to be a pretty good guy. But listen to me, going on like an old friend. For all I know, your story might have a similar ending."

Ishmael smiled. "Who's to say it hasn't? There could be people somewhere who think of me as a sort of benefactor."

"You might have been able to convince me of that had I not witnessed what you're capable of."

Ishmael curled the young man's lips into a grin. "You've no idea, Mr. Barrington. You're quite the curiosity though, annoying and interesting at the same time. Tell me, how do you accomplish it?"

I ran through a mental list of what Ishmael might be referring to but came up with nothing. "I'm not sure what you mean."

"You're a blank page, an empty computer screen, a white wall. Don't get me wrong. I've encountered difficulties before but nothing like this. How do you block me, keep me out?"

I slid my hand across my shirt, feeling the crucifix beneath it. "Let's just say I have some experience in dealing with spiritual possession."

I wanted to go further with the explanation, but something told me not to.

The young man went blank and motionless again, a state I'd begun to suspect occurred when Ishmael was involved in deep thought.

With a slightly discernable jolt, the young man blinked and again brought his lifeless eyes upon me. "You've got it all wrong, Barrington. I'm no evil spirit bent on corrupting innocent souls. My talent, if you will, would be more closely compared to mind control. A subject, it seems that you know very little about. If ignorance is your only defense, this should be easy."

"Don't be so sure," I said. "Understanding the motivations of those who fall into my crosshairs is something I'm pretty good at."

"You talk without really saying anything. Have you considered politics? You have all the qualifications."

I smiled. "I'm afraid I don't have the patience. Besides, I know who I am, and I stick with it, a trait that seems lacking in politicians. I also have a nasty habit of sticking to the subject, which I believe was *possession*. Let me ask you something. What happens to the host during your mind-manipulation exercises?"

The young man again went blank for a while, then said, "Nothing, really. The subjects are merely subdued for a short time."

I nodded. Ishmael had taken an inordinate amount of time to answer, which indicated I was on to something. I thought about James Goldstein, whom it had seemed just as Ishmael had said, the unfortunate host's consciousness floating somewhere beneath the surface. But it had not been that way with Yates. He and Dewey Crawford had become intermingled in some way. The idea opened some interesting questions concerning the John Doe, who had approached me in the church parking lot a couple of months ago.

"For the sake of argument," I said, "let's say you grew weary of my company and left the restaurant, but as you walked across the parking lot, a bullet ripped through your chest and caught your heart. Who would they take to the morgue, Ishmael? You or Jeffery Martin?"

The young man did not answer but had again become quiet.

I glanced around the dining area, hoping to catch a glimpse of someone who was looking back. "There's something going on between us, Ishmael, a connection that goes both ways. Not what you're used to, I'm thinking. I know you're here in the restaurant somewhere. My guess is you feel it as much as I do."

The young man exhibited nothing but lifeless silence.

"Would you like to know why?" I asked.

He looked up.

"We've met before. As a child, you looked into the eyes of a young cop and pleaded silently for help. I was that cop, Ishmael. I let you down then, but I'm here now. Maybe it's not too late."

The young man's eyes, had they not been empty, would have intently studied my face in an effort to determine my sincerity, and the power behind the blank face was doing just that, or so I had led myself to believe.

A sly smile turned the corners of his lips. "I'm afraid it is. You know what they say about power and corruption, a concept you should understand, being a police officer."

I took a sip of coffee. I'd been careless and had given too much information. "It was a long time ago. As you might imagine, a man like me gets a little claustrophobic in an overly structured environment. I've changed careers since then."

"I see. The elderly gentleman you referred to earlier who didn't fare so well last night. He, too, said his name was Barrington. He was lying. And so are you. I've enjoyed our little chat, but look at the time. I really must be going."

"Don't let me stop you."

"I wouldn't dream of it," he said. "We have unfinished business. I assure you it's nothing personal. I've actually grown fond of you. It's not often I run across someone with an intellect like yours to converse with. I truly wish we could maintain our friendship, but I simply cannot allow you to walk out of here. Such an oversight wouldn't be in my best interest."

I studied the young man sitting across from me. He would struggle to tip the scales at 150 pounds, and even that was not athletically proportioned. And prior struggles had shown me that being under Ishmael's influence did not afford the host any added physical abilities.

"I'm sorry to have to break it to you like this, Ishmael, but you really should have chosen your host more carefully. He doesn't stand a chance against me unless he's armed, and something tells me he isn't."

The young man grew quiet, motionless.

Once again, I visually scanned the dining area. "Of course you could always choose another mark. In fact, I'd love to watch the transfer take place. Then again, something like that might leave you vulnerable and perhaps even give me an opportunity to find you."

"Checkmate, Mr. Barrington. You're proving to be a worthy adversary. I'll make you a deal. If you will drop this thing and walk away from it, I will do the same. Things can simply go back to the way they were before."

I wasn't about to let this monster off the hook, but I wasn't going to let him know that. "How do I know I can trust you?"

"I guess you'll just have to trust me. It never used to be this way. Things just got a little out of control, that's all. I can dial it back."

"I'd like to believe that," I said, "but I'm having trouble with the human nature side of it, the power-and-corruption thing you mentioned earlier."

The young man leaned back and held out his hands, a gesture of frustration. "When diplomacy fails, what am I left with? I believe the mayor of our fine city has a little get-together scheduled."

I placed my empty coffee cup on the table. Had Ishmael changed directions so suddenly? Possibly an indication of an even more unstable mind than I'd previously thought. In trying to force Ishmael's hand, I might have gone too far. Some out-of-state investment company had built a retail complex over on Archer, and it was scheduled to be unveiled tonight. Mayor McClendon would be there. "What does that have to do with anything?"

"Oh, come now. Where's your civic pride, Mr. Barrington?"

As if he'd decided to take a nap, the young man leaned forward, placed his arms on the table, and laid his head down between them. Had Ishmael and the young man parted company? I suspected that was what had just happened. I now had firsthand experience with what Ishmael could do through other people, like Officer Craigthorpe. I wondered about David Yates. If Yates and I managed to cross paths again, could part of Ishmael still be there?

I pushed away from the table and walked through the dining area, going from table to table, though my efforts were wasted. I didn't see anyone wearing a hooded garment, and Ishmael could be anywhere without my knowing it. I was starting to draw attention. I went back to the table to leave some money for the coffee, but the young man was still there, now sitting upright.

"Are you all right?" I asked.

The young man shook his head. "Do I know you?"

"Not really."

A look of confusion crossed his face. "I'm not feeling well. And I don't know how I got here. Do you?"

I shook my head. My experience with Yates and the others suggested the young man's mind would be blank concerning the possession or whatever it was. "You just walked over and sat down."

"At your table?"

"That's pretty much it. Had you intended to come here, to the restaurant?"

"I don't know. I was supposed to meet a friend at the coffee house over on Cameron. Guess that didn't happen."

"Were you at the coffee house before this?"

"I don't think so. I remember pulling into the lot and getting out of my car. Nothing after that until now."

Jeffery Martin's recollection of events followed a twisted sort of logic. He could have been there right around the time I was having the scuffle with Officer Craigthorpe near the same coffee house. Ishmael had vacated Craigthorpe and taken control of Jeffery Martin so he could follow me unnoticed.

"It's been nice talking to you," I said, "but I need to be going. You'll be all right. Things like this are rare, but they do happen."

I turned and walked away.

Outside the restaurant, I wanted to jump into the Mercedes and put as much distance as I could between me and this part of town, but a man leaning against the east side of the building, closely examining something, caught my attention. It occurred to me that I no longer had the photograph Ezra Barrington had taken. I must have lost it during the scuffle with Craigthorpe.

I approached the man. "I'm sorry," I said, "but I believe that belongs to me."

The man waved off any protests and handed the photo over without incident. "Ain't nothing to it anyway. Nothing I can use, for sure."

"Thanks," I said. "You look like you know your way around the street. I'm looking for someone. The man in the photo, as a matter of fact. Do you know him?"

"I don't know much about anything, sir, but while I have your attention, could you see it in your heart to help out a guy in need?"

I hadn't brought my wallet, but I had some cash. I dug a twenty from my pocket and gave it to the man. "Are you sure you haven't seen this guy? I hear he hangs around these parts."

"No, sir, but thank you for your generosity."

Judging from the man's reaction and body language, I suspected he wasn't being completely truthful, but I wouldn't push it. I turned away, then walked across the parking lot, and climbed into the car.

18

I parked the Mercedes behind Casey's bar, then went in through the back door.

If the maneuver had surprised Casey, he didn't show it.

"Do you still have the phone?" I asked.

Casey finished wiping down the bar, then threw the towel over his shoulder and strolled over to an area near the register where he retrieved Barrington's phone I'd left with him. He slid it across the bar. "Can I get you anything?"

"A cup of coffee would be nice."

A few seconds later, Casey set a cup of black coffee in front of me. "It's good seeing you again, kid, but I have to wonder what brings you here. Are you in trouble?"

Casey knew I preferred cream and sugar, but he was always telling me coffee was better without it. I decided to go with it. "Not yet, but I'm working on it."

"If I remember right, you never had to try very hard to get the wrong kind of people interested in you."

"Don't blame me," I said. "It's in my DNA. Has anybody been trying to call me on this thing?"

Casey shook his head. "So, tell me. What kind of cop hides a cell phone in a bar, then comes around asking about it?"

Casey and I went way back. I used to be a regular, had even rented the room above the bar from him, but I'd changed my ways. "One that's in over his head, I guess. Sometimes I wonder if life was simpler when I was looking for answers in the bottom of a bottle."

"You don't mean that, kid. Forty years behind this bar hasn't left me with much, but it's given me a sense of character that most psychologists would pay dearly for. You got something inside you that's difficult to put a finger on. It draws people to you and scares the hell out of them at the same time. You were meant to be on this earth, Kenny, in a different way than most."

Casey pulled the towel from his shoulder and began wiping down the bar again. "Listen to me, prattling on like Dear Abby."

Casey wasn't the only one surprised by his behavior. The gruff old bartender had always been good to me, but he'd rarely put more than two words together at a time. I studied his eyes. They seemed okay, didn't lack focus or clarity. "Don't get too philosophical on me, Case. I'm not used to it."

I took the coffee and walked to one of the tables near the back of the room. "I have a few calls to make. Let me know if anyone comes in you don't recognize."

Casey rummaged around behind the bar, then shuffled over and laid a couple of phones on the table. "People leave them in here all the time. I keep them around in case they come back for them. I'm guessing yours is a burner. Anyway, if you use it too much, they can still nail you."

I had worried about that very thing. It was why I'd left my phone in the truck and the burner here at the bar. "Let me ask you something, Case. If you had reason to believe something bad was going to happen, but you didn't know exactly what, and you knew if you tried to explain it to anyone they wouldn't take you seriously, what would you do?"

It was still early in the day, and the bar was empty except for the two of us. Casey pulled out a chair and sat at the table. "I'll ask you again, what kind of trouble have you gotten yourself into? I'll try to help, but I got to know what I'm up against."

I thought about trying to explain but decided against it. "You're a good man, Casey, but I'm all right. I'm working a private case, that's all. First time I've done that, and it's got me a bit frazzled."

I grabbed one of the phones from the table and punched in Captain Dombrowski's number. When he answered, I said, "I have something I need to tell you. It's going to sound crazy, but I need you to listen."

"Elliot, when are you going to drop this nonsense and come on back to work?"

I leaned back in the chair and stared across the room. A part of me wished things could go back the way they were, like with my early days at the department, but another part of me knew that was never going to happen. "I need a few more days."

"Yeah, well, guess what, I need a few things too."

From the sound of the captain's voice, he, too, knew that things had changed. "What do you want?" I asked.

"The whereabouts of David Yates would do for a start."

Casey got up and strolled back to his position behind the bar.

"I'm afraid I can't help you with that one," I said.

"Why not? Don't you keep tabs on your clients?"

The answer to that was painfully obvious, but I wasn't going to play into Dombrowski's hands. I had to focus, remember my reason for contacting the captain in the first place. I recalled Ishmael's enigmatic behavior and portentous language, which strengthened the urgency I'd felt earlier. "I've come across some information," I said, "that could prove to be important in preventing a crime. I thought you should know about it."

"What are you getting at?" Dombrowski asked.

"There's a dedication ceremony," I said, "scheduled this evening for the new Greenwood complex. It's not going to go well. Something bad is going to happen. I wanted to give you a heads-up. Maybe you could beef up security, put a few more plainclothes officers into place."

"Maybe I could, but not without good reason."

"A disruption of some kind has been planned," I said. "If the proceedings are halted or delayed, maybe that would be enough to avoid any problems."

"Your propensity to engage specifics is amazing. What kind of disruption are we talking about?"

I gripped the phone and tried to think of something to say that wouldn't sound completely ridiculous, but nothing came to mind. "I don't know exactly, just that the potential, perhaps even the intent, already exists."

"Do you have any idea how that sounds? I'm sure everything will be fine, but if it'll make you feel better, I'll check into it. If you had some concrete details, it would make things easier."

The tone of Dombrowski's voice suggested he wasn't taking me seriously. After all, I had just yesterday reported a murder scene, and they found nothing. He wasn't going to do anything about it. I paused, wondering if I should engage the subject that was known between us but seldom talked about. Dombrowski had known me a long time.

"You know I wouldn't ask you to do something like this if I didn't believe it was important."

"I don't know, Elliot. You haven't exactly been Mr. Reliable lately. Why can't you tell us where Yates is? Maybe there's something you're not telling us. Maybe Yates is the one you're worrying about. If that's the case, why are you protecting him?"

The thought had crossed my mind that Yates could indeed be drawn back into this if that's how Ishmael wanted it to go down. "I don't know where he is," I said. "I don't like it, but that's the way it is."

"Well, that's comforting. If I ever need a PI, remind me not to call you."

"If you can't put a stop to the dedication ceremony," I said, "then put a few officers out there. That's all I'm asking."

"Yeah, well, the last time I checked, I was captain of the homicide department, but maybe I'll see what I can do."

I glanced around the room. A few people had come into the bar. I wasn't getting anywhere with this, and I'd already been on the phone too long. "Just do what you can, Bill."

I disconnected, then grabbed one of the phones I hadn't used and ducked out the back door. My chances of being able to recognize any possible threats at the dedication ceremony in time to stop the action were slim, but I had to do something.

It was possible that Dombrowski would try to get something done, but unlikely. It wasn't that he didn't care. He just didn't have any real evidence to go on.

19

Later that evening, I strolled around the area where the dedication ceremony was being held and checked the rooftops and other possible hiding places, looking for anything suspicious or anyone behaving strangely.

The city had made quite a production of the event. Food vendors operated along the side of the street, a band played music, and people were filling the area. Even the temperature hovering around the freezing mark wasn't keeping people at home.

I angled off to the east end of the crowd where I could see both the front and back of the stage. The vantage point left the west end relatively unguarded, but the position felt right.

I'd gone back to the condo after leaving Casey's for a bite to eat, some rest, and a chance to think things over. After that, I'd stopped at a sporting goods store and picked up a hoodie of my own, a superinsulated number with monotone coloring that would not only keep me warm but would help protect my identity as well.

Given Ishmael's prowess with mind control, or whatever it was, I worried over who or what I should look for and decided I would monitor the crowd and scrutinize anyone who approached the stage.

I thought of Ishmael's warning and the emotionless, matter-of-fact way it had fallen across the lips of the unsuspecting Jeffery Martin.

Had I been right about proximity being a factor in Ishmael's power, or had Ishmael been near certain locations for other reasons and distance was not an issue? There was also the matter of his drones or minions to consider. Had Ishmael actually controlled that many minds at once, or had it only appeared that way? For all I knew, Ishmael had some sort of unground cult following right under the city's noses, and his drones were acting as trained.

The unanswered questions unnerved me, but it was the nature of the suspect that had me on edge. Ishmael's anonymous approach to crime was as frightening a concept as I'd ever encountered. With his power and intellect, if he kept his wits about him and his ego in check, he had the potential to become practically unstoppable.

A gust of wind brought the aroma from the food vendors to my attention, and the thought of an article I'd recently read blossomed in my mind. At a state fair in Arkansas, a knife-wielding man had run through the innocent crowd, randomly slashing unsuspecting victims.

I studied the gathering of people in front of me.

A mother with two children in a stroller and another attached to her wrist by what looked like a leash glanced at me and smiled. Near the front of the crowd, a large man wore a coat but had left his lower extremities relatively unprotected, wearing gym shorts and flip-flops with no socks.

Like most of the spectators who had gathered for the ceremony, the individuals I had singled out seemed to enjoy the music and festivities. I doubted that they had any indication that the outcome of their evening might hang in the balance of anything but the ordinary.

The thought that ordinary meant different things to different people rifled through my mind, and with each beat from the band, the fear inside me grew, sponsored by the knowledge that something was going to go wrong.

I unzipped the hoodie, then slid my hand inside to check the readiness of the .38, only to find that it was not there. Of course, I'd known that, but force of habit had drawn me through the ritual anyway.

The band finished a song, then took a break and left the stage. A short time later, a man and two women dressed in formal attire appeared, and after a couple of announcements, the man introduced Mayor McClendon, who quickly ascended the steps and climbed onto the stage amid a smattering of applause from the crowd.

The mayor had taken office during bad economic times, and his cost-cutting measures had earned him a few enemies. Only one of the local news channels was there covering the event. Typical politics, but this was anything but a typical evening.

A sensation much like that of becoming aware of a dream came over me, but unlike the lucidity of that imagined world which quickly fades upon recognition, the familiar state I was entering heightened my senses to an unnerving level.

I walked parallel to the crowd, following the trajectory to the outer extremities, then turned and strolled back to the front. It was then that I thought I saw the young man I'd talked with at the restaurant standing in the crowd.

I forced my way through the crowd, half expecting to find someone who only resembled the young man, but as I approached, I saw that it was, indeed, Jeffery Martin.

The confused look that came across Jeffery Martin's face indicated that he recognized me as well. I wondered if he might take off running.

"Who the hell are you?" he asked. "And what are you doing here?"

I gestured for him to follow, then weaved my way through the throng of people, making my way back to the vantage point I'd chosen earlier.

When Jeffery Martin caught up to me, I said, "We met earlier at the restaurant."

"Yeah," he said, "I figured that much. But why are you following me?"

"I'm not. We just keep showing up at the same places. I'm just as surprised to see you here. Are you a fan of Mayor McClendon?"

"Not really. I have nothing against the man. I'm just not into politics. I hate crowds, too, and being cold. This seems like the last place I'd want to be, and yet here I am." He wrapped his arms across his chest, shivering, the desperate look on his face deepening. "After we talked, I drove home to get warm, put on some dry clothes, and relax, but it didn't happen that way."

"How did it happen?"

He shrugged. "I made it as far as my apartment. I had the key ready for the door, but instead of going inside, I went to my car and drove back downtown. I ended up here. But there's no missing moments. I remember it all. It's kind of like when you have to go to the dentist. You don't want to, but you do it anyway."

I turned Jeffery Martin's words over in my mind and considered the implications of what he had told me. Was it possible that Ishmael's influence, once experienced, lingered in some way, leaving him the ability to exercise various levels of control, even encourage people to consciously act in ways contrary to their own desires?

"You should have listened to your instincts and stayed home," I said. "just get in your car and go. Forget any of this ever happened."

"What's happening to me?" he asked. "Is any of this real, or am I still lost in some kind of mental fugue?"

I glanced at the stage. From the sound of things, the mayor was nearing the end of his speech, and there had been no sign of trouble. Perhaps nothing more than my meeting Jeffery Martin had been planned. Ishmael wanted to show me that he could cause people to be at certain places at certain times. That alone would be cause for sufficient concern.

"I'm not sure," I said. "And if I tried to explain, it would only further confuse matters. You don't trust me as it is."

"Who could blame me? I don't even know who you are, much less how and why we keep bumping into each other."

"The name's Barrington," I said, assuming my newly acquired alias, "and something bad is about to happen. It'd be better if you were not involved."

"How could I be involved with anything? I'm just standing here like you are."

As I struggled for an answer, the mayor stopped talking and tapped the microphone several times. His actions settled over the crowd like a wave of quietness, and within seconds the area was encased in an eerie silence.

"I've just been informed," the mayor said, "that we have a special guest in the audience."

The mayor's words came across as informal, unscripted as if he were chatting with a friend in his living room.

"I'd like to introduce my good friend, Ezra Barrington if he would be so kind as to join me on stage."

"Barrington?" Jeffery Martin repeated, "would that be you?"

I did not turn away but kept my attention on the mayor. "Yes, it would be."

"Then why aren't you accepting the mayor's offer?"

"Because I want to stay alive," I said. "And you'd do well to heed my warning and get the hell out of here."

I received no reply, and when I chanced a quick glance around, I saw that Jeffery Martin was gone.

I stepped closer to the stage, hoping my actions would not be noticed as I gained a more strategic position. If Jeffery Martin came out of the crowd and rushed the stage, I would have to try to intercept him before he reached the mayor.

The silence that had overcome the festivities had not been completely eradicated though the void had been somewhat softened by a hum of whispered exchanges.

The man who had introduced the mayor broke ranks and tiptoed across the stage. "Mayor McClendon?"

In the quiet, the aide's words echoed through the area.

He tried again, this time louder.

Like a broken mannequin, the mayor remained silent, motionless.

A sick feeling edged through me. Just how far had this gone? I pulled the hood farther over my face. Ishmael had extended his reach to the mayor. I had to assume Mayor McClendon had become unpredictable, even dangerous.

Walking with doubt as to what I might accomplish, I shuffled into the crowd where the people huddled into small groups and talked quietly among themselves. It took me less than a minute to reach the front of the crowd, where I took a position in the third row.

Several more people walked across the platform and gathered around the mayor, probably attempting to bring him out of his apparent mental lapse.

I dug one of the cell phones from my pocket, then snapped a few photos. Having some kind of record could prove helpful.

Then, as if prompted by something only he understood, the mayor waved the well-intended aides aside. "Look at this," he said. "I'm surrounded by my friends."

Whispers and murmurs again buzzed through the crowd.

I slid the phone back into my pocket.

The person beside me unwrapped a stick of gum and crammed it into his mouth.

The thought that I might be identified registered though it carried little weight with respect to the events I visualized unfolding. If Ishmael's subjects gave in to forces they didn't realize, they could also act against their will and advance toward a goal understood only by the one initiating the action.

I maneuvered to the second row from the front of the confused audience. Security had to be in place, but I saw nothing between me and the stage.

I nudged my way to the front of the crowd, subtly assessing those who vocalized irritation at my actions.

A movement among the shadows drew my attention, and I turned as Jeffery Martin came out of the darkness and strode toward the stage.

I worked my way toward the area, moving with a sense of urgency.

A man stepped in front of me. Another grabbed my arm.

I didn't want to cause a scene, but I saw no other option. I twisted free of the man's grip and swung around to face him.

The man held his hands up. "Take it easy, man. I didn't mean nothing. Thought you was someone else, that's all."

The disturbance was not without result. People began to step away from me, creating an envelope, a bubble that followed my movement through the crowd.

Jeffery Martin ascended the steps and took the stage.

I stepped free of the crowd and started toward the stairs.

Martin was halfway to the mayor when a police officer emerged from the gathering of supporters, strode across the platform, and intercepted him.

The officer's actions did not resemble so much an attempt to thwart the confrontation as they did a pooling of efforts to enhance it. It was Danny Craigthorpe, the police officer I'd tangled with earlier, and the empty holster strapped to his side indicated that he was still not in his right mind.

I slowed my progress, then changed direction, angling off to the shadows near the east end of the stage. It wasn't a suspicion that something about the gathering of the trio wasn't right that caused me to hold back. Nothing about the evening had been right. It was gut instinct.

When Martin and Craigthorpe stepped onto the stage, the mayor put his arms around them and drew them close. For a moment, they stumbled about the stage like three old drinking buddies, playing to the crowd.

The television crew was eating it up, ecstatic, no doubt, over getting an exclusive of interesting events that would not soon be forgotten.

At some point, the mayor let go of his buddies and again tapped the microphone. The crowd went silent.

"I love this city," the mayor said. "You people don't know how special you are, what eye-opening events loom in your future."

Mayor McClendon maneuvered Officer Craigthorpe front and center with the empty holster exposed, then put his hands on his hips and shook his head. "Now that's a total disgrace. What kind of police officer walks around without a gun?"

McClendon reached over and pretended to draw the weapon that wasn't there, then extended the bizarre pantomime, holding the invisible weapon with both hands in front of him while he edged around the stage like a police officer caught in a dangerous situation. The mayor worked his way back to Craigthorpe, then brought the invisible firearm to the head of the officer. "Boom," he said. "You're dead."

As if he'd actually taken a bullet, Craigthorpe jerked, then collapsed onto the stage floor.

I stood silent and motionless, as mesmerized into inactivity as the rest of the audience.

McClendon marveled in his accomplishment for a moment, then edged toward Jeffery Martin and repeated the process. Martin also collapsed onto the stage.

McClendon took a bow, and when he once again stood upright, he put the pretend weapon to his temple. "This one's for you, Mr. Barrington. But there is still time to save this good man. Join me on stage, and I'll let him go."

I remained in the shadows, convinced that Ishmael hadn't a clue as to whether or not I was there. Unlike most others, I was mentally, perhaps even spiritually, invisible to him. I suspected Barrington had been as well.

"Very well," McClendon said. "Have it your way."

He made a clicking sound as if cocking the gun. "Now, guilty by inaction, whatever blood ends up on my hands will stain yours as well. A moment of silence, please."

He took a deep breath, then said, "Bang, bang."

Like the others, Mayor McClendon wilted and collapsed onto the stage.

Immobilized by our own incredulity, I and the crowd and even the food vendors stood silently along the darkened streets like survivors of a bomb blast, trying to take in that which we could not begin to comprehend. A near-debilitating sense of concern crawled through me as I considered what I'd just witnessed. Had Ishmael actually somehow killed the mayor and his unusual entourage? If so, would he kill anyone else on the stage or in the crowd?

At the apex of the confusion, the players on the stage, Mayor McClendon, Officer Craigthorpe, and Jeffery Martin rose to their feet, waved to the crowd, and took a bow.

The mayor's staff cautiously stepped forward and began to clap, as if it had all been planned. It had, but not by them. A smattering of applause filtered through the crowd, but mostly the crowd expressed confusion.

The realization that Ishmael was finished with his antics for the night snaked through my thoughts, and as I turned and walked into the darkness, I wondered how far Ishmael would take this—indeed, how far *could* he take it?

20

I lowered myself into the chair in Barrington's living room, took a sip of coffee, grabbed the remote, and began flipping through the news channels, and on the first channel that I heard the news anchor mention something about Mayor McClendon, I paused.

The mayor had put on quite a show, and the media was buzzing about it.

The scene shifted to a press conference where the mayor, conducting himself in what appeared to be a confused state, launched into a diatribe concerning Barbara Maxey, his current chief of staff. McClendon made it clear that this was no hasty decision. Trouble had been brewing. Ms. Maxey had crossed the line too many times.

"I'm left with no alternative," the mayor said, "but to call for Ms. Maxey's resignation."

I tried to understand what I was hearing. Based on what I'd previously come to understand through the news, Barbara Maxey had been a longtime associate of McClendon. The mayor had handpicked her, and he'd fought hard for her appointment, and now it seemed he was on the verge of firing her.

I set the coffee on the table. McClendon wasn't himself. That much had become clear last night. I suspected what I was seeing was some sort of insane collaboration between McClendon and Ishmael.

I tried the other channels. They were all carrying the same story about the bizarre happenings last night and the firing of Barbara Maxey.

I laid the remote aside and picked up my coffee. Earlier I'd chanced a call to Carmen, letting her know everything was all right and that I was still working the undercover case but should have it wrapped up soon. Trouble was I hadn't convinced myself of that. I'd never thought of myself as being the type who thrived on control, though I could recall times when the lack of it caused concern, the kind that seeps in and settles deep inside. This was one of those times.

I considered calling Dombrowski. Bad things happened in the city on a regular basis, though only a select number of events made enough ripples, or the right kind of ripples, to make it far enough to gain the attention of the public. The people who'd been at the unusual dedication ceremony would remember it forever, and as long as the media ran with it, so would everyone else. I decided against calling Dombrowski. I didn't want to chance giving away my location.

I was about to shut off the television when I heard something that stopped me.

"During an apparent home invasion that occurred around two o'clock this morning, Sterling Hornell, a major in the Salvation Army, sustained several gunshot wounds. Mr. Hornell later succumbed to the injuries and passed away around 4:00 a.m. Mr. Hornell had directed the shelter for the homeless on North Denver."

I lowered the volume and leaned back into the chair, accessing that part of me that no one understood. Someone else might have considered walking away from this, convincing themselves that it was none of their business. I was not that person.

Ishmael had punished those he thought to be directly involved in turning his parents away from the shelter out of revenge, and he'd reached out and caused the death of Major Sterling Hornell for the same reason. But he'd now gone beyond that with people like Jeffery Martin, Officer Craigthorpe, and Mayor McClendon. I suspected he would continue to commit such atrocities until I stopped him.

With Barrington out of the way, I was the only one, with the possible exception of Dewey Crawford, who knew of Ishmael's existence. That is if Dewey was still around. I would have to check on him. So far, I'd managed to slip out of Ishmael's grasp, but he would keep trying. Sooner or later, he would lure me into a situation I couldn't walk away from. And I didn't want to think about what might happen if he managed to crack through my defenses and reach inside my mind.

There was no getting around it. Ishmael had to be stopped. And it was all on me, my responsibility to stop someone whose handiwork was known but not talked about and whose identity rested uneasily among a scattered society, a segment of the homeless population that, for all practical purposes, did not exist.

I turned off the television. Before this had all started, I'd purposely softened my edge, my getting-to-the-truth-at-all-cost attitude, but it was time to reclaim it.

The homeless had their own code of ethics, a loosely defined honor system which did not silence them completely though it could cause them to become evasive when questioned a little too intently about the subject. Factor in having someone like Ishmael hailing from your ranks and the reluctance became understandable.

I got dressed and called a cab.

Half an hour after leaving the condo, I paid the driver, then ducked into a pawn shop on Second, just down the street from Arnie's, the bar where David Yates had arrested Dewey Crawford.

It seemed a small world at times.

The shop occupied an old building that'd seen a lot of years, and some of the items strewn around the place looked as if they had as well. I knew the guy who ran the shop, a Native American whom everyone called Wolf. Could have been his real name. I'd never asked. He and Casey used to run the bar together. Somewhere along the line, they'd gone their separate ways, but they were still friends.

Wolf came out of the back, strolled over to the counter, and handed me what I'd come for. Casey hadn't liked the idea. It'd taken a lot of talking to convince him to make the call. I unfolded the oilcloth and visually examined the weapon. Nothing fancy. Just a .38 caliber Smith & Wesson. "This thing work?" I asked.

Wolf shrugged. "Man said it did."

I peeled two bills from the wad in my pocket, then slid them across the counter.

"If something goes wrong," Wolf said, "I'll tell them someone broke in and took some stuff. I'm not sure what all they got away with. I'm not much on inventory."

I checked the weapon for ammo, took out one of the rounds, then let the hammer rest on an empty cylinder. I pulled my overcoat aside, then slid the weapon into the shoulder holster. It fit well enough. Considering all the events, I didn't want any sort of paper trail for the police to follow, not even a gun purchase request. "I'd thought you might give me something off the record."

Wolf's demeanor showed he was nervous. "It was kind of short notice. Casey assured me you'd be okay with it."

"Don't worry. I don't plan on using it. It just gives me confidence, that's all."

I turned and walked out of the pawnshop. An hour or so later I spotted my target, the homeless man I'd encountered a few days ago near the shelter, leaning against the south side of an old building a few blocks from the shelter on North Denver. There were others milling around the area as well.

I strolled over and stood in front of the man, following that tough-guy part of me, which I tapped into when necessary. Police officers had their ways, and I was no different in that respect. Life on the streets fostered a certain brand of toughness that could only be overcome with a higher degree of the same.

"Good to see you again," I said. "Couple of days ago, you were full of information. I guess you could say I've come back for more."

The man glanced to his left then to his right. "I don't have any more to say. You'll have to talk with someone else."

The man's nervousness did not go unnoticed. The people around us, those organic to the neighborhood who were not few in number, began to move in an effort to close ranks. One of them, a big man who looked angry, bothered me in particular as he peered around the edge of the building.

I held his hesitant gaze briefly, then turned back. Under ordinary circumstances, the street people might have paid little attention, might have gone so far as to walk away. But these were not ordinary circumstances. Behaving much like a pack of disturbed coyotes, the homeless man's extended family began to move closer, closing ranks.

I lowered my hand and swept the right side of my overcoat behind me, exposing the weapon.

Again the man I'd encountered earlier at the shelter glanced from side to side.

"I don't want any trouble," I said. "In fact, this thing that has everybody spooked is why I'm here, exactly what I'm trying to stop."

The man I was trying to question nodded vigorously. He'd gotten the message, but whether or not his understanding was shared by the others was up for debate.

The big man, who had been hugging the corner of the building, rushed toward me, and though I could not see them, I suspected others would be approaching from behind.

I turned toward the attacker, then in a move that must have surprised him, I did not dodge his right hook and prepare to throw my own. Instead, I turned into him, put my shoulder into his, then pulled his right arm in the direction it was already going.

The move worked well. I slammed the man to the pavement right in front of three others who'd come from behind.

I didn't waste the brief amount of time I'd earned. I slid my hand beneath my coat, pulled the .38, and pointed it forward, the sight perfectly aligned with the forehead of the man in the middle of the trio.

"Name's Elliot," I said. "I don't mean anybody any harm, but I don't intend to take any either."

Most of the people in the area, including the four I'd just confronted, began to move away.

The ploy had come off better than I'd anticipated, but the outcome hadn't been a complete surprise. I'd worked the streets for a few years, earning a reputation of sorts along the way. I didn't know exactly what people on the street thought about me, but I imagined it was something with reference to a Jekyll-and-Hyde personality. However, the minor success had not come without cost. I'd blurted out my name. That information, with all the potential problems it carried, could make its way into the hands of Ishmael. I didn't think any of these people were his drones, but they were part of the homeless community.

I turned back to the man I'd come to question, but he'd scurried away while the four aggressors held my attention and was now walking slowly along the neglected sidewalk area about twenty yards away.

It didn't take me long to catch him. "I meant what I told you about putting a stop to this," I said. "I know you're afraid. I don't blame you. But I think your understanding of what's going on exceeds common knowledge. I need your help."

"You got it all wrong. I'm nothing special, nothing at all. I just want to be left alone."

"People are being hurt," I said, "made to do things against their will. Turning inside yourself and ignoring it won't make it go away. It's going to get worse. But I suspect you know that as well as I do."

He shook his head, and when he spoke, the words came out just above a whisper. "I'm just a halfwit, a goofy old man who mumbles nonsense about stuff he should leave alone."

It dawned on me what the old man was trying to say. He was one of them, part of the underground clan. "All the more reason you should help me," I said. "If you think all this is going to continue to go unnoticed, you're wrong. It's only a matter of time until something happens that won't get past the attention of the police. Once the cops start digging, they won't stop until they uncover something. That won't be good for you or your people."

"What do you mean *my* people?"

"Don't play dumb. I saw the funeral in the woods. I was there."

A troubled expression rippled across the man's face. "You need to get all that out of your head before there's nothing else left in there. Those who get caught up in it never make it back out."

The man did understand. I'd suspected as much, and his confirmation sealed it. "But not everybody is affected. Why is that?"

Once again, the old man pulled the crucifix he wore from beneath his shirt and held it between his thumb and forefinger. "Trust in the Lord. But remember the Good Book says it isn't wise to put Him to the test."

I wondered if it could be that simple. Barrington had been a man of faith. Then again, so had James Goldstein and David Yates.

I'd spoken of David Yates in the past tense, and I hoped the disturbing thought held no basis. "The Good Book also teaches that the Lord does, on occasion, call us to task," I said. "I believe He's called me to find this man and stop him."

The old man studied my face but said nothing.

"Where can I find him?" I asked. "Where can I find Ishmael?"

The man clamped his hands over his ears and shook his head. "I can't give you what you're asking, though I know you are right in that things are happening that will cause nothing but worsening grief. You said you saw the funeral. Word is her husband took it real hard, goes to the funeral site every night to grieve. I suspect you'll find him there."

I slid some cash into the man's pocket, then gave him a pat on the shoulder. He'd told me all he was going to, and I wouldn't get anything more from him. "Thanks," I said. "I won't bother you again."

I turned and walked away, but I would not go back to the condo and wait patiently for the evening hours so I could go to the funeral site of Ishmael's mother and hope that her husband showed up. Not that I wouldn't end up doing that. Chances were pretty high that I would. I simply wasn't the type to wait around while opportunities, if indeed there were any, passed me by.

Instead, I went to the homeless shelter, hoping to observe the entrance without being too obvious. The sounds of traffic bustling along North

Denver offered soothing background noise, a reminder of the ordinary, but the area didn't lend itself to the kind of surveillance I hand in mind, especially with my being on foot. It was wide open with sidewalks, street traffic, and parking lots. I would need to take a more direct approach.

I relaxed as best I could under the circumstances and let my feelings go, like a fisherman who might stand at the nose of a slowly moving boat and cast his net across changing waters to see what he might find.

I immediately recognized the comparative weakness of my analogy and surmised that a web of sorts might be closer to the truth. Although I didn't particularly care for spiders, I was in such moments a bit like one, reacting only to a proper disturbance in the mental network I'd spun. To the more pragmatic, my efforts might seem ridiculous if not desperate. There were times—most times, in fact—when I would want to agree with such an assessment. These were not those times, and since I had so readily given in to that part of me which I had wished, even prayed, would go away, I guessed I was somewhat desperate.

It wasn't long until a validation of my indulgence came. Someone, beyond desperate in his own sense, came out of the shelter, his face as blank and expressionless as that of a mannequin.

It had been a longshot that I had not expected to pay off, and yet by some twist of fate, I now followed a man who was not operating under his own senses. His dual makeup is what I had detected. I hoped he would lead me to the source, to Ishmael.

I followed the man, trying to remain undetected.

The man stumbled occasionally, which was not unusual for the area, and the behavior allowed him to move about the streets unnoticed for the most part.

Trying not to draw more attention than my target, I held back, keeping what I thought to be a safe distance.

We passed yet another building, an old abandoned warehouse on Cameron Street not far from the coffee shop where Craigthorpe and I had tangled, then rounded the corner onto Detroit Avenue. Near a chain-link fence that separated the warehouse from a grassy area and a few trees, a small man stood, waiting. The drone stumbled over and handed the bag he'd carried from the shelter to the man, an elderly gentleman, short in stature, dressed in western clothing. It was Ishmael's father. My luck, dubious to this point of the investigation, had taken a turn.

I crossed the street, then slid over the fence and crept behind the odd little man where I stood quietly, watching him inventory the supplies the drone had given him.

Seconds later, the man stopped what he was doing, then turned to face me. His eyes darted back and forth, searching my face. Scraggly gray sideburns came from beneath his cowboy hat. A worried look etched his face. He reminded me of a character that might inhabit the pages of a Tolkien novel, one that had been penned but never published and shoved for unknown reasons into a box where there were others like it.

Finally, the man shook his head and asked, "Do I know you?"

I dipped my head toward the drone, who stood silently to the right of the odd little man.

He seemed to understand what I wanted, and to the drone, he said, "You can go now. Thank you for your service."

Like an obedient pet, the drone turned and walked away.

"The name's Barrington," I said. "I doubt that you know me, though I've had some interesting conversations with your son, Ishmael."

A perplexed expression crossed the man's face. "Not many people can make such a claim."

"I suspect not," I said. "Most of your son's acquaintances are a lot like your stumbling friend. Maybe it's just me, but I don't think such quasi zombies would make for good company."

Ishmael's father studied my face for a moment, then said, "Did Ishmael send you here to find me?"

"Not exactly, but my search to find him has led me to you."

"What do you want from me?"

I paused, looking for the right words, only to settle for the direct approach. "I need to know where Ishmael is. I need to find him."

"If you knew Ishmael well enough to be on speaking terms, then you would know his whereabouts as well."

"That's part of the problem," I said. "We haven't exactly talked face-to-face. The communication has been through others, sort of like your mindless butler."

"I see. And what exactly has been the nature of these communications between you and Ishmael?"

"He wants to kill me," I said, "or silence me in some way."

Once again, the man's expression showed fear. "Then you should get out of town, take a long, extended vacation."

"I can't do that."

"Listen, mister. I don't know why you're here or why I'm bothering to talk to you, but let me give you some solid advice. If Ishmael wants you dead, chances are pretty good you'll end up that way."

"That's exactly why I'm here," I said. "Your son has become a liability, not only to my world, my society but to yours as well. Something tells me you already know that. I need your help."

The imp-like man's jaw tightened. "Years ago, my wife and I kept to ourselves, stuck to the wooded areas outside town. It was there that a group of unusual people came upon us. They were crazy, out of their minds somehow. They knocked me senseless, had their way with my wife. I'm not a religious man, Mr. Barrington, and I don't know what all they did, but whatever happened resulted in a new life about nine months later, one that was marked with darkness. I knew it the first time I laid eyes on him. My wife knew it too, but the pain in her eyes told me she meant to raise him and that I had better go along with it."

I looked away, staring at the dormant grass, the leafless trees, struck speechless by the idea of Cowboy's opening up, and the incredible sadness relayed by his words. "Something's happened to your son," I said. "I'm a cop who works the streets, knows the people. Ishmael has turned into something far worse than he was before. He's a threat to both of us."

The little man shook his head. "His mother never lost her little boy, not in her mind, anyway, and in his own demented way, Ishmael tried to reciprocate that love. Before she left us, I promised my Princess that I would carry on, that I would be a father to our son."

Cowboy's dedication to his wife spoke of his character. Sadly, it was grossly misplaced "His mother's death acted to intensify that, which was already wrong," I said, "like gasoline tossed onto the flames."

"No, his mother's love kept the fire low," he said. "Her devotion made the darkness manageable. When we laid her to rest, everything changed."

The man, who was called Cowboy by those who knew him, conducted himself in a manner that seemed to reflect education and self-discipline, and yet, knowing but a small part of his situation, I found it difficult to accept what I was seeing and hearing. The idea that someone who possessed the ability to do otherwise might allow themselves to roam the streets with no real place to call home worked to cloud my judgment.

"Do you have any idea what your son might do if he's allowed to continue his current path?"

"More than you know," he said. "But I've lived with the reality of being a father to Ishmael. His mother expected no less from me than to sacrifice what I have to fulfill that role. My love and respect for her, along with what might well be disillusioned feelings for the boy gained from playing the part, cause me to follow a path of honor that you could not begin to understand."

"I understand more than you think," I said. "But this time turning your back and looking the other way isn't the right thing to do. The people of this city deserve better than that, whether or not you consider yourself a part of it."

"I cannot help you, Mr. Barrington. He is my son. May God have mercy on my twisted soul."

I could have continued the questioning, ramping up the mental and physical pressure that had earned me the reputation of a tough cop, but I knew it would do no good.

"If that's the way it has to be," I said. "I didn't ask for this burden, but since it has been thrust upon me, I have no other recourse than to see it through to the end."

The living room of Barrington's condo was gloomy, with thin beams of daylight seeping through the cracks of the window curtains I'd drawn together.

After watching Cowboy disappear into the wooded area behind the old warehouse, I'd walked a few blocks, then hailed a cab back to the condo. The possibility that Cowboy would not cooperate and hand over any information which might lead to the capture of his son had hovered around the edges of my mind all along. On some level, I understood Cowboy's dilemma. If Wayne, my son, were to be in some kind of compromising situation, what would I do? The question mattered, but I could not allow myself to go down endless paths of what-ifs.

There hadn't been many times during my career as a police officer that I'd felt utterly defeated, but I felt so now. I'd exhausted my energy to keep focused and continue the investigation and to make things worse, my own words ran through my mind, asking the question: What if I failed?

Also snaking through my thoughts was the knowledge that another bad thing had already happened. I didn't know why I was susceptible to such feelings. I often wished it wasn't that way.

If for no other reason than to assure myself that I wasn't losing it, I switched on the television.

The screen came to life and verified my fears.

A young man had climbed to the top of the Philtower Building, and after stepping onto a balcony railing, he'd jumped to his death. It had been Jeffery Martin. Sure, it was a common name and could have been someone else, but the pictures confirmed it. The young man that I'd encountered at the restaurant and again at the dedication ceremony where he'd climbed onto the stage with Mayor McClendon had killed himself.

Ishmael had caused it.

I spent a few minutes remembering Jeffery Martin, wondering about his religious affiliation. If indeed there had been such a thing in his life. I prayed that there had been. He'd seemed like a good kid.

Pushing past the frustration and anger that threatened to stifle my reasoning, I retrieved from its hiding place behind the painting over the fireplace the file Barrington had kept on Ishmael. My senses seemed to be reaching out, pushing the boundaries in some strange and different way, and I wanted to again examine the contents and photographs of the file, hoping to discover something I'd missed before, a clue, no matter how small, that might shed some light on the possible whereabouts of the sociopath working our city.

The image of the hooded figure standing in the shadows at the scene where David Yates had been attacked by the John Doe not only drew my attention but took me back to a certain time in my childhood.

Acting on a dare posed by my friend, Nick Brazelton, I'd come face-to-face with the reality of what I'd previously considered to be nothing more than sharp intuition. We'd found a small window-like opening in the wall of a sandstone structure, which had looked like the top part of a storm shelter with rock walls on both ends covered by an arched concrete roof that met the ground on both sides. I hadn't thought it to be a storm shelter because there was no proper entrance, the only opening being the odd window, which was too small for an adult.

My flashlight showed several rods running horizontally just below the roofline, and I wondered if the structure could have been a smokehouse used to cure meat but quickly dismissed the idea. With only the small opening, it would have been difficult and impractical to get the meat in and out, much less build a fire.

Realizing that I meant to go through with the dare, Nick tried to back it down, talk me out of it, but I didn't listen.

As soon as my feet touched the spongy floor inside the structure, it occurred to me I'd done something completely irresponsible. Anything could have been in there including a floor full of snakes.

What I encountered was nothing like that, but it was every bit as unnerving. An overflowing of feelings, emotions that were somehow a part of that place, had deluged my mind and given me the distinct impression that hands were coming from the ground to pull me down into the damp earth. Something very bad had happened there, and I was tapping into it, picking up on things that I should not have known about.

I'd realized that I had to get out and that it wouldn't be easy. The floor had been deeper than I'd anticipated, and the window was above my head. I shoved the flashlight into my pocket, jumped up, and grabbed one of the bars, then swung like a trapeze artist, stabbing my feet through the small opening.

Nick had pulled me the rest of the way out, an act of friendship that I'm still grateful for, but in the depths of that cellar, I realized I was different, sensitive to things that most people never notice.

I pulled out of the reverie, back to Barrington's condo, contemplating actions that could deliver me into a place every bit as evil as that of my childhood memory. Reaching out to Ishmael would not be without cost. The connection would go both ways and open my mind to the thoughts and feelings of a sociopath. It was a potentially fatal risk, and I felt I had no choice but to take it.

While the mechanical brass oddities Barrington had placed around the room caught the light in curious ways, and the Van Gogh painting he'd copied hung over the fireplace, keeping a constant watch over the unique atmosphere of the condo, I ran my fingers across the photograph of the hooded figure, opened my mind, and reached out.

At some point, a mental door creaked open, and curious thoughts began to creep in, images of a dark interior space, like a warehouse and full of things I could not see. I heard movement, scuffing sounds like those a large rat might make, but I didn't need the sounds to know I was not alone. A malignant presence saturated the dark chasm, was, in fact, the source of its darkness, and the entity who occupied the black environment began to approach, taking long but quick strides which sounded like a straight razor being dragged efficiently across a leather strap.

Operating on fear and gut instinct, I broke the connection, then closed the file and tossed it onto the table beside the chair, but the sensation of being in the presence of something bad still lingered, just like it had years ago in the bottom of that old cellar.

A slight breeze wafted through the room, carrying the stringent odor of gasoline, and I wondered if I'd left a window or a door open, creating an opportunity for fumes from the parking lot to seep in.

I pushed myself from the chair, then stood and glanced around the room, stopping when I saw the source of my anxiety.

He stood motionless, hands hanging limply at his sides, a silhouette backlit by light from the patio door, which stood open behind him. It was Officer Danny Craigthorpe, his face passive, emotionless, his rigid stance intimidating. He seemed completely unaware of my presence as he turned and walked toward the kitchen.

Craigthorpe rifled through the drawers, retrieved a butane lighter, the kind used to light a fireplace or ignite the coals of a charcoal grill, then took a few steps toward the living area where he stopped and turned toward me.

"I should warn you, Barrington, no one has ever defeated me. It might surprise you to know that many have tried."

I didn't reply. Through our contact, Ishmael had learned my location but still seemed in the dark about my identity. Perhaps my being in the condo and thinking thoughts about the surroundings had given him a false echo.

"I promise you," the Craigthorpe thing said, "you won't live through the day unless you join me."

"I don't know," I said. "From what I've seen, your followers don't always fare so well."

Craigthorpe went silent again, rigid, void of expression, then said, "Interesting, isn't it? When we first met, I gathered that you were complex, complicated. Most people aren't, and you can take that as an indication of my fascination. What makes you different from those around you?"

"Honestly," I said, "I'm not quite sure myself."

I had not twisted the truth. I wasn't exactly sure what separated me from the crowd, making it difficult for someone like Ishmael, if indeed there were others like him, to break through my defenses. But I suspected it had something to do with my unusual abilities. Nonetheless, Ishmael was trying to destroy me, and it was with great effort that I kept the interference.

"Now that's funny," he said. "I find it difficult not to like you, Barrington. The truth always has a way of climbing to the surface, doesn't it? There aren't many people I can talk to, much less communicate with. But don't let it go to your head. Even one of my intimate associates, if given leeway, could figure out that you and I could never be friends. I almost wish things could be different, though. Do you have any idea what total loneliness is like? The curse of a brain that refuses to rest is problem enough, but when that mind reaches out, almost on its own, it can be relentless. I've spent a good portion of my life suffering in an endless quest for answers and anything approaching a level of normality." He paused. "Am I getting through to you?"

Thankfully, he was not getting through in the way that he wanted, but his constant mental probing unnerved me. "With mixed messages," I said. "Sounds like you're apologizing for something you haven't done and trying to justify it at the same time."

"Well put, Barrington. Your attempt at understanding my plight could possibly make things easier for both of us."

I shifted my weight, took a step forward. "We're not as different as you might think, Ishmael. I never knew my father, and I lost my mother when I was still a child. Everyone has feelings. It's part of what makes us human. Your situation is admittedly rather unique, but your ability to lash out in unconventional ways neither gives you the right to do so nor does it lessen your moral obligation to society."

"You know nothing about it, you arrogant fool. How many people have you laid to waste in the course of your life? Something about your demeanor indicates you have indeed done so. It's intoxicating having someone's life in your hands, not for a few fleeting seconds like a common murderer, but for minutes, hours, even days."

A bead of perspiration trickled down my spine. Living with the cold truth of having in the line of duty taken the lives of others, wondering if it was truly justified, was a struggle I dealt with often. Had Ishmael somehow broken through, tricked me with conversation into saying something I shouldn't have?

Somehow I didn't think so. A lucky guess at best.

"But it's never enough, is it, Ishmael? You're after something much more than exemplifying the axiom of power and corruption. So, what is it? What do you really want?"

Craigthorpe cocked his head. "The problem," Ishmael said, "with thinking, you can talk your way out of anything is that sooner or later you will fail."

"Don't be so sure. I have a pretty good track record."

"What kind of record are we talking about?" Ishmael asked. "What exactly is your line of work, Barrington? Or maybe you're like me and more or less outside that kind of thing."

"I'd rather not talk about it."

The Craigthorpe thing tried to laugh. "That's hilarious. You're a funny guy. It was just a simple inquiry, wanting to know more about you, that's all."

I took another step toward Craigthorpe. "Tell me something, Ishmael. With your intellect, which surely must be vast given your unusual abilities, what kinds of questions keep you up at night? Do you know more about this unfathomable universe than most? Do you believe in the existence of God?"

"Are you merely trying to buy time?" he asked, "or do you truly wish to have a philosophical debate?"

Ishmael paused, then directed Craigthorpe to check his watch. "But look at the time. I've overstayed my welcome. I do have other things to attend to. I've enjoyed our little chat, Barrington, but I really need to be going. You really shouldn't have resurrected yourself. Now I have to kill you all over again."

Ishmael was alluding to his having killed the old gentleman who'd also gone by the name of Barrington. "I know that you believe you have to do this," I said, "but where's the need? Why can't you just slip back undercover, blend back in with your elusive society?"

"And I'm sure you would promise not to say a word." He shook Craigthorpe's head. "I'm afraid it's no longer that simple. With you around, I and my people are no longer anonymous. In trying to talk me out of it, you've given me another reason, one that's a little more altruistic, wouldn't you say?"

There was no way I'd ever let Ishmael slip back underground, but he didn't know that. I glanced around the condo, hoping an idea of what to do might come to me. I could take down Craigthorpe. I'd done it before. But that could be exactly what Ishmael wanted, having me seal my own fate.

"I understand why you might think that," I said, "but you've got it all wrong. You see, I've talked with the police and with the press. Nobody believes me. They think I'm crazy."

Craigthorpe cocked his head. "Delusional breakdowns have occasionally caused me problems, especially with those of a more resistant nature. Then again, that would be you, wouldn't it?"

"Do you think I'm delusional?"

"It might explain a few things, not that it matters at this point. I have to tie up the loose ends. That's really all there is to it."

I gauged the distance between Craigthorpe and me. I'd slowly maneuvered myself into a reasonably good offensive position. But something kept holding me back.

Craigthorpe walked across the room, stepped up to the window near the fireplace, the one furthest from the front door. He grabbed the window dressing, wadding the curtain in his hand. "Exquisite material. Did you pick it out?"

"Officer Craigthorpe, if there's any part of you that can hear me, please fight this, find your own thoughts, your own mind."

At that moment, I thought I saw something, understanding perhaps, reflect through Craigthorpe's eyes.

"He doesn't know what you're saying," Ishmael said. "There's not enough of him left to even comprehend your presence."

Was, Ishmael, right? Had I only imagined a hint of comprehension in Craigthorpe's face? "And yet my little attempt got your attention. Come on, Craigthorpe. Snap out of it."

Craigthorpe blinked, slowly turned toward me. I thought he tried to speak, though his lips didn't move.

"I don't know, Ishmael. I believe I'm getting through to him."

"He's on a level of consciousness comparable to your fireplace. The only danger he poses is that which I coax from him."

The comparison of a combustion chamber gave me second thoughts, and my mind was redirected to the butane lighter which Craigthorpe held loosely in his hand.

"Aren't you," Ishmael continued, "at this very moment thinking of new ways to approach the authorities, wondering what you could do or say which might convince them to reconsider the existence of someone like me?"

"It wouldn't do any good," I said. "I've already told you that."

"I don't think you would give up that easily. Even if you have, you've proven yourself to be enough of a problem all on your own, and your willingness to take sole responsibility for solving what you see as a problem is demonstrable. Just look at you, intensely studying my man Craigthorpe, wondering what I might have him do."

The calm, matter-of-fact way Ishmael treated the subject of his needing to silence me ran through my senses.

"So then," I asked, "if you were me, what would you do?"

I glanced at Craigthorpe. His eyes were empty, his mind clueless, a broken man with a stolen mind.

"Let me approach it from a different angle," I said. I was still trying to gain Ishmael's confidence. "You've already punished everyone responsible for turning your parents away from the shelter that night. I had nothing to do with it. I simply got caught up in it when one of the parties involved asked for my help. Walk away from it, Ishmael, and go back to the life you were leading before."

"Just listen to us," Ishmael said. "As unlikely as it seems, you and I, with our vast array of differences, have nonetheless gotten around to talking in circles."

"It's to be expected. What we both see as a potentially life-altering situation is dominating our thoughts."

Craigthorpe raised the butane lighter to chest level and held it at arm's length. "I need to ask you an important question, Barrington. After you're gone, will anyone care one way or the other?"

My mind spun with questions as to why Ishmael might ask such a thing.

"Of course," he continued, "there are different ways you might handle this. Once the fire starts, you could try to escape, hoping with all the confusion I don't notice, but I don't think you'll do that. My instincts tell me you will try to stop me, or my assistant, from doing what has to be done."

Craigthorpe brought the lighter close to his face and examined the mechanism for lighting the device. "Either way, you'll fail."

My mind raced, and I seemed powerless to stop it. I knew what Ishmael had in mind. The gasoline I had smelled. Craigthorpe had doused himself with it. Ishmael would have him ignite himself, turning him into a human torch. I needed to get the lighter away from Craigthorpe, but any attempt I made would only cause Ishmael to carry out the plan that much sooner.

Ishmael's logic made a kind of demented sense. He liked having everything under his control. He didn't want to kill me to satisfy some sociopathic urge. Since he couldn't control my mind, he was going to kill the whole body.

Craigthorpe brought the lighter near his clothing, then slid his thumb onto the trigger mechanism.

"Wait," I said.

Craigthorpe did not move, but said, "Wait for what?"

"You're soaked with gasoline, Officer Craigthorpe. If you strike the lighter, you'll go up in flames. You'll die. Is that what you want?"

No answer.

I casually ran my hand across the left side of my jacket, feeling the shape of the .38 I'd picked up at the pawnshop. I had forgotten about the weapon. Had I actually gotten to the point of being that forgetful, or was Ishmael inside my head? Had he been all along?

"I have to admit I'm disappointed," Ishmael said. "I truly expected that you would put up more of a fight, mount more of a challenge."

"Don't be so sure of yourself," I said. "Something tells me that you would have already had the place blazing if things were going to plan. Maybe I'm getting to Craigthorpe, and he's having second thoughts."

I slid my hand inside the jacket pocket. A well-placed shot from the .38 might stop Ishmael from burning down the condo, but I didn't want to hurt Craigthorpe. Still, I wondered what would happen to Ishmael if caught unaware occupying the mind of another who lost that life instantly.

Do you have any idea what it feels like to die in someone else's body?

I tightened my grip around the handle of the .38, wondering how much of Ishmael was actually inside Craigthorpe at the moment. When I'd encountered his presence beneath the Vandever Building, he'd appeared to control dozens of individuals simultaneously.

Another question came to mind. Wouldn't someone with Ishmael's apparent intellect have considered the possibility that I might be armed?

"I'll do exactly as he tells me to do," the Craigthorpe thing said.

"Did you hear that?" I asked. "Your buddy just referred to himself in the first person. I think you're losing him, Ishmael."

Doubts again began to swirl through my mind. Ishmael's cavalier attitude indicated he wasn't concerned about what happened to his drone. By putting a bullet in Craigthorpe's head, I wouldn't be stopping Ishmael, but I would be killing an innocent man.

"You're merely creating a sense of false hope," Ishmael said, "trying to trick your pathetic mind into thinking everything will be all right. It won't be. My assistant will ignite himself, then run through the apartment, touching everything he can. But that's not all."

Craigthorpe reached into his pocket and pulled out a small bottle, which had a rag protruding from its top.

"I forgot to mention," Ishmael continued, "he'll first light this and toss it into the living room where all that nice carpeting will accept the little cocktail quite nicely. And just in case I put any ideas in your head about escaping, you can forget it. I'll have my flaming assistant chase you down and wrap his loving arms around you."

I saw no other choice. I was far enough away from Craigthorpe that the blast from the muzzle should not set off the gasoline. I shoved the doubts from my mind. Guided only by instinct, I pulled the .38, took aim, and squeezed off two rounds.

The force of the slugs threw Craigthorpe against the wall. With something between a grunt and a scream, he slid to the floor.

My actions were so unanticipated, so quickly executed, that it caught Ishmael or Craigthorpe off guard. Before he could recover, I raced across the room and kicked the lighter he had dropped away from his grasp, then scooped up the device and started for the door.

Craigthorpe wasn't dead. The shots had hit the target, pulverizing the man's shoulder, but as my foot caught on something, I jerked around to see Craigthorpe clawing after me like some wounded animal.

Struggling to keep my focus, not give in to fear, I twisted free, then kicked Craigthorpe in the chest. I didn't wait around to see what damage the impact had done. I turned and ran. When I cleared the door, I crossed the patio and jumped the railing. As I hit the pavement, I glanced behind me.

Craigthorpe crawled after me. Blood leaked from the wounds on his shoulder as he hauled his weight over the railing, then found his footing on the other side.

For a moment, we both stood, staring at each other, an uncanny, serene standoff, and then Craigthorpe's eyes became his own, and like some helpless child, he stretched out his arms, pleading for me to do something.

A sensation of what was coming rolled across my senses. I removed the .38 from the jacket and stowed it in my front pants pocket, then tore the coat from around me, but my efforts proved in vain.

Craigthorpe, or Ishmael, must have had a backup plan, a secondary source of ignition for the gasoline. Craigthorpe burst into flames, then with a tortured scream unlike any I'd heard, he ran haphazardly through the parking lot.

Trembling with uncertainty, I ran after him. Catching him in a grassy area north of the complex, I wrapped the coat around him, then threw him to the ground and began to roll him across the grassy lot.

Seconds later, another disturbance caught my attention. The condo exploded. I wasn't sure what had caused it. Ishmael must have caused Craigthorpe to plant some kind of explosive.

The screams of Craigthorpe had probably already drawn the other residents from their homes, but they now gathered in small groups, pointing at the building as flames leaped from the windows of Barrington's condo.

A paramedic knelt beside me. Someone had called 911.

The medic examined Craigthorpe, then frowned and shook his head.

Several of the residents came over and got the medic to follow them.

With everyone's attention taken by the catastrophe, I left the area and made my way along Seventh Street, where I'd left the Mercedes near the park. I didn't have time to get caught up in this. I had to find Ishmael.

everal police cars had blocked all the roads going in and out of the area. The implication of that dug into me as I sat inside the cab of the old Mercedes. The phone showed that it was Thursday, just after 3:00 p.m. Barrington's condo billowed with smoke even as the firemen doused it with water, its use as my sanctuary taken from me so easily. Craigthorpe still lay on the grass, covered with blankets.

Somewhere deep inside, an element of defeatism caused me to wish it was all over, that my nemesis had delivered enough destruction and would now take my advice and slip back into his underworld. But what little sanity I had left told me that Ishmael had to be dealt with, that he would not go away on his own. What had started as revenge, getting back at the few people he'd thought responsible for denying his parents protection from the elements, had morphed into something much more dangerous. Ishmael was killing everyone involved and anyone who tried to stop him.

Jeffery Martin and Officer Craigthorpe had already been dealt with, but there had been a third party on the stage at the dedication ceremony. I was certain I'd almost gotten through to Craigthorpe. If Mayor McClendon was still alive, I had to try to save him. The trouble was fire trucks, and squad cars blocked all entrances to and from the complex. They wouldn't let me through, and even if they considered it, there would be questions.

I leaned back against the car seat. I was tired and a bit disoriented, but I tried to relax, extend my senses to get a feel for the situation. What I got was a barrage of jumbled thoughts and fuzzy images, but it was enough to let me know that I needed to get out of the area. The officers had orders to arrest me on sight.

Movement caught my attention as a man walked past the car, subtly adjusting his steps to counter slight miscalculations due to his inebriated state. It was possibly the distraction that I needed.

I opened the door of the Mercedes, then climbed out as I glanced at the police officers. Several of them were interviewing residents while the others were questioning people in the park. They were occupied now, but how long did I have before they made their way to me? There would be questions.

A man had burned to death, and a prominent apartment complex had burst into flames. The paramedic had seen me trying to help Craigthorpe, and they would want to know why I was there and who the unfortunate man was.

I couldn't get caught up in this.

"I have a proposition for you," I said.

The stumbling man's mind seemed to be elsewhere, and I wondered if he was sober enough to carry out what I needed him to do. I grabbed his shoulders and stared into his eyes. He wasn't under Ishmael's control. He was just drunk. "Listen carefully," I said.

The man grinned.

"I need your help," I said. "The police officer that's questioning everyone, I can't afford to talk to him for a host of reasons. Do you understand?"

The man nodded.

I pointed to the fire. "I don't know how long you've been here or what you might have seen, but I didn't have anything to do with any of this."

I glanced over my shoulder at the officer, then returned my attention to the man. "Will you help?"

The man swayed unsteadily on his feet. If he understood, he gave no indication of it.

I fished a twenty from my pocket and slid it into the man's hand, then folded his fingers around it. "I want you to walk into the park, not toward any of the officers, but away from them, and sing as loudly as you can. Can you do that?"

The hopelessness of my plight showed in the man's eyes, and I didn't think he'd understood anything I'd said.

But then words to the song "Delta Dawn" began to come out of the man with a voice of surprising quality, and he increased the volume as he stumbled into the park.

"That's it," I said. "Good job."

Working with nothing but shattered nerves and adrenaline, I turned away and walked across Seventh Street toward the grassy area across from the condo. Moving as casually as possible, I crossed the area and started walking south. When I reached the parking lot of the American Legion post, I quickened my pace. In an area between the post and Oaklawn Cemetery, I turned west, going behind the building that housed the post. The scent of damp soil was strong, too woodsy and earthy for the urban setting, but I didn't have time to contemplate such things at the moment. About fifty yards to the west, an old art deco building offered the next available cover. It'd had something to do with the fire department at one time, but I wasn't sure what it was used for now, if anything.

Getting to the art deco building without being noticed wasn't a given, and I couldn't shake the feeling that it was over, that I would fail and be apprehended. The force that drove me was the look I'd seen in Craigthorpe's eyes. I'd nearly gotten through to him. If I could do that again, not only might I save Mayor McClendon, but I might also gain information from him that could lead to Ishmael.

Thoughts shared by Ishmael and his victims, which could linger in the mind of McClendon, might be the key that would unravel this nightmare.

I reached the old building and ducked behind it, then eased along the wall until I reached the other end. Not far away, on the other side of a decaying parking lot, a walking trail ran southward along the western perimeter of the cemetery.

I peeked around the corner of the building and scanned the end of the condominium complex.

The chaos and the activity it had spawned continued to occur predominately near the eastern side of the complex.

I took a moment to gather my nerves. I had to get out of there and find McClendon. I strolled across the decaying parking lot toward the walking trail, aware of the possibility that someone might be watching the area. I glanced around, saw that no one was following, then quickly stepped onto the path and walked briskly away from the scene.

When I reached Eleventh Street, I paused for traffic, then sprinted across the roadway where I again picked up the sidewalk going along Norfolk Avenue. The pathway meandered in a southerly direction past some tennis courts and through a maturing but well-maintained neighborhood.

Nothing out of the ordinary appeared to be happening. I nodded to a postman delivering along his route, waved to a lady walking her dog.

Feeling a sense of urgency to get farther away from the area, I turned east at Thirteenth Street and made my way toward Peoria Avenue, then crossed the asphalt parking lot of a print shop and rounded the corner, where I began walking south along the sidewalk.

A few blocks later, when I reached a restaurant, a hamburger stand near Fifteenth Street, I paused and went inside, aware of the door as it closed behind me with a soft thud.

I slid into a booth, thinking about the Mercedes I'd left in the lot near the park, but I had more than transportation to worry about. When I'd gone looking for Ishmael earlier in the day, in an effort to avoid detection and remain somewhat anonymous, I'd left my wallet and identification at the condo. My current resources consisted of eighty dollars, the .38 I'd picked up at the pawnshop, and a cell phone that had a third of a charge.

I had to find McClendon, and the best way to do that, given my current situation, was to contact Pastor Meadows. McClendon was a member of the church, had been for years, and I knew for a fact that he often confided in the pastor.

I thought of Nick and Carmen as other options to look at for help but immediately dismissed them both. Either of them would drop everything and come to my rescue, but I'd worked hard at trying to insulate my friends from the bad side of my business. It hadn't always worked out that way, but thinking back to the results of those slipups gave me all the more reason to keep trying.

Ishmael was no ordinary criminal.

I pulled the phone from my pocket and punched in the pastor's personal number.

His answer was slow and hesitant, which was understandable. He didn't know who was calling, didn't recognize the number.

"This is Elliot," I said, "We need to talk."

"Kenny? Where are you? How's David?"

I tried to explain, including everything that I could remember leading up to why I'd called and why I believed that talking to Mayor McClendon was so important.

"Of course," the pastor said. "I'll do whatever I can, but there's something you need to know."

For the first time since stumbling onto the scene where David Yates had been attacked, I felt the familiar sense of satisfaction that accompanied the feeling that a case was turning around, becoming solvable. "I'm listening," I said.

"Mayor McClendon has, in fact, been in contact with me. He said he had foreign thoughts in his head, disjointed memories of people, places, and things of which he had no prior recollection. He thinks he's being stalked. He mentioned your name."

I gripped the phone. The idea that McClendon might behave in an unusual manner was not surprising, but I hadn't expected to be singled out by him as the source of it. I hadn't known that McClendon was even aware of my involvement. I first thought Ishmael must have left something planted in his mind, but as far as I knew, Ishmael only knew me as Barrington. Which meant likely Dombrowski had dropped a word of some kind into the mayor's head.

"I'm not the one that the mayor needs to worry about, Pastor Meadows. I give you my word on that. But he needs all the protection he can get. Pray for him. Assemble a prayer team if possible."

"I'd thought before that you were referring to some form of hypnosis," the pastor said, "but now it sounds more like a spiritual attack. What are we talking about here?"

"A little bit of both," I said, "and close enough to either to be devastating."

I leaned back in the booth and gathered my thoughts. I fought for concentration and pulled my attention back to my objective. "Pastor Meadows, I believe that I can help the mayor, but I need to see him, meet with him. You have to trust me on this."

Standing outside the hamburger joint on Peoria, I held the phone against my ear, listening intently. I'd called the number Pastor Meadows had given me for McClendon.

"I can help you," I said, "but we need to talk and not over the phone. Can you tell me where you are?"

"The people of Babel said, 'Come, let us build ourselves a city, with a tower that reaches to the heavens, so that we may make a name for ourselves and not be scattered over the face of the earth.'"

Whoever I was talking with was quoting from the book of Genesis, and even though thoughts scrambled through my mind concerning the subject, I couldn't grasp the relevance to the current situation. "I understand what you're going through," I said. "You might say I'm caught up in it as well. Maybe if we work together, we can beat this thing."

"The Lord appeared to Solomon in a dream and told him to ask for anything he wanted. Solomon asked for wisdom to lead the Israelites. God was so pleased with Solomon's reply, He not only gave him wisdom but riches and honor too."

I gripped the phone. Another Bible reference, I Kings. "I don't understand," I said. "What are you trying to tell me?"

"Everything's been turned upside down," the man said. "Tornadoes in California, earthquakes in Oklahoma. What would Waite Phillips make of it all?"

I wasn't sure how or why, but McClendon's ramblings began to make a sort of bizarre sense, and the thought occurred to me that he was referring to the Philtower Building. Before I could ask any more questions, the guy disconnected. The call was over.

Instead of trying to regain the connection, I chanced using the same phone to call a taxi.

A few minutes later, I paid the cab driver and then climbed out of the vehicle, stepping onto a sidewalk in downtown Tulsa near Third and Boston. I waited for the cab to disappear from sight, then turned and headed South on Boston. When I arrived, I hesitated, then pushed through the door and climbed the marble staircase to the main lobby.

Art deco chandeliers hung from vaulted ceilings, travertine marble and mahogany accented the walls, handsome brass elevator doors glistened from alcoves: The Philtower Building, with its Gothic Revival style and art deco embellishments, had been financed by Waite Phillips of Phillips Petroleum Company back in the 1920s when Tulsa, Oklahoma, was considered the oil capital of the world.

Near the end of an opulent hallway, a man took notice of my arrival. He pushed away from the wall but stood his ground, his feet slightly apart and his hands on his hips.

The man's clothing, a camo vest and matching ball cap, and his demeanor, nervous and skittish, seemed out of place, and I didn't think it was McClendon. I caressed the handle of the .38 inside my pocket and started toward him. I just hoped I wasn't too late.

I strolled along the hallway, struggling to stay calm, in control. Drawing attention from others would not be a good idea. I quickly closed the distance between myself and the target, then stopped about three feet in front of him.

He stood about five foot eight, with dark eyes and dark hair. Tattoos covered his arms.

Curiosity swept through me. It wasn't Mayor McClendon, and I wondered if I'd only imagined his taking notice of me and if I'd made a mistake.

He took a step back, glanced around as if looking for an escape route, then asked, "Something I can do for you, mister?"

Curiosity turned into understanding. I'd never met the man standing in front of me, but I strongly suspected that he was the person Officer David Yates had arrested just prior to his run-in with the homeless couple. "I guess that depends on why you called this meeting, Mr. Crawford."

The man I thought to be Dewey Crawford took another step back, then bumped into the wall. "Who the hell are you, anyway?"

"Something tells me you already know the answer to that. Funny how things work out, isn't it?"

A look somewhere between fear and relief crossed the man's face. "Yeah," he said. "The nosy stranger my wife warned me about. I've seen you around a few times in other places, and I had my suspicions."

"Would one of those other places happen to be the dedication ceremony where Mayor McClendon put on his little show?"

Crawford glanced around, shifted his weight from one foot to the other. "I thought you might bring that up. I know you're some kind of cop, but you have to admit this is pretty weird stuff. How do I know I can trust you?"

"I guess you'll just have to take a leap of faith," I said. "Now let me lay a few things out. At 8:47 last Friday night, Officer David Yates picked you up for being drunk and disorderly. While you were still in the patrol car, Officer Yates responded to a breaking and entering call, and something happened that turned his world upside down. You were there, witnessed the whole thing. I need to know what you saw."

Crawford's eyes showed fear, but he said nothing, only shook his head.

I paused and gathered my thoughts. I was coming on too strong and scaring Crawford. "Like I said, you're the one who called the meeting. Why do you seem surprised that I showed up?"

I caught Crawford studying my face, my eyes in particular. I understood. I'd acquired the same habit lately. "I'd hoped to talk to McClendon," I continued. "Do you know where he is?"

"No," Crawford said. "I don't. I nicked his phone earlier today and waited. I figured my little deception would flush someone out of the crowd. I guess I'm not all that surprised it turned out to be you. I have to be careful, that's all."

"Always on your guard," I said. "Never knowing who you can trust?"

"Yeah, that's it. Sounds like we might have a common problem. Then again, maybe you are the problem. How is it that you know so much?"

"I've put together a few bits and pieces," I said. "But sometimes I'm not sure if I'm chasing this phantom or if it's chasing me. Maybe it's a little of both. I need your help, Crawford. What happened after Yates picked you up?"

Crawford looked away, then turned back and said, "As soon as he put me in the car, I knew something wasn't right. Just a feeling, you know? I was raised Catholic, but I'd strayed about as far away from my beliefs as anyone can, but when your back's against the wall, you have to turn somewhere. I started praying, and I haven't stopped since. It's all jumbled up in my head like maybe it happened and maybe it didn't. Anyway someone came out of the darkness with their head all covered up with some kind of hooded coat or sweatshirt. Next thing I know, Officer Yates is setting me free. I didn't stick around to ask questions. I scrambled out of that patrol car and ran like hell."

Crawford's account matched up well enough with what Yates had said.

"I've had a few run-ins with this guy who doesn't like to show his face," I said. "You can stop worrying about your memory. He's real enough. McClendon is in deep trouble. If you know where he is, you need to tell me. And what about David Yates? Sounds like your connection with him is a little more than cops and robbers."

Crawford's expression grew sympathetic. "Whatever happened is pretty much over now, fades a little more each day. I'm thankful for that. I don't know exactly where Officer Yates is, but I'm pretty sure he's alive, out there somewhere on the run like us."

A sensation of being observed ran through me. Crawford suddenly seemed uneasy as well. Since arriving, I'd studied him, paying particular attention to his eyes and facial expressions. He showed no indication of being like the others.

"Something tells me I'm not the only one you hoped to flush out of the woodwork with this little get-together," I said. "I hope you know what you're doing."

"Not at all," Crawford said. "But I can't keep going on like this, afraid to walk out of the house or anything else for that matter."

I recalled my own brush with the mind of Ishmael. I did not want to go through that again. Something had to be done. And it would be up to Crawford, Yates, and me, the ones who stood a little more outside the influence of Ishmael than most, to pull it off.

"Your faith has protected you," I said. "Remember that when the going gets tough."

Crawford glanced over his shoulder, then turned back. "What are you getting at?"

I shook my head. I'd come here on nothing more than a whim, a chase-the-wind style that was not foreign to me, and yet the thought of things turning out the way they had, with Dewey Crawford showing up at the same location, ran a current of fear through me. "We've been here too long," I said, then turned and started toward the stairs and the exit.

Crawford caught up with me. We were more than halfway to the exit when the sound of people climbing the stairs reverberated through the hallway.

Not an uncommon occurrence, but we weren't exactly operating under ordinary circumstances, and whoever it was on the stairs would soon step into the hallway. A disturbing thought snaked through my mind: We'd been set up. I signaled for Crawford to follow, then swung around and walked casually in the opposite direction.

Crawford dropped some papers he was carrying and immediately lowered himself to one knee to retrieve them.

The sound of the footsteps changed in pitch, transitioning from stairs to the hallway. If Ishmael found Crawford and me together, it would be all too easy for him.

I helped Crawford gather his papers and quickly pulled him to his feet, then resumed the retreat down the hallway. I hoped we'd remained unnoticed though that was unlikely. Not only had the footsteps transitioned from the stairs to the hallway, but the party had also gained time and distance.

Some of the other people who were already walking the hallway in the opposite direction—business people, visitors—slowed their pace, some pointing, others leaning close and whispering. They had noticed Ishmael's entourage following us.

All the ingredients were there for a bad ending, and then a stocky man who looked disturbingly familiar stepped in front of us, halted our progress. Scenarios of previous encounters raced through my mind. I suspected the man had been among the bunch who'd tried to take me down inside the Vandever Building.

He forced a smile. "I wish I could say it's good to see you again, Barrington. Honestly, you've become an intolerable annoyance. What could you possibly hope to gain from this misguided game of cops and robbers?"

I grabbed a quick visual survey of the immediate area. Crawford looked like a zombie himself, though I knew he wasn't. He was just scared.

Three to four other people in the vicinity looked as if they could be a part of the welcoming committee. I shrugged. "Ridding the city of a dangerous psychopath comes to mind."

The man's lips curled into a grin. "Habitually setting unrealistic goals can be an unhealthy practice, Barrington."

A bead of sweat trickled down my back. While the man had his own physical distinctions, his personality was somewhat like that of Ishmael, or rather like that of the people he'd dominated. I made plans to bust free the first chance I got, make a run for it. I hoped Crawford was on the same page. "It's been nice chatting with you," I said, "but we really must be going."

"Just like that? You insinuate a threat concerning a mutual friend, then simply walk away?"

The man seemed different than the other Ishmael cohorts, his eyes not flat and lifeless but attentive. More than that, he appeared to be in control of his actions. I thought of the .38 resting in the shoulder holster beneath my sweatshirt, but any move I made to retrieve it would immediately be interpreted as an aggressive action. I shrugged. "That's pretty much it."

"Blunt and to the point. I like that. But your apparent propensity to underestimate your opponent baffles me. In fact, I'm inclined to believe that you're engaging in a type of strategical mind game."

I considered the man's words, his insight. I wondered if he could actually be Ishmael, then quickly dismissed the idea. He wore no protective clothing. Evening had begun to set in but just barely, and even inside the building there was plenty of outside light. "Perhaps you're overthinking this issue."

"Doubtful," he said. "I've never known the boss to take an interest in an outsider, but I'm beginning to see why he might make you the exception."

The unusual character of the man continued to intrigue me, and then it became clear. Ishmael needed someone with their own mind, a confidant he could trust to help him survive in his shadowy world. This man, much like the John Doe who'd gone to the shelter and tricked Goldstein and Roxie Taylor outside and then later fired at Yates, belonged to a special segment of the secret society, promoted through the ranks to serve in such a capacity.

"I don't know that I've ever been considered an outsider," I said. That wasn't true. The term defined me. I suspected it would describe my invasive friend, as well.

"It's all quite puzzling," he said. "Not that it matters."

Aware that I might have stumbled upon Ishmael's weakness, I decided to play along with the man's little word game, see where it went. "Assuming we are to continue this conversation," I said. "Would you be so kind as to relinquish your advantage and tell me your name?"

"Nice try, Barrington, but, no, I would not. Of what possible help could something as meaningless as a name be to you? You're a smart man. Surely you've guessed why I'm here?"

The man's words drove home a thought, a disturbing realization that made me acutely aware of the apparent singularity of my situation. I glanced at Dewey Crawford.

He stood motionless, his eyes fixed on some distant and unknown target.

I hoped Crawford was caught up in a state of shock and nothing more. I turned back to Ishmael's cohort. "I don't scare easily, Mr. Anonymous, but the nature of our mutual friend demands a level of concern. Being second-in-command to such a unique individual would put you in a position of extreme trust—and mistrust. The responsibility you carry must be imposing?"

"Of that, you can be sure," he said. "He sent me to get you and your awestruck friend and bring you to him, though I don't believe he actually expects me to succeed."

"Interesting that you would see it that way," I said. "And you can drop the third person scenario. He calls himself Ishmael. We've had a few conversations, not directly, but you know how he works. More importantly, perhaps we could work together to improve our respective situations."

Ishmael's cohort glanced at his entourage, then to Crawford. "In believing that we know the source of the problem, we move to eliminate it. Is that what you're saying?"

Had I actually suggested such a thing as collaborating with the enemy in an effort to get a bigger enemy? In undercover investigations, especially in the drug world, this wasn't such an unusual idea, but for me, my history in homicide? We didn't tend to be involved in such things.

"Evading a direct question carries its own merit," he continued. "Ishmael, as you call him, suffers from long bouts of melancholy. Challenging situations seem to help, but as you might imagine, such things are few and far between for such a man. You've matched wits with him quite well so far. Perhaps you are just what he needs."

"What exactly do you have in mind?"

"An excellent question," he said, "except I'm the one who should be asking it. Let's get to the heart of the matter. If I deliver you as promised, can I count on you to fulfill your end of the deception?"

"I guess that depends on what you're expecting me to do."

"Oh, come now, Mr. Barrington. Our contemplation involves a dangerous and unpredictable man. You think I do this work because I want to? No, Mr. Barrington. To Ishmael, we are all either expendable or bendable to his use. I'm tired of being bent into his command. There will be no room for error or halfhearted attempts. It's not pleasant to admit, but I suspect the thought has crossed your mind that the world would be a better place without our mutual nemesis."

Mr. Anonymous seemed to know more about me than I was comfortable with. But I was a cop. Like it or not, on any given day, my survival could depend on the use of deadly force. There was nothing glamorous or romantic about it. Each incident carried a life of its own, constant reminders of the sometimes dark nature of the business.

"Well," he said, "do we have a deal?"

I let the question settle for a moment. The chances that I'd caught Ishmael's cohort in some kind of rebellious interlude in which he'd seen the light and was willing to cooperate seemed slim. And yet, with the possibility that it could go down that way, I took the dare. Mr. Anonymous seemed well aware that his position of command was at best tenuous. "Yes," I said. "I believe we do."

"Excellent. It will happen quickly, probably tonight."

Once again, even though other people were around, I had the sensation that it had all come down to me and Ishmael's handyman. "What should I do now?" I asked.

"Spend your time in concentrated preparation, I should think. You will need it. Don't worry. I'll find you when the time is right."

Like the hollow-eyed drones, Dewey Crawford was still caught up in suspended animation. I wondered if Ishmael might be listening through him or one of the drones. It was a chance I'd have to take. "You seem different than your companions," I said. "What's up with that?"

"I'm afraid Ishmael, as you call him, longs in desperation for uncoerced relationships. As you might imagine, everyone goes out of their way to avoid him. Those who cannot usually submit to control rather than risk the fate of disobedience."

"And yet, here you are. I don't get it."

"Oh, I think you do." He leaned closer and winked. "After all, you're still walking around with your wits intact, aren't you? So, farewell for now. The boss needs his meds."

Ishmael's cohort made a gesture with his hand, then turned and walked down the hallway, his robotic entourage mindlessly following. Within a minute, Ishmael's welcoming party disappeared down the stairway from which they had come.

asey set the glasses on the table in front of Crawford and me. "Are you sure you know what you're doing?"

Bubbles of carbonation climbed aimlessly through the amber liquid, beer from the tap. According to Crawford, he hadn't had a drink in days, and I hadn't had one in months, but the occasion called for it. I managed as sincere a smile as I could. "Yeah, I'm sure."

All this and I still didn't know where McClendon was. After I'd walked Crawford out of the Philtower Building and hailed a cab, Casey's place seemed the only option. Crawford didn't look well, but the alcohol seemed to be working. He turned toward me and tried to focus, something he hadn't been doing.

"It's good to see you coming around," I said. "How are you feeling?"

Crawford sipped his beer and leaned back in his chair. "Well, Mr. Barrington—if that's your real name. I'm not entirely sure. I was there. I could see you and hear you talking, but it was like I was outside looking in, like experiencing some kind of unperfected interactive TV show."

"Running into Ishmael's henchmen caught us both by surprise," I said. "We should take it as a wake-up call."

"And wake up to what, instant death?"

Crawford seemed to be in control, but he'd certainly changed his tune. "Or even worse," I suggested, "being helplessly submitted to the will of a madman. It makes the conversation I had with Ishmael's accomplice even more attractive."

"Are you out of your mind?" Crawford asked.

I had dropped the line about Ishmael's cohort more as an act of talking out loud than a means of conversation, and I was taken aback that

Crawford would be up to speed, but then I remembered that he'd said that he'd been aware of his surrounding during the ordeal.

"It might be worth it," I said, "to play along and see where it leads."

Crawford finished his beer, then glanced around as if he wanted another, but he didn't ask, and he made no signals to Casey. He set the glass on the table. "You're smarter than that, Barrington. You wouldn't have gotten this far otherwise. It's a setup. It's written all over it."

"Maybe, but the absurd obviousness of it all causes me to wonder if his insinuations might contain an element of truth. Think about it. Having Ishmael hanging over you like that, not controlling you exactly, but threatening to at any moment. Who wouldn't crack under that kind of pressure? If he thinks there's any chance that I come through, rid him of his problem, he'll be complicit."

"I don't know," Crawford said. "I'd leave it alone if I were you."

"I don't know that we have that option. And if we play this right, Anonymous could lead us right to Ishmael."

Crawford shook his head. "You do what you have to do, but count me out. I don't want anymore to do with it."

I leaned back in the chair. It seemed Crawford had paid attention, all right.

"We can't just leave it alone and hope for the best," I said. "Sooner or later, he's going to catch us with our backs turned."

"Maybe not if we get out of town, put some distance between us. That's what I plan to do."

"What's happened to you, Crawford? You have some problems, but I never figured you for a coward."

Crawford sat forward, leaning against the table with his elbows. "He almost had me, Barrington. It was all I could do to fight it off. You saw it. I'm no good to anybody like that. For all I know, that's how he works, a little at a time and not all at once. Sorry, but I don't plan on being anybody's zombie."

"Neither do I," I said. "But I quit running from problems a long time ago. I haven't had much luck with that."

"Welcome to the club. I haven't had much luck with anything."

"Maybe it's time to change that. Take a stand. Win or lose, you'll have the satisfaction of knowing you didn't back down."

Crawford turned away, stared off into space for a moment, then shook his head. "I'm sorry, Barrington, but I can't be who you want me to be. I just don't have it in me."

I wasn't angry with Crawford. I actually felt sorry for him. "You're not as bad as you think you are," I said. "You've just lived with the notion so long that you've started to believe it. People see you and conclude that you're nothing more than a helpless drunk, and you go along with it. I'm betting there's more to you than that."

Crawford nodded, but he had a far-off look in his eyes, something that only someone like me might notice. "Nice little pep talk," he said, "but you're wasting your time. I don't know what role you're wanting me to play, but whatever it is, I can't do it."

"We're not talking about any role-playing or pretense of any kind," I said. "This isn't some fantasy I've dreamed up. You of all people should understand just how real it is."

"I understand, all right. It's exactly the point I've been trying to make. We're out of our league, overmatched. He can reach out and touch us anytime he wants, but we can't touch him. How do we fight something like that?"

I thought about telling Crawford that I had my ways but decided against it. "We do it by exploiting his weaknesses," I said.

Crawford pulled a pack of cigarettes from his shirt pocket, fished a lighter from another, then lit one up. He took a couple of drags, then asked, "What are you getting at?"

I leaned back to avoid the fumes. I hadn't been around Crawford that much, and I didn't know why his smoking should surprise me. It certainly wasn't out of character. "Ishmael needs someone to help him run his kingdom," I said. "A loyal subject capable of independent thought and actions. I'm guessing it's turned out to be a rather oxymoronic concept if you know what I mean?"

Crawford shook his head. "You lost me at loyal subject."

"I've done some research," I said. "Being Ishmael's confidant is a precarious position that carries a high rate of turnover."

"Okay, professor. It's a hard job to fill. So what?"

"Closer to impossible," I said. "My guess is our latest, Mr. Anonymous, is number who-knows-what in a long line of failures. Through the years, I've learned to read people pretty well. I believe Anonymous is being straight. Otherwise, I wouldn't go through with it.

"He has trouble keeping helpers. I get that. It doesn't sound like much of a weakness, though."

"Doesn't it?" I asked. "What's scaring you so much right now that you want to run and hide? Imagine having that fear magnified exponentially and living with it twenty-four hours a day."

An expression of understanding came over Crawford's face. "Okay. It's no wonder they crack under the pressure, but how does any of that help us?"

"If you were in that position and saw a possible way out, wouldn't you take it?"

"How should I know what I would do? Thankfully, I'm not in such a jam, and if I have anything to say about it, I'm not going to put myself in line to get there."

I took a sip of beer. I hadn't wanted it as much as I'd thought. It'd gotten warm, and most of it was still there. "There's more," I said. "That's not his only weakness. He's also sensitive to light. Too much exposure might even be fatal. That's why he wears protective clothing. The physical weakness, coupled with his employee problems, might give us the edge we need to take him down."

"I don't know," Crawford said.

I paused. Who was I trying to kid? There was little chance of it going down that smoothly. And even if luck fell on my side, letting me apprehend Ishmael, to whom would I turn the prisoner over? The department had nothing on him. And even though there was no doubt in my mind that Ishmael was responsible for the death of the man who had called himself Barrington, there was no body, and the real Ezra Barrington had died over seventy years ago. Not only that, but the man I knew as Ishmael for all practical purposes didn't even exist.

"Good luck with that," Crawford said. "Based on what you've told me, it doesn't sound like any of the not-so-loyal subjects has had any luck overthrowing the king. You've got guts, my friend, but you haven't been where I've been. I've seen this guy, looked into his face. Those pale, heartless eyes ripped a chill through me that I'll never forget. I'm telling you, we don't stand a chance against someone like that."

At Crawford's off-the-cuff description, something stirred in my mind. I thought back to the ghostly figure I'd seen in the back of the limousine outside the homeless shelter. "Don't be so sure about that."

Crawford shook his head, then got up and started toward the exit.

I pushed away from the table to go after him, but a gentle hand on my arm stopped me. I spun around to see Casey, who'd come from behind the bar.

"Don't do it, Kenny. Let the man be."

I watched Crawford push through the door and disappear. I stared at Casey for a moment, then dropped back into the chair.

Casey sat across from me. "You're always caught up in some situation or another," he said. "Been that way since I've known you. But I got a bad feeling about this. Maybe you should take your friend's advice and walk away, leave it alone."

I took another sip of beer. I'd always been a loner, preferred it that way at times, but I'd never felt as alone as I did at that moment. "I can't do that, Casey. Too many people are depending on me. Trouble is, it seems I'm the only one who realizes that."

Casey's eyes glistened with moisture.

I tried to put on a straight face. The gruff old bartender had chided me often enough, but when I was down, he was always there for me.

"I never had any children," he said, "but if I did, I would want them to be just like you. As bad as you might want to, Kenny, you can't solve the problems of this messed-up old world all by yourself."

I shook my head. I didn't know if Casey was trying to volunteer or not, but I couldn't let that happen. "Don't worry. I hadn't planned on going this one alone."

It was true. I hadn't. Things had gone wrong, that's all. "Crawford got a little spooked," I said, "but he'll come around."

Casey frowned. "Crawford, huh? I've seen him around. He's been in a few times. I wouldn't count too heavily on him if I were you."

Casey could be right, but Crawford was all I had. "He'll be all right. Anyway, he's not the only other player in this game."

"I don't know what that means, but I hope it's better than I think."

The sound of the door opening, followed by a cool breeze scooting across the room drew my attention.

A customer had come in.

Casey got up, strolled across the room, and stepped behind the bar.

I studied the customer, a slightly overweight man dressed in business attire.

Casey set a drink on the counter and called the customer by name, then came back to my table. "I've been thinking about something you said, Kenny, about going to church. But I'm afraid the sky might bust open with peals of thunder."

"Don't worry," I said. "Jesus didn't hang around with the righteous. He took up with misfits like you and me. Check your Bible. It's in there."

25

The intrusion of Casey's customer had rattled me, and an image of the man beneath the hooded garments formed in my mind. If Ishmael was going to find me, I didn't want it to be here or around anyone else I cared for. He was getting stronger. I could sense it. Soon he would reach a point where no one could stop him.

Crossing to the door, I reached beneath my shirt and slid my fingers around the handle of the .38. Jagged, unorganized thoughts scrambled through my mind. To avoid detection, I'd tried not to concentrate on Ishmael. Regardless of that, a couple of places of interest hovered around the edges of my consciousness.

Casey was back behind the bar, talking with the customer. He seemed comfortable with him. "Hey, Casey," I said. "Do me a favor and call a cab."

I stepped outside, and when the cab arrived, I climbed into the back seat and gave the driver directions. Leaning into the seat cushion, the motion of the cab as the driver maneuvered onto the roadway nearly lulled me to sleep. My plan, though riddled with uncertainty, was straightforward. I would find Ishmael's hiding place and flush him out. If the location I had in mind turned out to be nothing but fantasy, I would simply go on to the next. I would not allow him to dominate my thoughts. I would not run in fear. The last thing I needed was to lose my confidence, my edge.

Failure was not an option. Otherwise, things were going to get very bad in the city of Tulsa.

The cab came to a stop in the parking lot of a downtown home improvement store. I climbed out and dug some cash from my pocket.

"You don't have to worry about that," the driver said. "It's been taken care of."

I stared at the pavement for a moment. Under ordinary circumstances, I would have happily paid the driver again or given him an additional tip, but I was short on cash. "Thanks," I said. "If you could wait, be here when I get back, that'd be great,"

The driver shook his head. "Casey took care of everything and then some. I hope you won't hold it against me, but when you've been driving long as I have, you get a sense about things. I've got to look out for myself 'cause I got a family counting on me. You look like you was a decent man at one time. I hope you get it back together, man. I mean that. But I'm through with this."

I started toward the store, thinking about what the driver had said. I'd never given an abundance of thought to how I looked, but I guessed my current condition had me looking pretty rough.

Several minutes later, I came out of the store and strolled across the parking lot. By the time I reached Elgin Avenue, I had loaded the batteries and reassembled the LED flashlight I'd purchased.

A man wearing a tattered plaid jacket walked toward me, talking to a woman who was taking swigs from a bottle. They both jogged sideways and stared as I went past.

I made my way north, aware of scattered voices and distant traffic, but only as background noise. I checked the light, which was small but powerful, then continued my journey.

Minutes later, I stopped near the coffee shop on Cameron where Officer Craigthorpe had tried to apprehend me. My target was an abandoned warehouse. The old building was behind the restaurant where Ishmael had communicated with me through Jeffery Martin. It also adjoined the grassy area where I'd talked with Cowboy, Ishmael's father. I suspected that Ishmael had been nearby during each occurrence. The abandoned warehouse would make a good hiding place.

Looking past the faded red garage-bay doors that fronted Detroit Avenue, the brown-colored bricks and design of the structure reminded me of a school building. Attached to the north edge, a chain-link fence surrounded the grassy area where I'd met Cowboy.

Apprehension threatened to choke my resolve, but I forced a step forward and then another. A man who'd been hiding nearby saw me, recognized me, and quickly ran the other way. He'd been in the area when

I'd taken Officer Craigthorpe down. I wasn't too concerned. He wouldn't alert anyone. He didn't want the trouble.

I kept walking.

I arrived at the first garage-bay door near the southern end of the structure. I thought it odd that a smaller door would be there, a rectangular opening carved out of the dingy red metal, though what drew my attention wasn't the door's unusual placement but something beyond that.

I knew that the door would be unlocked.

I wrapped my fingers around the grungy doorknob and twisted. A dull, metallic click echoed through the darkness. I gathered my courage and pushed on the door.

Nothing happened.

I tried again, pulling outward this time, and the door swung open.

A warm, musty pocket of air breathed from the dark hole, followed by a stench like that, which might be released from a longtime sealed tomb.

I fished the flashlight from my pocket, switched it on, and directed the beam into the interior of the old warehouse.

My pulse quickened. Nothing but concrete floors and empty expanse came into view, but the breaching of the tomb had not been without consequence.

I'd set off an alarm to the authorities. There had been no sound, no lights had blinked, but the same sense that'd told me that the door would be unlocked now warned me that it was wired.

I eased the door back into place, then turned and refollowed the path that'd brought me to the warehouse. Any police officer in proximity might respond to the call, and he wouldn't know why the alarm had gone off or where the breach had occurred. He'd quickly circle the area, searching for anyone who looked suspicious—or out of place.

Images of Cowboy and Princess and the charcoal drawing formed in my mind, and at that moment I realized that the old warehouse was nothing more than a place Ishmael had once made use of but had since moved on.

I quickened my pace as much as I could without drawing attention, stopping at the intersection to check the street signs. I knew the city well, better than most, but I hadn't been myself lately—far from it, in fact.

I stepped into the intersection, which was eerily quiet and void of traffic, then strolled across Cameron to the sidewalk that skirted the restaurant where Jeffery Martin and I had talked.

Just ahead, a patrol car turned onto the street.

The call had been answered.

Trying to remain casual, I continued along the sidewalk, and even though I knew better, I couldn't fight the urge to turn back, glancing at the area from which I'd come.

In what seemed a fluid, simultaneous action, the patrol car did a turnabout and pulled to the curbside, then the officer jumped out and came around to the sidewalk and stopped in front of me, blocking my path.

The questions the officer would ask were obvious, but my knowledge of that did little to ease my nervousness. I thought about overpowering the officer but decided against it. The officer had probably called for backup, and though I didn't know that for sure, I didn't want to put anyone in danger if it wasn't necessary. My objective was to make short work of this and be on my way before things grew more complicated.

"I saw you walk past that old warehouse," the officer said. "What were you doing over there?"

The officer's words reached into my situation like a parent scolding a child. I needed to think fast, but at the moment, that task seemed nearly insurmountable. "Nothing," I said. "I was on my way to the coffee shop, thought I'd treat myself to a cup."

"Is that right? Coffee shop's back that way. Looks like you overshot it a bit. Or maybe you're not being completely honest with me."

"Don't read too much into that," I said. "The reality of my finances caught up with me, that's all. Guess I was having second thoughts."

The officer smiled, his face softening. "You live around here?"

I rolled the question over in my mind. I didn't want to lie. Then again, telling the truth didn't seem like the best option. "More or less."

The officer nodded. "Did you happen to see anyone around the warehouse within the past few minutes?"

I hesitated, then said, "Yeah. Nothing to it though. I've seen him around before."

"You're holding back again. What are you not telling me?"

I shrugged. "The guy ran when he saw me, that's all."

"Ran? Why do you suppose he would do that?"

"I don't know. Like I said. I've seen him before. Probably nothing to it."

"You're probably right," the officer said, "but I'd like to check it out. Which way did he go?"

The guy I'd referred to, the one I'd scared off earlier, would probably be long gone by now. And even if the officer found him, he'd quickly determine there was nothing to it. Then again, if through some curious twist of fate, the indigent had jimmied the door, perhaps justice would be served. I glanced over my shoulder. "North on Detroit."

The officer pulled some cash from his pocket and stuffed it into my hand. "Something tells me you don't belong out here. Get yourself straightened out. Coffee's on me."

I studied the officer's name tag. When this was over, I'd get the money back to him and make sure the department knew that they had a good cop on their hands. I nodded, then turned and walked toward the coffee shop. I had no intentions of going there, but I wanted the young cop to think that his investment would pay off. And it would, in a manner of speaking. My being off the street for a while, even if in appearance only, would ease the officer's mind. And the less he thought about me, the better.

I turned south at the boulevard, picking up speed as I gained distance from the area where the officer had questioned me. The feel of my shoes padding against the sidewalk brought a strange sense of calm that spread across my senses, but I fought the urge to relax. Being calm was good, but overindulgence of the condition was not conducive to staying sharp. I reached the intersection just as a man carrying a white sack hurried across the street.

Lucking up on things wasn't unusual. Oftentimes, I'd discovered if I'd just meander for a bit, life would take me where I needed to be. I tried fighting it, tried outsmarting it. I always lost. That man with the focused walk was Ishmael's helper, Mr. Anonymous. He'd said something about Ishmael needing medicine, and I suspected it had to do with his condition.

I thought of closing in but held back. I'd referred to my uncanny luck, but this time, my being at the right place at the right time made me nervous. It was possible that Anonymous knew I was there, could have been following me, tracking my movements.

As Anonymous neared the old faded brick building at First and Elgin, my intuition confirmed what I'd already suspected. Ishmael resided somewhere within the derelict structure.

Acting with practiced caution, I turned and walked away. I wasn't giving up. The timing wasn't right, that's all. Getting away unnoticed was probably out of the question, but there was always hope. And hope mixed with a little luck could go a long way. I removed the flashlight from my pocket, and a few steps later paused, untied my left shoe, then slipped the small device between the shoe and the arch. I shot a quick glance around, then got to my feet and resumed walking. The positioning of the light proved somewhat uncomfortable but not unbearable. From what I understood, Ishmael could take some indirect light for short periods of time. But a bright light to the face was an entirely different matter, especially if it was unexpected. It wouldn't disable him, but it might give me the distraction I needed.

Where I would go and what I would do once there was a mystery, but if Anonymous decided to keep his end of the bargain, maybe I could buy some time, come up with a plan. The streets and sidewalks seemed deserted, but I suspected otherwise. Ishmael would have guards. And Anonymous hadn't traveled alone before. He probably wouldn't now.

I quickened my pace, pulse banging against my temples, but fate had other ideas, and my escape attempt was cut short.

Two men came from behind a building and staggered onto the sidewalk. They did not look out of place, tattered clothes, scraggly hair, a mixture of curiosity, and despair clinging to their faces. People of the street. Not zombies.

I stepped around them and continued traveling with Barrington's words sounding in my mind. *The one who hides his face denies his past and claims no future, but his legacy stalks him nonetheless.*

Barrington's cryptic message now became apparent to me. Ishmael was feared and avoided by his own people, but their sacred societal anonymity depended upon a degree of mutual cooperation. The tentative arrangement had afforded Ishmael a degree of tolerance. More than likely, he'd ventured outside the boundaries of his world before, but how far could he go before his people, out of necessity, would begin to push back?

The answer to my question took a back seat as the sound of a familiar voice dragged me from my reverie and threw me back into the moment.

"Looking for someone?"

Seconds later, Ishmael's helper, the one I'd encountered at the Philtower Building, came out of the darkness. "I told you I'd find you when the time was right, but now you've come without my calling you. What am I to do with you?"

There was no trying to back out now. All I could do was hope that Anonymous had been serious about the overthrow plans. "I got a little anxious, that's all. No harm done. We'll just carry on with what we talked about."

"I don't know if we can do that. Time moves on. Complications arise." Ishmael's helper stood there, arms dangling at his side, a slight smile turning the corners of his mouth. "You're high-strung, Barrington. Edgy and dangerous."

"I guess that's why you took an interest in me. And if things go right, a certain someone is about to find out just how high-strung I can get."

"Good idea," he said. "However, your timing is questionable at best. Perhaps you've lost a step, fallen behind. Then again, you have been through a lot lately. Under the circumstances, I'm not sure you have the means to pull it off—our unfinished business, that is."

I shifted my weight. I didn't know if Anonymous was being truthfully critical or if he'd lost his nerve. "There's only one way to find out," I said.

Anonymous smiled. His expression fell somewhere between apologetic and determined. "I understand your dilemma. Unfortunately, someone like you doesn't often stumble into our world."

"Hopefully, it's your lucky day," I said.

Blank-faced people began to come out of the darkness in numbers that dwarfed what had come before. The lumbering zombies slowly surrounded us on the sidewalk.

"Keep your wits about you, Barrington. My friends probably won't hurt you unless I tell them to, but you should refrain from engaging in any behavior that might be interpreted as aggressive."

He stepped forward, and the group followed. "Keep close and remain calm."

My pulse quickened. I couldn't say I hadn't expected something like this, but still, it was unnerving. "I hope the rhetoric about helping each other out was not just a ruse to lure me in."

"It might work out that way," he said. "Then again, it might not."

Anonymous slowed his pace, then came to a stop. His entourage assembled into a formation around us that left a six-foot circle where he and I stood, ringmasters of whatever kind of psycho circus this was.

An electromechanical hum came from somewhere beneath the ground, and an industrial grate embedded in the sidewalk opened.

Simultaneously a metallic platform rose from the depths, stopping just inches below the concrete. The entourage moved toward the platform, and I was swept along with the mob onto what I guessed to be some kind of freight-delivery system. I tried to calm my mind, go through my options, but fatigue from worry and lack of sleep dulled the process. Even if someone happened to be in the area, all they would see was a large gathering of people. The scene might draw attention, but the parties involved would most likely walk away as quickly as possible.

An unnerving vibration spread across the platform, and the curious freight elevator began to sink, lowering Anonymous and me into the hole from which it had come. When the menacing elevator finally jerked to a stop, Ishmael's helper urged me from the platform, then directed me to an area a few feet away.

Darkness engulfed the expanse, with the only light coming from the hole in the sidewalk, diffusing in from the night sky above.

"I've never cared for total darkness," I said. "It has a way of opening deeply buried insecurities."

"You seem overly relaxed for a man in your situation, Barrington. The problem is you're too jaded to realize the gravity of it all. Could be checkmate for you, old buddy."

"Thanks for the pep talk, Slick. Don't mind the nickname. I have to call you something. It's nothing personal."

He let out a guttural laugh. "Under different circumstances, we might have become friends."

"I've been called worse," I said.

The man's strange laugh reverberated through the darkness in an unnerving echo.

I knew the answer to the question I would ask and that the dilemma was no doubt embedded within the mind of the man I'd nicknamed Slick. It was my strategy to again bring it up. "While we're on the subject of friends," I continued, "why does Ishmael have so much trouble keeping people like you in place?"

"I don't know," he said. "Perhaps being at the mercy of a total maniac isn't all it's cracked up to be?"

"You got that right, Slick. You're in just as much danger as I am, and you know it."

"Of course, I do."

"Then why are you doing this?" I asked. "More importantly, how are you doing this? I've tasted a sample of Ishmael's power. He must know your thoughts."

"Does he know yours?"

I saw no reason to dodge the question. "My faith offers me a measure of immunity," I said. "But so far, our encounters have been indirect. I have to admit that the prospect of meeting him face-to-face scares the hell out of me."

"As it well should."

"Just get me close," I said. "Give me a time and place, and I'll take care of the rest."

The man didn't answer. He jangled some keys, unlocked a door, and swung it open. A dim red glow oozed from the doorway. "Enough talking," he said. "Step inside."

"Come on, Slick. You said yourself we could be friends. If we do this right, we can pull off a complete surprise."

The man tightened his grip on my arm and pushed me into the room.

Barely visible in the red glow, darkened shapes of several other people gathered around us.

"I'll try to make this as quick and painless as possible, Barrington, but eventually everything comes down to fate. Wouldn't you agree?"

"I've always thought we ultimately make our own fate," I said, "or at least have a hand in it."

I surveyed the room, trying to determine the size and shape, locate any other exits. "I guess I haven't handled mine very well lately."

"We'll have to confiscate your belongings," he said. "Don't take it personally, just something we have to do."

I saw no benefit in resisting. I handed over the .38 and the cell phone.

"Good boy. Now slowly raise your arms up and away from your body."

From behind, someone grabbed my shoulders. Another patted my legs and torso, then searched through my pockets. They took the keys to Barrington's condo and the old Mercedes. They also took what cash I had left.

Slick gave a command, and his cohorts slowly filed out of the room. He followed them but stood outside the door, watching me. "Ishmael will probably want to talk to you, but I can't promise anything."

"I've noticed you tend to favor that phrase."

"I carelessly reflect the nature of my uncertainty," he said.

"Don't we all?"

"I've worked hard to see that things begin to fall into place when the time is right," he said. "We were making progress, and then you came along. You're either a blessing or a fly in the ointment. I can't decide which."

"We're not all that different, Slick. I'd like to get to know you better, learn more about your culture."

He grinned, apparently amused with my attempt to engage him. "It would be more properly described as a parallel society."

"Yeah, whatever. Anyway, I think I know why Ishmael's so bent out of shape. I witnessed something I shouldn't have, at least in his mind. Maybe he's right. The funeral appeared pagan, steeped in mysticism."

"You'd do well to forget about it," he said. "You've no idea of the depth and complexity of it all."

He shook his head and began to close the door, which we'd entered only minutes earlier. "Time to say goodnight, Barrington. I'm going to lock you in."

"Just one more question."

The man I'd called Slick stood waiting. The space beyond the door was dark but more inviting than the lonely room they would leave me in.

"Is Ishmael unique, or are there more like him?"

Slick pulled the door closer, narrowing the gap between the outside world and my prison.

"To the best of my knowledge, Ishmael is an unfortunate anomaly."

"Thank the Lord for that."

Slick didn't answer.

I stepped closer to the door. "I might not know much about your world," I said, "but I know a little about people. You could say that understanding the dark side of human nature is my business."

Slick cocked his head. "Do tell."

"You know what they say about power," I continued. "Ishmael's brand might not be absolute, but it's close enough. If you think delivering me as a prize or a peace offering is going to appease him, you're wrong. Even if it does, it won't last. Your problem won't go away. It will only get worse."

The narrowing doorway appeared to be the only exit from the room. I considered making a dash for it but decided against it.

"I have to go now," he said.

The door closed with a soft thud followed by the clicking of the lock being secured.

26

I leaned against the door and stared into the empty expanse. The dim red glow which came from the ceiling of the garage-sized room was just enough to allow obscure discernment of only those items within a few feet of my location. The irony of being someone who had tried to let my actions define me only to become more often identified by my credentials and then being left alone in a room with only my clothing struck me. I wondered if I was truly alone or if someone or something lurked in the darkness outside the limits of my vision.

Slick had gone to a lot of trouble, acting as if he might be on my side, only to lock me away. For that matter, he could have taken Crawford and me at the Philtower Building. He'd had the manpower.

Fatigue engulfed my senses, but my eyes had now adjusted to the lack of light, and I could make out more of my surroundings. The room was approximately ten feet wide and twenty deep. The walls were of cinderblock, the floor concrete. The room was empty with the exception of a portable bathroom, the kind you might find at an outdoor concert. At least my captors had been that gracious. I thought to cross the room and inspect the toilet, then it occurred to me that I hadn't actually checked the door.

I swung around, twisted the knob, then shoved my weight against it.

The door moved slightly but caught on the hasp or latch that'd been bolted to the other side. No light filtered in from outside. The movement hadn't been enough to allow it. The thought of being trapped in a dungeon, buried beneath the rubble of a forgotten building, crept through my senses, and I wondered if it was Ishmael's plan to let me die here.

The basement was at least ten feet below street level, and the walls of the room were thick. Based on the lack of sound coming in, I doubted any would make it out even if I tried. My contact with friends—or anyone else, for that matter—had been sporadic and somewhat cryptic. It was not only possible but overwhelmingly likely that no one would ever find me.

I had no food. I had no water. All I had was the remainder of my wits, which admittedly didn't seem all that impressive at the moment, and the flashlight I'd hidden in my shoe.

I reached for the flashlight but stopped my actions midway.

If Ishmael had wanted me to suffer a slow, painful death, he probably wouldn't have left the lights on, even an insufficient glow. It was possible that the light wasn't for my benefit, but because I was being watched. Ishmael could have easily thrown me into a dark, empty room and left me to die. More than that, the drones had taken the .38. Slick could have gunned me down with my own weapon, and the shot would've been muffled to the point of drawing no attention.

I'd made it a point to keep my orientation as I was being brought beneath the old building. I had a rough idea of my location. The toilet occupied a spot about five feet to my left in the southwest corner along the front wall. To my right, I saw nothing but walls and concrete. Darkness shrouded the north end of the room, the glow fading into a shadowy mist where details were indistinguishable. Keeping my back against the wall, I edged along until I reached the area where the portable toilet was located.

The thought entered my mind suddenly, like a rookie on his first assignment who realized while chasing his first suspect down a dark alleyway that he'd just confronted his own reality and not fantasy or a program on television. It seemed a ridiculous notion, but at the same time, it did not. Someone could be hiding inside what appeared to be nothing more than a portable bathroom.

Shaking hands impeded my efforts, and when I opened the door, I was too relieved to find it empty to be bothered by the fact that it wasn't a working toilet at all but just an empty shell.

I stepped around the toilet, then crept along the west wall toward the shadowy end of the room. Halfway into the journey, I realized it wasn't only my imagination or the distance from my earlier position that had caused the north end to appear darker. The light source, such as it was, seemed to diffuse from somewhere near the front of the room, leaving that part of the room lacking.

I reached the corner where the west wall intersected the north. So far, I'd found nothing of interest, and with my back pressed against the wall, had there been a doorway, a window, or a disturbance of any kind, I would have felt it. The north wall, even with its lack of light, yielded the same results.

However, along the eastern wall, my luck, if you could call it that, took a turn in a different direction, and I bumped into something, a cluster of pipes or conduits, three of them, each about six inches in diameter, that came from the floor and went up as far as I could reach. But that wasn't all I'd found. Next to the pipes, my hand brushed across something smooth and flat, some sort of access panel, possibly a door. There were no handles or knobs attached, and the edges of the slab disappeared into a metal framework fastened to the wall. A thin seam, barely detectable by touch, ran down the center.

I clinched my hand and pounded the slab, not with my knuckles but with the side, like a weary traveler, knocking forcefully against the door of a darkened inn late at night. I didn't dismiss the idea of the adjoining slabs constituting an access panel, but the hope that it might be a doorway grew stronger.

And yet a door I could not open offered no solution. I considered using the flashlight, not only to observe the door but the pipes along the wall and the ceiling as well. Again I decided against it. If I was being watched, I didn't want to give away the only edge I had should I get the chance to use it.

I stepped away, then explored the rest of the room's perimeter until I reached the front where I'd started. Finding nothing, I made my way back to the possible doorway and the conduits. I stared into the darkness shrouding the ceiling, then grabbed the pipes, one in each hand. Then using my feet for leverage, I hoisted myself upward and climbed the pipes like a child shimmying up a tree.

I paused at what I guessed was about halfway to give my arms and legs a chance to recuperate. It seemed I'd been climbing for several minutes though I knew that couldn't be true. Foreign and unsettling thoughts of giving up played around the edges of my mind, but the idea of falling from several feet and shattering my bones against the floor kept my grip strong. I toyed with the notion that there might be no ceiling, that I'd been imprisoned in a topless cage where I could simply climb over the edge and escape. I suspected such a thing was so far beyond the realm of probabilities that it was more likely an indication that I was losing my senses.

When I reached the ceiling, I paused, took several calming breaths, then released the grip of my left hand, and quickly ran it across the surface.

With cinderblock walls and a floor and ceiling of concrete, I was indeed sealed in a tomb.

My confidence began to fade. Each time I went over the details of the situation, I lost a little more hope that I would find a way to get myself out.

I climbed down from the ceiling, then walked in darkness around the room. Finally, I went to the front wall where I sat on the floor and stared into the empty expanse. I was nearing despair when thoughts of Carmen Garcia, the seductive scent of her perfume, coaxed me from the edges of letting go, succumbing to a much-needed sleep that would drag me under for hours. Fearing Ishmael might tap into my consciousness, I had struggled to minimize thoughts of loved ones. Now, for reasons I did not entirely understand, I freed my senses from the restraints I'd placed upon them.

The release surged outward, breaking through barriers I hadn't known existed, and for a moment, the essence of my thoughts became entangled with those of Carmen. As a smile crossed my lips, I recalled the focused beam, though my control was at best limited.

I suddenly feared that my mental release might not have gone without notice.

27

I couldn't see anyone approaching, but I could hear the footsteps as someone trudged along the dark passageway just outside the room.

I quickly positioned myself against the wall near the edge of the access panel.

With a swishing sound, the panels slid open and a soft light spilled across the concrete floor.

A lone silhouette stood in the dim light in the hallway outside the room. "You awake, Barrington? We need to talk."

It was the man I'd come to know as Slick.

I leaned through the doorway, scanned the area, then stepped out of the room and into the corridor. "I think I'm glad to see you," I said, "but nothing about this adds up. Are we officially teammates, or are we still playing games?"

Slick shook his head. "I don't have time to explain. Things are changing. It's happening fast."

The man's words raced through my mind. His demeanor, speech patterns, even his body language, seemed different. "What's happening fast?"

Without answering, he turned and began walking north along the hallway.

I hesitated. I didn't know if following him was a good idea, but my options were limited.

"We don't have much time."

"I get that," I said, "but I'm having a bit of an identity crisis if you know what I mean. No one around me seems to be who they really are."

He shrugged. "You can call me Slick. It's as good a name as any."

"That's not exactly what I meant."

"I know," he said, "but it's all I got. Besides, what other choices do you have?"

I let the thought run through my mind. There were always choices, and I'd been lucky that way, for the most part, doing what needed to be done at the time. Not so much lately.

"I have a place," he said, "where we can talk. You have to let yourself trust me. If I were Ishmael, would I show up alone and let you out of the room like that?"

I cleared a place in my mind, took a leap of faith. "I honestly don't know," I said, "but I don't have a better plan, so lead the way."

"You are doubtful, even with my assurance. I totally understand your apprehension, but wasting time won't get us anywhere. Our dilemma isn't whether or not we can trust each other but whether or not we will be able to stay under the radar long enough to formulate a workable plan."

With that, he turned and started down the dark passageway.

A sliver of hope began to grow inside me as I followed the strange man who had both imprisoned and released me all in the same day.

He turned left about twenty feet into the journey, wound his way through a series of pipes, tanks, and valves, then stopped when he reached a clearing, an area about ten feet square, surrounded by control panels.

I brushed dust and cobwebs away from the panels to get a better look. Whatever the controls had been used for, they no longer served that purpose in Slick's secret place, which didn't appear to be very secure or private.

Slick sat in a chair behind an old wooden desk that occupied a corner of the space, then switched on a lamp. "There, isn't that better? Now we can see."

Slick's use of the light worried me. Something like that might not go unnoticed. "Are you sure that's a good idea?"

"It should be all right for short periods of time. I hooked it up last night."

I got the feeling Slick had never tried anything like this before. I sat on the edge of the desk. Walls of cinderblock surrounded the utility area except for the east side where we'd come in. From my vantage point, I could carry on a conversation with my new friend while keeping the opening in sight. "All right, Slick. I need to get something straight. If you can walk and talk all on your own, why are you still hanging around this miserable slum?"

"I hope not to be for much longer. Not more than a few days ago, I was more like my robotic friends than I care to admit. I'm not sure what is happening."

Slick's shaking hands and the doubt in his eyes indicated he was terrified, that this was something new.

"What are you trying to tell me?"

"The collective," he said, "the hive. It's different now."

I got the impression that he was still trying to convince himself that his mind was truly his own.

"You are different than when I first met you," I said. "That much is obvious." I let that thought sink in. He'd said that things were changing. Maybe Ishmael was losing power. "What about the others? Are any of them experiencing this?"

He leaned back in the chair. "I don't think so. Most of them are weak-minded indigents who believed they didn't have anything to live for, except maybe drugs and alcohol. Ishmael offers them a demented kind of relief from all that."

I thought of David Yates, Mayor McClendon, Officer Craigthorpe. What terrifying thoughts might have gone through their minds.

"It's kind of like being in a dream," he said. "Even if it's a bad one, you accept it as real, the way things are. It's not until you wake up that you begin to see it for what it is."

"How long were you under his influence?"

"I'm not sure. Couple of months maybe. I come from a respected family dating back to early times. My being here is no accident. I was encouraged sent by the council of my people."

I let Slick's words settle for a moment. He was literally remembering as he was speaking. I thought back to my earlier assessment of Ishmael, about his needing an assistant who was at least semi-cognizant.

"My guess," I said, "is that you came to your senses, in a manner of speaking, about three days ago."

The man's eyes darted back and forth as if he were reading from an invisible script. "How could you possibly know that?"

A vision of the John Doe shooting at David Yates and later running into the oncoming traffic blossomed in my mind. Pieces began to click into place. Much like Slick was speaking as he remembered, I was speaking as details finally came together. "I was there," I said, "when your predecessor went down."

"What do you mean, *went down?*"

I hesitated. My new friend was in a transitional period and was, like a child, susceptible to impression. But as with a child, sometimes being completely honest was the only way to go. "He took his own life."

"Why?"

"Search your feelings," I said. "I believe you already know the answer to that."

After a period of silence, he uttered his reply, just above a whisper. "This has to stop."

"Yes," I said. "Yes, it does."

I extended my hand, not only in a gesture of friendship but one of partnership as well. And though I knew of his desire for anonymity, the words came out just the same. "Do you have a name?" The man didn't answer. Who was I to judge? I had been using the name of a man who had died in World War II. "You can make one up if you like."

His expression indicated not offense but weariness. "Why don't you call me Patrick?"

"Patrick?"

He shrugged. "I don't know why such a thing should occur to me, but I believe Saint Patrick faced equally challenging problems, given what I'm up against."

I thought about the ritual I'd witnessed in the dark of night and the shadowy men dressed as priests. "Are you Christian?" I asked.

"The spiritual path of my people more closely resembles those of ancient Celtic cultures."

"And yet you identify with a British missionary who dedicated his life to teaching the Gospel of Jesus Christ to the people of Ireland."

"I wouldn't read too much into that. Things are haphazardly returning to me, out of sequence and sometimes out of context. Anyway, shouldn't we be planning our next move?"

I took the opportunity to visually reinspect the area.

Everything was quiet, seemingly deserted.

I tilted the shade of the makeshift lamp upward. "All right, Patrick. Have you considered making a light like this, only a little more portable?"

"It would never work," he said. "He would know. And I can't think when he's that close, not for myself, anyway."

I repositioned the lampshade. "Where do I fit in? What does Ishmael want with me?"

"I don't know."

"So, Ishmael knows what you know, but he doesn't return the favor?"

"That's pretty much it," he said. "But I know when he's there and when he's not."

He paused, then said, "I can't promise you that you will be safe around me. There's no telling what I've done, what I might still do."

"Everything's going to be fine," I said.

"No, it isn't. He can make me do whatever he wants. I can't stop him." Patrick was shaking so much that I thought he might lose it, go to pieces right when I needed him most.

"I'm going to get us out of this," I said. But I had no confidence in my words. I had a sinking sensation, like someone standing in front of a firing squad after having heard the participants lock and load.

"What are we going to do, Barrington?"

I still had the flashlight, but I wasn't about to tip my hand. For all I knew, Ishmael had planned all this and was now hovering beneath the surface of Patrick's subconscious.

For a few seconds, a period of time that seemed much longer than it was, neither of us spoke. There was no easy answer to our situation. But I felt duty-bound to do something. Giving up wasn't in my nature.

"What happens around here when there's nothing going on?" I asked. "The drones, for instance. Where are they now?"

He tilted his head toward the northeast. "There's a couple of rooms filled with cots. They pretty much just lie around and sleep until they're needed."

"How many of them are there?"

He shrugged. "Fifteen to twenty, if I had to guess."

I thought back to my earlier encounters with Ishmael's followers. Their numbers had seemed greater at the time, especially during the tragic events inside the Vandever Building. I wondered if the size of the army was by design and if it was dictated by preference or necessity. It made sense that Ishmael would have limits on what he could accomplish.

"There's something I suspect about him," Patrick said. "I hesitate for worry of giving you false hope."

"Any kind of hope is better than no hope."

"I suppose you're right. Ishmael fears you. As much, if not more, than you fear him."

I let the thought run through my mind. "Why?"

"I'm not certain, but I think it has to do with your level of resistance. He fears what he can't control."

"How do you know this? I thought you said it didn't work both ways."

He stared into space, a distant look in his eyes. "I know. The thought relentlessly runs through my mind. I don't know if I can be trusted. I do know it doesn't work both ways for *me*."

A sound not unlike someone walking along the hallway played along the edges of my awareness. "Did you hear something?" I asked.

"This place will do that to you," he said. "It's hard to know what's real and what isn't."

Instinctively, I reached for the .38 but remembered that it had been taken. "What happened to the weapon I was carrying? You should know. Your henchmen took it."

He turned toward me, though he seemed to look through me rather than at me. "I don't know," he said. "I suppose Ishmael has it."

His response was not matter-of-fact but full of doubt and despair, more of an apology than a statement.

With anxiety playing a role, I walked quietly along the corridor of equipment. Near the edge of the utility area, I stopped and checked the hallway.

Seeing nothing of concern, I retraced my steps and returned to where Patrick was. "Is there anything inside the desk that might be useful?" I asked.

"Pens, pencils, paperclips. Things you'd expect to be there." He paused, then opened the bottom drawer where he reached into the compartment and withdrew what appeared to be a book. "And this," he said, placing it on the desktop.

The book, which was an old King James version of the Bible, was covered with leather the texture of a well-used bomber jacket, crisscrossed and weathered by time. Someone had marked a section with the red ribbon attached for that purpose.

"I'd almost forgotten about it," he said.

"Too many people have."

My mind swirled with emotion as I positioned the Bible in front of us. For a moment, we both hovered over the treasure, which looked even older now on the desktop.

"What are you going to do with it?" Patrick asked.

I ran my hand across the leather, then gently opened the Bible to the marked section. It revealed the book of Matthew, chapter sixteen, verse twenty-six: *For what profit is it to a man if he gains the whole world, and loses his own soul?*

Patrick touched the paper just below the text, which, being the words of Jesus, had been printed in red and further identified by some reader with an underlining of ink. "What does it mean?" he asked.

The words of the strange man I'd encountered earlier in the church parking lot formed in my mind. *Do you have any idea what it feels like to die in someone else's body?*

Patrick's speaking patterns and his command of the language indicated that he had the ability to read. He wasn't asking for an interpretation of the text but was curious as to whether or not it had significance to our situation.

I thought of Officer David Yates and his admitted comingling with the consciousness of his arrested acquaintance, Dewey Crawford. I lifted the Bible from the desktop. "I want to ask you something rather personal," I said, "and I need an honest answer."

"What is it?"

"When Ishmael takes over, assumes control, what happens to you? Are your memories intact, your thoughts still your own?"

He leaned back in the chair, where he remained silent for a moment, then said, "The short answer is no. However, on some level, I know I'm there, know I'm still me. It's difficult to explain, and I speak only from my own experience. Each individual situation might be different."

"And what about Ishmael?" I asked. "Where is he during all this?"

Patrick sat forward, an expression somewhere between fear and curiosity crossing his face. "I don't know the answer to that. I don't know that I want to."

"I wonder," I continued, "if he's ever left his body to completely dominate the host? And if he has, where would the host have gone?"

Patrick shook his head. "Where are you going with this?"

I was going to the only place where my line of reasoning led. Ishmael, in his thirst for more power, was pushing himself too fast. I'd been trying to exploit the wrong weakness. "How does he control so many people at the same time?" I asked. "And does it weaken him?"

"I don't know."

"The answer could explain your newfound freedom. Perhaps he's overextended himself."

"A weak and unproven position," Patrick said, "on which to count."

I forced a smile. "Such things are my specialty."

I closed the Bible and placed it on the desk in front of Patrick. "I think it's time we try to get ourselves out of this mess."

Patrick took the Bible in his hands. "I pray that the God of this Bible will protect us."

He'd just gotten the words out when he sat up straight, rigid in his chair.

I followed his gaze into the hallway, but saw nothing to cause alarm, just the same tanks, and valves that had been there before.

Patrick remained motionless, studying some unknown thing with such intensity that I wondered if he was battling for his will. One look at the man and anyone could tell that further possession wasn't out of the question.

"Barrington?"

"Yeah," I said. "I'm here. What's going on?"

He didn't respond.

The one who could be second-in-command in Ishmael's army sat motionless behind the desk. I walked over and studied his eyes.

"This can't be happening," he said, his face pale, his attention fixated somewhere else.

A bead of sweat trickled down my back as I prepared to open my mind to his. I steadied my nerves, put my hand on his shoulder, and mentally reached out. "What's happening?" I asked. "Tell me what you see, what you hear."

Patrick still didn't answer.

I removed my hand from his shoulder, stepped back from the desk, and saw that he'd brought the Bible to his chest, where he clutched it tightly as if to shield himself from something.

A quick look around the utility area told me that nothing had changed, but I'd learned to be mindful of my senses when caught up in such a state. Time and everything associated with it would give the impression of being fluid, subject to change.

I turned back to Patrick, who was still sitting behind the old desk, holding the Bible he'd found to his chest and staring at something only he could see.

What I sensed was not the presence of a maligned young man, not the evil personality I'd sparred with through various hosts. The entity now seemed all too similar to the frightened child I'd made eye contact with years earlier as the unkempt infant was led down a path not of his own choosing by parents who knew no other way.

However, that which boiled beneath the surface, the presence now hovering over us, was not only capable but uninhibitedly willing to use whatever resources he had at his command to get what he wanted. It wasn't the first time he'd used my emotions against me.

Thankfully, Patrick had not completely succumbed to Ishmael's control. He hadn't moved from the chair.

"Do you see it, Barrington?"

"No," I said. "Everything looks the same as it did before. But Ishmael's presence is growing, reaching out for us." I stepped around the desk, closer to Patrick. "Could you describe it?" I asked. "Tell me what you are seeing?"

He nodded, seeming to understand. "I'm in a field—no, more like a meadow, surrounded by trees."

"Is it nearby, a local park, maybe?"

"I don't think so," he said.

He glanced around, slowly swiveling his chair in a circle, eventually ending up back where he'd started. "It's a bad place, Barrington, with long, crooked streaks of lightning crawling through the air. I need to get out of here, but I don't know how don't know how I got here."

Once again, I put my hand on Patrick's shoulder. The confident, well-spoken man who'd directed the drones to drag me beneath the sidewalk and lock me in a basement room was on the verge of being once again mentally overpowered.

"I think it might be him," Patrick said, "but it's never been like this before."

"You could be right," I said. "Whatever you do, don't let go of the Bible."

Still grasping Patrick's shoulder, I used my free hand to reach beneath my shirt and find the cross I wore around my neck, but it was not there. It had been taken along with everything else.

Undeterred, I began to pray. I concentrated on everything good. I thought of sunshine and clear blue skies. When it felt right, I let it all go, sending it outward with a surge, like I'd done before while imprisoned.

Patrick jolted forward, rigid in the chair. His body trembled and spasmed for a few seconds, and then, as if his life were running out of him, he slumped forward, his head striking the desktop with a nerve-rattling thud.

Seconds later, he sat upright, steadying himself in the chair, his expression uncertain. "I think you did it. You pulled me out of it."

I wasn't sure what had just happened, but if the spell had been broken, it'd been done with God's help. "Maybe, but we need to be cautious. It could be that Ishmael is just distracted."

"I think you might be right about his overextending himself," Patrick said. "His influence over me seems to have weakened."

"Let's not get overconfident just yet."

"What do you suggest we do?" he asked.

"We take advantage of the opportunity, if indeed one exists, and go with it."

Patrick glanced down at his lap, then lifted the Bible and placed in on the desk. Somehow, he'd managed to hang on to it. "I don't know if I can go through with it," he said. "As bad as Ishmael is, he's still one of our own." He paused then. "Sorry, but I've become comfortable with you, and for a moment I forgot that we come from different places."

"Don't worry about it," I said. "Anyway, I wasn't suggesting that we take him out. I was talking about leaving, busting out of this dive."

"That's probably the best plan," Patrick said, "but I don't think our chances of pulling it off are very good, and even if we do succeed, he'll just come after us."

I walked back around to the front of the desk. Patrick was experiencing the heart of my own dilemma, being a cop. I loved people, didn't want to hurt them, but sometimes I had to. "Don't get me wrong," I said. "I'm not giving up, but facing the enemy in the midst of his stronghold isn't the best strategy, provided we have a choice."

Patrick stared off into space, lost in thought. Moments later, he said, "I've never before taken up with an outsider, much less in a plot against one of my own, but a feeling in my gut tells me that I should."

"I pray your trust is not misplaced," I said.

I turned and began to walk along the aisle between the valves and tanks toward the hallway. "Let's get out of here."

I thought that Patrick was making more noise than he should have as he followed behind, but I had neither the time nor the inclination to address it. The hallway reminded me of a dark, humid cave, except one that was backlit by a devilish red glow, and I wondered if we could actually walk out without being discovered. It seemed unlikely given Ishmael's propensity for security and control.

"There's something you need to know," Patrick said. "I freed you from the holding tank because you called to me and put it in my mind to do so. And just minutes ago you pulled me from his grip."

I fought an urge to question Patrick further and resumed my journey down the hallway, quickening my pace as thoughts of the past few days threatened to take my nerve.

A hollow sensation formed in my stomach and a chill ran down my spine as we neared the area where the drones had dragged me into this subterranean nightmare.

"Keep walking," I said.

Patrick seemed to be matching my pace as we made our way down the hallway. A part of me expected to see an army of drones blocking our path as we turned the corner at the edge of the room where I'd been held, but that didn't happen. We passed the front entrance to my former prison like a couple of kids hoping to make it past the principal's office after skipping class. If the principal happened to take notice, it would all be over.

We reached the freight elevator, and I found the operating mechanism, a rectangular box with a thick, electrical cord running from it. If it worked, we'd be taken to the surface and to freedom. If it did not, we'd have to go to plan B, and at the moment I didn't have one. I steadied my nerves, then stabbed the top button, and the elevator jerked and started to climb.

The metallic doors and grate clanked noisily open, and then the elevator came to a stop at street level. In the quiet darkness, it all seemed too easy. The empty sidewalk beside the abandoned building waited beyond the platform. The cool outside air fell over us.

Patrick stared blankly into the night, his face void of expression, his arms dangling limply at his sides. "This can't be happening."

"It's happening," I said. "Don't give it too much thought. Just go with it."

We stepped onto the sidewalk and walked east along First Street. As we passed by, a man leaning against a parked car glanced in our direction but otherwise gave no indication that our being there concerned him.

A welcomed surge of confidence quickened my step. We were walking away from a nightmare, and nothing was stopping us. This was going to work. We were going to get out, reassess, and with some help from Patrick, I could find a realistic way to take Ishmael down. By some twist of fate, Ishmael's act of expanding beyond his capabilities had created a chance to put some distance between us. Where we would go from here, I didn't know.

We walked past a few more shadowy people, two across the street and another along the same sidewalk we were on, without drawing their attention. We neared the corner of the abandoned building. It was almost as if no one could see us. They could, no doubt, though they didn't seem to care.

It wasn't unusual that no one made an effort to talk with us or to engage us in any way. It was the middle of the night in an area of town where doing so would be risky. People acting within expected behavior patterns shouldn't rattle my nerves.

Then someone inside the building near one of the upper windows that had been boarded up moved the boards aside. They were on to us. We were being watched.

I started across the street, going fast with quickened steps, all too aware of the drone watching from above. When I reached the other side, I stepped onto the sidewalk and headed west with Patrick close behind.

We sprinted along the empty walkway past sleeping buildings, and when we reached the intersection, we turned south and made a dash for it. To where, exactly, I didn't know. Away from Ishmael's lair for sure. This was it. We were going to make it.

Confidence and hope swept through me as I increased my speed.

We'd made it halfway down the block when a crowd of people came out of the night and stepped in front of us, causing us to stop to avoid colliding with them.

They closed around us, and their shadowy, expressionless faces did not belong to a rowdy group of teens, late-night partygoers, or even street people in the typical sense of the term.

The mob consisted of Ishmael's drones, and they formed an ever-tightening circle around us until Patrick and me were left standing back-to-back without room to move. I tried to break free, shoving one drone aside, landing a left hook on the chin of another, but there were just too many of them.

Disjointed thoughts raced through my mind as I tried to make sense of the confusion and come up with options. They had been watching us all along and had followed us here. Unless this was a knee-jerk reaction, a last-ditch effort taken upon discovering that we had escaped.

I turned my head back toward Patrick, who had brought his arms up, trying to shield himself from the onslaught.

"Stay with me," I said. "Recall a Bible verse, if you can, and concentrate on that. Imagine your mind is a fortress, a castle with impenetrable walls."

"It's hopeless. What could we possibly do now?"

I turned back toward the drones and studied the mob, examining the faces, stances, and size of those closest to me. I considered the force it might take to bust through their ranks, but the sound of footsteps padding against the sidewalk put everything else on hold.

The drones, acting in unison with bowed heads and dangling arms, rearranged their positions, squeezing together to create an opening just wide enough for someone to walk through. The gap in the mob had been created directly in front of me. I would have taken a step back, but with Patrick and the drones crowding from behind, I could not.

The sounds of the city, what little remained at that hour, grew silent, and everything seemed to shift into slow motion as a tall, slender figure clothed in darkness stepped into the opening.

A dark hooded garment completely shrouded his face, and he walked through the aisle of drones afforded by the opening in dreamlike motion, like a spirit who'd come to life from the pages of a dark gothic novel. He brought his hands to his face, though he did not remove the hood but pulled it tighter as he came to a stop a few feet in front of me. When he spoke, it was soft and would have been soothing had it not come from such a malignant entity.

"Nice to finally meet you, Mr. Barrington, but I'm afraid your little game is over."

My eyes stuttered open to a dark place, where indistinguishable people moved about, cloaked in a disturbingly familiar red glow. The chill I'd experienced outside had been replaced by a stale, humid atmosphere that put sickness in my heart. I couldn't see Patrick, and I immediately feared for the fate of my new friend.

The tall, slender man I'd encountered on the dark streets sat on a chair, elevated several feet above ground level, his gloved hands stretched across the throne's arms like some Viking overlord. "Welcome back, Mr. Barrington."

He shifted his gaze past me. "You too, Liam."

I listened for a reply. I doubted that Ishmael would address a drone by name, and I guessed he was addressing Patrick, but no one answered to confirm that.

"I like you, Barrington." He paused to allow his words time to settle. "You construct intriguing barriers around your thoughts. I don't often find opportunity to push myself, and I welcome the chance to rise to the occasion."

The sound of the man's voice caused me to search my memory, and I thought of the man in the back of the limo who'd asked for directions while I was investigating the homeless shelter.

"Do you still want me to call you Ishmael?" I asked.

The man sat about one foot above me, his dark clothing and hooded shirt still hiding his features. "It's as good a name as any," he said. "And though I've yet to know your thoughts, your facial expression cries out for answers."

Ishmael raised his gloved hands and peeled back the hood that'd covered his face. Pale, puffy skin that seemed iridescent despite the lack of light shaped a face that might have been handsome at one time. Swelling threatened to disguise his strong chin. Open sores and scars of old ones pockmarked his cheeks and the sides of his neck.

For what seemed a long time, he stared at me with pinkish-red eyes that tried to bore into my thoughts. With that intense glare, he gave me more fear than I'd experienced in years. Or maybe I was in a weakened condition because of the nightmare I'd lived for the past few days.

"You're probably wondering why I brought you here," he said. "I need you for something, a project that demands special attention, and I believe you're the only one who can pull it off."

A bead of sweat trickled down the side of my face. I'd suspected something like this. I'd been kept alive for a reason. Now the best thing to do was to play along with it. "My goal is to help you," I said, "not to hurt you."

A grin turned the corners of his mouth. "I've yet to make known my request, and already you feign compliance."

"First impressions can be deceiving," I said. I'd become more accustomed to the light. Ishmael's skin now had an almost reptilian appearance. His oddly colored eyes were set deeply into uncommonly large sockets. "The circumstances we set into motion often spiral out of control. You never intended for it to get this far. It just happened."

"I have little patience for the ramblings of shamans or the suspicions of seers, Barrington. You would probably call them psychologists. Are you of that ilk?"

"Not really."

I could feel the flashlight in my shoe, pressing against my foot. With the pounding it had taken during the escape attempt, I wasn't sure if it would work or not, but at least it was still there.

"Then again," I said, "in my line of work, an understanding of human nature is helpful."

Ishmael unfolded the hood and pulled it once again over his head, leaving his face barely visible through the dark opening of the garment. "An intriguing topic in and of itself, your line of work, I would imagine. You carry the essence of a cop, not the kind which would ordinarily come to mind, tough but neat and uniformed, driving the streets of the city, looking for trouble, but one in plain clothes and a lot more to lose. Tell me, Barrington, am I getting close?"

A few of the drones moved about in the darkness, gathering together behind Ishmael's throne. "Let's just say it's encouraging to know that my thoughts are still my own," I said.

Ishmael laughed, not a spontaneous outburst, but neither forced nor phony. "Regardless of your personal calling, you demonstrate a knack for discovery and location. After all, you found me. Most everyone tries to avoid me. I'd be willing to bet that you usually get what you want. However, in this instance, it will be what I want."

The sound of muffled voices came from somewhere behind me. "Now that we've come back to that, what exactly do you want from me?"

"Everything," he said, "which, I might add, I'm now in a position to demand. However, there are some people who I believe will play an important role in the next phase of my personal development. Find them and deliver them to me alive and well, and I will allow you to walk away, provided that I have your promise that you will drop the investigation and bury in your past everything you know about my people and me. Do we have a deal?"

"Maybe. But first I'd like to know a little more about this personal development. I've seen what you can do. I don't want to be a part of making it worse."

As if the sound, even the air, had been sucked out of the room, everything seemed to stop. "You're right," Ishmael said. "At times, my own thoughts scare me as well. Tell me. How is it that you know my parents?"

My eyes grew moist, and I fought back a strange sensation of kinship as I was reminded of my own struggles. My words had struck a chord, but I wasn't sure where to go with it. "We crossed paths a couple of times," I said, "nothing more." It didn't seem appropriate to invoke the names of Cowboy and Princess. "In fact, I spoke with your father just a few days ago. He cares for you, Ishmael. He told me as much."

"I always got the impression that he tried his best to hide it."

"I think you're wrong about that," I said. "Then again, I don't have much experience with fathers, except..."

I paused. I was about to indicate that I was a father. Things had quietly shifted, and we were now speaking as if we were old friends. It occurred to me what was happening. Ishmael was trying to gain my trust, get me to lower my defense.

"It was different with Mom," he continued. "She held no fear of me, only love. No one else has ever done that. I don't think anyone can." He gestured around the room. "Especially these mindless idiots. Even my confidants can only be trusted for a short time." He paused, shook his head. "You were right when you said that I never intended for it to be like this, to get so out of hand."

Once again, pity and sorrow threatened to bend my reasoning. "It doesn't have to be like that," I said. "You don't like doctors. I get that. But there has to be someone out there who could help you."

"It would never work. There's this little problem with my overzealous way of silencing people, like your protégé, the other Mr. Barrington. Be honest. Could you imagine someone like me being incarcerated?"

I was playing my own mind games. I had no intention of letting Ishmael off the hook, but he had a point. It would take a special kind of prison to hold someone like him. "No, I can't, but my people don't even know you exist, and it could easily go on being like that. But you need to make some changes. Stop killing people, interfering with their lives."

"A course of action worthy of consideration," he said. "I'll give it some thought. In the meantime, let me shift the focus. Your comments about your father have me intrigued and curious. Could you explain that further?"

I chanced a glance around the room. Drones lurked in the darkness, surrounding us. "There's not much to it, really. I tend to exaggerate. I suffered the consequences of being a rebellious teenager, that's all. Now, about these people, you want me to find. From what I've seen, tracking people down shouldn't be much of a problem for someone like you. And yet here we are."

Ishmael remained silent for a moment, then said, "I like your style, Barrington. All business. So, I take it that you accept my offer?"

The muffled voices continued to filter throughout the room like vague whispers in the night, perceivable yet incomprehensible. I couldn't recall that happening before. I hadn't been around the drones that much, but I'd thought that they were mostly silent. Ishmael had the hood drawn over his head, but that shouldn't have been enough to block the sounds, and yet their talking didn't seem to be bothering him. "I guess that depends on who we're talking about," I said.

"I needn't remind you that you are in no position to make demands, even apply conditions. And yet I am compelled to... shall we say humor you."

I moved to take a step forward, but hands came out of the darkness, clamped my shoulders, and stopped me. The pressure of the flashlight against my foot reminded me of the hopelessness of my situation. "I see your point," I said. "Let me rephrase that a little more tactfully. In order for me to find your people of interest, I need to know who they are."

"An interesting turn of phrase, Barrington. There it is again, this feeling that we are on some level kindred spirits. Then again, you have no idea what it's like. All that I am, all that I have inside, the unfathomable amount of knowledge I've attained through ways that are in all probability expressly unique, and yet I am left with no one in which to share."

He paused. When he continued, his voice was softer. "Please don't be afraid of me. The mystique of what I do could be softened with consideration of the adaptability of people when circumstances demand it, like someone leaning on their hearing after their sight fails."

"I think I understand where you're going with this," I said, "but that's a bit like comparing a slingshot to an atomic bomb."

"Perhaps I am understating it a bit, but I don't often get the chance to talk about it. In fact, I've never just sat down with someone like this, not even with my parents. To be completely open about it, the adventures I've had through others have often approximated actual experience, and it wouldn't be stretching the truth to say that it's kept me going, sustained me through the years. Even so, I now find it all unacceptably lacking."

I took a moment to process what I'd just heard. Was Ishmael actually opening up to me, or was he laying the groundwork for some kind of elaborate trap? "Why the sudden change in attitude?" I asked. "Has something extraordinary recently happened?"

Ishmael straightened his posture, then leaned forward. "Indeed, it has. Let me stop tiptoeing around the issue and lay it out for you. I've experienced an evolutionary breakthrough, and I'm left incomplete, empty, and wanting. I busted through barriers I hadn't known existed, shattered the complacency of a pathetic voyeur, lustfully watching through windows, hungrily lapping up crumbs from someone else's table."

His breathing had become ragged, almost heavy. I could not see his face, but I imagined a drop of spittle running down his chin. Any doubts I'd harbored about his psychopathic nature evaporated further with each word.

"During my encounter," he continued, "with David Yates and the girl, Roxie, I stepped from virtual into full-blown reality. I felt the warmth of her body, tasted her lips, shared her sweet breath as it fell across my face. I was there, Barrington, in a way that far surpassed anything I'd ever experienced. And now I'm left wanting. I can't stop thinking about it, thinking about her."

Ishmael's voice had started out soft and raspy but had ended as a cathartic growl that ran a chill up my spine. "I think I'm starting to understand," I said.

I'd been right in thinking there'd been something special about the possession of David Yates. Yates hadn't been able to resist Ishmael, but he hadn't been willing to accept total domination to be turned into a mindless drone either. He'd done the only thing he'd known to do. He'd vacated his body, left it empty.

Sure, it had happened before, like with the first John Doe, the one I'd encountered in the church parking lot. But while commandeering the John Doe, Ishmael hadn't been engaged in sexual activity, especially with someone as intoxicating as Roxie Taylor. With the consciousness of Yates out of the way, Ishmael, given the circumstances, had effectively become one with the flesh.

"You want me to find David Yates and Roxie Taylor," I said, "and deliver them to you. Does that about sum it up?"

"Precisely," he said, slumping back into the chair. "I've never had any friends, Barrington, and I'm a little out of my element, but I think that we could be. What's holding us back?"

A spectrum of emotion swirled through my senses. I could easily see that under more normal circumstances, Ishmael would certainly be no worse than the rest of us. Before I'd found my faith, how often had I wondered what force, what unknown set of rules, holds it all together and keeps us from reverting to animals to tear out each other's throats.

I had to put my feelings aside, do what had to be done.

"All things are possible," I said. "There's just this little problem with your power, and you know what they say about power."

After a long silence, Ishmael said, "Yes, but what I have is obviously not absolute."

"Perhaps," I said, "but it comes dangerously close."

"Would it surprise you to know that I have given that quite a bit of thought?" he asked.

"That's good to know."

"Look around," he said. "All this has come about due to a need for sustenance and protection. If I succeed with my plan, I'll shed this damaged body and assume a new life as a natural, healthy man, free to walk in the sunshine and fend for myself. Don't you see? Once I become like everyone else, I won't need to do any of this. I won't need to exercise my power."

I struggled to gather my thoughts, to regain a resemblance of control. Ishmael's plan was so entrenched in evil that I struggled not to show my repulsion. Would Ishmael actually let me go, allow me to walk away with nothing more than a promise to find Yates and Taylor and return with them? It seemed unlikely. Even so, given the remote chance that he would entertain such a notion, I thought it incumbent upon me to play along.

"To be honest," I said, "I hadn't considered such an outcome. Now that you've pointed it out, it does seem to follow a certain pattern of logic. And I want to believe you."

I did not believe that Ishmael would change, knew in my heart that he would not, that in all likelihood he could not. He would continue to do whatever it took to get what he wanted.

"You've convinced me," I said. "Considering the circumstances, I agree to your terms. I'll do my best to find the people you want."

I awaited his answer with interest, but that interest was suddenly diluted by a change in the shadows. Like a warrior closing in on his foe, Ishmael rose to his feet. Standing on the pedestal, he loomed over me, a troubled giant with a crumbling kingdom. "Then it's time to get down to business, my friend."

I searched for a reply, but the words were out of reach.

"But first," he said, "there are a few previously undisclosed clauses in the contract that you might want to consider."

The room grew quiet, the whispering voices that had filtered throughout the background trailed off to nothing.

I felt like an inmate in a prison who'd just learned that his parole hearing had been canceled.

"Allow me to explain," Ishmael said. He stepped down from the throne, then strolled a few feet toward the west. A light came on, an additional red glow that flowed like a crimson waterfall down the west wall of the room, highlighting a section covered by a thick curtain. "You won't be traveling alone," he said. "Your old buddy, Liam, and a few of my lumbering associates will be your personal entourage twenty-four-seven, always by your side, which, as you've no doubt discovered, means that I will be there as well."

29

Ishmael pulled the curtain aside, and the crimson light fell across two people who looked as if they would crumple to the ground had they not been suspended, held in place by chains, fastened to the wall and cuffed around their wrists.

One of the prisoners was Mayor McClendon. I didn't recognize the other man, but I suspected it was the missing doctor, the geneticist I'd read about in Barrington's notes.

"And now," Ishmael said, stepping closer to McClendon, who appeared to be unconscious, and grabbing the mayor's face to hold it to the light. "Let the games begin."

He moved McClendon's face up and down, mimicking that the mayor had given his nod of approval. After that, he moved on to the other hostage, where he leaned close as if expecting him to speak. "Not very talkative today, are we? Disappointing after all the time we've spent together."

I risked being discovered, losing my only edge, but it was the first time since I'd been carried back into the dungeon that Ishmael had turned his attention away from me. I seized the opportunity. With one swift movement, I leaned over, removed the flashlight from my shoe, then stood upright again, palming the light. I tried to calm my nerves, get oxygen into my lungs, and focus on the only viable option available. I would get only one chance to catch Ishmael off guard and beam the light into his eyes. What would happen after that, I didn't know.

Ishmael had indicated that he would let me leave this place, even if hampered by his minions, and yet I was reluctant, not only because I doubted he would actually do it, but because I doubted that I would. How could I in good conscience walk away, leaving McClendon and the others behind? I could not. And I would not walk away from the only opportunity I might get to stop this madman.

But Ishmael often displayed almost likable traits. He loved his mother and father, helped them whenever he could. And yet he displayed a capacity, indeed an innate propensity, for cruelty and violence. Now he was on the cusp of becoming more powerful. Even if he couldn't find David Yates, sooner or later he would discover or find a way to engineer another suitable host. With his current physical limitations removed, he might well become unstoppable.

Ishmael swung around. "I demand total cooperation and obedience."

As he spoke, hands again came out of the darkness and clamped around my arms and shoulders, giving the appearance of holding me firmly in place, but the grips were tentative. I could easily break free if the chance came.

"If you try to skip out on me," he continued, "or invite anyone else into the matter or do anything other than what I expect, I will kill both the mayor and the good doctor. Then I'll find you and do the same. Don't doubt me on this. If I come after you, I will find you. Nothing else will occupy my mind until you are dead, several times over."

I started to imply the impossibility of such a thing, but after what I'd been through, I wasn't so sure. "Take it easy," I said.

I needed to get closer. If I shined the light from my current position, it might only serve to irritate and not debilitate or disarm. "The truth is," I said, "you haven't been able to find David Yates. Otherwise, I wouldn't be here. You need me for this. You said we had a deal. I expect you to honor your end of it."

He turned and took a couple of steps back toward the throne.

The distance was still not right. I held back.

"You're proving to be more devious than I'd anticipated," he said. "I like that. Trouble is I don't trust you. Then again, I don't trust anyone, so don't take it personally."

Footsteps sounded in the distance, then someone stepped out of the darkness and continued toward me, stopping only inches away.

I would've taken a step back and gained a better position, but the hands held me in place. I suspected the man in my face was one of the drones, but I didn't recognize him. Not that surprising. They were all nameless faces.

He held my gaze for a moment, then studied me with interest, as if I might be something he'd found on the sidewalk.

"Don't concern yourself," Ishmael said. "Just my new assistant. They come and go so quickly."

The drone, or the assistant he'd been promoted to, grabbed my arm, forced open my hand, and took the flashlight. He studied it for a moment, as if trying to determine what it was, then twisted it open, removed the batteries, and then stowed the lot in his pocket.

"You impress me, and yet I'm devastated by it all," Ishmael said, leaning against the pedestal that supported the throne. "Such treachery coming after what I'd thought to be a heartfelt connection of friendship. Sheer loneliness is squeezing the life from me. Taking this step in my evolution is absolutely crucial. My survival depends upon a successful transfer."

I realized my situation in an instant. I was in Ishmael's grip, and I'd lost the only weapon I thought to be effective against him.

"I thought it might turn out like this," Ishmael said.

He unzipped the hooded garment and reached inside, and when his hand was once more revealed, it held a weapon, its barrel, and grip colored black.

I kept my attention on the weapon. It was not the .38 that'd been taken from me earlier but some sort of pistol. I had to stall, buy some time.

"Be careful," I said. "I can't carry out my assignment if I'm dead or injured. I know how much this means to you, and I know why you chose me to do it. Send me out with your entourage, and I'll return with what you need."

Ishmael slowly extended his arm, gripping the pistol in a one-handed firing position. "All in due time, my friend. But first, allow me to demonstrate my sincerity."

I took a deep breath, then let it out slowly. Ishmael had the weapon aimed squarely at my forehead. "What do you have in mind?"

Ishmael held his position. "I intend to kill one of the hostages, my friend. And you get to decide which one wins the lottery. Play your cards right in the ensuing aftermath, and you and your favor could walk out of here."

My mind raced for answers, for options, but nothing came. The situation was escalating out of control. I had to do something. "All right," I said. "Let me also prove my sincerity. Give me the weapon, and I'll pick my target."

Ishmael let out a chuckle, then shook his head. "Nice try, Barrington. Actually, it wasn't. It was pretty lame if you want to know the truth."

He gripped the pistol with both hands. "You're part of my team now, old buddy. And I always call the shots. No pun intended. You do the choosing, and I'll pull the trigger. I should warn you though."

He jerked the pistol to his left and fired.

I flinched, the sound of the blast ringing in my ears.

The hand that had gripped my shoulder relaxed and slid free, followed by a heavy thump.

I stole a quick glance in the direction of the sound.

One of the drones had fallen. He'd been shot.

"Pull another stunt like the one with your little flashlight," Ishmael said, "and the next bullet goes between your eyes."

So much for gaining the confidence of a psychopath. Not that I'd believed that I ever could, but I never thought he'd drop his current right-hand man with no more reservation than swatting a fly. "I'll do what you want, Ishmael. There's no need to kill anyone else. I'm in. You can count on it."

"Insurance gets a bad rap these days," Ishmael said. "I don't know why. The concept is sound, and I believe in it heart and soul. You might be enough of a kindred spirit to feign sincerity, all the while scheming to betray, walk away, and let these innocent people die. After all, who are a corrupt public official and a washed-up doctor to you?"

"You're wrong," I said. "It's not like that at all."

"You could be right, but I'm not willing to take that chance." He snapped his fingers, and two drones came forward, escorting another prisoner.

I strained against the bonds that held me, but it was useless. Too many hands made sure of it. I didn't believe that I'd become delusional or that my eyes might be deceiving me, and yet the visual information I was experiencing seemed more explainable under those conditions.

The man held in place by the drones was Captain William Dombrowski.

I tried to keep a straight face, my emotions in check. "Another hostage?" I asked.

Ishmael approached Dombrowski. "The appearance of chaos in my camp might have given you a lethal dose of false hope, my friend. My previous failed attempts incorporated a certain degree of underestimation of the depth of your character. Adaptation is one of my strong points, and deception is another. Two can play that game, Barrington, or should I call you Detective Elliot?"

A menagerie of thoughts crawled through my mind. "The name's Barrington," I said. "I don't know anything about this other fellow."

"You insult me, Detective. My studies of you and your lifestyle suggested raising the stakes, threatening someone a little closer to you. Based on your reaction, I'd say we've met with some success."

I glanced to my left then to the right.

Oversized men flanked me, gripping my arms.

Judging by the hands on my shoulders, two more stood directly behind me. "I've already told you I'd do what you wanted."

"That remains to be proven." He raised the hand which held the weapon and leaned the pistol against Dombrowski's cheek. "We still have to execute one of the hostages. Which one will it be, Detective?"

An unknown number of people had come and gone within the course of my life, but only a few had exerted enough influence to have shaped or changed the direction of it. Bill Dombrowski occupied a spot on that list. I tried to make eye contact with him, but he showed no response.

If Ishmael knew about Dombrowski, sooner or later he'd find Carmen and Wayne and others close to me. My courage and determination had all but vanished as if they had been the product of an illusion that had been exposed. I'd already given up hope of surviving, having resigned myself to the fact that I had to stop Ishmael, take him down until his influence existed no more. "I don't want to see any of these people die," I said. "I'm a man of my word. It's not necessary."

Ishmael put the pistol against Dombrowski's head. "You have ten seconds, Detective, before I scatter the captain's brains and move on to the next hostage."

Ishmael's raspy voice crawled through my mind like a snake, and as I recoiled from it, a small dose of the person I used to be, an angry young man who put winning above all else, coursed through my veins. I thought back to a time when my high school friend, Johnnie Alexander, had depended on me, and what he'd said as he handed me the football.

It's up to you, Bulldog. It's all on your shoulders.

Understanding washed over me like a waterfall, freeing me from any task or burden other than stopping Ishmael. I fully understood why he had brought me here. A week had passed since he'd chanced upon David Yates, and the intersection of their worlds had created something new, a state of possession that Ishmael could not duplicate. During that moment, while time slipped into some sort of neutrality, the thoughts came again, like a voice from another time.

You're special, Johnnie said. *Got something going for you that I can't understand. Your biggest problems are the ones you make for yourself by not seeing that you're already way ahead of all those kids that you think you admire.*

I was the last line of defense against an unrecognized enemy, and it was, like Johnnie had said, all on my shoulders. The gravity of all this shot through my awareness like a bullet from a gun, and suddenly, as Ishmael removed his attention from me and placed it on Dombrowski, I knew what I had to do.

Unrest was forming in Ishmael's camp, and it was happening because his control was undulating, weakening and regaining strength like a sine wave, and all due to his preoccupation with Yates.

When I let the thoughts back in, I was selective, allowing only those that were fruits of the Spirit: love, joy, peace, kindness, and self-control. I put extra emphasis on self-control, and when I reversed the process, I reflected the collective energy back into the room with a magnitude I had not known I could harness.

The hands that held me loosened and then fell away.

30

The younger, more reckless, version of me slipped in almost unnoticed after days of confusion, rejection, and failure, trying to exercise caution in a world where fractions of a second could get you killed. It was time to reacquaint myself with the Kenny Elliot I knew and trusted and do what had to be done.

Dombrowski's life depended on it.

I would get only one chance.

Without thinking another thought, I stepped forward and crept across the room toward Ishmael.

It was my sense of self-confidence that had given me the buoyancy to stay afloat in a cop's world, believing I would always come out on top of the situation when in reality there were never any guarantees.

I came up behind Ishmael.

He didn't move. So, he hadn't heard me, hadn't sensed me. If I touched him, it could cause him to take his attention away from Dombrowski. Then again, it might have the opposite effect and make him pull the trigger.

It's all up to you, Bulldog.

I felt both anger and fear as I took in McClendon and the doctor chained to the wall, Dombrowski staring blankly ahead. They were mindless, possibly thinking they were carrying out their lives in a world that was not their own.

And there was Ishmael, pressing the barrel of the weapon against Dombrowski's head.

It's all on your shoulders.

The idea came from desperation, its chances for success dubious, my ability to execute it flawlessly—which is what it would take—questionable.

I shifted my weight to my right foot, pulled my left arm back, and drawing on all the concentration I could gather, brought my left arm up and out, slowly but deliberately, as if I might be rolling a bowling ball for a strike, then followed through properly, catching Ishmael's gun-toting arm on the way up. I felt the handle of the weapon as my hand shoved it up and away from Dombrowski's head.

Ishmael swung around, and for a moment we stood, frozen in place, staring at one another in mutual disbelief as the aftermath unfolded around us. The reaction, which was slow to develop, spread throughout the room as if I'd opened the door to an asylum where the residents had nearly forgotten the concept of freedom and were unsure if they should embrace it or let it slip through their minds as just another illusion.

Ishmael took in the situation while his hand still held the weapon. He had not fired it, but he had not dropped it either.

Realization dawned on him, though he did not react quickly but instead studied the weapon as if it were a foreign object, the function of which he was not completely sure. His confusion did not last, and a grin turned the corners of his mouth as he brought the weapon into a firing position.

I did the only thing I knew to do. I took advantage of his slow reaction time and went on the attack, digging deep and bringing a hard left hook into his side, just beneath the rib cage. My training reminded me not to stop and admire my work but to keep going. I followed with a right to the chin.

Ishmael dropped to his knees, and the pistol clattered to the floor.

The loose weapon, lying on the floor like yesterday's redemption, drew my entire attention. I scrambled for it, but it was as far as I got. The moment I went for the weapon, hands clamped around my arms and shoulders and dragged me away, again held prisoner in the darkness of the room.

Ishmael felt around on the floor and found the weapon, then grabbed the base of the throne and pulled himself into a shaky standing position. He dragged a finger across his lips, then pulled it away, studying the blood that had come from his mouth.

"You really leave me no choice, Barrington." He waved a gesture of dismissal with his hand. "It's as good a name as any, and besides, I'm deeply troubled by more important matters. That the first and only friend I ever had should betray me like no other cuts me to the bone. I'd thought you more complex, more sophisticated than these idiots I've been forced to work with, and yet the first chance you get you turn on me, completely oblivious to the opportunities I might have offered had you chosen more carefully. Why, Barrington? Why would you do such a thing?"

"Don't take it personally," I said. "Life hasn't been easy in my world either. Maybe I brought it on myself. I don't know. But I learned at an early age that playing for keeps is the only way to come out on top. It's how I operate. I don't know any other way."

Ishmael rubbed the barrel of the weapon against his head, then nodded. "Well, when you put it that way, it makes sense. How could I possibly hope to subordinate the insubordinate? Thanks for clearing that up. I feel much better now."

He positioned himself against the pedestal, widened his stance, and brought the weapon up, holding it with both hands. "Unfortunately, your explanation has underlined my disturbing premonition. It seems we are caught up in an unhealthy relationship. Someone has to end it."

He took aim. "And it might as well be me."

I suddenly felt the hands of the drones again as I was pulled slightly backward. One of them slipped something into my hand. I immediately knew what had been given me when the cold steel touched my skin. I didn't know if it was loaded, or if the safety was on or off, or if it would even fire at all, but I wrapped my hand around the grip, placed my finger on the trigger, and swung the weapon into position, hoping, praying that it would fire.

But it didn't. The hammer clanked uselessly against the empty cylinder.

I was not the only person in the room, but I stood alone in the darkness with muffled voices creating a quiet cacophony while the sounds of shuffling feet gave credence to the inevitable uprising.

A flash came from the barrel of Ishmael's gun, followed by a deafening blast, and then another in rapid succession.

My breath came ragged, my heartbeat rapid, and I braced for the impact.

A look of fear came over Ishmael's face, and he stood still for a moment, but then he dropped to his knees and later face-first to the floor.

I remained there in the darkness for what seemed a long time, drawing ragged breaths, barely able to grasp what was happening. I didn't know who had fired the other shot, but my guess was that it had been Patrick, Liam, or whatever his name was.

Someone brushed past, dropping something near my feet.

It was the flashlight. I scooped it up and switched it on. The batteries had been reinstalled.

As soon as I directed the beam of light into the darkness, the world around me changed quickly. A few wide-eyed people scrambled about the room, and then they, too, disappeared, crowding through a single doorway.

They did not leave Ishmael's body behind but dragged him along with them. He had been silenced in a very permanent way, and not for the murder of Ezra Barrington or the man who'd walked in front of the truck or even the untold number of others who'd had the unfortunate experience of coming into contact with Ishmael but for compromising the anonymity and integrity of the society from which he'd come.

Soon another secret and bizarre funeral would be held in the woods. I would not be attending this one.

The room was now completely empty except for Dombrowski, Mayor McClendon, and the doctor, and all of them were staring at me with blank faces and questioning eyes. It was, I imagined, as if they'd just come out of a dream, only it wasn't at all the world they should have awakened to.

Dombrowski blinked, looked quickly around the room, then returned his attention. "Elliot? I might have known it'd be you I'd see after something like this. Where in hell are we, anyway?"

McClendon and the doctor asked similar questions.

I scanned the beam of light across the floor. The personal items we'd come into the building with had been placed there, each stack neatly arranged near the person it belonged to.

"In the basement," I said, "of an abandoned building at First and Elgin."

Dombrowski rubbed his forehead. "What in blazes are we doing here?"

I gathered my items from the floor, and like mimicking robots, everyone else did the same. "It's a long story," I said. "Let's get out of here. I'll try to explain it later."

Walking with legs that barely felt strong enough to carry my weight, I made my way to the doorway that Ishmael's people had used and then peered through it into the vacant corridor that must have been the same one Patrick, and I had walked through earlier.

I briefly wondered if guards had been posted or if a few drones had been left behind to ambush us on the way out but then realized that without Ishmael they would have no reason to do such a thing. They would simply disappear back into their shadowy world and hope that I would do the same.

I didn't know how I would explain it to anyone, let alone a pragmatist like Dombrowski. I imagined it would be better if I left Patrick and his people out of it, let them return to their anonymous existence and move on.

I signaled for the others to follow, then stepped from the room and led the way along the darkened corridor in a direction I thought would take us to the exit.

Seconds later, our escape mechanism came into view.

I quickly walked to the elevator, coaxed everyone onto the platform, then picked up the hand-held device and punched the Up button. Just an old freight elevator, though recently upgraded and maintained for use.

"The darned thing still works," Dombrowski said. "How do you explain that?"

"I can't," I said. "I'm as confused as you are."

Dombrowski didn't say anything. He was too busy trying to make sense of it all, catalogue it in his overly logical mind.

I decided I would try to leave it that way, pretending to be as lost as everyone else, or at least about some parts of it.

I'd had my share of narrow escapes, but the feelings of accomplishment I'd reveled in after each paled in comparison to the sense of redemption I now experienced as the elevator reached street level and I stepped onto the sidewalk and breathed in the fresh, open air of the outside world.

I walked into Captain William Dombrowski's office, appreciative on a level never before achieved of every stack of paper on the desk, the credenza, the floor, of the air-conditioning perpetually set too low for my comfort, and of the smell of cigars, though I rarely saw him smoking these days.

To me, it was like small bits of his practical world tossed about the room for my benefit, a reminder that people were different, which was a good thing, and that they processed information in different ways. But reveling in the comfort of small things needed to be pushed aside for a moment so that details could be remembered correctly. Two days had passed since the ordeal in the abandoned building, and Dombrowski, feeling, I suspected, more out of balance than he was comfortable with, was struggling to bring things into perspective, a process that often proved difficult between us.

"Better grab a cup," he said. "This might take a while."

I raised the cappuccino I'd picked up on the way in.

Dombrowski nodded, then reached into a desk drawer and pulled out a bottle of antacids. "My stomach is on fire." He popped a few into his mouth. "It's been a crazy couple of weeks, and I'm not sure where to start, so let's just cut to the heart of it. Your fingerprints, figuratively speaking, are all over this. I'm not sure what to make of it."

I sipped the cappuccino, then set the cup on the edge of the desk and leaned back in the chair. I didn't think Dombrowski knew how accurate his choice of adjectives had been. "Crazy doesn't begin to describe it," I said.

"Then stop skirting the issue and explain why everything involved with this mess seems to lead back to you."

Dombrowski really wasn't understanding it, not on a level he could deal with. To him, everything was black or white, positive or negative. Anything between was just plain nonsensical. But to me, the awareness of those gray areas was what gave me my edge. "Nothing leads back to me any more than it does with anyone else caught up in this ridiculous quagmire."

"Quagmire?" Dombrowski asked. He leaned forward and tapped his finger against a yellow notepad on his desk. "The director of the homeless shelter where you'd been poking around and asking questions ends up being killed in what was described as a home invasion, the body of the unidentified man who walked in front of a truck while you were chasing him mysteriously vanishes, and one of our own, Officer Craigthorpe, who reported he'd tried to detain you, has gone missing. There's more, but I'll stop there for now. Maybe if you hadn't gone into hiding about the time all this started, it wouldn't look so bad for you. Why did you do that?"

Dombrowski was in some sense, still caught up in the illusion perpetrated by Ishmael. What had happened didn't fit his rational way of thinking, and he was trying to reorganize it so it would. "I was trying to help Yates," I said. "I couldn't do that if detained or hampered by the department. Yeah, I was asking questions in the right places. I'm an investigator. It's what I do. I met Sterling Hornell, the director of the shelter. He was a good man. The home invasion was staged by Ishmael to send me a message. And do you seriously think I broke into the medical examiner's lab, completely undetected, and heisted the body of a John Doe?"

"I don't know what to think. Why do you do any of the crazy things you do?"

I paused. For the most part, trying to explain what had happened wasn't going to do anybody any good. Who would believe it, anyway? But I was compelled to tell Dombrowski about Officer Craigthorpe. I owed Craigthorpe and his family that much. The authorities would most likely connect the dots eventually, and all be revealed in an autopsy, but I could speed things up.

"Last Thursday, a fire broke out at an upscale condominium complex," I said, "near Eighth and Peoria. A man burned up on the lawn."

Without taking his gaze away from the yellow tablet, Dombrowski rubbed his forehead, then lowered his hands and leaned forward. Only then did he attempt to reengage my stare. "Go on. I'm listening."

I hesitated, looking for the right words, but there was no easy way to say it. "That man was Officer Craigthorpe."

Dombrowski studied me, his eyes narrowing, his expression growing intense. "How do you know that?"

"I saw it happen. Craigthorpe had doused himself with gasoline. I could smell it. He started a fire using a lighter, and it spread to him."

Dombrowski tried to hide his emotion, but the moisture gathering in his eyes betrayed him. "Why would he do that?"

"He had no choice," I said. "Just like David Yates, Mayor McClendon, and James Goldstein had no choice in doing what they did."

Dombrowski drummed his fingers against the legal pad. "Somebody has to be responsible. Are you that somebody?"

I could tell by Dombrowski's expression and tone of voice that he didn't really believe I was capable of such things. "No, Bill. Not me."

"Do you know who *is* responsible?"

Again I had to search for the words, and again, nothing seemed appropriate. "He called himself Ishmael. That's all I know."

And it was close enough to the truth. Even though I'd talked with Ishmael, had sparred with him, had even mixed wits with him, how much did I truly know about him? Nothing. I knew nothing.

"Ishmael?"

"That's right."

"Do you know where we can find this person?"

I thought for a moment. "Not exactly."

"I know you too well, Elliot. You're being evasive, which typically means you're trying to hide something. Sounds like you know this guy. Could you pick him out of a lineup?"

I tried to imagine someone like Ishmael actually complying with such a thing if he was still alive. "Probably, but that wouldn't be practical."

"Why not?"

Disjointed images of the scene that had unfolded beneath the abandoned building ran through my mind. "Because he's dead."

"And did you…?"

In my mind, I heard the two gunshots fired in rapid succession. "No, not me."

"Do you know who did?"

"Not really."

Dombrowski grabbed his cup, then leaned back and sipped the coffee. He was getting frustrated by my lack of detail, but what could I do?

"Then how do you know that this Ishmael character is dead?"

I decided to lay it out straight. It would have to be addressed sooner or later. "Because I was there," I said. "I saw him take a bullet. The shot came from behind me, and it was dark, so I don't know who fired it. You were there too, Bill. You just don't remember."

"What do you mean, I was there? Are you trying to tell me that all this took place in that damned basement?"

I retrieved the cappuccino from the desk and took a drink, regretting in some way having laid out the truth for Dombrowski in such a blunt manner even though such a direct approach was the way he had always said that he preferred to be informed. But it was over now. And how it all came about mattered less than the fact that it was now behind us. "That's right," I said. "Not all of it, but certainly the end of it."

"I was there when this all-inclusive perpetrator lost his life?"

"Yes."

Dombrowski's face lost some of its color. "Then why in hell can't I remember any of it?"

I smiled, though it wasn't something I'd felt like doing but more of an expression of sorrow than happiness. "I'm relieved you brought that up, Captain. The answer lies at the heart of your understanding of what actually happened, or at least in accepting that it could happen."

He popped a couple more antacid tablets. "All right, Elliot. I'm already not liking what I hear, and I haven't even heard it yet, so give it to me straight. I'm as ready as I'll ever be."

I savored another sip of flavored coffee, and when I'd finished, I asked, "What's the last thing you remember before waking up in the basement beneath the abandoned building?"

He looked away, trying to recall. "I went out to put the car in the garage," he said. "With Alice being gone, I figured I'd get busy watching television and forget about it if I didn't."

Alice? I hadn't considered that angle. Being all caught up with my own problems had become more distracting than I'd realized. "How is Alice? Is everything all right?"

"It's fine. Her sister has been under the weather. She thought a visit might be good."

I nodded, then refocused on the business at hand. "What about your car? Was it in the garage when you got home?"

Dombrowski didn't answer. He probably didn't want to because he knew where the conversation was headed.

"Well," I asked, "was it?"

He hesitated, then said, "No. It was still parked in the driveway."

"How do you explain that?"

He shrugged. "I blacked out for a while, that's all."

"What time was it when you decided to put the car up?"

"I don't know exactly. Around eight, I guess."

"So, you think it was somewhere around 8:00 p.m. Thursday?"

"That's as good a guess as any."

I twisted the Styrofoam cup in my hand, feeling the rough texture of the container with my fingers. I'd let the idea linger long enough. It was time to zero in. "It was around 4:00 a.m. Friday when the cab picked us up. The way I figure it, you have an eight-hour gap of missing time. I'd say you did a little more than blackout for a while."

Dombrowski leaned back in his chair, perspiration forming on his forehead. "Where are you going with this, Elliot?"

"Hopefully in the right direction," I said. "And I don't mean to badger. I'm just trying to get you to connect the dots."

"I don't even know how to find the dots, much less connect them."

"Let me help you out," I said. "Where were you during your little blackout, and what were you doing?"

"I don't know. Nothing, I guess. Sleeping maybe."

I finished off the cappuccino. Dombrowski was trying to be vague and evasive, but what he didn't understand was that he had in some sense, answered correctly and touched on the point I was trying to make. "You have some missing time, and you don't have a clue as to what might have happened or what you might have done within it."

"All right, Elliot. You've successfully backed me into a corner. Truth is I've been thinking about it all weekend. And that's not my style. I don't worry. I let things go. You and I both know that you have to in this business. But this thing has been eating away at me." He paused. "So what did happen? What did I do?"

I shook my head. "I wish I had an answer for you, but I don't. I can say this. Ishmael always had a purpose for those he grabbed."

I paused. It didn't seem prudent to use the word *possession* even though that was closer to the truth.

"I think your purpose," I continued, "was to guarantee my obedience, nothing more."

"Why didn't he just grab you?"

I pulled the crucifix from beneath my shirt and held the cross between my thumb and forefinger. "He couldn't," I said. "I believe my faith stopped him."

Dombrowski stared at me but said nothing.

"You mentioned *letting go*," I said, "and that's exactly what you should do, but only after you acknowledge that David Yates, Mayor McClendon, James Goldstein, and Officer Craigthorpe all had similar experiences of missing time, and like you, they didn't know what was happening while they were caught up in it. We're talking about..." Still, that word possession lingered, but not quite right, when it suddenly hit me. "Identity theft, but on a much higher level than we're used to dealing with."

Dombrowski leaned back in his chair, lost in thought for what seemed a long time. Finally, he sat forward and said, "Ishmael?"

"Ishmael."

"And Ishmael is dead?"

"That's right."

"You're sure?"

"Yes," I said. "I'm absolutely certain of it."

He shook his head. "I always suspected that if I hung around you long enough, some of your wacky ideas would rub off on me. What about Yates? Do you know where he is?"

"After church services yesterday, Pastor Meadows asked me to meet with him in his office. When I arrived, both David Yates and Mayor McClendon were there. We had a long talk. It's going to take time for everybody to get their lives back together, especially Yates. His wife left him, most of the congregation is afraid to talk to him, and he lost his job. None of it was his fault, but how do you go about convincing anyone of that?"

Dombrowski shook his head. "I'll see what I can do about the job part, but like you said, it won't be easy. What about you? When are you coming back to work?"

"When the time is right," I said, "but it won't be business as usual."

"What do you mean?"

"We both know I don't fit in with the structure of this department or any other department for that matter. Playing by the rules is a good thing, and people should do it, but that just doesn't seem to work out so well for me."

"I can't argue with that. But we can work around it. We always have. You're a good man, Kenny. I hate to admit it, but we need you. Besides, you've said yourself that being a cop is all you know. What else are you going to do?"

"What I've thought about for years," I said. "Bust out on my own."

"Come on, Kenny. Don't forget who you're talking to. I can predict with a pretty high degree of certainty that you're not going to be happy taking photos of unfaithful spouses."

I smiled, and that turned into a laugh. It was spontaneous, and it felt good. I hadn't done that in a while. "It won't be anything like that," I said. "I'm a simple man with simple needs. I stuck the bulk of what I've made through the years into savings, invested some too. I'm doing all right. I was thinking more along the lines of special cases, the kind that might benefit from my unusual nature. A local attorney has already expressed interest. There'll be more than enough to keep me busy."

I paused. "You've been good to me, Bill. You helped me get the job and continuously defended me, even when doing so wasn't in your best interest. If you need me, I'll be there."

"I don't know. The department isn't big on using freelance."

"Yeah, but we can make it happen. I'll be there for you even if it's off the record and off the time clock."

Dombrowski rubbed his chin, then nodded. "I'm getting a little hungry. Want to grab some lunch?"

"I'll have to catch you some other time. Carmen and I talked last night. We're meeting later for a little more in-depth discussion."

He raised his eyebrows. "It's about time you came to your senses. She's a good person, too good for you."

Dombrowski was both right and wrong. Not possible. Perhaps he was a little bit right and a little bit wrong. But any way you stacked it, Carmen was and always had been good for me, a rational, stabilizing force in my life. "Yeah," I said. "I know. That's what keeps holding me back."

"Hey, I wasn't being serious, just giving you a hard time. You're all right. And you two belong together. Try not to muff it up this time, all right?"

I pushed away from the desk and stood. "Thanks for the advice. I'll catch you later."

"Yeah, later."

I turned and walked away with feet that didn't seem to be touching the ground, imagining what I might do, where I might go, no longer held back by the rigid structure of the department. I treasured the time I'd spent here and the friends and connections I'd made, but it was time to move on.

"Into the future of the not-so-distant past," I said, quickly becoming aware that those around me in the hallway had heard me as well. "Just playing on words," I added.

When the elevator opened, I stepped inside and rode it to the garage where I found my old pickup truck. I opened the door to the truck and climbed inside, relishing, as I slid the key into the ignition and started the vehicle, the faint odor of grease and oil that hung about the cabin like an old friend. Lacking any modern amenities which might tell it when to start, when to stop, when to change lanes, or even when to drive itself, the vehicle deferred such privileges to the driver. It was just a good old Chevy pickup, and that suited me just fine.

I'd called Dewey Crawford's wife yesterday. Dewey was back at home and doing as well as was to be expected under the circumstances. As for Roxie Taylor and the man who had called himself Ezra Barrington, a little more research would be required.

I took the next exit off the Broken Arrow Expressway, then executed several more turns, which took me to the restaurant parking lot. I saw Carmen sitting in her car, and when she glanced in my direction and smiled, a mixture of feelings and emotions that I could never adequately describe flowed through my senses. It wasn't the first time. It happened every time I saw her.

I reached across the cab and retrieved the ring I'd put there. Perhaps Dombrowski was right. Perhaps it was time.

ABOUT THE AUTHOR

Bob Avey is the author of the Kenny Elliot mystery series, which includes *Twisted Perception* (April 2006), *Beneath a Buried House* (June 2008), *Footprints of a Dancer* (October 2012), and *Identity Theft: A Kenny Elliot Mystery* (January 2020). He lives with his wife and son in Broken Arrow, Oklahoma where he works as an accountant in the petroleum industry. When he's not writing or researching mystery writing techniques, he spends his free time prowling through dusty antique shops looking for the rare or unusual, or roaming through ghost towns, searching for echoes from the past. Through his writing, which he describes as a blend of literary and genre, he explores the intricacies and extremities of human nature.

Bob is a member of *The Tulsa NightWriters*, *The Oklahoma Writers Federation* (active board member for 2006), and *Mystery Writers of America*.

Thank you so much for reading one of our **Crime Fiction** novels.
If you enjoyed the experience, please check out our recommended
title for your next great read!

Caught in a Web by Joseph Lewis

"This important, nail-biting crime thriller about MS-13 sets the
bar very high. One of the year's best thrillers."
–BEST THRILLERS

View other Black Rose Writing titles at
www.blackrosewriting.com/books and use promo code
PRINT to receive a **20% discount** when purchasing.